A Handful of Earths

Book 1: The Analogs

Sansoucy Kathenor

Multiverse Press

MultiversePress42@gmail.com

Editor: Louise Koren
Managing Editor: Madona Skaff
Interior Design: Éric Desmarais
Cover Design: David Koren

Legal deposit, Library and Archives Canada, September 2021

Paperback ISBN: 978-1-7778259-0-4
E-book ISBN: 978-1-7778259-1-1

Literary Executors: Madona Skaff and Valerie Kirkwood

MultiversePress42@gmail.com

Sansoucy once said, "If you write, you *are* a writer. Don't let anyone tell you otherwise."

On behalf of Sansoucy Kathenor, I'd like to dedicate this book to all of the struggling writers.

Madona Skaff

Character Sketches by Sansoucy. Top to bottom; Mayne, Ithleen, Jonno

In this universe, all the persons, places, and organizations in The Multiverse Trilogy are imaginary.

In their own universes, of course, they are all perfectly real, and we are imaginary.

Sansoucy Kathenor

CHAPTER 1

Infinity

A happy childhood. A traumatic adolescence. And finally, as his world's most famous physicist, Jonnan Mayne had reached a triumphant maturity.

But his state of surface contentment had crusted over with an unacknowledged restlessness. A need which he sensed only as a craving for new experiences, fresh fields of study to explore. He no longer felt any struggle, or excitement, or sense of adventure in a life that had once been spiced with them. His life had gone unbearably flat.

He enjoyed his success, but he wanted to risk the unexpected again.

None of this lessened his absorption in his immediate task as he sat at a workbench in the main room of his lab, working alone after hours as usual. His two technicians would have cheerfully stayed overtime if he had wanted them to, but there was no urgency about the day's pursuit. He scorned social activity; he had had more than his fill of it in earlier years.

In his teens, he had built a defensive wall around his emotions. Though trained in social ease, he had also learned to act impersonally, never allowing acquaintance to develop into friendship. Among his co-workers, he remained polite and pleasant, ready with his own help and generous with credit for others' help; but he retained his reserve, rejecting the socialization he had come to despise, and devoting himself entirely to his work.

That work had been acclaimed the most impressive in the world. Though only in his early thirties, what was left now to achieve? He had added to his fame and prestige by further discoveries, but with ambition fulfilled, some of the challenge had faded from his life. His subconscious was seeking new stimuli, new risks, to counteract what he felt was mental stagnation.

Sitting this summer's evening with the electrodes of the telekinetic micromanipulator — or TKM — at his temples, he was breadboarding an image circuit. Aside from an occasional reference glance at his designs on the display screen tilted up out of the bench top in front of him, he faced blankly across the room, his attention entirely on the mental process of experimenting with the circuit's arrangement.

So intent was his concentration that his unfocused gaze rested for some five seconds without so much as a blink of surprise on the figure that formed and solidified in that time, well beyond the other side of the workbench. The height of a short adult human, and of appropriate width for one, it was sheathed from presumed head to presumed feet in a shimmering, silvery shielding, and stood completely still. Beyond height and width the apparition was shapeless, like a cloth draped over a pillar, or a stir of glitter particles flickering in a vial.

As the import of what his eyes were registering suddenly struck Mayne, the manipulator skittered out of his control and impressed a jumble of components into the ruined circuit; but he disciplined his racing pulse with habitual iron control and kept his outward calm as he slipped the electrodes off and regarded the newcomer.

"Greeting," said the figure. "I mean you no harm, but I have the means to protect myself if necessary."

A multitude of questions thrust and tumbled through Mayne's mind. He pushed them all firmly down and said soothingly, "You're in no danger here, so far as I know. What can I do for you?"

"We are seeking help in exploring the universes."

Mayne cut off his rampant thoughts, and asked with assumed detachment, "Was that a plural on universe?"

"Yes. We do not know if their number is infinite, but we assume so."

Without a referent, it would be useless to ask, 'Which universe are you from?' or even 'What's yours like?' in an effort to gauge the visitor's difference from himself. Mayne settled for, "How many universes did you have to work your way through to reach this one?"

"There is no need to pass through the universes one by one. In fact, it is not possible to touch the closest ones. In any case, since we discovered that the type of personality we are seeking can be found among the human-inhabited Earths, we did not consider it necessary to try to find a suitable closer species."

"What's *your* species?"

"We do not have names for either our species or for individuals. Among telepaths, a collective image for each person is possible and more expressive. Why are you surprised?"

"I hadn't realized you were speaking telepathically," Mayne said, excited at the realization. "Our only means of telepathy is by machine; and it's very crude and limited. Your transmission is so clear my mind registered it as speech... Couldn't you read all that in my mind, without asking?"

"I could, but prefer not to. My people have natural shields which enable us to maintain our division into individuals, a state we value. Since you humans do not have this ability, please continue using speech, or at least form conscious speech patterns. It clarifies your thoughts and gives me a means of restricting my attention to what you intend to communicate. If you want me to look deeper to understand something you cannot articulate, make a specific request for me to do so."

Accepting that with a nod, and mentally filing his speculations about implied ethics and mores, Mayne went back to the previous question. "Since I can't handle these concept-identifications, do you mind if I invent names for you and your people?"

"That has already been done, by our first full-contact human, who seems to think as you do. For my species, she chose 'wexter', and for myself, 'Spen'."

"Fine." Mayne went back further to pick up another point. "Did you imply you're limited to Earths, in all universes?" An infinity of other Earths, he thought, allowing his inner excitement a moment's reign, would be scarcely less interesting than a universe of alien planets. If this being really meant to offer him a chance to see some of them...

"So far, yes. Some of them may have interstellar travel, but we do not. That is one of the many things we would like to know about."

"We're barely interplanetary in this universe, so we can't help you there."

"We think that you, personally, can help us in more than that one query."

"How?" Mayne managed not to snap out the word in his eagerness.

"We are seeking an explorer, to collect data about the multiverse for us. If our reading is correct, you have the personality to relish meeting the unknown, accepting the risks which we prefer to avoid."

Mayne kept his tone judicious, "Is moving between universes so risky?"

"Not the transplacement itself. But who can tell what one may meet in another universe? Our psionic instruments enable us to seek out personality types; but we cannot identify the circumstances in which they live. To actually explore a world we require a being who is intelligent, courageous, resourceful, and honourable. Our selector identifies you as such."

"What do you hope to gain from the explorations?" Mayne asked, forcing his mind to consider the possibility of ulterior motives. His own Earth's people had been exploitative for most of their history, and some still were. The impression he was receiving from the wexter was of readiness for nervous withdrawal rather than for aggression, and of hopeful friendliness rather than slyness; but how could he tell whether these were true inclinations or projected lies?

Spen was unhesitant: "We seek knowledge. It is so valued among us that we take the risk of offering you, in return, the possession of a transplacing device which you may use independently of our control — although we do ask that, on worlds where transplacement is not yet known, you limit even knowledge of its existence to carefully screened people."

Mayne noticed a reservation: "You'll give me the device itself, but not information about the technique?"

"We recognize that this may be a delaying tactic only: since we asked for a personality with high intelligence, we are aware that you may eventually work out the principles for yourself. But we also specified that our explorer should be a trustworthy person; and long before you can master transplacement psionics, we shall either have confirmed your character or removed from you both the device and all memory of it. You must agree to this condition before we will give you the transplacing device."

Both their willingness to trust him with unsupervised use of interuniversal transplacement and their concern to avoid indiscriminate spreading of the technique argued that these people were trustworthy themselves. And at a subconscious level, the wexter's formality of expression, matching Mayne's own inclination towards precision, created a feeling of alliance in Mayne and disposed him to accept the word of the earnest and unaggressive being. So it was more curiosity than caution that now prompted him to probe further into motives: "Why are you so worried about unselected people getting into the other universes? Are you afraid unscreened people might invade your own universe?"

"We have arranged defence against that possibility, of course, but we prefer to avoid even the threat. Moreover, we are a responsible people, and do not approve of turning loose unsavoury personalities on any other peoples in the multiverse who may not be able to defend themselves, as we can. Nor do we wish to upset societies not prepared for inter-universe contact. So we will keep our knowledge exclusive as long as we can."

Mayne absently ran a hand through his rumpled light brown hair. "Surely, in infinity, there must be many other people who have inter-universe travel; so your knowledge can't be exclusive even now."

"This danger is what we are most anxious to investigate — what made us decide to make this contact. We originally believed other transplacers to be unlikely, but the human theorist Ithleen has demonstrated a fallacy in our logic."

"That's the first-contact person you mentioned, the one who named you?" Mayne noticed a lack of any title with her name, as he was used to.

"Yes. We sought the best theorist within this part of the multiverse so we could obtain opinions on points of interest about the multiverse from someone of another species, whose thoughts would be bound by a different mind-set from ours. This being, Ithleen, is capable of extremely high-level intuitive reasoning, a form of psi talent; she is able to make a valid judgement on the basis of data that would be insufficient for ordinary logic. She has agreed to continue to aid us with independent studies; but she has also convinced us we need to have a different quality of data than our robot probes can collect, the kind that only a live investigator can bring us. If you agree to be our explorer, I will take you to the theorist Ithleen for any further information you may want."

It was the moment of commitment or withdrawal. Infinity... and the chance to exchange ideas with a brilliant mind from a wholly new culture, if everything Spen said was true. That or a safe but routine life of ever-diminishing achievement, examining the corollaries of his major discovery... this was exactly the sort of excitement his restlessness craved.

The wexter remained as still physically as ever, but Mayne caught the mental impression of discomfort over the duration of the visit to this strange world, and an intention to end the interview. Almost without awareness of making his decision, Mayne said quickly, "Let's go see this theorist, then."

"You agree to our conditions?"

"Yes, certainly; they're reasonable. Where's the transplacing device?"

"The one for you is just being made. It had to be designed to suit the human mind. For now, I will transplace you any time you need to move."

"When do you want me to start the independent exploration trips?"

"We are eager, but have no immediate urgency. Since yours is a world without advanced psionics, it is one where you must restrict knowledge of the multiverse. Ithleen said that means you must conceal your absence from your Earth. How long will it take you to arrange that?"

"No time, I'm not accountable to anyone. I'll just leave a note for my lab assistants." Mayne flicked off the telekinetic micromanipulator, turned to a computer on an adjoining desk, and typed: "Away indefinitely. Will call when I return. J.M." He hit the print-out key, retracted the computer neatly into the desk, and stood up. "Let's go."

***

The sensation of transplacement was not intrinsically unpleasant. The scene about him faded out in about three seconds, to an impression of white opacity lasting just long enough to sense. Then another scene faded in around them, taking about five seconds, during which time they found themselves positioned exactly at floor level in a clear area. Mayne let out the breath he had been holding in spite of his determination to accept this intoxicating development as merely impressive.

The large room was furnished half as a study, half as a lounge. At one end were thickly upholstered chairs and sofa, draped in throws of sea-green with swirls of misty white, grouped around an elegantly shaped wooden looking table. At the other end, amid floor-to-ceiling shelves of disks and books, was a curved desk, like a chunk of torus, fitted with an elaborate computer keyboard, several monitor screens, and other peripherals.

"Greeting." Spen's telepathic announcement of their presence seemed to be on general broadcast, so Mayne caught it too.

The woman at the desk, who was facing one of her monitors, startled slightly, but spoke with a casualness that Mayne suspected covered a keyed-up anticipation. "Hello, Spen. Did you find him? Did he agree?" She finished a few keystrokes, pressed a final key, and turned with a smile, before coming to her feet in a definitely startled movement. Obviously, she had not expected the wexter to bring "him" here immediately. She drew a quick breath, then crossed to join them.

Mayne's first impressions of her were of graceful movement, brown hair with a soft wave, worn in a short, brushed-back style that needed no attention, and a thigh-length green jacket over matching slacks and a white, silky blouse.

The wexter announced unnecessarily, "Here is the explorer."

Mayne noted with a touch of amusement that Spen had forgotten that humans liked to use names and hadn't even thought to ask his. "I'm Jonnan Mayne."

The woman extended both hands in greeting, and said warmly, "Welcome, Jonnan Mayne."

As he took her hands, Mayne observed with greater precision that she was in her mid twenties, tall, less than a head below his own one-ninety-one, and had grey eyes. From her ease of movement he judged her to be slim and athletic, but could not tell directly, for her clothes were loose and much bepocketed. A pocket-stuffer himself, Mayne smiled at their common taste.

She was looking at him with equal interest, and he wondered fleetingly what she was making of his own body — its strength masked by his well-tailored clothes — his face with its habitual expression of distant politeness, and his aging grey-green heather jacket which, his early training belatedly reminded him, he should have changed before going visiting. He was out of the habit of giving consideration to social niceties. The thought was fleeting: a habit he did have was self-assurance. And anyway the situation was too interesting to leave time for trifling matters.

The woman smiled back at him, her own flustered moment past. "My name is Ithleen Danir. We no longer use titles of any sort, but we used to. I take it your world still does; what's the correct one for you?"

"I'm a plennor."

Adapting politely to his world's customs, she said, "I'm looking forward to hearing about your world, Plennor Mayne, and to showing you some of mine."

The wexter, still immobile, let an impression of restlessness interrupt them, and abruptly said, "I will leave you to your discussions now, and collect your reports as usual. If the explorer remembers anything that must be done in his own world to ensure its ignorance of the multiverse, I will come to transplace him."

Ithleen nodded casually, and said, "Thank you, Spen." The wexter faded out, and Ithleen, with a sympathetic smile, murmured, "Poor old Expendable."

"That's what you derived the name Spen from? Why Expendable?"

"As a penance for precipitating the wexters into their quandary over the multiverse, Spen's been assigned to be their contact with the outer darkness, which is to say, us — and is shivering under ner shiny silver shield every moment because ne knows they'll cut nem off from the wexters' home universe if anything threatens that universe."

"You're not using 'he or she', you're using the neutral 'ne'," Mayne noted. "I take it you've never seen any of them more clearly than I have?"

"No. They don't want us to know anything about their physical appearance, or their home Earth. It's part of their defence against invasion; their transplacing method allows one to go to a visually known place or person. They don't seem to care what we learn about their minds; in fact, they seem pleased to be able to make comparisons with ours. I think they feel vulnerable physically but not mentally. That roughly humanoid size and shape we see may be partly illusion: the wexters may be a little smaller and physically weaker than humans, and want to appear less so — like cats fluffing themselves up and bushing out their tails."

"Sounds reasonable. Why did you decide to call them wexters?"

"A blending of 'we' and 'ex'. The 'we' tries to express their combined unity and individualism; they share thoughts and emotions more completely than we can quite grasp, but they determinedly keep from coercing anyone's else's thoughts or actions — treasuring individuality. And the 'ex', of course, is for their preference for doing their observing from outside."

"Have you known Spen long?"

"On and off for some weeks now. Come and sit down." Ithleen led the way to the lounge end of the room. As he took a chair, Mayne noticed several books on astrophysics lying on a table, as if kept handy for recreational reading.

Ithleen sat across from him and resumed, "The wexters are intensely interested in the multiverse: they have a consuming curiosity, backed by a high intelligence and an ingenuity in invention. They also have a certain difficulty in theoretical reasoning, perhaps because they've never needed to develop it, with their great psychic abilities, and a great nervousness about contact with other people."

"Spen mentioned something about doubts of ner people's hypotheses forcing them to consult with an other-species theorist."

"Yes. Like cats again, they're driven to investigate even what frightens them, because of both curiosity and the need to know what dangers there may be. But they have the same caution of preferring not to be noticed except by people they've found they can trust. They hesitated a long time over the suggestion of enlisting an explorer who might draw attention to them."

He glanced around. "Your world has obviously reached at least the electronics level. Are you further than that?"

"What's left of my world is just holding at that level. We had a global war, fifty years ago, and this community, Geode, is all that survived. We've never found any other survivors."

"How did your group survive?"

"The city was supposed to be simulating the technological and sociological conditions of a space colony for study before we really tried to establish one. We were completely sealed off and equipped with decontamination facilities because of it."

"Supposed to be?"

"It was actually a voluntary genetics experiment by an international group who thought that breeding ourselves with as much care as we give to plants and animals might pay off just as well. They'd had breakthroughs in identifying some of the gene combinations of personality, and they wanted to see if they could produce children with an augmented inclination towards altruism, intelligence, and so forth. But the world had worries about superhuman mutants enslaving the rest of the people or killing them off; so the group had to disguise itself as the sealed-city experiment. Then the worriers killed *themselves* off. Of course, it was traumatic for the first-generation Geodans who had friends and relatives outside. My age group — I'm twenty-seven, second generation, first Geode-born — and the one growing up now are inclined to mutter 'poetic justice', quite unfeelingly, as we've never known a broader life."

"You've never been out of your city, then?"

"Actually, I'm one of the few Geodans who has been out since the catastrophe. Most of us are victims of a version of agoraphobia, but by some genetic quirk, I'm not; so I volunteered to become one of our pilots when we built survey planes to gather data on how the surface world is regenerating, and to scout for suitable raw materials for our robot vehicles to collect. I think one of the reasons the wexters selected me out of infinity was that I understand a fear of Outside but don't share it.

"My main work is teaching advanced physics and helping to organize the miscellaneous information in our library. Except for specialized biological and engineering data, our collection was ignored for at least a generation. We've lost other sciences, history, literature, things we can't even guess, so we're indexing what we do have, for our older people to work on, adding whatever they can still remember." Her words came faster as she neared the end of the explanation of her personal history. Excited as she was to get to his part of the information exchange. "Our people strongly encourage physical fitness as well; I do karate, gymnastics, dancing, and high-wire work, myself."

Leaning forward eagerly, Ithleen said, "Now, tell me about your world. I had to fight off some of our sociologists when they heard you'd be coming!

If you want to avoid being mobbed on future visits, you'd better bring along books about your world. But I'd like to know your own life."

"You can have a book on that, too, if you want," said Mayne, trying to screen the distaste out of his voice.

"You've had books written about you?"

"Two biographies that I've heard of, sections in biographic collections, and an assortment of articles."

"Tell me some of it now."

Mayne made a dismissive gesture. "My life hasn't been all that eventful." He went on, "I'm a physicist, now working in psionics. I achieved my plennorate four years ago. There's nothing else really worth mentioning."

Ithleen considered him thoughtfully. "You don't like to talk about your life, do you?"

"You're perceptive." He braced himself a little.

Sensing his discomfort, Ithleen said quickly, "Right now, tell me about your world and your work, and what a plennorate is."

Mayne relaxed somewhat. "I think we're at roughly the same technological stage you are, or were. We also came near destruction, back when we had a lot of individual countries; but we were luckier: we've had reasonably secure peace for a generation or so now, thanks largely to the International Science Complex, the institute I work for. It's an independent commercial empire, run as a co-operative by a collection of scientists. The ISC became rich and powerful and, inevitably, somewhat political. With its wealth, it was able to attract top scientists and continue to turn out useful technology; and the Regions soon drew up treaties that guaranteed ISC's permanent independence and agreed to the rules of behaviour it laid down: if any Region threatens or exploits another, ISC can cut it off from the distribution list for new technology, putting it at a disadvantage. The mere possibility has so far kept all the Regions honest with each other as well as with the ISC. They're especially careful to pay royalties on everything we've invented," he added drily.

Ithleen laughed. "I can see they would."

"Of course, the ISC has no control over what any Region does within its own boundaries, except for insisting that anyone who wants to may apply to work at ISC and, if accepted, must be allowed to come."

"What was your own plennorate for?"

"Proving psionics was possible by making a psi amplifier which, in turn, made immit technology practical."

"I'm not familiar with that term."

"A method of creating errorless 3-D sub-nanostructures by controlling the material and the construction environment during fabrication: the image circuit, or immit. The smallest structure we've been able to make."

"Our physicists were discussing nanotechnology at the time of our disaster, but we hadn't achieved it. And, now, of course, it's all we can do to maintain our technological level, never mind increasing it. I'm one of our few research physicists, and my work is strictly theoretical, not experimental. If you can teach us practical nanotechnology, our engineers will inscribe your name in platinum."

"I'll bring you texts that go beyond nano."

Ithleen sighed. "Your Earth sounds marvelous. But it surprises me. I wouldn't have thought it possible to teach a whole planet's population to support science."

"They don't. The ISC is tolerated because of its constant fallout of technological benefits. There are still occasional outbursts of protest groups, even in Varidor, the Region that gives us the most support. And in the past, some areas had violent anti-science movements."

His face must have revealed more than he usually allowed it to, for she asked, "You've had personal experience with them?"

"Yes." He made his voice dismissive, hoping her vaunted intuition would warn her off the subject.

Apparently it did, for she said only, "And in spite of it, you've become a plennor. I can see why the wexters' caltor chose you."

He lifted an eyebrow, and Ithleen explained the derivation of her term: "Their caller-personality-searcher-selector, developed from their equivalent of a phone. A psi tele-finder/communicator. This caltor is what they used to search for personalities that turned out to be you and me."

"And what do you know about the multiverse?" he asked.

"When the wexters discovered the multiverse, they began sending out robot probes to find out what was on the other Earths. They expected to find near-repeats of themselves in the first universes they contacted, with gradually less resemblance in others; but they never found any such beings in any universe. At first, in fact, all they found were Earths where no intelligent life had ever developed. They speculated that some psychic law prevented contact between universes with sapients.

"Spen is neither a scientist nor a manager, but some sort of intermediary. Ne selects and programs the scientists' experiments into equipment, such as their probes.

"Spen implied it was an accident or slip of some sort, but I suspect ne put a little genuine desire into the probes' instructions to look for intelligence. The probes are psionic, of course, and I think the ones previous expediters had sent out had picked up the general wexter fear of finding people intelligent enough to pose a potential threat. But Spen's probes returned news of what appeared to be intelligent, non-psi beings so different from themselves that they were dismissed as incomprehensible and offered no threat. They grew a little bolder; willing to accept a bit of psi, in people they could actually communicate with. And their probes turned up humans. By this time, they had several times as many hypotheses about the multiverse and its peoples as there were species in their records, and their confusion was steadily increasing."

"One would expect a telepathic people to reach a consensus easily."

"As I said, they prize individuality, and condemn any attempt to impose ideas on another person. Although they're weak in logical thought, logic is the only thought-pressure they approve," Ithleen said.

"An attitude that resembles human inconsistencies. Perhaps humans are the nearest analogs to wexters that they can reach, if they're cut off somehow from real neighbours. But your world and mine are now in touch," he said. "Are humans better able to stand one another than wexters are? I find that surprising."

"I doubt we're more amiable," said Ithleen drily. "I presume the wexters are more sensitive. They had already discovered that they could touch more than one human world. They risked a little manipulation: mentally broadcasting the idea of such contact to these worlds and observing the reaction to it.

"The people they experimented with were at the industrial-age level, and were able to grasp the concept of multiple universes. But the wexters found that, although some of these people could actually relish the thought of visiting other human worlds, and even of meeting deceased friends or ancestors there, they shied away from the idea of meeting duplicates of themselves or their living acquaintances.

"The wexters concluded that no people who were powerful enough with psi to initiate contact with other universes could ever touch one occupied by another such people.

"This emboldened them to the point of considering actually communicating with a reachable species – humans. That was when they adapted their existing specific-person-locating device, or caltor, to search for a specified type of personality instead, combined it with a probe and, with this caltor, set out to look for a suitable theorist."

"Co-operative, imaginative, non-xenophobic – "

"And harmless: not only low-psi, but also of a people who would be powerless to attack the wexters physically. Geodans are just surviving; even if we were aggressive, we'd be in no shape to express it, so everyone here was eventually allowed to know about the multiverse. A number of us volunteered to permit a deeper probing of our minds than the conversational level. We reasoned that either Spen had not already done it without permission, and so was honourable and trustworthy, or else ne already had probed, in which case we weren't letting ourselves in for anything new. In return, the wexters gave us as much data as they could interpret on the human mind."

"The wexters aren't the only ones driven by curiosity."

"I think humans and wexters are fairly close analogs. We have quite a lot in common, including courage, for all the wexters' apparent timidity."

Mayne nodded. "Courage is not being fearless, but going ahead when you are afraid; and they certainly do that, even if their principle is to avoid danger."

"A rational principle, when you remember how closely their minds are linked. An injury to any one of them would hurt the whole population; many hurts could threaten their species' existence."

"So it could. Depression might spread like a plague, infecting more with each one struck down."

"Spen and I discussed the wexters' discoveries and their speculations about the multiverse. Whether all universes originated from one, splitting off constantly or at particular choice points; or whether all the universes existed from the start, with similar ones being just statistical run; whether all possible versions exist or whether some principle of cohesion or exclusion limited them. With so little hard data, it's difficult to exclude any possibility, of course..."

"Spen said you have a psi talent for reasoning from insufficient data."

Ithleen smiled. "It always seems adequate to me. Perhaps it *is* psi; Geodans just call it a hunch."

"So what's your hunch about the multiverse?"

"Multiple origins and chance resemblances, like convergences in evolution. The wexters clung at first to their earlier ideas, arguing for their hypothesis of a psychic law that severs potential contacts among universes touched by major psi people. They even speculated that there were no other such people; that they themselves were the only possible initiators of contact, and perhaps they were even creating the other universes rather than discovering them. I called this their single-ripple theory."

"Did you point out they were generalizing from a sample size of complete insignificance?"

"Yes, although I couldn't push that too hard when I'd made my own choice with no larger a sample, and second-hand information at that!"

"But you have that ability to reason with psychic sureness."

"Regardless, I concentrated on their logical fallacy of assuming that because they couldn't reach truly close analogs of themselves, then no such analogs could reach them. Just a slight difference in attitude might affect the ability to make contact.

"In the wexters, curiosity overrides fear; in their analogs, the balance could be the other way, making them want to reach and destroy rivals, or at least to destroy their ability to touch other universes. Or they could be fearless and foolhardy, carelessly spreading knowledge of transplacing methods, to the harm of the weak and benefit of aggressors. In the face of such possibilities, the wexters had to give up their comforting conclusion that no one would ever come to them."

"And you suggested that, since their robot probes can't react to things they haven't been specifically programmed to notice, the wexters had better use a live explorer to do some scouting."

Ithleen nodded. "I'd have liked to volunteer myself, but my background is so limited that I might not notice important things either. So I suggested they use their personality locater again. They finally agreed, but then found they couldn't even imagine the sort of personality they needed. So they got me to tell their caltor what to look for, and set it to find them — well, another expendable."

Chapter 2

Suspicion

Mayne had boasted of his independence from supervision, but had forgotten that every person's actions cause ripples. The reactions to his absence started the next day in his lab with his two full-time technicians, who had arrived to find the building empty and no explanation except the cryptic note from Plennor Mayne on the computer printout.

The assistants were recent assignees to the lab, casually requisitioned by Mayne when his previous pair had left to work on the commercialization of the TKM. The current technicians, a woman named Vandrai Sartyov and a man named Davith Kamalua, were both twenty-three, earnest, cheerful, and full of youthful enthusiasm for their work. They had met during the extra year of training ISC gave to all its accepted college graduates, and had become friends over their common interest in sailing. Later, they had been pleased to find themselves teamed in this, their first steady assignment, after some weeks as fill-ins on different projects. They had arrived in pleased excitement, but also in some worry and apprehension, with a high resolve to endure whatever quirks this particular plennor might have, in order to keep such privileged positions.

Van, who was so light a blonde that her fine, pixie cut hair looked almost silver, had sky-blue eyes that looked on the world with bright interest and frequent amusement. She was of medium height, athletically slim, and full of energy. In her work she cultivated a no-nonsense air but in her personal relationships she indulged in gentle teasing. She was quick, competent, and intelligent. She enjoyed being part of a project team but had no desire to lead one, so had chosen to become a technician rather than go for a higher degree. Her work clothes were a shirt with the sleeves and collar neatly cut off, and jeans of various muted colours.

Davith, though he enjoyed Van's teasing, was serious by nature, striving not only to do his work well but also to match Van's city-bred sophistication, in spite of his rural Oceanic background. He admitted to a liking for adventure literature, but tried to conceal a sentimental streak. He wore his wavy black hair long, framing his bronzed face. He was medium-height and sturdily muscular, toughened by a childhood on a ranch. His work clothes now imitated the plennor's: a grey heather jacket and grey slacks. Like Van, he had a quick mind but a preference for work that involved his hands as well. Rather modest about his abilities, he had been as surprised as pleased to find himself swept into psionics, the newest and most exciting field of science.

On this Thursday morning, Van and Davith read Mayne's note, then looked at each other in surprise that shaded into disbelief.

After their first few questioning remarks, Davith said firmly, "It's not like him."

"We can't say that for sure," Van cautioned. "We don't know him that well yet."

"In the six weeks we've been here, he's always been careful to tell us where to reach him when he's gone out during the day."

"He's only gone out a few times. And it was always business — checking on work he was having done for him in other labs, things like that. Maybe this is social."

"Our plennor?" cried Davith. "He doesn't know what social means."

"He does so. Don't you remember how smoothly he turned down that Varidoran official the other day, the one who wanted him to head some Regional committee?"

"So he's got good manners. I've never seen him go to any social event in Neithon, for all the invitations he gets."

"Seen him? Since when have you travelled in the same social circles as a plennor?"

"You know what I mean. The news media always show the guests at those big affairs."

Van grinned. "Yeah, okay. He's on my computer's clipping-service list, too. But if it's not work, and not social, where has he gone?"

"I can't imagine. That's what's bothering me. We know he planned to continue with the telepathy amplifier upgrading today..." Davith picked up the electrodes of the TKM and had the analogram screen show what the plennor had been working on after their departure the previous day. "Van! There's a jumbled mess in the immit he was forming. He never leaves things untidy — and he wouldn't make a mistake like that in the first place unless something had interrupted him — violently."

"So he's been called away suddenly? Illness in the family, maybe?"

"He hasn't got any family. No, I mean real violence. I think he's been forcibly removed."

Van gestured at the print-out. "But he says — "

"Somebody says! Anybody can type a note."

Van conceded the point, but demanded, "Why would anyone want to grab our plennor?"

"Maybe some communication company's against psionics."

"They're falling all over themselves to get into the field."

"Well, maybe one of them figures it'll get a jump start by making him work for them."

"He wouldn't help them," Van said firmly. "ISC always plays fair."

"There are ways of forcing people."

"You've been watching too many thrillers on your E-cube."

"All right, maybe I'm an idiot; but I'm going to call Security." Absent-minded in his worry, Davith reached automatically for his pocket phone before remembering that all wireless devices were left outside the lab area.

As Davith moved instead to the nearest room phone, Van asked, "You're serious about this?"

"I am. I'd rather look like a fool than risk losing our plennor."

"When you put it like that.... Make the call."

***

Davith's message was received by Security with neither doubt nor excitement, but with the standard operating procedure of reserved judgement. Within ten minutes a small group of field personnel was at the lab applying equipment for holographic photography, laser fingerprinting, collection of dust particles, examination of the premises by infra-red, ultra-violet, gamma, and X-rays, and assorted kits for chemical, radiological, and physical on-site tests.

The man in charge of the group introduced himself as Captain Marquif Simao. He was a handsome man of twenty-five with light brown skin and short, neatly styled black hair, a ready smile, and a quiet air of authority. He wore civilian dress with a well-cut summer-weight moss-green suit and a white shirt with a fashionable speckle of apple-green threads. He allowed himself a single touch of unconventionality: a bola tie bearing a fire agate cabochon.

After quietly setting his staff to work, Simao turned to the two lab technicians. "You last saw Plennor Mayne when you left here after work yesterday afternoon?"

"That's right. Van and I left at the same time. I think it was about seventeen-thirty."

"Plennor Mayne remained in the lab?"

"Or came back out after supper — He lives in the apartment at the back."

"Was this customary behaviour — working after hours?"

"If he had started on something he wanted to finish off."

"What was he doing when you left?"

"Designing a piece of apparatus, using the computer over here, the one with the note on its print-out."

"Did he mention his plans for the evening?"

"No, but he must have gone on working, because the design's been copied into the TKM — the telekinetic micromanipulator — and there's an image circuit partly made there." Davith waved at the machine.

Simao looked at the TKM, built into a desk-sized piece of workbench. There was little to see except the analogram display screen in the top surface; the sides were enclosed by dust-proof panels. "That's his most recent invention?"

"No, the TPA's the latest — the telepathy amplifier."

"But he's still experimenting with this one?"

"Not really. We use it to make immits for other things."

"Still, he is an experimenter. Could it have malfunctioned and injured him, so that he might be acting randomly, in shock?"

"His designs don't malfunction," snapped Davith.

Van said, more practically, "That machine's been in use here for months, and it works perfectly. Anyway, Davith checked it this morning — That's how we know Plennor Mayne had been building an immit with it."

"Nevertheless, we'll look into the possibility." He turned to face one of his men. "Sergeant, do we have word back from the hospitals, yet?"

"Yes, sir. No report on an injury," said Sergeant Wolfric Tansk. He had an old-soldier look of relaxed alertness; but, like the captain, he wore plainclothes rather than uniform. The breast pocket of his dark blue suit bore an embroidered badge: ISC Security Service's emblem of two crossed keys overlying the base of a lit candle.

Simao asked him, "Did you get his medical records?" The technicians knew that in ISC Territory, medical histories were not private: people were valued for their abilities, and any defects were cured or compensated for or, in the extreme, honourably pensioned off. Only stupidity, wilful ignorance, or prejudice were considered reasons for scorn or discrimination.

"Yes, sir. Seems his only contact with them is his compulsory annual pilot's medical. The doctor said he's boringly healthy."

"And mentally?"

Tansk snorted. "Just, 'Well adapted to his environment'."

"Hmm. Limited, but positive. Take a look through the entire building, the ground outside, and the neighbouring buildings."

"We've already looked through this building," Davith put in.

"For a — an active person," Simao said delicately.

Van said tightly, "That's right. We weren't looking for a body."

"Or an injured man who might have crawled under something, ma'am." He turned back to Davith. "Now, sir, you said the plennor uncharacteristically left no clear word about his absence?"

Davith gestured at the print-out. "It's not even handwritten. Anyone could have typed that."

Simao nodded and turned to one of his staff. "Check the entire area around the computer and this psionic apparatus for trace deposits of any known knock-out gas or spray, and blood-splatter traces or scuffle marks." To another, "What have you got so far on fingerprints?"

The green-uniformed woman glanced up from the phone console where she was waiting. "On the apparatus in this main room, only the plennor and these two. In the attached living quarters at the back, the same, plus the two people who run the cleaner machines and bring in supplies. But none from the cleaners in here, oddly enough."

Van said, "Nothing odd about it. The plennor doesn't want anyone unfamiliar with our apparatus working around it. Davith and I look after cleaning this room."

The police officer made a murmur of understanding. She continued, "We found other prints on some stuff in one of the small labs but they're dusty. I've just fed them through to Records — Ah, here comes the answer." She scanned the report on the phone's monitor, and summarized, "Two former assistants of Plennor Mayne, still working for ISC."

Sergeant Tansk, carrying an infra-red detector, reported back in. "No live body in the area, sir. We're continuing to search for a dead one."

"Carry on." Simao turned back to the lab assistants. "Does Plennor Mayne have any enemies?"

"We've never heard of any," Davith said.

"I don't think he would," Van pointed out, "because he doesn't have personal relationships. Unless someone's envious? Or feels slighted because the plennor's ignored him? Would those be strong enough motives?"

"For some people they are."

"What about somebody kidnapping him to work for them?" Davith put forward.

"Don't worry, we'll check into that possibility fast. *That* would be serious."

"You call that more serious than the possibility of murder?"

"Yes. If he worked secretly for a Region or a commercial company, it would reflect on the ISC; and that's more important than any one scientist, even a plennor."

Gradually the Security staff reported in. No body; no signs of violence; no evidence of preparations for an absence. "We can't tell what clothes may be missing, of course."

"Razor?" Simao's tone held little hope.

The other man shrugged, "He's had his beard roots permanently inhibited, according to medical records."

"Toothbrush?"

"Disposables."

"And he's too healthy to require medicine; how about recreational drugs?"

"None on record; no traces in the building."

"A very independent man," murmured Simao. "And so no way to tell whether his absence is voluntary or not. Well, we'll get on with the routine." To the lab assistants he said, "We'll talk to you again. But if anything more occurs to you, phone me immediately."

The Security team moved out again and split up, some to do further physical examination of the area around the lab, some to question the personnel of the neighbouring labs. Simao returned to his headquarters and made his official report. Before he sent it to his superior he made an entirely unofficial duplicate of it.

***

Simao sat looking at the extra copy of his report; but he was not thinking about it. He was remembering a conversation he had had recently with a man named Tyrus Polminander, a small, neat, fifty-five-year-old man with sparse grey hair and a guarded expression, who dressed in a noncommittal grey suit and navy tie. Administrator Polminander was an official whose proper concerns had nothing whatever to do with Security.

"Has it ever occurred to you," Polminander had asked at one point, "how little control ISC has over these plennors and laudors? The vennors at least have limits on them, even if they're allowed to putter at their own interests. But the others can ask for anything they want and get it."

"Control? Doesn't Admin look after keeping their records, even assigning professional writers to bring clarity to opaque reports? Isn't the whole setup meant to free up the scientists from petty paper-pushing, so they can concentrate on their work?"

"Petty!" Polminander looked scandalized. "The money involved! These top scientists not only have their own labs and research teams, they have priority use of every other ISC facility, whatever might have been planned for it."

"That's the intent, to free them from boxed-in thinking and rigid budgets. By definition," Simao added in mild rebuke, "every plennor and laudor has already made a valuable contribution to ISC — and the world."

"So they deserve reward — but not this unlimited power and unquestioned demand on our resources."

Simao shrugged. "Most of them are reasonable in their demands. ISC gambles some of them will come up with additional major discoveries. They all continue to produce useful work of some kind."

"But how many real breakthroughs have come from this generosity? One 'repeat' plennor and two plennors upgraded from laudorates."

"Don't you think the work of those alone has been worth the gamble? — Not to mention the laudorate-level work many of them have added to their previous accomplishments. That's not routine stuff — It's breaking-wave."

"But think how much more we would have if their research had been *directed* at things we desperately need — medical cures, food and ecology studies, industrial techniques — nobody finds any of these things just puttering around. Who knows what we might have had by now if our resources had not gone to the whims of these self-centred geniuses!"

"You sound like the anti-science protestors."

"So they think — They've tried to recruit me. I won't have anything to do with them: they're extremist fools. But that doesn't make their basic argument invalid: we waste resources on their foolish blue sea research: research that doesn't go anywhere and has no end."

"Have you argued all this out with the Council?"

"Argued! The Council doesn't listen to administrators, or anyone else who sits far enough back to see the whole thing in perspective. Policy, remember, is entirely in the hands of scientists. And mind you, it's not ones who have retired or moved into administration, where they could learn something about values and priorities, but practicing scientists. And not even elected, but appointed for only a year at a time, and the selection done by random choice among those who haven't been on the Council lately. There's just no way to establish influence when they're constantly changed and don't need election support — and you don't even know who will be appointed next!"

Simao rubbed his chin pensively. "Does seem a strange way to run an organization, when you stop to think of it. I always assumed they were mostly token figures — that they'd take advice from experienced people like you, the way governments do from civil servants."

"They do not. And one of these days the whole institution is going to come crashing down around us, unless they can be convinced of the error of their ways and persuaded to amend the system in time."

"You think so?"

"I know so. Because you can't give unlimited legal power to a group as technologically powerful as the plennors and laudors and expect all of them to stay forever preoccupied with their studies."

"What would you put in place of the present system?"

Polminander waved a hand. "What else but an elected Council with administrative advisors? Why should all the people in ISC —like you and me, not scientists — why should we not be represented in our own government?"

"It's still a company, not a government."

"It's much too large and important to be considered as a company at this point. We're independent from all the Regions, so we're the equivalent of a Region ourselves. It's our right to have democracy."

"I've always presumed we would eventually — that running ISC as a company was just until everything was established."

"Once a ruling system is established, it won't let go until someone from outside jolts it into changing."

Simao frowned thoughtfully. "Yeah, they say that in history classes. So what would you do to kick in some change?"

Polminander leaned forward, oratory flowing. "The key to it all is the plennors and laudors. Not just because they have a vested interest in the system, but because the ISC's whole prestige and faith is bound up in them. To the layperson, they are scientific super beings, benevolently producing miraculous new technology — even though most of them are really engaged in basic research, not technology at all. To other scientists, they're an elite: idealized or envied, as may be, but looked up to as the giants in their fields. To the ISC, they are life itself, for they are what the ISC has that no Regional government, no university, no commercial company has: the acknowledged best scientific brains in the world... and further, they're seen by the world as a group of people who are devoted to their work, to helping humanity, and to increasing knowledge – models of integrity, above politics, and all the rest of it. *That* is what holds up the ISC."

"I'd say there's a little more to it than that. The Regions support the ISC because it ensures a balance, an equality of technological power among them."

"Quite true – but only as long as it continues to attract and hold the best brains: the people who become the laudors and plennors. And the flow depends on the reputation of the existing ones: the devotion, integrity, et cetera." Polminander became crisp: "Shatter that, and you've shaken the credibility of the ISC."

Simao was shocked. "You can't do that! We'd be back to anarchy – wars!"

"Don't worry; the fall of one plennor or laudor wouldn't be enough to topple ISC from its position – but it would shake it enough to make the Council listen to reason – to make them shift control to a firmer, democratic base."

Somewhat reassured, Simao considered that, but said rather challengingly, "So you want to ruin the reputation of a plennor or laudor?"

"I want to expose one. In your job, Captain, you must realize better than most people that no group of humans is wholly composed of honest and upright people."

"No large group, I agree. But there are only eight living plennors in all the fields of science, and only about a hundred laudors; and they've been selected for special qualities."

"Of intelligence and intellectual integrity – or blind luck in making a discovery," Polminander added cynically.

"As any investigator learns, it takes intelligence to recognize what you've stumbled over."

"Very well, grant them all the brains, and the integrity too if you want, but only in their work. A person who would never dream of falsifying a scientific report might still cheat someone in a business deal, or murder ner spouse."

"Not good enough for what you're after," said Simao, with professional judgement, beginning to settle in to Polminander's ideas. "Unless ner crime was associated with ner work ne'd be seen as an individual, not as a representative of ner class. You'd have to find one who really was selling out the ISC somehow."

"Such as how?"

"Leaking discoveries to a Region or a company before ne turned in ner official report to the ISC. Working privately for one. Devising a weapon to set nemself up in control of a Region. Taking pay to suppress a discovery that would lose a company money."

Polminander fixed his gaze on the other man. "Well, if you found a plennor or laudor had done one of those things, would you be willing to help me use nem against the Council, and not let them sweep it under the rug? In order to achieve democracy?"

Simao thought for a long moment, then said, "One of those things, yes. The ISC can't run on phony integrity. Whatever the danger to the Complex itself, it would be worse to conceal a crime like that."

Polminander steepled his fingers and smiled. "Then it remains only to find our sell-out. I am convinced there will be at least one. Because they are above suspicion no one has ever looked into their lives. They can get away with whatever they want to — and it's beyond belief to me that none of them have ever succumbed to the power of ner position and used it to ner own advantage."

"Well, you could be right," Simao conceded. "I've always thought of them as woolly-headed putterers, brilliant but impractical, not interested in anything much beyond their studies, families, and hobbies. But of course, they are human...and I suppose if you can have everything else for the asking, you might start craving the only things forbidden — things that could harm ISC."

"You have access to their records — not just the public part, but everything ever recorded about them, however private it's classified. I'm convinced that if you go through those records with the eye of suspicion, you'll find at least one of them whose behaviour has at some time been suggestive of something questionable or covert."

"And if nothing suspicious has ever been recorded?"

"Then we'll concentrate on the present. The more successfully one has covered any past misdeeds the more confident and careless ne will have become. It's harder to hide the present than the past. We watch for any break in any of their established patterns of working or living, any behaviour that's more than the usual amount of odd, even for one of them. And when we spot it, we'll close in on that selfish little genius and find out what ne's up to."

***

The question was, thought Simao now, staring at his report, whether being missing without explanation was sufficiently odd behaviour for a plennor to substantiate Polminander's cynical suspicions. Plennors and laudors set their own schedules; a few of them wandered off around the world on some whim of research or recreation without any formal notification to anyone of their going. This one's assistants insisted it was out of character for him; but they had not known him long...

Simao got up and went to see Mayne's former assistants.

Later, he dropped in casually at Administrator Tyrus Polminander's office with a plausible excuse. The administrator greeted him with equal casualness, but flicked on the room-privacy switch and regarded him expectantly.

"We've had a missing-person report on a plennor," Simao told him.

"Indeed. Which one?"

"The most famous one we've got — J P L Mayne, physicist. Now listed in this new science of psionics he founded."

"The man the news media like to call the triple plennor. You've caught a big one, Captain. Tell me more."

"Here's a copy of my report on the case — barely started, of course."

Polminander read it and frowned. "There seems to be a lot of doubt that he's missing at all. He may turn up tomorrow and say he went fishing, or off on a holiday with his mistress, or out somewhere to test a theory."

"Perhaps. But the few people who know him personally think it unlikely. And he hasn't made any casual mention of travel plans. Most people do, even high-and-mighty plennors who can't be bothered giving formal notice of anything."

"So what do you think has happened?"

"Since there was a note left, he presumably hasn't just met with an accident somewhere; but we checked that out routinely. Negative. There's no ransom message, so he hasn't been kidnapped. Murder seems unlikely

— he appears to have no enemies, and no one stands to gain by his death: he doesn't seem to be in anyone's way; and his estate is willed to ISC.

"All the known anti-science fanatics are under steady surveillance, of course, and they haven't had any surge of activity lately. It's true that we can't rule out the spontaneous eruption of a psychotic new terrorist, but it's unlikely such a person would try to hide a murder by leaving a put-off note. When one of that kind kills, they generally want the deed and reason broadcasted far and wide.

"His assistant Kamalua thinks Mayne's been abducted for forced scientific labour. Highly unlikely, but we're checking that too. All these things are still possible, but the most likely explanation, just as it looks, is that the plennor's gone off on his own initiative for some reason he doesn't want to state publicly — which is probably perfectly legitimate."

"But it could be something he needs to cover up?"

"That's among the possibilities, or I wouldn't have bothered coming to you. We need further evidence before we can begin eliminating possibilities; but I checked with his former assistants, and they agree with the present ones on both points: he's tidy in his work and explicit in giving information. To leave things in a mess and to give no word as to where he can be contacted are both out of character. I think we may assume at least that something unusual has occurred."

Polminander leaned back. "If he's dead, we'll have to look for another subject. If he stays missing, we can eventually talk to the Council about a — what was that word, back when scientists belonged to nations? — *defector*, that's it. But that could only be a back-up case, if we had no further information on him; we'd need a stronger one with it. And if he turns up with an account of some perfectly traceable activity, however unreasonable by ordinary people's standards, we're out of luck. But if he comes back with a cover story that we can break, we may just be onto something. In that case, we'll need every scrap of information we can get on him. What do you have so far?"

"Well, to begin with, here's his official record." Simao passed across a data slip.

Polminander slid it into a drive, called up the single file, and ran through the identification and biographic data: "Jonnan Parringer Lethe Mayne

— photo, fingerprints, voice-print, iris-print, blood type, DNA profile, et cetera. Height, one-ninety-one centimeters; complexion, fair; eyes, hazel; hair light brown — worn fairly short, I see from the photo — "

"In line with his policy of being unencumbered," guessed Simao.

The administrator resumed reading the description: "Four centimeter, straight-line scar on back of left wrist; no other distinguishing marks." Polminander spent another moment looking at the pictured features: intense, alert eyes, set in a face whose lines spoke of seriousness, self-reliance, and accepted responsibility — topped by slightly curly hair, quite tidy for an official photograph.

He moved on to another section: "Born seventh of June, 'seventy-eight. Father was Laudor Kennard Parringer Mayne, physical chemist, and mother was Plennor Derin Cavendale Lethe, geophysicist. That would have to be *the* geophysicist, I suppose?"

"Whose work is the basis for all geology since, yes."

"Hmm. Both parents died the same year."

"Same day. I looked it up. They were among the victims of the anti-science riots at the Penhaster Conference. The boy was twelve; he was sent to live with distant relatives of his father."

"ISC slipped up there, not looking after a child with that genetic potential!"

"If you'll recall your history, there was a period of considerable confusion after that massacre. That's when Security was reformed into the strong force we have now."

"Too bad they didn't get administrative procedures better organized at the same time. If *I* had been in charge then, I'd have spotted a potential loss like that! Lived in Berley, Varidor Region with these relatives. Haven't I heard of that city, for something unpleasant? Where is it?"

"It was and is a centre of anti-science feeling, dogged conservatism, and bigotry out in the prairies. It had a slum district called the Marmiche that had a nasty reputation. Of course, in those days, violence wasn't as common, or as vicious, or as... sophisticated as it is now, but for its day the area was considered rough. I checked Mayne's address, and it was just outside the Marmiche. His area contained mostly genteel-poor, but they went in for the bigotry and technophobia enthusiastically."

"Surprising he managed to stick to science, then. But makes it even more likely he picked up doubtful morals."

In mild disagreement, Simao mentioned, "His relatives seem to have been high-principled people, who lived by their beliefs."

Polminander shrugged and went back to skim reading. "Scholarships... universities... ISC appointment... image circuits... telekinetic micromanipulator... telepathy amplifier... more awards... honorary degrees... thirty-five of them! And it appears he writes his own articles, of which there is quite a list. A shining success story, in spite of ISC's goof," he concluded. "No wonder his name has become a byword for brilliance."

He closed the file, removed the data slip, and looked up. "So much for the official record. What can you tell me about him on a personal level?"

"So far, very little. He seems to be uninterested in the usual human vices – no drugs, no binges, no pick-ups. He also has no hobbies. He doesn't take vacations. Doesn't belong to any clubs. He's a member of professional societies, but never been active in any of them. Rarely even attends meetings, unless they're held in Neithon. His assistants claim he scorns social activity – gets lots of invitations but throws them out."

"Shy? Awkward?"

"No, just can't be bothered being sociable. He's been polite enough to attend ceremonies where he's been getting an award. The videos of the affairs show him looking perfectly at ease, but well-mannered rather than interested."

"Got anything else on him?"

"He takes time to keep in shape by karate practice, but doesn't go in for any competitions or team sports. Strictly independent, all the way."

"Very annoying of him. How about past friends or lovers?"

"He seems to have rejected people from the time he got dumped into that anti-science ambience as a child. The nearest he came to social relationships was to outfight a set of fist-and-knife bullies by learning to do proficiently what they did by instinct."

"Proficient indeed, to pick up only one noticeable scar."

"What little he's interested in, he learns to do well."

"Well, he must associate with his assistants. See what you can get out of them."

"There won't be much there, I'm afraid. They've only been with him a few weeks, so they won't know much about his past. Not only are they intensely loyal to him — to the point of hero-worship — they also seem to have vivid imaginations which run along the lines of spy-thrillers. If we try to pump them, they might jump to the right conclusions and put him on his guard."

"Can we get anything on them?"

"They're both fresh out of tech college, and they both seem to have been quiet, serious students."

"You never know, perhaps one of them cheated in an exam, or has a craving for something we can supply. Check them out. The earlier assistants, too, and whoever Mayne worked with before he got his plennorate."

"And if it turns out his past is blameless, do we drop him?"

"Not unless this absence is accounted for beyond any possible doubt. If this break in his behaviour pattern is voluntary, it's significant and it can't be any petty crime: plennors can have anything they ask for; they've no need to get or do anything on the sly. Either the whole thing is a confusion about something perfectly legitimate, or he's up to something that even a plennor doesn't dare admit to: and that pretty well narrows it down to anti-ISC activity — in which case, we've got our man."

"If his absence *is* voluntary, there's no way Security can demand further information about it. Beyond the normal records, a plennor's privacy is inviolable."

"I know of a way to get some information myself, Captain. Completely legal, and ideal for this situation. Casual chattering is a human instinct, and when a man cuts himself off from it, he becomes a perfect set-up for the proper stimulus."

"What are you going to do?"

Polminander smiled to himself. "I'm going to put pressure on a certain biochemist I know about, named Haldis Gythstrom."

***

The following day Davith Kamalua reported that someone had removed the printed out manual of Mayne's telekinetic micromanipulator — the copy the plennor had kept for handy reference. Kamalua insisted that he could identify the copy by a coffee stain, and that it was no longer in the lab, and that he himself had checked something in it on the very day he had reported the plennor missing, when he had cleared the TKM for routine daily use. Simao informed Polminander.

"Is this information a new piece of research?" pounced Polminander.

"No. It's published stuff. Highly technical specifications for building and using the apparatus. But the information's available in any library and in hundreds of labs, some of which have already built the machine for their own use."

"Then it doesn't make sense."

"If we could only find some definite evidence of a criminal act, by or against him, Security could put more intensive effort into the investigation, and into checking on the plennor's own behaviour; but as long as his actions appear to be voluntary and show no overt signs of illegality, we've got to be careful. Protecting the privacy of plennors and laudors is one of Security's jobs."

"Well, if he shows up, let me know and I'll send in my own agent."

CHAPTER 3

Attack

When Mayne returned to his own universe after nearly eight days in Geode and only a brief trip back home, he had a transplacing device and a small amount of knowledge about it. The wexter had pleaded personal incomprehension of its technical aspects, but had spoken willingly about its effects.

It was about six by nine centimeters, three millimeters thick, and very simple in appearance: a flat, smooth case of deeply greyed green with rounded corners. Towards one end, was a scattering of twenty-four slightly darker dots, looking like nothing more than happenstance irregularities of shade.

On Ithleen's suggestion, the wexters had patterned a checkerboard in dark and light squares on the opposite side, to provide an excuse for carrying the little object, and had given the whole thing a slightly homemade and worn look – with one corner not quite matching the curve of the others, and a scratch across the game board – to make the object look valueless. Neither the telepathic wexters nor the tiny Geodan society had much experience with theft; but the Geodans read and wrote mystery and adventure stories set in "the old days", and the wexters gave prompt consideration to any suggestion of even remote possibilities of danger: so the precaution had been added.

Mayne commended both the original dullness of appearance and Ithleen's additional camouflage; he did not want his transportation – perhaps someday his life – to depend on an object that was likely to interest a casual thief. To transplace at random, he would place fingers across the patch of dots. To transplace to any particular universe he would run a fingertip through a sixteen-point pattern among the dots, while concentrating on where he wanted to go. Pressing the end of the case nearer the dots would return him to his home fast.

The wexters, as usual, had no name for the device, so Ithleen had decreed it to be a rifkey: a key for crossing the rift between universes.

"Why the dot pattern?" asked Mayne. "Why not a straightforward button or just the mental commands?"

"An additional safeguard in case the rifkey should fall into the wrong hands," returned Spen. "A button can be pressed by anyone, and a mental command given by anyone who can conceive of the idea of transplacement. We have built the rifkey so that it will work only if operated by an organic sentient being who is touching it and willing the transplacement at the same time. This means it cannot be tested by any computer-automated device. It takes five seconds to operate the rifkey, so with the greatest number of trials that could be made in a year the chance is approximately ten to the sixth, in your math."

"You seem to have an adequate safety margin there," said Mayne, allowing his touch of amusement to surface. Then another thought struck him. "But what if I run into telepathic people, who could simply draw the knowledge out of my mind?"

"We have considered that possibility, and the further one that you might someday, because of injury, have to have someone else use the rifkey for you, thus spreading knowledge of its operation. We have therefore built into the rifkey a control which will affect the mind of anyone who uses it, causing a reluctance to pass on the operating pattern and a complete resistance to having that information taken without consent. If your mind reaches the point of yielding up the information involuntarily, the information itself will be wiped out of your mind before it can be passed along. We regret the fact that this will strand you in whatever universe you are then in; but we must maintain defenses against the possibility of any hostile being learning to use the rifkey's directed transplacement."

Mayne nodded soberly. "I did agree to be expendable." He went back to exploring the rifkey's abilities and limits after a moment. "How selective is it? Is there any way to preview where you'll land? Suppose, for instance, it deposited me next to some paranoid dictator in ner bath."

"The rifkey, being psychically operated, is able to incorporate an emotional sensor which blocks you from a situation where your presence would be unwelcome. It also prevents you from transplacing to a location where your arrival would put you in danger. It operates through a 'temporal phase-shift sampling of probability events'. I am not a theorist and do not understand how this works."

He turned the rifkey over in his hands, considering the limitations placed on it. "That probability sampling sounds like a brilliant protective invention; but it's also a drawback. No way to land in the middle of a band of enemies and take them by surprise."

"Who would want to emerge among enemies?" cried the Spen with startled incredulity.

Mayne probed further into his new tool's capabilities instead. "How do I will myself to a particular universe?"

"There are two ways: if you have been there before, you simply select it in your memory. Or you may will yourself to go to the location of any person you know in another universe."

"How well must I know the place or person?"

"You need to have seen nem personally, or have at least a memory tag of identity, such as 'third world after that tropical one.' The rifkey can tap your subconscious mind, but the information must be in your mind as personal experience, not as hearsay."

Spen continued the briefing. "In random selection, the arrival point is also random. If something begins harming your particular body chemistry, the rifkey will automatically return you to the safety of your home base. It can detect such dangers only in the immediate place and time of landing; it could deposit you near a physical danger, or a moment before one."

"How much can I carry with me?"

"If it is not sentient, anything within your arm's reach. You can transplace only one other person at a time, and that person must be willing to accompany you, not a reluctant person. Not even if the person became unconscious: as I have told you, the rifkey senses into the subconscious. You could however move an animal, which would not have the comprehension to resist."

"Any other limitations on it?"

"You cannot move a person or thing that is in the grip of another transplacing device. As well, the automatic emergency homing mode will move only the user nemself home, not a companion, although the homing mode in deliberate use can be willed to take a second person."

"Interesting." He ran his thumb over the rifkey. "How is it powered?"

"We are unsure exactly. We only know that it draws power into itself. We believe it may be connected to Ithleen's theory of what she has named the diaphane fluxate."

Mayne and Ithleen had spent hours discussing her theory. Ithleen herself had said, "I always assumed the diaphane to be a pure thought construct, as imaginary as mathematics, until Spen came to tell me about the multiverse. Ne said ner people got excited when they studied my equations: they think the diaphane is what they've been calling non-space, an otherness they've discovered that supports and divides the universes. They haven't learned much about it because those who tried to linger in it came to a nasty end."

"Spen said transplacement isn't dangerous." Mayne's quirked eyebrow had made it a question.

"So far as they know, it's not. It's only the trying to stop partway through that's disastrous."

Mayne thought about that conversation now. The wexters might know more than they realized, and simply not have sorted out their practical experience into logical patterns yet. And one should never pass up a possible source of knowledge because of assumptions. "Spen, if I could talk to your theorists..."

"They are not willing to make contact with an alien."

"How do they expect to learn anything from Ithleen's studies then if they won't talk to an outsider and you don't understand enough to carry her ideas to them?"

"We have another device, capable of recording directed thought. Ithleen calls it a wexcorder. It is a one-way device, delivering thought-records only to beings with our particular brain structure. When our theorists have studied a discussion Ithleen has recorded for them, I bring her their specific questions or data. We have made one of these recorders for you as well, so that you may tell us what you discover of the universes; but I doubt if the theorists would be willing to send answers to your questions unless the answers become necessary for your task. It is not our intention to hasten the development of psionics in a world not yet prepared to handle it."

Mayne sighed. "How often do you want reports?"

"They need not be regular. Report whenever you have data you think may be of interest to us. We suggest you do some random sampling first, to give us a broader base of knowledge about sapients' Earths; we will then consider your observations and see what ideas they suggest. Meanwhile, familiarize yourself with the use of both the rifkey and the recorder; go where you please, and report whatever is of interest to you, whenever you wish. We will collect the information at our convenience."

"You'll come for it?"

"No. The wexcorder sends its data with a signal to a random, empty universe. We trace the signal later and move the data by other random transplacements, eventually delivering it to those in charge of this project for distribution."

Mayne picked up the second device, which the wexter had caused to appear on Ithleen's desk. It was a four-centimeter, roughly spherical object with one flattened spot for standing, and no controls of any sort. A dark bluish grey, with no markings or variations in colour, it was smooth but not highly polished or slippery. It looked like a cheap paperweight.

"How do I use it?"

"When you want to give us information, simply think of doing so. We prefer directed thoughts, but it is capable of absorbing impressions of its immediate surroundings. However, it takes considerable effort to analyze that level of background noise and we would prefer only to expend the energy if necessary. You need not be touching the recorder, but the closer it is to you the clearer a record you make."

After looking the wexcorder over briefly, Mayne put it into a pocket, and took his rifkey back out as he cast a final glance around Ithleen's study.

The theorist herself came forward. "I'm as interested as the wexters in what you discover in the universes. Come again and tell me what you find, and more about your own world, too."

"I will. And I'll bring all the books and journals I promised. A pity our disks and microfilms won't fit your readers."

"You've already taught us a great deal. Your psionic apparatus has intrigued several of my engineering students into switching to basic science. I had meant to show you the city and the labs..."

"Another time."

"I'll look forward to it."

He smiled at her and pressed the end of the rifkey. Ithleen and Spen faded out into white opacity. Five seconds later, he was standing in his own living quarters at the back of the lab.

"So, it works," he said. He hesitated before slipping the rifkey into a pocket again. "Before I start playing with this, I suppose I'd better check to see if any important messages have been left while I've been away. I seem to recall ordering some data from the Central Library." How long ago and unimportant that felt now!

He walked along the corridor from his apartment, through the airlock doors that helped keep dust out of the working area, entered the big main lab room, and stopped short. Two men he had never seen before were talking with his assistants.

The younger one was in ISC Security Service's forest green uniform; while the other was in civilian dress but wore the embroidered crossed-keys-and-candle badge of Security on his jacket's breast pocket, surmounted by the rank marker of a sergeant. They both wore an air of calm and solid authority.

Jumping to the conclusion that he had indeed been missed, Mayne wondered if he had lost months in the days he had spent in Geode. He walked forward with a casual air. "Do you have the right time, Davith?"

All four whirled to face him.

"Plennor Mayne! I, yes, it's fourteen-oh-two."

Mayne's watch agreed perfectly. So time was probably parallel, and the Security personnel had nothing to do with his absence. Worth the bluff, anyway. He gave them an inquiring look. "What's the problem here?"

"None, apparently," snorted the sergeant. "Davith Kamalua reported you missing, sir."

"Missing? Didn't you see my note?"

Flushed with embarrassment, Davith replied, "Yes, sir, we did; but we - I thought it was a fake."

Van came to Davith's support, insistently sharing the ridicule. "We thought you'd been kidnapped. I'm sorry for the trouble we've caused."

The sergeant smiled at her, his craggy face lightening. "Never mind. If it had really happened, it would have been helpful to get on it right away. I'll call off the hunt." He hesitated. "Care to state, for the record, Plennor, where you've been?"

Mayne gave him a frosty look. "No, I do not."

"Okay, sir. No need."

The uniformed Security man gave him a courtesy salute and the two men left. Davith and Van stood like penitent children. Davith blurted, "It was all my fault. Don't fire Van, too."

"I've no intention of firing either of you. But what on Earth —" This Earth, Mayne thought, with a rush of private joy — "made you think I'd been abducted?"

Davith explained about the circuit and Mayne nodded. "Good deduction, Davith. As a matter of fact, I *was* interrupted. If I'd realized I had a budding detective here, I'd have taken time to write by hand. Well, let's get back to work. Van, have you completed installing the scintillation plates in that new detector?"

"Yes, sir."

"Good. Davith, have those Briach stabilizer coils I asked you for come in?"

"They weren't up to specifications, sir. I sent them back with a pointed note about quality control. Supply promised to have good ones here by today."

"Get after them and make sure they do. Van, make me a new printout of the TKM's manual while I go through my designs again." Since it would obviously be indiscreet to vanish again immediately, Mayne calmly fitted himself back into his routine. He seated himself at his computer console and set it running through his three-dimensional views of the proposed circuits.

The assistants sighed, half in relief that things were back to normal, half in disappointment at being told nothing, and resumed work. Neither appeared to notice Mayne's slip in referring to the absence of the old copy of the manual, which he had left in Geode for the engineers. Wisely, he let the mention stand once realizing his mistake, instead of calling attention to it by an invented explanation as to how he knew it was missing.

***

Captain Simao phoned Polminander. "He's back and refuses to say anything about where he's been."

"Does he now? Then there may be something there to find out. Well, no man is as self-sufficient as this arrogant plennor thinks he is; and the agent I've been saving will soon get some information out of him." Polminander switched off and went to put pressure on a certain vennor.

***

"It's good of you to take the time to see me, Plennor Mayne."

"You said it was important to you, Vennor. What can I do for you?"

Vennor Haldis Gythstrom was a short, white-haired, normally brisk woman of sixty-seven; but now she was hesitant. When she had phoned the previous evening to ask to come see him, Mayne had noticed that she sounded disturbed over something. Thinking she might want to hold her discussion in a room with privacy, he had cleared an accumulation of temporarily stored items off the desk and chairs in the office that he had designated as his own. He rarely used it, since he preferred to do even his computer work at a desk in the central lab room, where he was close to the hands-on work he loved; but he believed every worker should have a quiet retreat available. When he had chosen the lab building his position entitled him to, he had made sure there were a number of these retreats available, even though he planned to stay uncluttered by having any work that required a large staff done elsewhere: he liked to think ahead to possible contingencies.

Leading the vennor into his own private niche, Mayne seated her with formal courtesy before taking his own chair.

She twisted her hands together, then raised her eyes and said, with effort, "I want to ask a small but perhaps annoying favour."

"What is it?"

"Could you endure having a teenager in your lab for a brief time?"

"Not if it's the sort of child who handles things."

"Oh, she wouldn't do that. She's been underfoot in my lab often enough to have it drilled into her to keep her hands off what she doesn't understand."

"Why do you want her here?"

She hesitated. "The child is my grand-niece, Robinaire Filyk. My niece married a popular singer, who had a beautiful face, a pleasant voice, and a better vacuum in his head than any I've ever achieved in the lab. No, I take that back. The space was completely filled with self-interest and egotism."

Mayne shifted impatiently during the recital of these obviously long-standing resentments, but did not interrupt, guessing that the vennor was trying to work her way towards whatever it was that was really bothering her.

"Robinaire takes after her father in being self-centred and worldly, but she's been managing all right in school. With her mother now passed on and her father always away on tour, I've had to look after her education," she digressed. "I've never been able to interest her in science; she prefers things she can memorize. But she does well enough. It's only recently that I learned she's been struggling with mental illness."

With that sentence she began to speak carefully, as if she had rehearsed the part she was most reluctant to say. "There's a psychiatrist who has adapted your psi amplifier into a clinical tool, which he wants to apply to Robinaire. But he says the treatment could be a shock to her unless she's first indoctrinated with the idea of using psionic tools in a non-clinical atmosphere."

She drew a deep breath of relief at having got the statement over. Mayne wondered why an educated woman should find it so hard to speak of mental illness in the family. Or *was* it embarrassment? He was not good at analyzing people's emotions, but it seemed to him there was a touch of anger or resentment in her. Not against the child: her voice had been warm when she spoke of her. And surely not against treatment. What, then? The need to ask a favour?

But her voice was more relaxed as she went on, "So what I'm asking is whether you'll let her come here a time or two and observe the use of your psionic equipment. She wouldn't know the real purpose of the visits; the excuse would be for her to write an article on your discoveries, for the Junior Writers section of the *Neithon News*. She'd be willing to do that: she's keen on celebrities. Of course, she prefers pop-culture heroes, but even she has heard of you, Plennor Mayne. Will you do this for us?"

Mayne stirred uncomfortably. "Isn't there any other way to treat her?"

"This is what the psychiatrist wants. She wouldn't be in your way, Plennor; and she does what she's told. It wouldn't take much of your time. Just let her watch. You could forget she was there. It does mean so much to us."

There appeared to be no way out of it. In any case, he expected to be absent himself from the lab – the world – for much of his time these days, so the nuisance should be minimal for him. "All right then. Let her come. Ms Sartyov, my senior technician can show her around."

Vennor Gythstrom stood up. "I'll send her tomorrow then. Plennor Mayne, I don't know how to thank you."

He rose with her. "No need, Vennor."

As he escorted her to the door, she suddenly turned back and touched his arm. "You'll take care of Robinaire, won't you? See that no harm comes to her?"

He was surprised. "Of course, Vennor. We're not doing anything remotely dangerous here."

"I'm fond of the girl; and I don't understand this business. But I know I can trust you to look after her."

"I will, Vennor."

"Thank you."

After she left, Mayne returned to the central room, telling Van to be ready to do a guided tour the next day, and explaining the situation. "I haven't heard anything about this psychiatric adaptation of the amplifier," he said, "so I presume it's still experimental and unpublished. Maybe that's why Vennor Gythstrom was worried. It certainly sounds unorthodox."

"Maybe the psychiatrist's a plennor!" said Van excitedly.

"Psychiatry isn't eligible for plennorates," Davith quenched her. "It isn't a science; it's a medical art."

Mayne said, "Keep an eye on her to be sure she doesn't damage either herself or any of the equipment; otherwise, treat her as the budding journalist she's supposed to be."

"Okay, Plennor."

As Mayne moved away, Van looked at Davith and said, "Well, we're certainly having our little excitements. Though going from detecting to nursemaiding is rather a let-down!"

"Don't grumble," said Davith. "Be thankful we've got a let-down instead of a loss!"

"I am, Davith," Van said seriously, "and not just for the sake of still having a job; did you notice how — in spite of the worry — how dull it was with the plennor away?"

"You're homing on harbour there, Van!"

***

Mayne spent the evening testing the rifkey in brief random hops, observing but not moving about on several Earths. He tried to select particular types of worlds but found, as the wexter had claimed, that one could not pre-determine circumstances. But apparently the rifkey picked up his intended caution, for it placed him in fairly isolated locations, where interaction with others was unlikely.

He experimentally directed the rifkey to take him to Spen; as he expected, it simply did not work, confirming that it needed the user's sight-memory to work in the person-directed mode. He wondered whether his attempt was a complete nullity or whether it had rung alarm bells on Spen's world. If it had, could the wexters tell immediately that it was only their agent testing out the limits of the rifkey?

He hoped they understood the principles of an experimenter: to take nothing for granted merely because it had been stated by authority. Otherwise, Spen might find nemself in yet more difficulty, having to defend the trustworthiness of ner selected agent. Belatedly, Mayne thought into his wexcorder the reason for his action, and an apology for any disturbance he had caused. Not that it would have made any difference, he realized, even if he had taken that precaution first, since Spen had indicated that the wexters would collect his messages only at random intervals.

Whether or not the wexters had taken note of his attempt, no one came to demand the rifkey's return, so Mayne tried the person-centred command again, this time using Ithleen as target. The rifkey made no difficulty over this choice, and promptly deposited him in her study.

He had intended just to drop off the books he had promised; but once there, he lingered to tell her what he had seen so far. To his surprise, he eventually found himself telling her about his psi discoveries, in a degree of detail he had never offered anyone before.

"We found that there would be a limit to how small we could make our transistors, down around the fifty nanometer size because of natural quantum effects beginning to interfere with their functions. However, these results weren't entirely consistent. I noticed that the inconsistency depended on who was doing the construction. I, and a few others, were steadily more successful than the rest of the experimental group; and I began to wonder if there was a psi factor involved," He told her.

"What we couldn't do at a macroscopic level, we might be able to achieve at an atomic or nuclear level. So I borrowed technology from some neurologists who were experimenting with biofeedback to control computer programs. Once we grew accustomed to the notion of controlling things mentally, we also tried hypnosis, convincing our subjects that they *could* influence the construction of nano components by telekinesis. And we found it worked. Those of us who knew exactly what we wanted the circuits to be and do, increased our success rate noticeably.

"We found two things: that eventually we were actually constructing patterns at the nuclear level, where an additional set of laws begins to operate; and that one of the patterns I formed experimentally was able to feed back a resonance into whatever part of the mind was applying the psi influence. When we got it hooked it up to macro equipment, we had a crude psi amplifier. Using that, those with enough psi talent and knowledge of physics to form a perfect image in their minds were able to make components. We called them image circuits — which soon got shortened to immits."

"I'm impressed," murmured Ithleen. "Psionics has been purely theoretical here. Less than that: fictional. Has it changed your society much?"

"Not at first. Only a few people could make the immits, so it remained in the lab for a while. But as the knowledge and ability spread, it became obvious that immits were going to have as big an effect as transistors or steam or electricity did in their day; and ISC awarded me my plennorate. Most people tend to say it was for devising immits, but I like to feel it was for proving psionics was possible; I think that opens up a bigger field. Not that we've got very far in understanding what we're doing. The development has been strictly empirical; all attempts so far to work out a theory of psi get tangled up in violations of the principle of causality. Your fluxate theory may well be the key to understanding psi."

"What about your later inventions?"

"Once I got my own lab, I was able to construct a psionic device specifically designed for forming and handling. That's the telekinetic micromanipulator that I showed your engineers how to build. It can be used even by someone with no more knowledge than a technician: all they have to do is visualize the function of the image circuit, not the actual structure, and the TKM will construct it."

Ithleen grinned. "Perhaps even I could use it, though it's years since I've done any hands-on physics."

"Of course you could; you have the knowledge of what you'd want to make. The psi-activating part is now incorporated into the machine; and we've found very few people with absolutely no ability to be touched by that."

"The wexters did say some of my talents were forms of psi," Ithleen mused. "So, does everyone on your world use TKMs now?"

"No, we don't yet have mass production. The TKM can make multiple copies of any design, but each still has to be guided by an operator who knows what ne's doing, even when it's working from the model of a previously-made immit."

"How long have you had the TKM?"

"About two years. They're now being built commercially and — more importantly — in many labs, which means there'll be a lot of good minds applied to the problem of what's in that deeper level."

Their talk ranged on, mostly about their differing backgrounds and present circumstances — things they had had little time to discuss during Mayne's previous visit, which he had spent mostly with the Geode engineers, teaching them as much as he knew about psionics.

Mayne even found himself telling her about finding Security men in his lab on his return. Ithleen looked a little uncertain, and asked, "Is that police or some sort of guards?"

"Basically it's a community police force which looks after the ISC Compound itself and Neithon — the city that was built to accommodate ISC personnel. Besides ordinary crime, it pays particular attention to the lunatic fringe of anti-science activity, though we haven't had much of that lately. That overlaps with protecting plennors and laudors who have become famous enough to arouse tourist curiosity."

Eventually fatigue made Mayne notice the time. With hasty apologies, which Ithleen brushed off sleepily but cheerfully, he took his leave and returned home for a few hours of rest.

He decided he should postpone further testing of the rifkey for a day or two: it would be prudent to get his routine re-established until any unusual interest in him on the part of Security faded away. His training as a physicist also told him to do his experimenting with the unknown in steps; so he held a firm check on his yearning to devote his whole time to exploring.

***

By the next day, Mayne had half forgotten the proposed visit to his lab. He had spent the morning installing the Briach coils in the latest experimental model of his telepathy amplifier, and was now, in the early afternoon, hovering over one of its paired consoles with a piece of test equipment, while his technicians observed. "If this corrects the distortion in the test pattern —" A chime interrupted his discourse, and he looked around in surprise. "Did one of you set a timer for something?"

"Doorbell, Plennor," Van prompted him.

"Who could it be? Oh, yes, Gythstrom's grand-niece. Bring her in, will you?"

A few moments later Van returned from the front hallway ushering in a fifteen-year-old who walked with a poise beyond her years. The girl had cornflower-blue eyes and a heart-shaped face; her light auburn hair fell about her shoulders in a smooth tumble of half-curls. She wore an expensive looking sleeveless blue and white dress. Her only ornament was a pin in the shape of notes on a music staff; but the notes were, in fact, the markings of a radio dial: it was the latest fashion fad, a radio-brooch. Fortunately, she had been polite enough to turn it off before coming in.

Van presented her in a voice so carefully neutral as to hint at disapproval. "Plennor Mayne, this is Robinaire Filyk."

"How do you do, Ms Filyk?"

She approached and said, "Please call me Robinaire."

"As you wish. Ms Sartyov will show you around the lab."

"Oh, won't *you*?" cried Robinaire.

Mayne was taken aback. He had grown accustomed to having his most casual decision accepted as law. But he remembered that she was his guest and even more, his responsibility, on his promise to Vennor Gythstrom.

"Yes, certainly," he said.

"Supra!" Robinaire exclaimed.

So with a good grace Mayne put down his test equipment and led her around, describing the various pieces of apparatus in simple terms.

Van giggled softly to Davith. "Not exactly what he expected, is she?"

"He's coping," said Davith, "Nothing ever fazes him."

"Unlike a certain tech, who would get a somewhat clearer reading if he turned that meter *on*," Van said.

Davith flushed and flipped the switch.

"And onto the right scale." She changed it for him. "You should be conducting the tour. You've got point-nine of your attention on it!"

He met her teasing smile. "I'm not the celebrity." He sighed.

Robinaire was more interested in the cartoons Van had taped up around the lab than in the apparatus. Looking at one decorating the TKM, she said to Mayne, "That's you, isn't it? I've seen you in others."

The cartoon showed a group labeled "ISC Council" waving around papers labeled "Next Project" and "Current Needs" and "Wanted Yesterday", and a thin, rumpled-haired man in a lab coat, wearing three medal ribbons from each of which dangled a letter P, who had one hand on a computer keyboard and the other holding a simple screwdriver, and who was saying nonchalantly, "Sure; what size universe would you like?"

Mayne shrugged. "Yes, that's the cartoonists' standard depiction of me."

He had grown so used to seeing this particular cartoon beside him as he worked that he had ceased to notice it. Reading it anew, he thought, I can't make them, but I can visit them! And a bit more warmth than usual was in his voice as he showed Robinaire the rest of the equipment.

They completed their circuit of the room back at the telepathy transmitter he had been modifying. Van and Davith stepped back.

"What's this?" Robinaire asked. "Why is it opened up?"

"That's what we're working on right now. It's called a telepathy amplifier, or TPA for short. By wearing these electrodes, you can send a message to anyone who's plugged into a receiver. It's just like radio, except you don't talk: you think in clear, simple words or pictures. So far it can link only nearby stations, and we're trying to find a way to extend its range. Since we don't yet understand psi, our work has to be empirical, by trial and error, that is."

"Aunt Haldis said you know more about psionics than anyone else in the world."

"Very likely; but that's still not much."

"How does it work?"

"We don't yet know. We're in the same position as the early workers in electricity or radioactivity. We've found a phenomenon and a few ways to manipulate it, but we don't really understand or control it."

"How can it work if you don't understand it?"

"In the same way your radio-brooch will work for you when you switch it on, even though you don't understand what little theory we've worked out on the image circuits that run it. Here, sit down and we'll show you how the TPA works." He checked that the machine was in operating condition, closed it up, and gestured his assistants to the receiver portion behind him, halfway down the room. They moved to the other machine and Van reached for its electrodes while Davith began adjusting the controls.

Robinaire obediently sat at her own machine and Mayne turned back to face her, picking up a pair of electrodes from the workbench. "You just slip these onto your temples; the band holds them in pla—"

From behind him came a sudden brief pulse of light, reflecting from the apparatus and walls at his end of the room. Robinaire's eyes, focused beyond him, narrowed against the moment's flash, then widened in startlement. Mayne twisted to see what was going on. He never completed his turn.

Chapter 4

Deportation

Mayne came slowly back to consciousness on the floor of his lab, his perceptions hindered by random firings of his sensory neurons — coloured flashes, rumbles and squeaks, a salt taste, a musky smell, and a crawling under his skin. His head ached, and his muscles would barely, painfully, work. He dragged himself up on an elbow, trying to force away the pain and phantom sensations, and stop the twitching of his muscles.

"Van! Davith!"

"Here, Plennor," came Davith's voice, faint and confused.

"What happened?" asked Van, equally shaky. "I'm all pins and needles, and I'm seeing great flashes of colour and smelling scorched popcorn..."

"Something seems to have stunned us."

"Something or somebody?" demanded Davith.

"I've no idea. All I saw was the reflection of a light. It was behind you, too?"

"Yes."

"Robinaire, you were facing it; what did you see? Robinaire?" He tried to peer around, and rubbed a hand irritably across his eyes. "Robinaire, are you all right?"

There was no answer.

"She must have run out," said Van. "She couldn't have been hurt any worse than we were: she was farther from the light, and we were only knocked out."

"Can you move yet?"

"Yes, but it hurts."

"Stay put, then, for a while." Setting his will against his own pain, Mayne forced himself to a sitting position. "What did you see?"

"Just a light flash," said Davith. "I thought it was an explosion."

"What was it, Plennor? Is anything damaged?"

"Yes," said Mayne sharply, as his sight cleared enough to take in his surroundings. "The TPA! It's gone. So is half the workbench, and Robinaire's chair." He got a grip on the edge of the workbench and hauled himself to his feet, clenching his jaw against the renewed surge of pain and dizziness. "And not through an explosion: the part of the bench where the TPA was has been sheared away. No charring, and it's absolutely smooth. Nothing I know of in this world could do that."

"Do you mean it was something out of this world?" cried Davith. "Another dimension? Time travel? Those things aren't really possible, are they?"

"Anything's possible," Mayne said absently.

"But some things are very unlikely," Van finished the familiar saying. "What do you think did happen, Plennor?"

"I think people from... somewhere else have removed Robinaire and the TPA. It seems to have been deliberate... though they may have taken more than they meant to, in their hurry. Their technology must be highly advanced: why would they steal an experimental amplifier that barely works? Whatever they wanted, it may have been Robinaire. Of what importance could she be to them?"

The assistants had managed to sit up, huddled over and leaning against a console and a chair. Davith asked hesitantly, "Should we call Security, sir?"

"No. There's nothing they could do about it. This may be connected with something that must not become generally known. I think I'll have to tell you two about it, however."

He looked at them and stressed, "You must prevent anyone else from learning any of this, unless I give permission, or your judgement tells you the revelation is justified and urgently needed."

They both murmured, "Yes, sir," with solemnity to match his.

Mayne glanced at his watch, and said with concern, "We must have been out for two or three hours. I'll have to give you just an abstract now."

He began determinedly to flex his still-stiff muscles, forcing life back into them.

"You've read speculation about an infinite set of universes? Well, it appears to be fact. The evening I began working on the new modification to the TPA, a being from one of the other universes appeared here."

"So that was what interrupted you!" exclaimed Davith, deductive triumph overriding surprise for the moment. "I knew it was something big!"

"The being, of a species who've been named wexters, asked me to become an explorer of the multiverse for them, in return for a means of inter-universe travel. I agreed." He continued methodically working out his stiffness.

The technicians stared at him. They accepted his words as truth; not yet associating it with their own reality.

"I visited a place called Geode and after talking to their scientists came back here for the TKM printout and the specs to make the immits for the psionic core. Then I built them a TKM to have experiments done on."

"In a week?"

"The Geode engineers used my printout to build the rest of their machine, and promptly started in to make a second one, using the first to make the image circuits. They were so pleased over learning the technology they gave the project priority, and promised they'd do the same for anything I ever wanted made."

The technicians helped each other to their feet and stumbled over to him. Davith said, "If you're working with these wexters, they wouldn't be the ones who attacked us..."

"No, they'd have no reason to. And their control is so exact that I don't believe they would have to slice through objects to reach a target, nor pick up anything beyond that target. It would be too much of a coincidence for a contact from somewhere else to occur just after the wexters'. Even a second contact from the multiverse seems coincidental — unless it was triggered by the first contact, somehow. Ithleen was concerned about that possibility. Well, speculation can wait. I've got to get Robinaire back."

He took out his rifkey. "If Vennor Gythstrom should inquire about the girl, tell her Robinaire and I have gone on a field trip somewhere; you don't know where. That'll be the truth; I don't know myself where it is."

"Then how can you find her?" Van asked.

"This device can locate her and take me to her."

"But Plennor, you're not going just like that, are you?" demanded Davith. "Those people could be dangerous. They could have worse weapons than a stunner. Shouldn't you take a gun?"

"Whatever makes you think I own one?"

"But you could get one!"

"After days of form-filling and waiting."

"They'd cut that down for a plennor. You could get it in an hour, I bet!"

"I doubt it. And it's been hours already. I can't make Robinaire wait any longer."

"Can we come along and help?"

Mayne shook his head. "I can't move more than one other person, and that will have to be Robinaire herself." He traced the required pattern on the rifkey, and faded from sight.

Van and Davith caught their breaths, staring.

They simply stood and waited.

And waited.

Finally Van said, "It's been twenty minutes, Davith."

"Maybe the transplacement takes time."

"He spoke as if it were instantaneous."

They waited again.

The rest of the afternoon dragged by. Their usual leaving time passed.

"Davith, what'll we do if he doesn't come back?"

"He will," said Davith stoutly. "Eventually."

"But, uh, till then?" Van accepted his refusal to lose hope.

"What can we do? There's no way we can go to help him! The only thing we can do is what he wanted, cover up what's happened till he gets back."

"I suppose we should go home, then, to make things look normal."

Reluctantly, he agreed.

***

The next morning they both came in early, eager for reassurance; but there was no sign that the plennor had been back. They doggedly carried out the pieces of work they had pending, and puttered around with other things, to keep busy as well as to keep up appearances. And minute by minute, hour by hour, the day passed with no sign of the plennor's existence.

***

The pulse of light had snatched Robinaire's attention from the plennor to the scene behind him. Three men stood there, all dressed in jeans and work shirts. One, a middle-aged man, stood staring ahead in dull indifference; the other two acted simultaneously. The second man, indeterminate of age, stolid of frame, and grim of expression, aimed a pistol-shaped device at Plennor Mayne, who collapsed even as he was starting to turn to see what had alarmed her. The pistol whipped around to the assistants and they too crumpled. At the same time, the young, nervous-looking man wearing a heavy pack of equipment on his back pointed straight at her a cone-shaped device that was attached by cable to the blank man.

There was another burst of light, this one right around her; and the world vanished.

She was too startled to react as the light enveloped her. Her scream rang out only as a new scene appeared around her. It too was a lab, a large room filled with machines bearing banks of monitors, gauges, and digital readouts.

In front of her stood a well-built man in his mid-thirties, with a short, silky brown beard, cut spade style. His hair was not so rich a tone, it was, in fact, the same as her own natural colour, a shade unkind people might call mousy. Unused to seeing beards in ISC Territory, Robinaire wondered if this man wore it to distract attention from the blandness of his hair. And why didn't he just dye his hair, like any sensible person? He was dressed in black corduroy trousers and a silky white turtleneck sweater, which she thought gave him rather a casual air; but in spite of that, he had a look of physical and mental competence, and an air of firm command.

Ignoring her cry, he looked instead at the three men who appeared beside her in another flash of light. He flicked a brief, pointed glance at Robinaire. "What's this?" His voice held sharp disapproval.

"Sorry, Zar Haughn. She was in the way," said the young man as he dumped his heavy equipment on the floor. "I thought we'd better not wait. There might have been others around with weapons. Shall I put her back?"

"And let her tell her people about us, while her trail is still fresh? Don't be a fool."

"What do we do with her, then?"

"Anything you like, so long as her trail doesn't end in our universe. Donate her to Aresette." Haughn shrugged the matter off and turned to the equipment his men had brought back from their raid. He lifted it free of its collapsed piece of workbench and heaved it easily onto a table.

"If we put her back in some uninhabited part of her own world, her trail would be circular," suggested the young man, "and it would be a long time before she could talk to anyone."

"And how many tries would it take you to find a suitable spot, Geeling? By the time you did, you'd have made so many contacts their clairvoyants would have an easy job spotting us."

The stolid man with the stun pistol spoke up. "We had enough trouble just getting ourselves back. Teleporters can't do a bunch of transplacements in a row. This one's about used up for today anyways." He motioned vaguely to the third blank looking man who was swaying on his feet.

He was answered sharply by the remaining occupant of the room, a small man in a black suit cut to suggest a uniform, though it was devoid of insignia. He wore a crewcut, a cultivated sneer, and a blustery manner that attempted to assume authority. "Then take him back to the psychics' quarters and fetch another teleporter. Get out another booster, too, and plug in that one to recharge."

The two men who had done the transplacing gave him the resentful looks of people being instructed in the obvious; but neither answered, and the older one went off with the blank man who seemed to be the teleporter.

Zar Haughn, absently stroking his beard, was still examining the stolen amplifier. "Let's see what you've brought back, Geeling. If it's not something that will enable us to improve our system, I'm going to wring that clairvoyant's neck. She's sent us on two fool's errands already this year."

Geeling, the lanky young man with straggling blond hair untidily pinned back, answered, "Well, this time at least it was a lab, with a machine being operated by electrodes. Maybe Xabis has got her wires uncrossed at last. Uh, as long as we fetched the operator of the machine, wouldn't it be useful to question her about it?"

Haughn gave him a look of impatience. "How much do you expect an operator to know about the principles or construction of ner machine? How much do you know about the equipment you've just been using? And you're a technician. I don't expect to understand any of this machine myself, even after all the years my experts have been trying to drum psionics into me."

He turned to the small, sneery man waiting in the background. "Porduc, I want the analysis of this apparatus done here in my private wing. Nothing's to be taken out of this lab. Tell Doctor Cazl she's to select two teams for double shift work. She'll no doubt claim she's working on something vital; tell her to drop whatever it is and report here with the first team immediately." In a sarcastic tone he added, "You may assure her that it's not a weapon and is interesting."

As he paused, Robinaire came out of her fear-induced paralysis and ventured to ask, "Who are you? What's going on?"

Haughn ignored her, his attention back on the amplifier, which seemed to fascinate him, like a man yearning over a food he couldn't digest, Robinaire thought.

Geeling, the young technician, said quickly and quietly to her, "Don't bother him, girl. He's the Zar of Kinnasoor!"

"What's that?" asked Robinaire uncomprehending.

"The most powerful man in the world. His word is law; and if he wants to he can have you tortured or killed, and nobody could say a word against it. So don't make any trouble!"

Robinaire swallowed. "Does he do much of that?"

Geeling shrugged. "There aren't many people foolish enough to oppose him. Or his personal aide," he shot a glance at Porduc, "who enjoys disciplining people. So don't make trouble!" He said again.

"But what's going on? Where am I? Why did you shoot the others?"

"We just stunned them, so they couldn't interfere. And we got you by accident. You're in our world now, and you'll never get back to yours unless the Zar decides to send you; so do whatever he says."

"I'm not on Earth?"

"Of course you are. But not your own Earth. You're in a different universe."

"I want to go back!"

"Then keep quiet and hope he changes his mind."

Haughn, continuing to examine the amplifier, said, "We may have something this time, Geeling. It's nothing like any of our own boosters, and it seems to be a stand-alone device, not hooked up to a base machine. If it really is psionic, this new world's technology may be beyond ours."

Geeling looked worried. "Then do you think they'll be able to trace us, on just one contact?"

"Not unless their clairvoyants are better than ours." Haughn continued to delve into the machine. He seemed to be talking to himself now, and Robinaire wondered if he kept his underlings around the way some people kept pets, just as an excuse to talk. "Electrode jacks, tuning controls, yes... but why does this section, which looks like the focus of the whole thing, have no input or output lines? Even nanotechnology needs connections of some sort to its manual controls. Hmm. Telepathic controls?"

He glanced sharply at Robinaire, then shook his head. "No, the operator's not an idiot, so she can't be a psychic. Can some genius on that world have invented a purely psionic machine that doesn't need to be tied in to a psychic? Or is it within the bounds of imagination that, on their world, not all psychics are mental deficients? Well, Perine may not have been able to make anything like this, but she should be able to analyze it..."

The other assistant returned with a bored-looking youth. He was less blank-faced than the previous teleporter or psychic, but exhibited neither interest in nor comprehension of either the activities or the apparatus around him. He obeyed direct orders, sullenly and with the same lack of interest.

Haughn looked up briefly again from his rapt examination of the TPA. "Send the girl off, Geeling."

Leaving his heavy pack on the floor, Geeling picked up the cone and spoke to the teleporter, gathering his attention and reminding him to work only on the person indicated by the cone's marker light.

Robinaire broke her obedient silence to ask hopefully, "Are you going to send me home?"

Geeling glanced inquiringly at Haughn. Porduc snapped, "The Zar has already told you Aresette!"

Haughn nodded absently, his attention remaining on the TPA. "Aresette will do. Anyone tracing her there is welcome to that world."

Geeling shrugged, aimed the cone at Robinaire, and touched his other contact to the teleporter. The marker light was blotted out by the dazzling, silent explosion of the operating light.

Robinaire abruptly found herself in an almost deserted street of grimly grey buildings. A passing vehicle swerved to the curb beside her and came to an abrupt stop. A man in a dark grey uniform jumped out and came back to her.

"Name and number, soldier! What are you doing out of uniform?"

"Me?" cried Robinaire. "I'm not a soldier!"

"Then let's see your maternity dispensation."

"I don't know what you're talking about!"

"Get in the car!"

"Please, I want to go home!"

"Get in!" The man drew a handgun from a holster. Robinaire got in. The man followed suit and drove them along the road at a fast pace. In a few minutes he was herding her into a building staffed by dark-grey-uniformed people in a multiplicity of offices. He took her into one and turned her over to its inhabitants.

"Deserter. Possibly a mental case."

They took her fingerprints and fed the data into a machine. She tried to talk to them, but they wouldn't have it. The machine spewed out a brief answer. The staff looked at it, consulted, re-printed her, and again queried the machine. After getting a second negative answer, they took skin flake samples and fed these into a different machine. After a longer wait, another negative result came back. The staff members looked at one another.

"She's not recorded," said one blankly.

"I've been trying to tell you!" burst out Robinaire. "I'm not one of your people! I'm not even from this world!"

"Send her to Colonel Stavvic."

She was hustled out and taken to another office, where Colonel Stavvic, a middle-aged, tired-looking woman in the inevitable dark grey uniform, was told that, incredibly, here was a person not recorded even in the genetic identification files. "Possibly mad," added her guard. "Keeps saying she's from another world."

"Okay, leave her. Sit down, girl." The colonel actually looked at her as if seeing an individual. "I'm in Intelligence, and I've heard there are other worlds. We can't touch them, but one of them has contacted us. They recruited some of our soldiers to be a special bodyguard for some ruler there, in return for some weapons we hoped would give us an edge in the war. Tell me what you know about this universe-hopping."

"I don't know anything! Someone called Zar Haughn took me out of my own world by mistake. I asked him to send me home, but he said he was sending me to a place called Aresette instead."

"That's the name of our country. Since you're here, I'm afraid you're stuck. We can't treat you any differently from our own citizens. We're in a state of war: everyone is under arms; and unless you have special knowledge or skills, you'll just have to go into the ranks, or be executed. We can't afford to keep useless people around. Do you have any special abilities? Training in electronics, medicine, chemistry, bacteriology...?"

"I'm still in school. I don't know anything special."

"Well, as a female, you still get one other choice. If you don't want to be a regular soldier, you can become a production-line mother. With our attrition rate, it's just as important a job."

"You can't be using children in your war!"

"Not till their teens; but we have to keep the supply flowing."

"You mean you expect to be fighting still in the next generation?"

"Unless we make a weapons breakthrough, or the other side beats us to it."

"I thought nuclear weapons could finish off a world in days."

"Not since we got force field defences. It's a stalemate in all our sophisticated weapons. We fight mostly at the tank and rifle level, that is, hover tank and thermal-lance rifle, of course," she explained, "and both sides try to perfect the one weapon that can break. Hmm... Just a moment."

She sat in thought for a minute, then asked, "This inter-universe travel: it's psionic, isn't it machines?"

"The Zar was using human teleporters; but he also talked about machines."

"That's what we thought. Now, we've been trying to work on this combination, too, though not for inter-universe travel... Would you like to try to get home, even if it seems risky?"

"Oh, yes!"

"We are trying out a new miss— vehicle: a sort of jet, which needs psychic guidance. You'd just have to sit there and will the controls to stay in their settings."

"Why?" asked Robinaire, at a loss.

The colonel was patient. "Because the enemy is jamming all our remote control, and can send their own signals into any pre-set program. We think this psionic idea may beat them, but we're not experienced in the field. We seem to have been short-changed on psychic energy in our universe," she concluded bitterly.

Robinaire was confused. "How will guiding a jet get me home?"

The colonel remained patient. "It's the only psionic device we've got to even the experimental stage. We can't hope to transplace you out till we succeed in controlling at least one such device."

"Oh, I see. You have to sort of practice first."

"That's right. And our own people don't have the psychic power to hold the link with the machinery when they're under stress. There's a chance that you can. And if you do, you get special status instead of going into the fighting or breeding ranks." Colonel Stavvic smiled. "Are you willing to help us, in the hope that we can eventually help you get home?"

"I guess so. I sure don't want to stay here in a war."

"Fine." The colonel switched on her phone and tapped out a set of numbers. "Major Quabbol, I have a volunteer to test your new vehicle, the XPM-1."

"Vehicle?" came the major's voice.

"That's right," said Stavvic evenly. "The XPM-1. I understand it's in a state of readiness?"

"Has been for weeks!" grumbled Major Quabbol. "We still haven't found anyone rated high enough to hold concentration long enough to reach the tar-"

"I think you'll find that this volunteer will. Her concentration and motivation may both be stronger than we are accustomed to. I'll send her to you right now, then call you back with more details." The colonel broke the connection, and signalled for a pair of guards to come in.

Robinaire was whisked out of the building, across the city, and through a long tunnel. She was met by Major Quabbol, a harried-looking little man, in another office. He was not quite as uniformed as the rest, having shed his jacket and tie and rolled up his sleeves; but he seemed just as grim and earnest as the others, and even wearier than Stavvic.

His smile was not as natural as the colonel's, but he welcomed Robinaire with careful politeness and offered her a cup of coffee. Seeing her expression as she tasted it, he said enviously, "I suppose you have real coffee where you come from?"

She nodded, got down a swallow, and gave him back the cup. Grumpily, he remarked, "No use offering you our food, then, either. Let's get on with the mission."

Robinaire hoped it wouldn't take them long to figure out how to send her back home if their food was that bad, but she kept the thought politely to herself. She went with him and the guards through a long series of corridors, across a walkway, and finally into a small, metal-sheathed compartment with an acceleration couch; she recognized its function from her world's entertainment-cube programs.

As they strapped her in, the major explained that all she had to do was to hold in her hands the knob he was putting into her grip, and to keep willing the vehicle to perform according to its program. He checked that the cable from the knob was secured, then followed the others out, and sealed the door behind him.

Robinaire felt the ship being moved about and heard, faintly, a noise like a massive door above her sliding back, then something like the muted roar of a jet engine. The acceleration was gentle, calculated not to disrupt concentration. She clasped the knob of the psionic device and willed the vehicle to follow its instructions.

Chapter 5

Malfunction

"Robinaire. Are you all right?"

"Plennor Mayne!"

He had materialized in the tiny space beside the acceleration couch, and surveyed the scene in a sweeping glance: the military markings and warning signs, the unfinished look of expendable material, the feel of the acceleration, and the draft from unsealed cracks.

"I've come to take you home, Robinaire. Now, I want you to relax —"

"But shouldn't I finish this first? They were going to try to send me home, so I promised to help them test their jet. The enemy's jamming their remote signals, so they need someone in the vehicle to make the psionic equipment stay working —"

"Vehicle? Robinaire, it looks to me as if they're tricked you into a suicide mission in a war missile."

"Missile? You mean it's going to blow up?"

"Yes, but we won't be on it. I'll take you home."

"Oh, yes, *please!*"

"Forget whatever they've told you to do. Just relax, and we'll go." He pressed the homing end of the rifkey. The missile faded around them...

***

"This isn't home!" cried Robinaire, in bitter disappointment.

They stood on an open plain, flat and treeless in all directions. It was not, however, without feature, for it was spotted with metal-grid towers some twenty meters high, top-heavy with equipment on small platforms.

"At a guess, we're on a world that uses broadcast power."

"Why didn't we go home?"

"I'll have to guess again: the device you were holding on the missile — you said it was psionic?"

"Yes, they said I was to will it to work."

"And you were still holding the device when we transplaced. Perhaps you were still thinking of their instructions. Since it wasn't a transplacing device, it didn't stop our leaving, but its interference threw off the working of my rifkey." He showed her the small device in his hand. "Well, it just gives you a quick look at another world. We'll go home now." He pressed the homing circuit again. Nothing happened. Frowning, he traced the transplace pattern. Again nothing happened. A second try, carefully precise, had the same lack of result, as did a press of the random-choice mode.

"Are we stuck here?" Robinaire worried.

"Not yet. We're very near one of those broadcast towers. Their power may have a psionic component, and the rifkey may have automatic circuit breakers that have acted to protect it from such massive power. If we walk far enough out into the space between towers, it may re-set itself. If not, we'll have to try to get to an area completely away from —"

He broke off as his glance caught a sense of movement. "Something's coming towards us... a ground-effect vehicle," he added, watching the wheel-less truck riding its dust cloud above the surface of the plain.

"I hope we're not still on that planet where everybody's at war," said Robinaire.

"We've moved to another universe. Exposed towers like these would never last on a planet at total war."

"Then the people here must be peaceful?"

"And technologically advanced, too: so we should be able to get help if we need it."

The vehicle abruptly changed its oblique approach to a straight one, its noise rapidly growing. "They've spotted us," Mayne remarked.

"Are you sure they'll be friendly?"

"No, but there's no hiding place, so we haven't much choice about meeting them. However, the chances are they'll be friendly."

The hovertruck settled to the ground beside them, and Mayne's optimism was instantly proved unjustified. Three men in rough clothes, carrying guns, piled out.

"City people, all right!" growled one of the men.

"What are you doing here?" demanded another.

"Where's your vehicle?"

"We had a breakdown," replied Mayne, with a kind of truth; "and we were hoping to walk to where we could get help."

"What are you out here for?"

"We're here by accident," said Mayne, again truthfully.

"Don't give me that. Either you're Power Officials, or you're bounty hunters after us Homesteaders!"

"We mean no harm. You can see we're not armed."

"Then you're Power Officials, out here playing with your foul toys!" His gesture swept at the nearest tower.

"We have nothing to do with officials of any sort."

"Shut up." The man turned to his companions. "They must have sent their vehicle back for something. We've got to get to work before their friends come back."

Another man spoke worriedly. "We still gonna...?"

"Blast the key tower," confirmed the first. "We just stick this pair on the top of it before it falls. They'll look like clumsy fools who got caught in their own blast, and that'll delay the hunt for us. You two. Into the truck!"

The guns prodded them in. The vehicle lifted onto its air cushion and roared across the land, to brake abruptly by a tower.

"Out! And start climbing!"

As Mayne hesitated, gauging the chances, the leader added, "Or we leave you out in the plain, too wounded to crawl, but not dead. You can wait to see whether the sun or the ants finish you off first!"

One of the men kept his gun trained on them as they climbed, while the other two busied themselves about the equipment at the base of the tower, taking bundles out of the truck and placing them in selected places, connecting them all by wires. Their work was hurried but efficient.

Robinaire looked down, and clutched more tightly at the railing of the platform. "Can't we get away?"

"If we try to climb down when they leave, we'll just be getting closer to their explosives. Judging by their hurry, there won't be a long delay before the explosion. But they obviously expect to interfere with the power broadcasting system: they spoke of a key tower. If the broadcast stops, the rifkey may work again. It's a small chance, but appears to be our only one."

Robinaire looked at him. "You're not scared. You must know it will work."

He shook his head. "It's not even a guess, just a hope. And of course I'm frightened, but getting excited about it won't help, while keeping calm might."

"They're going!"

The men piled into the truck and fled.

Mayne brought the rifkey out of his pocket and held pressure on the end of it. There was a flash below them and a blast of sound. The top of the tower lurched and toppled... and faded.

***

"Are we home or dead?" asked Robinaire, and opened her eyes.

"Neither, yet." Mayne looked around the jagged landscape. "Craters, I think. If they're radioactive, we'd better get out of here fast. At least the rifkey's working again, after a fashion."

He pressed the end. Nothing. "I spoke too soon. Well, let's try the direct mode with the pattern."

The world faded to white.

***

"Now where are we?"

"We appear," replied Mayne judiciously, "to be in a swamp. Be careful not to step off this ridge of solid earth." He looked at the rifkey. "The homing mode doesn't work; the direct mode randomizes; let's see what the randomizer does." He placed a palm across the dots. Nothing happened. "So, two modes gone. This could get serious."

"Serious! What do you call the dangers we've been in?"

"Just dangers." Mayne was trying to find a way to look into the rifkey. "I haven't been able to get this thing open to get a look at the workings. But perhaps I didn't try hard enough when I was just curious..."

Robinaire screamed and cowered back. Mayne whipped a look around

71

and saw a large animal of unidentified species but with undoubtedly carnivorous teeth advancing towards them. There was no time for pattern and concentration. "Run!"

They raced along the relatively solid ground, and managed to increase their distance from the lumbering dental display behind them, which seemed ill fitted for the slippery footing. A little more and they could risk a pause. But at that moment Robinaire's feet hit water — the ridge had run out. The drag of the water tripped her. Mayne made a grab to save her and lost his own balance on the slimy edge.

To lurch through the impeding water to another ridge would simply use up their lead. In an instant decision, Mayne sat firmly still as the jaws opened above him, and carefully traced out the sixteen-point pattern on the rifkey.

The closing jaws faded into nothingness around them...

***

...And the luminous white opacity shattered into dim tiny pieces — the icy, stinging whiteness of a blinding blizzard.

The water in their clothes steamed out like their breath in the dry, frigid air, whipping their body heat with it. Wind slashed at them, coating them with driving snow that mixed with the water into slush, and refroze. Urgently, Mayne ran his numbing finger over the transplace pattern. Nothing. He peered at the rifkey, trying to hold it steady in his shaking hands, and saw that a coating of ice was insulating the dots from his touch. Locking his arms against his body for steadiness, he lifted the rifkey, and with breath and the aching flesh of his palms warmed the ice layer away.

Robinaire was crying and shuddering beside him, gasping at the bite of the cold in her lungs. Carefully, forcing his cramped, numb hands to obey him, Mayne traced the pattern.

***

The snowy landscape faded. High, distant walls appeared around them, enclosing rows of huge machines.

Mayne shoved the rifkey into his pocket and held Robinaire's shivering form against him, speeding their recovery with shared body warmth. It was long minutes before she was able to take any interest in the new situation. When her teeth had stopped chattering, she looked around fearfully. "Where are we now?"

"A factory, from the look of it. Apparently automated. I don't see any workers."

"Why can't we get home?" cried Robinaire, in protest rather than question.

"I haven't had a chance to look into the rifkey yet. In fact, I haven't been able to get it open yet." She was still clinging to him, a semblance of protection in an increasingly unstructured situation; he put her gently to the side and took out the rifkey again. "Even if I can get it open without breaking it, I may not be able to fix it. I've no idea of the principles of its design. I can only hope it turns out to have some sort of fuse system that's obvious enough and simple enough to be fixed by someone with only a trifling knowledge of psionics..."

"But you *can* fix it?" Robinaire had not quite followed his mutterings. She had caught a hint of doubt, and wanted reassurance.

"The wexters did expect me to figure it out in time. Perhaps they underestimated human ingenuity because we have so little natural psi, compared to theirs. Maybe I'll be able to see some of it right away, if I can just get the rifkey open..."

He broke off and pushed Robinaire into a space between two large machines, throwing himself after her. "Out of the aisle. Here comes a delivery truck, or a cleaning robot, or something."

The large machine zoomed down the aisle and swished to a stop opposite them. Underpads mopped up the water they had dripped. Then an antenna swivelled towards them and jointed metal arms reached out.

They dodged further back and ducked under projecting parts of the stationary machines. "It's after us!" gasped Robinaire.

"We're foreign matter in the system — dirt!"

The groping arms were unable to make the necessary twists at their hinges to quite reach the humans. The machine went still, keeping them trapped by its waiting arms.

"Has it given up?"

"Probably calling for help."

"I don't hear anything."

"It wouldn't use light or sound signals, since there aren't any people here. It will call by radio. Yes, here come other kinds of robots. There's a smaller one, and one with flexible tentacles; one or the other will be able to reach us. Nothing for it but to try the rifkey again, I'm afraid."

Robinaire clung to his arm and shut her eyes. "Go ahead, quick!"

***

"You can open your eyes, Robinaire," said Mayne with equal parts of sympathy and amusement. "There's no immediate danger."

They were standing in a small town with a run-down, patched-up look. The only vehicles in sight were mule carts. On another road in the distance a number of pack-bearing humans trudged on foot.

"Doesn't look as if we'll get any technical help here," murmured Mayne. "Still, if I can just find a spot to sit down quietly for a while and examine the rifkey, I might at least be able to tell whether I have any hope of fixing it, or whether we'll just have to go on making random jumps, hoping to find a psi-using society where I might be able to learn what I need to know."

Robinaire shivered in her still-damp clothes. The synthetic material was regaining some of its fullness, but its powder blue and white were overlaid with brown and green stains from the swamp. Robinaire was so miserable with cold that she paid no attention to her appearance, not even to her bedraggled hair. "I wish we could go somewhere warm."

Mayne was also shivering. His jacket was quick-drying, summer-weight synthetic, but it had retained more water than Robinaire's dress, though its staining was less visible. "We can at least get out of the wind if we go over to the side of this house or —"

"You two there!"

They turned to see two overalled men with shotguns advancing on them.

"What's the trouble?" asked Mayne easily. "Are we trespassing? We've got ourselves lost, and could do with some help."

There was a slight relaxation on the part of the townsmen, who had been braced for resistance; but they kept their guns steady. "We've had a spate of technolegging around here lately," explained one; "so every stranger's under suspicion."

"What's technolegging?" demanded Robinaire.

"Bootlegging technos, of course." As she still looked blank, he added, "Selling technological objects from city ruins."

"It must be hard to keep down," said Mayne, fishing for information. "Hard to draw the line as to what's allowed and what isn't." He nodded towards their weapons. "Even guns could be called technological. In fact, anything more complex than a hand-axe could."

"Are you one of these right-back-to-the-earth types?" demanded the second man, scowling.

"By no means," said Mayne, picking up his cue. "I'm just thinking how tough your job is, weeding out what's too technological."

"Not too hard: if it's strictly mechanical, or simple-chemical like gunpowder, it's all right. Nothing mechanical can wreck the world's economy again."

"Now," said the other, "suppose you two step inside here and empty your pockets onto the table." The men thrust their shotguns forward a bit.

Mayne's quick mental inventory concluded that he had nothing obviously technological with him; so he nodded acquiescence and ushered Robinaire into the house indicated.

One of the men kept his gun trained on them. The other put his weapon down behind the first man and came to examine the objects Mayne put on the table, pausing first to slap at Mayne's pockets to be sure they were emptied. Straightforward items like keys and wallet he shoved back immediately, but lingered admiringly over a kit of miniature tools: tiny screwdrivers, fingertip wrenches, an angled mirror on a telescoping flexible shaft with a magnet on its other end, tweezers with attached magnifying glass, a pocket-microscope, a graver, a tape measure, and a knife with a variety of blades. "I bet *that* kit's pre-Depression!" he commented. "Still, it's all mechanical."

He picked up the rifkey. "What's this?"

"A checkerboard. Do you play? I don't have any pieces with me, but we could use pebbles."

"Forget it." The man tossed the rifkey back, then looked at the wexcorder. "What're you carrying this rock for?"

"Good luck piece."

"Okay, you seem clean. Wait a minute, let's have a look at that watch you're wearing. It looks mighty complicated."

Keeping his expression calm, Mayne shoved up his sleeve and thrust his arm forward instead of taking off the watch. "It has a few extras, but they're mechanical. This elapsed-time ring turns by hand. The window shows a calendar. The buttons are for a stop watch," he demonstrated it, "and an alarm."

"Well – okay."

Mayne was careful to show no sign of relief or relaxation. The watch was battery-powered and immit-run, but its outward appearance mimicked an old analog aviation model he had worn in the days while he was building hours for his senior pilot's licence. He had taken himself to task for the touch of sentiment that had led him to choose the matching style, but he was thankful for it now. Seeing dials and buttons, the investigators had not thought to check for a winding stem to confirm the apparent mechanical state of the watch. Mayne let his sleeve fall back down and re-pocketed his possessions.

"Now you, miss."

Robinaire had left her purse in the lab, and her stylish though now begrimed dress had only one pocket, which held nothing but a handkerchief. Her watch was a genuinely mechanical one, designed for fashion rather than accuracy; but the searcher's eye was caught by her radio brooch. "What's that thing?"

Before Robinaire could answer, Mayne said, "An ornament, of course, what does it look like?"

"I don't know. Hand it over."

Robinaire looked at Mayne, who nodded. She unpinned the brooch and gave it to the searcher, who turned it over in his hands. He pushed on the music note station selectors, then on the treble clef on-switch.

Nothing happened. As Mayne had guessed, there were no broadcasts on this world.

"I don't know," said the man again. "It seems harmless, but somehow..."

The other man said, "Let's go ask my brother. He'll know."

"Okay. You two, into that room. If this thing's okay, we'll let you out, with apologies and an invitation to dinner. If it isn't, you're dead." They were herded into a windowless storage room and through the thick oak door. They faintly heard a heavy padlock scrape on solid iron and snap tight.

CHAPTER 6

Precedence

This world might never have heard of image circuits, but Mayne knew he could not depend on the chance that the townsmen would drop their suspicions of the radio brooch just for lack of proof of its function; if they broke it open and saw the tiny leads connecting the manual controls to the apparently featureless core that held the invisibly small immits, they might decide the brooch was a smuggled "techno" even though they had no understanding of it.

The fugitives would have to transplace again, now, while they could.

Standing close to the lantern their captors had hung just inside the door, Mayne spent a few minutes examining his rifkey, but could still find no way to expose its presumed inner workings. As their waiting period dwindled, he sighed and accepted the fact it would have to be another blind jump.

While his eyes and fingertips had been exploring the surface of the rifkey, Mayne had had, for the first time, the chance to think about the situation as a whole. Until he had managed at least to study the workings of the rifkey, he would not admit to helplessness; but he did face up to the possibility that he had lost the ability to return to his own world, or to any other of his own choice; that the best he could hope for was to find one safe enough to stay in — or at least to leave Robinaire in until he might be able to come back for her; he felt that he himself might prefer to go on randomly exploring rather than stay in a society where the science that was his lifework was too far behind or ahead of his own for him to contribute.

Acknowledging the strong possibility of being trapped in an endless series of random worlds, he also accepted it as being the result of his own decision, not blaming the wexters for the equipment failure, or for their policy of not trusting their explorer with the knowledge necessary to repair that equipment. He had agreed to those conditions. Reminded of his bargain, he kept his side of it by directing his thoughts to the recorder in his pocket while he went through what had happened, concluding with his determinedly optimistic hope of finding a way to repair the rifkey, and a promise to continue reports whenever the situation allowed, through however many worlds they survived.

"Robinaire, stand beside me; the rifkey doesn't have much range."

She obeyed; and once more he touched out the pattern.

***

They were standing near a road, in a pleasant green landscape. The field they were in appeared to be a pasture. As they made their way to the road, they saw crops on the other side.

A small, horse-drawn wagon was approaching and soon reached them. Its driver, who was wearing a sun-bleached, coarse linen smock, flower-embroidered in faded colours, jumped down and saluted them with a touch to his forehead. "Had a break-down, sir?" he asked with apparent concern.

"Yes, we have," responded Mayne.

"You must have walked a long way. Where did your car come down?"

"I don't know exactly where we landed."

"Would you like a lift to the village, sir? You could wash up while you're waiting for the repair truck to fly in."

"Thank you; we could do with a wash!"

It was a short ride to the village. As Mayne and Robinaire got out they were surrounded by a small crowd of respectful but curious peasantry, dressed like the driver. The group was bustled back by a man carrying a heavy metal staff of office, who was wearing a smock of somewhat finer weave than the rest, its embroidery design suggesting a logo or coat-of-arms. He introduced himself as the village reeve, Jussub.

"Welcome to Ocerat, my Lord, my Lady. We're sorry to hear of your mishap, but honoured to have you stay in our village, however briefly. You'll find we've kept the public guest house spotless, though it's been many years since any Lord was here."

Mayne was so accustomed to the respect given to a plennor in ISC that only now did it occur to him that the deference he was being shown went well beyond what peasants, even humble and hospitable ones, might be expected to show to strangers. And the title — he seemed to have been mistaken for a person of high caste. Why? Had he done or said something that asserted the claim? If he disabused the villagers of their belief now, would that spark resentment? Perhaps it was wiser to follow their lead until he could find people of the senior caste and see if these had more advanced technology than he saw here... or until he knew he must give up and try another random transplacement.

The villagers escorted their guests ceremoniously into a building containing a comfortable lounge. The reeve bowed them through an inner door into a smooth-walled room equipped with generously proportioned cubicles with shower heads in their ceilings.

"Spotless!" boasted Reeve Jussub.

"I sure need a wash, after that swamp!" declared Robinaire, crossing to look at a cubicle. "But — there aren't any taps," she exclaimed.

"Foot pedals, Robinaire. And the water comes in at the top."

"Oh."

"And according to these labels, you have a choice of liquid or sonic cleaners for your clothes in these adjoining compartments." Mayne turned back to the half dozen people who had come in with them. "It is indeed spotless, Reeve Jussub; and now we shall appreciate the opportunity to wash up." He hoped the local customs did not class the peasants with animals, who need not be removed during the washing. He had used communal showers, but washing as entertainment for watchers would be weird; and he guessed that Robinaire would find it offensive.

Apparently the villagers considered themselves human: by degrees they bowed themselves out, as Mayne, guessing by the pictures and symbols on the controls, said, "Here you go, Robinaire. This handle will close the cubicle. This pointer must select the temperature of the water. Pressure on this pedal will adjust how fast it comes out...and this will be an air blower. Here's a robe to wear while you put your clothes in the cleaner."

In the lounge, the villagers closed the door and huddled together, whispering. "She doesn't know how to use a shower!" "I don't think she'd ever seen one before!" "She's not a Lady!" "But he's a Lord, isn't he?" "Maybe they're both impostors!"

"Quiet!" The reeve took charge. "There are two possibilities. Either he's a Lord who's picked up a pretty girl from some back-country village – Yes, I know the Lords frown on such behaviour, especially taking her around as if she were a Lady; but it's still done! Or else they are both ordinary people, impersonating a Lord and Lady, whose clothes they must have stolen. Perhaps there *was* a car-crash and they robbed the bodies. Or – perhaps they are murderers as well."

There were shocked breaths drawn as he voiced this worst suspicion, and cries of "What shall we do?"

"If there's the slightest chance of their being murderers, we must take action against them. The Law says that anyone suspected of murdering a Lord – even another Lord – must be imprisoned immediately, and handed over to proper authority."

"It's a terrible responsibility. We can't imprison them unless there's *some* evidence."

A woman said, "If he's a Lord, he'll know more than I teach here in the school. I have a book of mathematics that I won as an award many years ago; I can't understand it, but there are answers given to the problems. I'll copy out a problem and see if he can solve it. If he can, he's got more than a village education."

"It wouldn't quite prove he was a Lord – Sometimes the Lords give more education than usual to somebody they want to serve them..."

"But if he can't do it, we'll know he isn't."

"Okay. Go get the problem. For the rest of it, we'll just have to watch how they behave."

When Mayne and Robinaire returned to the lounge, in a much cleaner and drier state of clothes and body, they were met by the same small group of people, still respectful, but with an air of determination.

"Sir, we have here a mathematical problem for which we need an answer. It's beyond village ability. Will you graciously work it out for us?" They proffered him notebook and pencil.

"What's the problem?" Mayne was accustomed to using computers or calculators for math, and hoped he could remember whatever it was they obviously wanted worked out by hand. As he took the notebook, a graver doubt hit him for a moment: the notation looked strange to him. Then he realized it was just the curlicue style affected by the writer.

Robinaire peered around his shoulder. "What is it?"

"Just algebra." Mayne began to work it out. He checked his figures, and handed back the notebook.

"Thank you, sir. May I offer you refreshments at my own house? It would be a great honour." Jussub passed the math problem to the schoolteacher, who surreptitiously compared answers.

"Thank you, Reeve Jussub," Mayne accepted. A meal would be a good idea. No telling when they would get another.

The schoolteacher caught Jussub's eye and nodded. A relieved sigh breathed faintly through the group, as the reeve indicated the way with a flourish of his staff. They had an excuse for postponing action.

Although the ignorant young woman was obviously no Lady, she was not their concern as long as the man was a Lord. His behaviour should perhaps be reported, but there was no urgency; and by carefully not giving the man occasion to mention his name, and certainly not being rude enough to ask it! — the reeve could even avoid having to make a direct accusation in his report.

But *was* the man a Lord? He was at least educated, and they had done their best to test him. If no further reason for doubt came up, the villagers were justified in accepting him at face value. But if both strangers were false, then more than a misdemeanour must have been committed, and it was the villagers' clear duty to go to any length to apprehend the criminals.

Yet what else could they do to check the man's authenticity? They themselves knew too little of the Lords' society to catch him out on questions of news from the City — which he might know, in any case, if he worked there for the Lords. And if he *was* genuine, he must not be offended. In spite of the relief over their reprieve from action, the responsibility continued to weigh on them, and they cast nervous glances at Mayne as they escorted the guests through the village.

They reached the reeve's house and one of the group sprang forward to hold the door open, while Jussub posed beside it in a welcoming manner. Mayne automatically stood aside for Robinaire to precede him, then followed her. The reeve stiffened in a startled realization and then, in one move, swung around and slammed his heavy metal staff down on Mayne's head. The plennor crumpled to the ground.

Amid horrified cries from the others, the reeve declared shakily, "No Lord would ever give way to a villager, no matter how fond of her he was! They're both impostors! Lock them in the town hall tower and send a messenger to the City."

"What will happen?" cried one of the villagers.

"They'll send out guards who can check on identification. As soon as they prove these two are impostors, they'll execute them."

***

To a worried Robinaire, it seemed hours before Mayne stirred. She had never before in her life witnessed a head blow, and could not understand why he remained dazed. In the entertainment-cube dramas, the knocked-out hero always sprang up a minute later and resumed violent activity, brilliant deductions, and witty repartee.

She crouched beside him, pulling at his arm. "Plennor Mayne! Please wake up!"

He mumbled something.

"Oh, please!" In the previous dangers, she had not had time to worry: only moments of fright. But since they had been imprisoned, fear had had time to settle in and bite deep; and without his conscious presence, she had been dreadfully alone. "Please, Plennor!"

"Robinaire? What's happened?" he asked groggily.

"The mayor hit you!"

"Any idea why?"

Robinaire quoted the reeve's words in full, and added the information about the summoned guards.

"So, no trial," Robinaire said. "And it's a capital offence... for... for anyone but a registered ruler... to wear anything but... a peasant smock."

"You mean they're going to kill us because we're dressed differently from them?" With an effort, Mayne managed to push himself up against the wall of their prison. His words grew more coherent as his mind cleared a little. "We'll have to get ourselves out of here...before these guards arrive."

"Can't we go now? Please?"

"Sorry, I can't see yet."

"Can't see! What's wrong?"

"It can take a while for your vision to clear when you've been hit on the back of the head."

"Oh, I didn't know that. Can't you transplace us by feel?"

"Only the pattern mode works; and I have to see the dots to follow the pattern. They aren't raised or depressed: I can't feel them." As much to distract her as to gain information, he asked her to describe the room and the building they were in.

"We're in the town hall. It's got a tower, and they brought us up to the fourth floor. There's no furniture in here — I guess it's another storeroom; but nothing's stored in it just now. There's only one window. It's too small to get through; and there's no way to climb down anyway, it's a straight drop." Robinaire's watching of adventure flicks on her E-cube had enabled her to investigate the obvious hopes of escape. But reciting the forlornness of those hopes made her voice tremble.

Mayne pulled out his rifkey and tried to peer at it. His initial sensation of sheer blankness was beginning to alter to faint awareness of light and dimness, but he could not detect even the largest of shapes yet, far less make out faint dots on the same-coloured background of a small object.

Robinaire could see the dots, but she did not know the pattern. If the dots had been laid out in an orderly array, he could have given them an arbitrary numbering system and had her count out the sequence; but the dots were in an irregular spread, to make them look like happenstance blemishes in the material; he could not think how to designate them clearly.

He tried to visualize the array; perhaps he could gesture the pattern, and have Robinaire follow it on the actual dots. But he found it difficult to concentrate on anything, and impossible to focus on a visual image.

With a sigh, he slipped the rifkey back into a pocket, to be sure he would not mislay it. "I'll try again as soon as I can see something," he said, careful not to mention his concern over whether he could fully remember the pattern even if he could make out the dots, nor to speculate on whether he would recover before the summoned guards arrived.

Robinaire huddled against him. "Oh, Plennor, I wish I'd never come to your lab. I thought it would be fun to boast about it. Everyone in Neithon thinks so much of all the scientists, especially the plennors; and those of us who like the arts instead are just nobodies; and Aunt Haldis has always been so disappointed in me. She thinks I'm stupid because I don't know any science."

The mention of Vennor Gythstrom stung Mayne with a memory of his promise. He said ruefully, "I haven't done a very good job of looking after you."

"I don't want to die!" cried Robinaire.

He shoved himself further up the wall and put his arm around her. She began to cry against his shoulder.

"We're not finished yet. I may be able to work the rifkey in time."

Then, through the open window, he heard voices approach the building, and the creaky opening of the big main door, and knew that time had run out.

CHAPTER 7

Overconfidence

"Plennor Mayne!" said a new voice. It sounded, incredibly, like the clear, warm contralto of the theorist with whom he had recently enjoyed long discussions of infinity and anything therein.

"Who is that? I can't see."

She drew a quick breath of alarm at the statement, but wasted no time on questions or exclamations. "It's Ithleen. The wexters told me your rifkey is malfunctioning and allowed me to come to see if you need help."

"Urgently." Heavy steps were mounting the stairs. "The approaching noise is likely to be an execution squad. Take Robinaire first."

"You're much more valuable to the multiverse."

"Granted. Take her anyway."

"Very well. Robinaire, come here, quickly. Do you understand that you must want to go with me?"

"Oh, yes!"

There were twenty-six seconds of tense silence inside the room. Mayne heard his jailors come clumping up the last of the stairs and puffing along the top hallway. They paused while one of them sorted keys and wrestled with the storeroom door's stiff lock. It clicked over —

Ithleen's voice said, "Ready, Plennor?"

The handle turned.

"Let's go!"

He thought he heard the fading sound of the door opening, and then there was Robinaire's voice again, and Ithleen was guiding him to the sofa in her study, saying hurriedly, "Relax. I'll call a medic."

She crossed to the phone. "Medical emergency!" She gave crisp identification of her location. In a few minutes there was a bustle of activity about him, a diagnosis of mild concussion, and orders for an overnight stay in a hospital, reinforced by the administration of a quick-acting sedative.

***

He awoke feeling fit, and was checked over again by Ciath, Geode's chief medical officer, a small, serene woman of thirty-four, with smooth black hair, dark eyes, buff skin, and the carved-ivory look of beautiful facial bone structure. Under an open white lab coat, she wore a rose-hued sheath dress with a gold-and-pearl pin in the shape of a clump of lily-of-the-valley. Like the table he had seen in Ithleen's lounge, the pin was beautifully made; and Mayne remembered that Ithleen had told him many Geodans devoted spare time to artistic creation.

Not even the multi-purpose diagnostic tool slung around Ciath's neck detracted from either her sophistication or her quiet grace as she went smoothly through her checks. In her presence, one felt confident that her world — or at least her part of it — was under control. The night before, she had assured Ithleen that she would have the visitor back in shape within a day; and Ithleen had accepted the promise as a guarantee.

Ciath concluded her tests and gave him the pleased smile of a teacher or parent whose child has done the right thing. "You're in very good condition, Plennor Mayne. If you promise to take it easy for a day or two, I'll go sign you out now. Ithleen's on her way here to collect you."

As he waited, running his own mental checks to be sure he could now visualize the transplacing pattern again, remember events up to the reeve's blow, and juggle facts and figures with his normal dexterity, Mayne examined with mild interest the diagnostic and treatment devices built-in around the bed where he had spent the night, and guessed, though his knowledge of things medical was limited, that this world was far ahead of his own in that field. Ciath's confidence was probably based on more than her own skill.

He heard Ithleen's voice in conversation approaching along the hall: "I quite agree with you, Karby; but remember he's a guest, and furthermore he's not used to our ways of thinking. Don't forget the attitudes that prevailed on our own world in the old days; his might be like that, too.

He'll probably be here again later, and you can put your request; but please don't spring it on him now."

There was a grumbling acquiescence in a male voice, then, "If you'd seen the chart, Ithleen!"

"I can imagine it," said Ithleen drily. "Go back and pant over it. You can talk to him later." A thin, bouncy, white-haired man walked by the open door, with a lingering, wistful look in; and Ithleen, giving him a grin and a little push on along the hallway, came in.

"You're looking better," she greeted casually.

"What was that all about?" Mayne inclined his head towards the corridor.

"Our chief geneticist, Karby. You were routinely recorded, and he likes your genetic profile."

"Oh, yes, that's your specialty here, isn't it?"

"Yes; and of course he's excited to see outside material, from another world at that! It's this way to the travel tunnel. Do you feel up to walking? We have electric carts, but we normally walk, to help keep fit."

"I'm fine; let's walk. How's Robinaire?"

"No ill effects. The medics looked her over, too, just in case."

They arrived back at Ithleen's quarters and found a restless Robinaire in front of a video-library screen in the study. As Ithleen fetched some snacks and cups of herbal tea, Robinaire whispered to Mayne, "Their entertainment cubes aren't cubes at all; they have flat pictures like a phone screen instead of projections. And their videos are quite *amateur*. And they broadcasted a *news* program on the E-cube instead of on a phone channel, and it is the dullest stuff — all about somebody's latest technique in something-or-other to do with cells. No *real* news at all!"

When they were settled with their drinks, Ithleen asked Mayne, "What went wrong with your rifkey?"

"It got jammed on the random setting — crossed with the dot-pattern mode of operation. In the occasional moments I had to look at it, I couldn't even get it open to see if I could do anything with it — couldn't find any trace of a control, or a crack to pry at. If the rifkey does open, it must use a mental command, but it needs more than just an order — I tried that. It didn't open on the dot pattern, either. I didn't expect it to, but tried anyway.

I suppose there's another pattern, to add a few trillion more possibilities for an investigator to try out."

"No, you use the same pattern, but you add the mental image of a symbol."

"The *same* dot pattern? The wexters are willing to use a code twice?"

"In this case, yes. They felt that having two patterns in memory might cost their agent a hesitation or mistake someday when ne had need to make a fast, directed transplacement, say, to move something dangerous without using the homing mode."

"Did you deduce this, or did Spen tell you?"

"Spen explained it when ne brought my rifkey and apologized for not giving us the information earlier. Ne didn't say whether that oversight was due to forgetfulness or reluctance. Or whether it simply hadn't occurred to them that you might need to know; they have great faith in the reliability of their devices. Or, of course, they might have been testing your ingenuity further, since they made the symbol suggestive of the multiverse."

"Are you allowed to show me, or am I still being tested?"

"Oh, definitely allowed." Ithleen grinned. "The wexters don't want to expend their explorer this fast! I think they're a little mortified, too, that their device malfunctioned, so they may be sort of paying a forfeit by letting you have a look at it without having to figure out how to get into it." She crossed to her desk and touched computer keys. "This is the symbol."

On the screen appeared an image of overlapping, interpenetrating spheres, with latitude and longitude grids on them. Worlds that were the same and yet were separate entities, Mayne thought, and were also unreal ghosts of worlds.

He tapped in the dot pattern on his rifkey as he looked at the symbol and pictured the rifkey open. In a moment he held it in two flat parts.

Ithleen asked, "Do you think you can make anything of its innards?"

"If the wexters think enough like human engineers to put something to act as a fuse in their equipment, and if that fuse is no smaller or more complex than an image circuit, I might. I certainly want to have a go at it before asking the wexters for help. They seem to have given me tacit permission to try. So either simple repairs are within my ability, or they're so far beyond me that the wexters just want me to see it will remain hopeless until my technology is a lot further developed." As Ithleen nodded to his summing-up, he added, "I'll need to use a TKM..."

Ithleen turned to the phone. "As we promised, you get first priority." She phrased her words on the phone as a request, but there was authority in her voice, and the agreement was immediate, though it sounded wistfully reluctant.

As they walked to the lab, with Robinaire trailing disconsolately behind, Mayne said, "I appreciate the privacy, since I don't know what I'm doing myself, this time." He added, "Please convey my thanks and my apologies to the engineers for interrupting their studies."

"You sound a bit embarrassed. Aren't you accustomed to having your every whim catered to?"

"At home, yes. But I realize that in Geode, you're living precariously, so your own concerns have to be given priority."

Ithleen grinned. "We'll let you know if we have an emergency."

"Do you have many?"

"Enough to keep us alert; not enough to keep us in a state of anxiety."

In the cleared-out lab, Mayne put the rifkey down on a workbench. "This is likely to take quite a while, since I've no information on the rifkey's principles, nor even any circuit diagrams."

"Will this help?" asked Ithleen, taking her own rifkey out of her pocket. "The wexters let me keep it."

"A working model! Much better than diagrams."

"Can I help in any way? I can't offer any hands-on experience, but I can stand by to send for anything you want, or hand you things..."

"Thanks, but I'm used to working alone, and the TKM is all I'll need, if I *can* make any sense out of this."

"Then I'll take Robinaire on a tour. I'm afraid she finds my reading and viewing matter dull, even the fiction."

Robinaire, who had come as far as the doorway, asked, "What's there to see in this place?"

"Not much, really. It's just this one city, and it's mostly devoted to biological labs. We have a number of gyms and sports fields, a theatre, some parkland, a sunroom, some factories, and some stores. I can buy you a few souvenirs to take home. They would be from another world, you know."

Robinaire brightened. "Maybe I could get —" Then she looked at Ithleen, who was wearing a pantsuit, turquoise instead of green but otherwise the same as the one Mayne had first seen her in. Simply cut, of quiet, solid colour, cluttered with pockets, and devoid of any ornamentation. "Does everyone here dress like you?"

Ithleen laughed. "No, of course not. Come and see what we can find for you."

"Supra!"

They went off, and Mayne promptly lost himself in his investigations. He used the TKM to scan both rifkeys. After making analograms of everything the TKM could report about the transplacing devices, he set the machine to making an equally careful comparison of the two rifkeys, and had soon located the breaks in what must be the homing and random mode paths and the fused crossover between the direct and random modes. He suspected that there was "circuitry" as far beyond the immit level as that was beyond transistors, for what he could analyze of the immit parts suggested their function was strictly auxiliary. But since they had, obviously, served as fuses, he was encouraged to hope that no damage had been done to the deeper levels of the rifkeys.

He set the TKM to the delicate and precise job of restructuring the damaged portions of his own rifkey to match the equivalent parts of Ithleen's. It was harder than making complete new immits but necessary, in order to retain whatever finer structure might be incorporated into the same flecks that formed the smaller circuitry.

Finally, he made new analograms of the repaired rifkey and did a new comparison. As far as he could check it, he had a perfect match. He made hardcopy imprints of the whole set of analograms to take with him for future study.

He was tired but jubilant as he finally rejoined the others back in Ithleen's quarters; and he returned her rifkey almost with a flourish. "I think we're back in business."

"That will impress the wexters, though perhaps not entirely favourably."

"They needn't worry. I still haven't the faintest idea how the transplacing process works."

Robinaire asked with excitement, "Does that mean it's fixed?"

"I think it's fixed; and we'll soon find out. Even if I'm wrong, it can't do any worse than randomize us again. The wexters are too safety-conscious to make anything that could damage the user. If I've done anything wrong, the rifkey probably won't work at all. But I think it'll take us home this time."

"I'll be glad to get home," sighed Robinaire, in weariness more of spirit than of flesh, since she had had a good night's sleep and an easy day.

"Are you ready to go? Got all your shopping done?"

Robinaire nodded enthusiastically "Would you like to see what I've got?"

"Ah. You can show it to Van when we get back."

"Before you leave again," put in Ithleen, "tell me what happened. Is Robinaire another of your assistants, or did you find her in another universe, or what?"

"No, Robinaire's from my world. She came to my lab to get material to write an article —"

"That was just a story," put in Robinaire.

"You knew it was untrue?"

"Sure. The other one's just a story, too — the one about the psychiatrist."

"It... is? What's the truth, then?"

"I don't know all of it; but that man Polminander told both stories to Aunt Haldis. They didn't know I was listening."

"Who's Polminander? And why did you come, then?"

"I've no idea. But I thought it would be supra to meet you and be one up on all those science student snobs from school. And besides, I thought I'd better help Aunt Haldis out of the spot she was in."

"What spot was that?"

"That Polminander was blackmailing her. Years and years ago, she helped my mother commit suicide."

Both of the scientists regarded her with amazement as she made this calm statement.

"Aunt Haldis always thinks I'm too dumb to know what's going on; but you don't have to be able to do mathematics to notice things about people. I've known about my mother for years. I didn't know about Aunt Haldis, though, till Mr Polminander talked about it."

"What else did he say?"

"He said, 'I want your grand-niece to meet Plennor Mayne.' She said, 'Why?' He said, 'Never mind why, just arrange it.' And then he told her the two stories. Do you want me to repeat them?"

"No, they don't matter. He didn't give any indication of why he really wanted this arranged?"

"No. But I didn't care. I thought it would be fun to come. And now that we're safe, I'm glad I did."

Mayne turned to Ithleen. "After we showed her around my lab, we sat her down at a TPA; then I saw a flash of light reflected around us; something stunned us, and Robinaire and the TPA vanished. What happened then, Robinaire?"

"There were three men standing where the light had been. One had a gun, and another had something shaped like a megaphone. The first one shot you and the others, then there was another burst of light, all around me, and then I was in a huge room, full of machines — more and bigger than I've seen in any lab at ISC. But it didn't look much used. It was like a dressed set, or a rich man's hobby lab. I saw one of those once, with Aunt Haldis. She said, 'Only in ISC Territory would a lab out-prestige an art collection!' But maybe it did there, too."

Mayne gently prodded her back to the subject. "Can you tell us more about who you saw, and what happened?"

Robinaire nodded. "There was an *intense* man in charge there who reminded me of an actor I once saw playing an old-time navy officer, with a beard and a jump-when-I-say-move look. He was old — over thirty, maybe forty. I thought at first he was *really* old, but I guess not." In ISC Territory, beards were currently so unfashionable that only a few men of the oldest generation wore them, so to Robinaire they betokened near senility; but she had also sensed in Haughn a vitality which she associated with youth; the combination confused her normally good observation of people. "He seemed strong, and everybody did jump to do what he said. He looked at me and said, 'What's *this*?' in a snarky tone, as if I were something that had crawled out of the baseboard. And one of them said, 'Sorry, Zar Haughn…'" She recounted the entire conversation.

At her third quoted sentence, Mayne pulled out his wexcorder and sent a glance of command to Ithleen, who read it and snapped on an ordinary recorder as well. When Robinaire reached the point of Mayne's reappearance in her story, he gently stopped her, and Ithleen played back the part about Zar Haughn. Then the two scientists regarded each other.

"Psychics plus machines — a clumsy system. So he's trying to find a better one," Mayne commented.

"His clairvoyant spotted your practice transplacements and pinpointed your universe," Ithleen reasoned.

"Haughn's a tyrant, and he's expanding his empire. So he's dangerous."

"But limited, so far. He fears you'll trace him. He must be still vulnerable. And he thinks your world is ahead of his, technically."

He added on to their back and forth, "And if he plans to expand his empire beyond his own world, he'll fear we could get in his way, leading him to the idea of striking first."

"Is inter-universe conquest even possible?" Ithleen asked.

"Well, the wexters have prepared defences against it — but that may be simply their excessive caution — I don't think it's very practical. Cheaper to find an uninhabited Earth and exploit that: unlike the wexters, Haughn seems to be able to select for situations, rather than personalities."

Ithleen considered, then shook her head. "The impression I get is, rather, that his clairvoyant can trace the use of transplacing energy in the multiverse. His first contact with Aresette must have been random, since the Aresettans can't transplace; but his limited means won't allow him to hunt indefinitely until he hits an unoccupied Earth."

"You're right. And, anyway, megalomaniacs aren't always logical or practical. He might prefer conquering people to owning a brand new world."

"So the wexters will want to know more about him. You didn't actually trace Robinaire to his world?"

"No, she was on the Aresette Earth before I could get to her."

"But she could take you back, if you taught her to use a rifkey."

They turned to her, and Mayne said, "It's very simple, Robinaire. All you do is tap out the pattern you've seen me use, and will the rifkey to take you and me to Haughn's world."

"No! I won't go back there ever again!"

"But I'd be with you, Robinaire; and you could come back home again right away. It would just be for a few seconds, so that I could have been there myself, and be able to go again."

"No!"

Mayne shrugged, and said to Ithleen, "It takes the will. Perhaps she'll change her mind later, if we don't press her."

Ithleen asked, "How much will Haughn learn from the amplifier he stole from you?"

"About transplacement, nothing. About psionics — depends on how much his world already knows, and how good his scientists are. My first thought is that he must know a lot, since he has a transplacing system of his own. But since it depends on natural psi, perhaps he really knows very little. Even so, he does have amplifiers; and the TPA is simply an amplifier specialized for telepathy. So I don't think he'll learn much from it, unless he lacks immits and has to use nano circuits, made the hard way."

"Is he likely to make another raid?"

"Depends on how he analyzes my situation. If he decides the TPA is the best I've got, he may cross me off his list of suppliers."

"But if he suspects you have other lines of merchandise, particularly, a means of transplacement?"

"Then he might try again. I must ask the wexters if they can spare one of their inter-universe burglar alarms," he added whimsically.

After a pause that acknowledged their inability to carry the speculation further, Ithleen asked, "What else happened to you yesterday? You haven't reached the malfunctioning."

"Robinaire was hooked up to the psi circuits in the missile, which threw off the rifkey. We landed in a world with broadcast psionic power which apparently triggered circuit breakers in the rifkey. It resumed working at a critical point when the broadcast power was interrupted — irregularly for an instant, before it went completely. That's when some of the rifkey's operating circuits blew. Robinaire, you tell the rest."

When she had finished, Mayne put away his wexcorder and said, "Robinaire's memory of conversations is perfect. Significant?"

"Data collection for Polminander?"

"But why?"

"Perhaps if we knew who or what he is, we'd be able to guess the why."

Mayne shrugged. "I've never heard of him. Perhaps he's in Security? But I can't see why they — or anyone — would be interested in me. It's true my assistants told them I was missing for a few days — the time I spent here — but they stopped their investigations as soon as they saw it was a mistake. And if the news media heard anything about it, they must also have heard it was a simple misunderstanding. No one on my world has any way of knowing I went anywhere interesting. And anyway, this scheme has to have been pre-planned; you don't find a walking recorder like Robinaire at a moment's notice."

He turned back to Robinaire. "Have you ever been deliberately introduced to anyone this way before?"

"No."

"Is it well known that you've got a good memory?"

"I guess so. I suppose I show off a bit."

Ithleen turned back to Mayne, "Could it be that Polminander lined up this situation as a sort of general trap, and that you happened to be the one to walk into it?"

"General trap for what?"

"For people in your Territory with some sort of information he wants, who would automatically select themselves by some action."

"That still doesn't fit. Until Spen came, I'd done nothing non-routine for weeks; and Polminander had Robinaire's visit lined up by the day I returned at the latest. What information could he be after? All my work is published; and there's nothing hidden in my past — especially with hungry biographers combing through it," he added, with remembered resentment. "And there's no way he could even suspect the multiverse."

"What about some sort of local intrigue? Do you have politics?"

Mayne hesitated. "Not in the ISC itself. In order to get high enough to be on the roster of scientists who take their turns on the Council, one has to produce a lot of good work; so one doesn't have time to devote to the practices of influence-building, like committee work, editing, reviewing — any of the mutual back-scratching or back-stabbing that still marks university staff structures. In fact, most of that non-research work at ISC is done by support staff; and they are completely outside the power sphere."

"Could it be that Polminander is seeking to gain illegitimate power? Investigating some of the most prominent scientists, to see if he can find something to blackmail them over? The timing might be coincidental."

"I distrust explanations that involve coincidence; but it's possible. Or he might be working for an outside group. There's plenty of politics left outside the ISC."

"Or perhaps Polminander is a straightforward blackmailer, merely after money. A plennor would be a rich source of that for him."

"In my society, a plennor can do no wrong. About the only thing I can think of that could undermine a plennor's position would be the discovery that ne hadn't really done the work for which the plennorate was awarded."

Robinaire said, "Nobody could think that about you. Not with all you've done since."

Ithleen continued to reason out Polminander's assumptions. "Is a plennor as immune to moral pressure as to legal consequences? It might not be coincidence that the person he chose to send to you is an attractive young woman."

"I'm not concerned over what anyone thinks I do, because I learned to ignore the opinions of others, in the science-hating sub-culture I lived in. So I wouldn't care what a blackmailer threatened to tell the public I had done, however well he had framed me."

"But he might not realize the strength of your indifference to public opinion. Or he might just be hoping you'd talk freely to Robinaire, and mention some other facet of your life which you don't want generally known."

Mayne shook his head. "I've never had any secrets, guilty or otherwise, in my life."

"But you have one now. Or, as I said, maybe you're just one of a number of prospects to him, and Robinaire just one of his methods. It still leaves you in the trap: and Robinaire does know about it."

Mayne nodded thoughtfully, and considered Robinaire. "Do you understand the situation, Robinaire?"

She said hesitantly, "You think Polminander wants to blackmail you, and you've got a secret about the multiverse, and Ithleen says I know it, but I don't know what it is."

"It's the very fact that there is a multiverse. It would be very bad if Polminander or the general public learned about it. A lot of people would want to rush out to other Earths. Some of them would kill or exploit the people in less developed worlds. It would be like the old days before we were born, with wars and rioting."

"You mean like Aresette? Could our people be that bad?"

"We're not that far from the days when we were very like that, Robinaire. Some Regions still keep armies, and the more unscrupulous entrepreneurs are still trying to get around anti-exploitation laws as fast as they're made. Our people are still too fearful and too greedy to trust with instant contact with societies at vastly different levels from our own. It's not the same as our hope of contact across space someday: that would not be instant, and some control could be kept on it — And besides, by the time we achieve it, we may be many generations more practiced at keeping the peace among ourselves and curtailing our exploitative inclinations."

"It would be awful to live like Aresette. Everybody in uniform... And they don't even have coffee!"

"Then will you help to keep the multiverse a secret?"

"Well, sure."

"Can she?" asked Ithleen softly.

Mayne kept his attention on Robinaire. "It's sometimes hard to keep a secret, even when you really want to. But I could help you do it, if you like. Would you be willing to be given a hypnotic suggestion to keep the secret?"

"You can hypnotize people?"

"It's simple enough, if you're willing. May I?"

"You wouldn't make me do anything silly, like running around clucking?"

"Of course not!" Mayne was offended by the suggestion he would be so frivolous.

"Okay, then."

Mayne's voice lost its moment of stiffness and became soothing. "Then sit back and relax. Close your eyes and listen to my voice. You are comfortable and relaxed, hearing only what I say..."

When he brought her back to full alertness, he assured her, "You'll still remember everything, and you can talk to people who already know about the multiverse; but you'll find you don't want to talk to anyone else about it, or about anything you've seen or learned away from your own Earth."

"But I *can* talk to you about it?"

"Yes, provided there's no one around who shouldn't hear about it."

"Supra. It's fun to have a secret, but a lot more fun if you can talk to someone about it!"

Ithleen remarked lightly to Mayne, "When you learned hypnosis to encourage your colleagues to believe they could work psi, you can't have dreamed you'd be using it someday to protect a secret as vast as the multiverse!"

He matched her smile. "No — psi itself was the extent of vastness I thought of then! But actually, I had already learned hypnosis in my teens, when I first had the idea of using it to elicit psi phenomena — well before I got the chance to do the experiment. I've always believed in preparing early for what I want. But, as a matter of fact, it came in handy right away: a demonstration of my alleged mind power got a bully off my back once." He suppressed his unusual inclination to elaborate on his experiences: the event had no bearing on the current concern of protecting the multiverse secret. A fainter thought said he could share the story with Ithleen at some later time. He dismissed that as well.

Although she looked interested, Ithleen did not press for details, seeming to respect his reticence. "What do you intend to do about Polminander?"

"For the moment, nothing. If he's just fishing blindly, as you suggest, perhaps he'll give up on me if I appear to carry on as usual. If I try to investigate him, in turn, it might convince him his attention worries me, and make him think I do have something to hide. And speaking of worries, Vennor Gythstrom may be concerned about Robinaire by now, though I told my assistants to assure her Robinaire was with me."

"Oh, she won't worry. She'll think I've gone home. I stay in my father's apartment most of the time and Aunt Haldis moved out to a place of her own in the Compound, like you."

"Then your father must be worried."

"He's never there: he hates ISC Territory. It was my mother's apartment originally, and he just kept it on to have a place to leave me. When he's not on tour, he lives in Bruza Region — He's got homes in two cities there."

"All the same, we'd better get back. Collect up your souvenirs." As she went off, he commented to Ithleen, "She seems to have had rather a tough life."

"No worse than your own, from what I gather."

"I was never neglected."

"I don't think Robinaire has been, either. She has a natural talent for getting people to look after her — I felt it myself. From her descriptions, her great-aunt mothers her; and even her wandering father made arrangements for her. She's a little cynical and self-centred, but I don't think life has scarred her as deeply as it has you. In spite of her normal adolescent emotional upheavals, she's basically happy and optimistic: she's not afraid to make friends."

There had been a shade of emphasis on that last pronoun; but before Mayne could claim equal comfort in encounters, Robinaire returned, stuffing her parcels into a bag; so the others dropped the subject.

"Keep me informed of what happens," requested Ithleen, rather wistfully. "My studies are beginning to seem a bit dull in comparison to all this adventuring. Even my tiny taste was exciting."

"That reminds me, in the enjoyment of discussing things with you, I've completely forgotten to thank you for rescuing us."

"It was quite literally my pleasure."

He smiled. "I'm afraid I hope it's a pleasure you won't have occasion to repeat."

"I agree there. It was sheer good luck the wexters checked your recorder in time. I know they don't monitor mine steadily. Perhaps their curiosity has led them to make frequent checks on yours."

"Well, I'm thoroughly grateful to that chance, and to you. Ready, Robinaire?"

"Ready."

"Thanks for your hospitality, Ithleen. I'll come again soon."

"In less urgent circumstances, I trust!"

Robinaire clasped her bag nervously and stood close to the plennor.

"Home, this time, Robinaire." Mayne operated his rifkey.

The moment of whiteness came, and cleared.

It was not home.

CHAPTER 8

Confrontation

Just for a moment, Mayne thought they had made it: they were in a lab very similar to his own. But a second look told him he was wrong. For one thing, there was no TKM taking up a central space. There were many familiar pieces of test equipment, but they were arranged in a different order from the one he found convenient; and there were also a few items he did not recognize at all.

"Robinaire, I'm sorry."

"We're not home?"

"Not yet."

A dark-haired young man with a slightly rumpled look got up from a workbench in another part of the large room and came around to them. Mayne tried to think. Had he seen him somewhere before? "Where did you come from?"

"We seem to have taken a wrong turn and come in here by mistake," responded Mayne.

"Oh. Can I help you?"

Mayne hesitated. To check the rifkey again, he would need a lab; and he had an instinctive inclination to accept the young scientist's offer of help: the sight of papers jammed in a pocket and a pair of test leads dangling from a lapel by their alligator clips gave Mayne a feeling of fellowship towards him. But he pushed away the absurd thought of confiding in a stranger. Perhaps he could find an unoccupied lab or, although it went against the grain, simply somewhere unobtrusive to wait until he could appeal for help again through his wexter recorder. "I'm afraid not. We'll just have to go out and try again."

The other man said, "Perhaps I can direct you; I know most of the ISC layout."

"The ISC!"

"International Science Complex. Didn't you know what the place is called?"

Robinaire turned to Mayne and cried, "Plennor Mayne, are we home or not?"

"Easy, Robinaire. Not yet."

"Mayne?" said the other man.

"Jonnan Mayne. This is Ms Robinaire Filyk," responded Mayne with automatic manners.

The other man looked at them each in turn. Then he said, "I'm Jonno Mayne. Seems to be a coincidence. And you're a plennor, too? I haven't heard of you. What field are you in?"

Mayne experienced a brief flare of rejection of what was becoming obvious, but his interest overwhelmed it. "Physics and psionics. You?"

"Physics and dabbling in psionics. The chances against such a coincidence are extremely high. Adding in the chance of my never having heard of you, it becomes unbelievable."

Mayne's revulsion towards the situation had vanished under his surge of curiosity and his pleasure in new knowledge and experiences; and in any case, Jonno had enough evidence to begin suspecting the truth. And who, thought Mayne, did he have better justification for trusting? He said deliberately, "Not if you add in one more factor."

"Which is?"

"Multiple universes."

Jonno considered the point. "Are you offering a hypothesis or telling me a fact?"

"Fact."

"You'd better come over and sit down." Jonno almost matched Mayne's outer calmness. "It seems we have a lot to talk about."

"Plennor Mayne —" said Robinaire.

They both turned to her.

"— what's going on?"

"Robinaire, I've just met an analog of myself. In a sense, it means that Jonno is another me."

"But he doesn't look like you at all! At least..." She hesitated, looking between them.

"He's not a duplicate; he's a different person. But he fills the same niche in his universe as I do in mine."

She digested that, and then asked, "Is everything in this world like ours? Including all the people? Is there —" She faltered. "Is there a me here, too?"

Mayne's look of inquiry passed the questions on to the resident plennor.

Jonno shook his head. "We don't yet know; but I've never met anyone with your name or appearance, Ms Filyk."

With a deep sigh of relief, Robinaire turned her attention back to comparing the two men. Like "the real" Plennor Mayne, as she thought of him, this one was dressed in a light heather jacket and grey slacks, though his jacket was a blue-grey instead of a green-grey; and he wore a pearl grey silk scarf in the open neck of his pastel blue shirt instead of a dark green tie over a white shirt. He was younger than her Plennor Mayne — at first glance she thought by half a dozen years, though a later exchange of data between the two plennors reduced this to two. He was about three centimeters shorter, and well-built, though he also looked a little thin for his height. His hair was dark brown, with the same touch of curl; and his eyes were the same hazel.

More of his innate warmth of personality showed in the normal expression of his clear-cut features than Plennor Mayne allowed his to reveal, and he was less intense and incisive, lacking both the air of assurance and the unconscious dominance that marked his analog. The two men were similar in feature though, now that she looked past the superficial differences like hair colour.

"Call me Robinaire," she said. "I'm glad there's no me here. I think it would be horrid to meet someone who would be living in my apartment and wearing my clothes, as if someone had cloned a whole body of me. Who would I be, then?"

"The same person as ever, Robinaire," Mayne assured her. "It would be no worse than having a twin sister: she wouldn't *be* you. Less than that even: more like having a cousin. You can see that Jonno and I are different people."

"That's true," Robinaire agreed, comparing them again. "And, anyway, people on other Earths aren't real, so actually they don't matter."

Jonno raised an eyebrow, a faint smile quirking his lips, but he said nothing.

Mayne was about to comment on relative viewpoints, but he realized that Robinaire's attitude could be simply that of a teen whose sense of reality only included the world around her, so he too let it pass.

Jonno led them to his apartment at the back of the building, to a room that had been furnished for leisure, but whose sofa, chairs, and entertainment cube were all crammed towards one side, making space for a computer desk and several bookcases and tables, all bearing piles of hardcopy sheets and books, discs, data slips, and an assortment of unidentified gadgets. "Now, let's hear your story."

Mayne described the events that had deposited them on this ISC Earth, again letting Robinaire detail the parts she had experienced. When they had finished, Jonno said, "This has been a shock; but now I must admit I'm glad your rifkey malfunctioned again, however big a problem it is for you. I wouldn't have missed this for the world — for any of the worlds. Are you in a hurry to get your rifkey fully repaired and go home, or have we time to exchange a few ideas? You seem to be more advanced in psionics than I am. I'd like to hear about that."

Mayne's conscience told him he should get Robinaire home. But the possibility of discussing psionic technology with a scientist of another world intrigued him. "Well, it'll take some time to get the rifkey fixed, anyway, so we'll have to stay that long. I'm afraid you'll have another wait, Robinaire. And we can't let you go out on this world."

"Oh, well, at least nothing's trying to kill us here," she said, with resignation, "and it can't be any duller than Geode." She turned to Jonno. "Are your E-cube programs any better than Ithleen's?"

"I presume they'll be similar to the ones on your world. Why don't you try it and see?"

Leaving her ensconced in front of the entertainment cube, the two plennors moved back to the lab. Mayne felt some anxiety about telling this man about the process of displacement, but ascribed it to the effects of the rifkey itself that Spen had told him about and pushed past it. Mayne opened the rifkey and pointed out to Jonno what he had figured out of its workings:

"Three travel modes, a power unit, and an unknown number of circuits for its psi-sensing activities, placement operations, and so on. The actual breaks were here and here, and the crossover here, all in image circuits." He went into his belief that there were finer components in the rifkeys than he could find, and that the immits had acted as fuses; then he took out his analograms and placed them in a viewer.

"These show how the rifkey looked before I worked on it. This set is after; and this set is Ithleen's rifkey. Can you see any place where the last two sets don't match?"

They studied the analograms under extreme magnification in a blink comparator, section by section, but could find no difference between the repaired rifkey and Ithleen's.

"How much of the circuitry have you actually identified?" asked Jonno at last, rubbing tired eyes.

"Just the auxiliary immit parts immediately connected to the breaks and the crossover, except that I suspect this portion here is the power control."

Jonno ran a hand through his hair. "Where and what is the power itself, in this tiny device? Surely you need an immense amount for inter-universe transplacement?"

"It's not self-contained. It draws power from an outside source — psionically."

"What source?"

"Ithleen, the theorist I mentioned, thinks it taps the diaphane directly."

"What's that?"

"In a sense it's everything: it contains the universes, it *is* the universes, it divides them, connects them, and is the fundamental substrate that comprises all the regular and dark energy and matter and space that we know and all the states and phases in between them and itself. She calls this substrate fluxate energy, and suspects that all psi is powered by it, to the extent the person or machine is capable of tapping it."

"A rationale for psi!" Jonno drew a deep breath of excitement. "Does she have data to back up this theory, or is it just an idea?"

"Equations that led her to the belief. No experimental work until the wexters brought her their data on the multiverse. They consider her a genius for making sense of their observations — before she'd even received the data!"

"I'd agree with them. But getting back to the rifkey... Can it tap any other source of energy?"

"It doesn't seem to take any from its immediate surroundings: there's no drop in air temperature or in current to electrical appliances such as lights or to any of my psionic machines. But I think it *can* pick up psi power that's being broadcast either deliberately or as leakage from some other device. It seemed to get an overdose on that world with the broadcast towers."

"I should have thought the wexters would have built in a cut-off for such a circumstance."

"They did, and it worked at first. But the rifkey began operating when the power began fluctuating from zero to full at the last moment. The wexters probably thought that only distant suns — unreachable from our Earths — have power that is both extremely strong and highly variable. No doubt all their own power is docile, under their natural psi control; and they seem to be somewhat lacking in imagination."

"They must be."

"I suppose that, in spite of their strenuous efforts to remain individuals, they suffer even more than humans from the tendency to take old ideas for granted and not question what everyone else accepts. That's why they wanted an other-species consultant, and need an other-species explorer."

Jonno nodded. Looking again at the rifkey, he remarked, "There doesn't seem to be enough circuitry here to handle all the things this device does."

"That's the main reason I suspect the wexters have something even finer to work with than immits, something sub-sub-nuclear — down closer to the pure patterned energy of the fluxate — which they can incorporate right into the structure of the grosser components like immits."

"If that were true, how could you have replaced the immits and still have the rifkey work at all?"

"I didn't replace; I mended. All I had to do was to have the TKM match up my rifkey with Ithleen's."

"What's a TKM?"

"You haven't made one? A telekinetic micromanipulator."

"No, I haven't. I've just started looking into psionics. I made a psi amplifier, and with that I was able to create image circuits directly instead of through standard hit-or-miss nanotechnology; but I've nothing as automated as your TKM sounds. Tell me about it."

Mayne began describing the machine's functions and construction, and a desk was soon littered with notes and rough sketches. As they finally surfaced from technicalities, Jonno sighed and said, "I wish I had one of those."

"Our lives seem to be parallel, except for your being two years younger; so you'll be developing it yourself, soon."

"Not in two years." Jonno shook his head. "My ISC isn't as generous as yours seems to be. To keep my facilities here, I have to keep coming up with new discoveries for them. That means concentrating on filling in the gaps of structured knowledge — which limits the time I can spend on looking into the real unknowns, like new fields of psionics. In fact, I also have to spend a lot of time making gadgets to give the Council something to impress the public with. I may end up better known as an inventor than as a scientist!"

"Your Council must have fools on it."

"My ISC is a little less securely established than yours, I think. It needs to give the public the occasional toy."

"As long as it doesn't make the mistake of letting that public expect and then demand the toys."

"No, we keep the emphasis on basic science as a whole. I just made the error of admitting that I rather enjoy making gadgets; now the Council — or rather, the bureaucracy — is expecting and demanding them mostly from me instead of spreading the task around. I could refuse to make more, but I keep getting intrigued by the idea for another one; and knowing they're needed, I just make them. So if I'm able to create a TKM, it'll take me longer than it did you."

"Well, look here, if I can get home and back, I'll bring you my specs. You can catch up to where you should be, and if you put it in your reports a bit at a time, you'll show the bureaucrats you're too busy to make their toys; and you'll be able to work on your own interests as you please. By the time you've given them the whole TKM, you'll have had time to get well into the study of psionics."

"You tempt me," admitted Jonno. "I'm twitching to get my hands on a TKM. But first we have to get you home, so let's get back to the rifkey. Now, we can see that you've made a successful repair on the level we're able to detect, so the fault must lie at the finer level..."

"But the TKM can sense into that level, even if it can't work there; and it recorded that everything in my rifkey had been adjusted to a perfect match with Ithleen's — and hers worked perfectly when she found and transplaced us."

"Wait a minute, I think I caught the glimmer of an idea there," said Jonno, "if I can chase it down. Psi control operates the settings in the circuits, right? Including the unidentified circuits that search out universes or people..."

"Right."

"And your TKM is psi-operated. And it matched up everything in your rifkey to Ithleen's. How was hers last set?"

"To go home, I suppose."

"She was in a hurry; she'd have used the homing mode for that. The main control, the pattern one, how would that have been set?"

"To go to the world where Robinaire and I were trapped... No, she'd have set it to search for me: she didn't know the world." Realization was washing over Mayne. "And I used the homing mode when I came here."

"The rifkey must have been locked in the search mode by your TKM, searching for you, which was backed by your intense determination to get an exact match, and your continued hoping that it was the same..."

Mayne nodded slowly. "Now that I know what happened, I can unlock it and it should function normally again."

"Any way you can test it?"

"Only by using it."

"Why not use your recorder to ask a wexter to come and check it for you?

For that matter, why didn't you ask one to check it before you transplaced here? Or to make the repairs in the first place?"

Mayne flushed guiltily. "I wanted to delve into it myself; and its malfunction gave me an opportunity to do so. And then I was convinced I had it fixed, when the TKM said I had a perfect match. I realize I was over-confident, criminally over-confident, in that I brought Robinaire along on what should have been a test trip. But I'd still rather manage this on my own, if I can, instead of asking for wexter help. After all, I'm supposed to be their bold and competent agent; I can't go yelling to them for help every time I have some trouble."

"You can when the trouble is a breakdown of their equipment, which they refused to train you to deal with."

"I suppose so, but I think this time I *am* justified in believing it's serviceable again. Still, I'll try it alone this time – I'll see if I can get home and back."

"Just a minute," exclaimed Jonno. "The least you could do is let me experience transplacement, too, and a different world."

"After I make the test trip. After all, it might not work right."

"That's why I want to go along the first time – just in case it's my only chance."

Mayne could understand Jonno's craving for the excitement of new worlds, new fields of study. He himself had gone off with the wexter on a moment's notice rather than risk missing such an experience. At worst, the rifkey would randomize them again, and he could call for help through the wexters' recorder. Jonno – unlike Robinaire – would be a help, not a responsibility, through whatever happened during a wait for rescue. And Ithleen could come collect the three of them if necessary. "All right." He closed up the rifkey.

Jonno had another thought. "Your world won't feel much different from mine. Why don't we go to Geode, instead? I can meet this theorist. She sounds worth knowing."

Mayne hesitated, feeling a sudden resurgence of that wish to reject the whole matter which he had experienced on discovering he was in an analogous world: but this time it was less a sensation of losing his individuality than a reluctance to share Geode – a part of his personal past that wasn't already Jonno's. But that wasn't rational, so he firmly dismissed the feeling, and agreed.

Jonno let told Robinaire know that they were leaving for a short time and reminded her not to go outside. She was quite happy to stay where she was and explore this world's entertainment.

Mayne fixed his thoughts on Ithleen, and touched out the pattern.

The shock of again shattered confidence hit him momentarily as they materialized not in Ithleen's study but in a room cramped-full of machinery. Then he saw Ithleen beside him, turning briefly from watching half a dozen people in coveralls who were wrestling with something in the depths of the machinery.

"What's going on?" asked Mayne.

"A minor engineering crisis in one of the life-support systems," Ithleen explained. "In Geode we take even small malfunctions seriously. I'm not of any practical use here, except to hold test equipment." She gestured slightly with the dial-laden, lead-trailing box in her arms. "But I'm the only hard-science person on this year's governing council, so I'm expected to 'supervise'. I'm glad to see your rifkey's operational again. I worried a bit, though I was sure you knew what you were doing."

In spite of her disclaimer of uselessness, her attention had gone back immediately to the repair work.

She went on. "Did you just come back to reassure me, or do you need something? If there's anything pressing, I can leave here, but otherwise — " "No, I'm just continuing to test my repairs," Mayne assured her.

"You've left Robinaire at home? Who is this with you?" Ithleen asked, then turned away to obey a word from one of the engineers. She adjusted a control on the piece of equipment in her hands while watching for the other woman's nod.

"I'll bring you up to date later," Mayne said quickly. To Jonno, who seemed about to join the conversation, peering around Mayne in the cramped space to get a better look at the theorist, he said, "Let's get out of their way." Jonno acquiesced, looking regretful.

Mayne successfully transplaced them back to Jonno's lab. The younger man shook his head, between wonderment and regret. "That was so brief I can scarcely believe I've been out of my own universe. You might have taken long enough to introduce me!" he complained. "She seems to be an interesting person, but all I got was one quick look at her."

"Another time," said Mayne shortly. "We were in the way."

"Well..." Jonno turned to the analograms still lying on a workbench. "May I copy these? I want to see how much of a rifkey I can figure out and put together."

"I don't think you'll get far, even when you've built a TKM to work with." Again, that resistance to share the knowledge of displacement reared its head, but Mayne was practiced at tamping it down now.

"I know. I'll still try."

"I expect I'll be trying, too," admitted Mayne.

They looked at each other and suddenly smiled. "How could we not try?" said Jonno, "Being who we are!" He glanced at his watch and remarked, "We've been at this for more than two hours. I hope your friend hasn't been bored."

"She probably is. She's already had twice as long a wait as when I was working in Geode." The thought of Robinaire re-awoke Mayne's guilt over his irresponsibility in taking her on the first trip with the repaired rifkey. And on taking this second trip without telling her. He hurriedly tidied Jonno's test equipment and went back to her. But Robinaire had found the entertainment on Jonno's world to be much the same as she was used to on her own and was concerned only with being hungry. Mayne was more than happy to stay for a little while longer, so they retired to the kitchen and gave orders to the food processor. Over the meal, the two scientists resumed their discussion.

"For all your wexters' fail-safe mentality, they seem to have made a mistake or two in their rifkey."

"Well, these are the first field trials. They made this type of transplacing device specifically for human use. With their natural talents, they can probably repair instantly anything that goes wrong themselves. I've told them about the breakdown. Perhaps they'll devise a more easily replaceable 'fuse'. That reminds me: I'd better tell them I'm operational again. Unless Ithleen has reported to them, they may think I'm still on Geode with a broken rifkey, too stubborn to ask for help."

He took out the wexters' recording device for Jonno to look at, and explained its simple operation and how the wexters collected their data. "The wexters can rejoice that everything about this recording device is still baffling, even if I've learned a tiny bit about the rifkey."

"Have you tried looking inside it?"

"It won't open." Mayne ran fingers through his hair. "There are no controls; and no mental command or combination I've thought of to try — including visualizing the rifkey's dot sequence and/or the multiverse symbol — has any effect on the wexcorder. I presume its opening is attuned to wexter minds only, just as the deciphering of the recording is. So we'll have to do without seeing into it."

"Perhaps not. There's always my latest failure."

"What do you mean?"

"I've been trying to make a matter duplicator. It won't work. All it does is analyze the innards of things — composition and position. We can build a three-dimensional computer model from that, though it'll take weeks of computer time to interpret it, unless I requisition time on a major system. Even so, I don't think I can justify that, even if we wanted to risk drawing attention to the analysis."

"A matter duplicator!" marvelled Mayne.

"A failure!" said Jonno bitterly. "I have a lot of them. A lot more than you do, I think."

"Maybe," said Mayne; "but anyone who can even attempt a matter duplicator is in the front ranks, Jonno. I wouldn't have any idea where to start."

"It seems I didn't, either," Jonno gloomed.

"But you've got an analyzer now."

"It's never been useful before. I've never had anything that couldn't be CAT-scanned, or opened, or thin-sliced, or couldn't spare a tiny chip for standard analysis."

"You under-rate yourself, Jonno."

"I take it you don't," said Jonno wryly.

"No."

"Well, I wish I had your self-confidence," Jonno returned, ignoring Mayne's recent display of gross over-confidence.

"Start by being proud of what you've accomplished, instead of being embarrassed at not having done more," Mayne advised him. "Lots of things aren't useful when they're first made or discovered. If I'd made your analyzer, I'd chalk it up as useful experience, at the very least."

"You have, I think."

"Have what?"

"Built the analyzer. Given our similarity of mind, I'd guess it's a better version of this that you've got in your TKM to scan the deep levels of circuits. Yours, at least, is useful."

"Then yours is going to be, too. You're well on your way to making your own TKM. My first attempts weren't successful, either."

As they both paused, Robinaire said, "Plennor Mayne, do you ever watch the program 'Planetfall'?"

She was addressing her own plennor, so after a moment's thought Mayne answered, "I believe I've heard of it. Space-exploration fiction, isn't it?"

"Yes. It's lots of fun. They have practically the same program here. The actors are different, though, and some of the roles, so it's kind of confusing, but it's got the same sort of stories." She began to describe the one she had just watched. Mayne, aware she had been left out of the conversation and activity, listened courteously, though Jonno was restive.

Mayne was rewarded by being reminded of something, when Robinaire narrated how the explorers had had their communicators taken from them by enemies. When she had finished recounting the story, and he had exchanged a comment or two about it with her, he turned again to Jonno. "That group of anti-technology people we met while we were shunting around searched us for contraband, and actually confiscated Robinaire's radio."

He turned back to her with the aside, "I'll get you a new one, Robinaire," then addressed Jonno again. "It occurs to me I might run into similar problems of people wanting to take away tools or weapons for one reason or another. It would be useful to have some powerful but inconspicuous tools, that look nothing like weapons or like anything else to fear or covet. They wouldn't be as vital to hang onto as the rifkey, but they might make it less necessary for me to depend on transplacing out if I meet hostile people while I'm trying to investigate some interesting phenomenon."

"There's no artifact that wouldn't stand out in some type of society: a tin can in a primitive culture, a shaggy-pelt tunic at a formal ball."

"Granted, but I suspect the technological cultures will be more useful to investigate, so I'd settle for something that would pass unnoticed there."

"Hm. Tools that are powerful enough to use as weapons if necessary, but which look like something perfectly innocent and reasonable to carry. We might think of a few. Maybe you could ask the wexters to invent some, too."

"I will. I'm also going to ask if they can make their rifkey small enough to fit into some casual object we might be expected to carry. And whether they can create a transplacing device that will move more people at a time."

"That's a load of requests."

"I think they like inventing new psionic devices — it's what they're best at."

Robinaire asked, "When are we going home, Plennor?"

"In a few minutes, Robinaire — as soon as I've made a recording."

"All right. I'll get my souvenirs."

Mayne recorded his message to the wexters while Jonno gathered a selection of professional literature for Mayne to compare with his own. Then Mayne called Robinaire back, reminding her to stand close to him for the transplacement.

"Come again soon," Jonno urged, handing Mayne the armload of books and disks.

"I will," Mayne promised. To Robinaire he said, "This time for sure." Shifting his grip on the armful of information, he operated the rifkey.

Chapter 9

Surveillance

The room in which the transplacers found themselves was very like Jonno's living room, with its computer desk, shelves, reference books, and print-outs making it look more like a study than a room traditionally used for entertaining visitors.

Robinaire raised worried eyes to Mayne's, but he gave her a reassuring smile. "It's all right, Robinaire. We made it this time; we're in my own quarters." He glanced out a window, noticing that a pair of the little electric scooters ISC supplied at the bus depot for travel around the Compound were still parked beside the building. "It's seventeen-fifty. Let's go see what's keeping Van and Davith here so late."

He led the way through the airlock passage to the main lab, making sure, before entering the central room, that this time there were no potentially curious visitors. The two technicians were desultorily carrying out routine work in a showing of normalcy. They greeted the wanderers with excited cries.

"You made it!"

"You found her! We knew you would!"

Then Van's worry shattered into sharpness: "What happened? What took so long? It's been the better part of two days!"

Robinaire was looking blankly at them. Mayne said, "It's all right to talk to these two any time, Robinaire, provided no one unauthorized can hear you."

"Supra," said Robinaire. "I've been to eleven worlds! And," She waved her bag of packages, "see what I've brought back!" She had been promised that Van would look at her souvenirs; now she could recite her adventures, too.

Van and Davith looked to Mayne, but he delayed them, seeing Robinaire's eagerness. "Later. Let Robinaire tell you her experiences first."

Letter-perfect, Robinaire recounted her story before getting to, "They were going to kill us, and Plennor Mayne couldn't make his rifkey work: but a woman called Ithleen came from the wexters and took us to her world. I went shopping with her, and see what I've got!" She began taking things out of packages.

"How did you buy them, Robinaire?" asked Van. "They can't have used our money there."

"They don't use money at all. Ithleen just put her fingerprint on the window of a machine."

"What's Ithleen like?" Davith asked curiously.

"Oh, she's a baggy old woman. She must be at least twenty-five. She's nice, though."

Van and Davith, who were both twenty-three, looked at each other across the head of the teenager, bent over her packages. Then they looked at Mayne. "What is she like, Plennor?"

He considered, giving thought to what he had taken entirely for granted before. "She seems to be a kindly and generous young woman. She's twenty-seven. It's quite true she likes clothes that are made for comfort rather than style, which shows sound judgement on her part. Since she went out of her own universe at a moment's notice to help people who were involved in unknown dangers, she's courageous. She gives duty preference over what she likes to do, so she's conscientious. And she is refreshingly intelligent to talk to."

Robinaire resumed her story, describing Geode's stores and its lack of interesting news, and then continued: "Plennor Mayne fixed his rifkey, only not quite, because it took us to a wrong world again, but a good one. There was a lab like this, and Plennor Mayne met his cousin there."

"His cousin!"

"Not a real cousin. Not even a real person, actually. They're just sort of imitations, those otherworld people, like in a video game where you program yourself into the role of one of the characters. But Plennor Mayne said it felt like having a cousin." Robinaire quoted fluently, "An analog of himself; he fills the same niche in his universe as Plennor Mayne does here.

And he's called Plennor Mayne, too, but his first name's a bit different, and he's different, too, except not entirely..." Here she floundered. "It's like someone who didn't really know Plennor Mayne programmed him into the VR."

Again the assistants looked to Mayne for enlightenment. "Yes, we reached a world analogous to this one." He hesitated. "It's hard for me to describe Jonno. I also had the feeling that he was both like and unlike me. I probably noticed more differences than similarities; but I did feel kin to him. Apparently the rifkey considered him to be very like me." He explained about the rifkey's final malfunction. "He's ahead of me in some things, behind in others," he concluded. "We exchanged some ideas, and I'm eager to get to work on the material he gave me." He gestured at the pile of disks, data slips, and hardcopy he had unloaded onto a workbench.

"If you want help, we can stay."

"No, not tonight. It'll take time to read all this material. You two should have been off home an hour ago, anyway."

"Well, we kind of wanted to see how things came out," said Davith, "so we've been staying late and coming early."

Van was more direct. "We've been worried blue, and would have stayed here day and night, if we hadn't had to cover up."

"It — it was good of you to be concerned," said Mayne awkwardly. Personal concern over his welfare was something he was no longer used to. "But go get some rest, now. I'll work on my own this evening." His glance fell on Robinaire and responsibility touched him again. "I'll take you home first, Robinaire."

"We can look after her, sir, when we've tidied up here," Van offered.

Mayne hesitated, but conscience won, prodded by his guilt over the test transplacement. "No, I'll do it myself." He took Robinaire out to the garage as the technicians packed away their work.

"What's he doing?" asked Davith, with prompt suspicion raised by Mayne's over-compensating attentiveness. It wasn't usual behaviour for him.

"I think he's just being kind, Davith, not just polite, for all he's so stand-offish most of the time."

"Somehow I don't think he's been so stand-offish with the kid."

"Because she is a kid, for windsake! And he promised to look after her."

"If he's busy being kind with a kid now, do you suppose he's thinking of settling down?" Davith considered for a moment before answering his own question, "No. He'd get bored as soon as the fog cleared; but he could be hooked and gaffed while it was still there — and miserable for the rest of his life."

"We can't let that happen to our plennor. Think 'pre-emptive strike'. We bring someone in while there's still time. An attractive woman, with brains."

"Going to advertise for one in the physics journals?" Davith asked sarcastically.

"No need. We know about one already."

"Who?"

"That theorist, Ithleen."

"How do you know she's attractive? He didn't say she was."

"He did, you know: he said he enjoyed talking to her; and that's the most important and lasting part of any human relationship. And everything else he said about her was approving, too."

Conceding the point, Davith asked, "But how can you get him to bring her here?"

"She's supposed to be solving the riddle of the cosmos or something for these wexters, right? And she lives in a little sealed city with hardly any resources. Where's her experimental data to come from? You can't theorize in a vacuum. Why not move her here where there's more recent data, better facilities, and Plennor Mayne handy to do any experimenting she needs, to test a hypothesis?"

"Well — you can try," said Davith.

"The idea has merit," came a new "voice".

They whirled to face a silvery draped-pillar shape.

"I... think it must... be a wexter, Van."

"Your assumption is correct. I have come to speak to Plennor Mayne about his recent report. I sense that he is not here, but observe that he has trusted you two with knowledge of the multiverse; so I will speak to you. We will work on the problems he has put to us about the rifkey and the tools. And we will invite the theorist, Ithleen, to work in this universe. Please tell him these things." The wexter faded out.

"Whoosh!" said Davith. "That's quite a thing, that wexter!"

"I've got cold shivers running up and down my spine," admitted Van. "But it's worth it!"

"Slap on!" cried Davith again. "We're part of the action, at last. And some more of the action is coming to us!"

***

When Mayne returned, he found his two assistants still present, and waiting with such an air of excitement that it was obvious something had happened.

"What is it?"

"The wexter came!"

"Ne seems to be getting bolder — extending ner acquaintance. What did ne say?"

"The wexters are going to work on the problems of the rifkey and the tools."

"That's good news." Their level of excitement had not dropped. "There's something more?"

"They're going to send Ithleen here!" Van firmly put all the responsibility on the wexters.

"Why?"

She launched into her argument.

"I wonder why the wexters suddenly thought of this. They've known all along that Geode is very limited," Mayne said.

"Well, they didn't have anywhere to send her, before." Davith took up the explanation. He also did not want the plennor to guess they had been talking about his private affairs. "So they probably didn't think about it. We were comparing worlds when the wexter came. Ne decided on the spot."

"She can stay here, can't she?" suggested Van. "You've got a couple of spare rooms; and she shouldn't have to plunge out into our world right away. Besides, she doesn't have any identification or rental history; she'd have a hard time getting a place of her own."

"I could give her enough money in cashcards to cover temporary accommodation, but it probably would be easier for her to stay here, and just visit outside. We'll let her decide for herself when she arrives."

"Do you think she'll come right away?" Davith asked.

Mayne considered. "She's keen to investigate the multiverse, but she's also conscientious, so I'd say it depends on how long it takes her to get leave of absence from her duties. The Geodans make sure no one is irreplaceable, and they seem to be co-operative in the multiverse research, so they'll probably be prompt in making the arrangements, which means it might be only a day or two."

Van asked innocently, "Will you let us know as soon as you find out?"

Mayne raised an eyebrow. "What's the hurry?"

"We're interested," said Van simply.

That was a feeling Mayne could empathize with. "All right. If I get news during the weekend, I'll phone you."

***

The next morning Spen visited briefly with a new rifkey and a request to take back the first one for checking. "We do not belittle your accomplishment," ne told Mayne; "but it is better to be quite sure there is no remaining fault."

"I wouldn't want you to worry," said Mayne drily, and made the exchange. "Any word from Ithleen?"

Spen confirmed that she had agreed to make an extended visit and expected to arrive late that same afternoon, as soon as she had briefed a replacement for her Council position and handed over her teaching work to one of the few other physicists in Geode. Mayne nodded with satisfaction. It was always a pleasure — he explained his feelings to himself — to observe competence, and both efficiency and the ability to improvise were requisites in Geode.

Spen then requested guidance to Jonno's world. Mayne learned that the wexters had been even more amazed than he was by the contact. Defective though humans were in psi senses the wexters had been convinced that not even one of that species could make a contact with so close a personal analog; and the wexters were eager to examine the analog themselves.

Before guiding Spen, Mayne took a few seconds to call Van's home number, as promised, and tell her recorder, "Late this afternoon," cautiously giving no other information. He had thought of getting his assistants active anti-tapping devices for their phones to supplement the automatic passive testers routinely installed on communication equipment throughout ISC Territory, but had decided it might catch Polminander's attention; so he had merely warned his technicians to be oblique in conversation.

With his promise to Van fulfilled, Mayne picked up the return load of data recordings he had promised Jonno and made the transplacement, the wexter either accompanying or following him on ner own.

The two plennors told Spen what little they had discovered so far about the similarities and differences in their worlds; then Mayne returned home, leaving the wexter with Jonno, still engrossed in the hard-to-believe similarity of the two worlds.

An hour later, Van and Davith quietly let themselves into the building and came into the central lab room. Mayne regarded them without comment, and Davith began to mumble something about wanting to finish a piece of work.

Van stopped him with a gesture. "We can't wait to meet Ithleen," she admitted cheerfully. "But we will get some extra work done, while we're here. And you don't have to give us time off to make up for it."

Mayne let them see that he was a bit amused by their impatience to become part of the multiverse activity, but was equally pleased by their offer. "I've been designing some tools; you can start making them. Here are the specs; you can shape the casings first. After Ithleen gets here I'll probably be talking to her for a while, to get her settled in, so you can use the TKM to make the immits."

As they began collecting up the necessary materials, Mayne turned back to his own work. He was attempting to probe further into the rifkey, pushing the TKM's scanner to its limits, and tiring his own mind even further.

The technicians worked dutifully for the next three hours, but whenever Mayne took a much-needed break from his concentration, he saw them looking at their watches. Their suspense and anticipation finally began to affect even his steady nerves, and he caught himself looking at his own watch and wondering at what hour Ithleen's "late in the afternoon" arrival would occur. Annoyed at himself, he put the TKM's electrodes back on and closed out the surrounding world.

It took him longer than usual to regain his concentration. He reminded himself that annoyance was counter-productive, and spent a few moments clearing his mind of emotion by a touch of self-hypnosis. But he had only another half hour of work time before excited cries from the assistants pulled him back. Ithleen had arrived.

Mayne quickly put down the electrodes and joined the greetings — as was only courteous, of course. He introduced Van and Davith to Ithleen, and showed her the office they had cleared out for her. Remembering her enthusiasm for the subject, Mayne had stocked a shelf with books and disks on astrophysics; and he showed her how to call up more information from the ISC Library and elsewhere.

Ithleen was touched by the thoughtfulness of his gesture; and she readily accepted Van's suggestion that she ease her transition by sheltering in the plennor's home. She remarked that she had come braced to live in an "outside" and was looking forward to seeing the ISC world; but she agreed it would be handier for work to live here, and would require less adjustment to a world where she would be undocumented.

The apartment attached to the lab building boasted — besides its half-converted living room — a kitchen, three bedrooms with attached bathrooms, and a further room meant for dining, which Mayne had long since turned into a library. The kitchen was only a little less automated than the Geodan ones; for meals Mayne had only to speak or type commands into the food processor which occupied one wall, and return dishes to it for recycling. The cleaning staff restocked the processor weekly from a standard list Mayne had given them; he invited Ithleen to experiment with a greater variety of food, but she remarked that they seemed to share a general indifference to what they ate.

She was glad to see that the ISC world practiced recycling of materials; re-use was one of Geode's most basic principles, and to go straight into a wasteful world would have been upsetting, she declared.

To abundant energy she was accustomed; her little world was utterly dependent on that. But assorted weather was a novelty — She flew only on days of good weather, her cockpit tightly sealed against the possibility of contamination — and the night sky fascinated her. She had read all of Geode's few books on astronomy; but an observatory was still on the "someday" list for her people. When she learned that this Earth had two large observatories on its moon, as well as a scattering of telescopes in orbit, she declared that any last trace of agoraphobia in herself had just been conquered; she wanted to get out there and see for herself!

Ithleen had brought a portable computer and stacks of disks full of wexter data. As she began arranging these in her new office, Mayne impatiently put to her the problem of Jonno's world.

"Is this the man you had with you the last time you came to Geode? I noticed it wasn't Robinaire, but not much else, I'm afraid. I couldn't see much of him anyway, and I really had my attention on the repairs. You should have brought him back the next day; I'd have liked to meet him, if he's your analog."

Mayne brushed that aside with a gesture. "Plenty of time for that. He's completely immersed in building a TKM right now. The important thing is the fact that I got to his world at all. The wexters were sure it was impossible — so sure that I accepted it, and never tried."

Ithleen considered. "Are you sure that was the only reason you didn't try? The wexters say there's a psychic resistance that could have been operating, too."

"I'd rather believe that than that I was so short-sighted and unprofessional as to not bother to test out something I'd merely been told," admitted Mayne ruefully, running a hand through his hair. "Any experimenter worth the name checks things for nemself. But that brings us back to the wexters' question of how I overcame that resistance and got into Jonno's world."

"Yes. We humans have no difficulty in reaching another human world if it's different enough, but..."

"But this one isn't."

"It's not just this one person? The worlds are really alike?"

"Everyone in his background is the equivalent of mine, though those in his present environment seem to be not quite the same, slightly different people in ISC positions, for instance, but not different enough to affect his life. And up to the last year or two, his history is the same as mine, barring a slight shift in some dates. Universities, Regions, ISC, customs, the state of science, everything that's been major in our lives is the same. Even his world's fiction programs seem to be similar enough."

"And you felt no resistance to going there?"

"I didn't know I was going at the time. Come to remember, when I realized what had happened, I felt a sort of lurch. I put that down to disbelief, and then got so interested that I forgot it. But, thinking back, I believe it was a feeling of wrongness, rejection, maybe even panic. But it vanished, as I say."

"And you never felt it again?"

"I'm not sure. There was something later, not quite the same, I think, but some sort of reluctance. It was when I agreed to take Jonno on a transplacement to Geode. But that might have been worry over whether the rifkey was really fixed that time. I'd just taken Robinaire through another malfunction."

"You had no trouble in the Geode transplacement or in returning Jonno to his world?"

"No, nor in going back there myself, nor in guiding the wexter to it."

"Have you tried to reach any other analog?"

Mayne was startled. "No. I didn't even think of it just now when I mentioned having neglected to test out the resistance hypothesis!"

"What's your reaction to the idea now that you have it? Suppose you could get into a universe where you had an analog so like you that only some trifle were different — say, one of you had just had his hair cut while the other hadn't: all the rest of your lives and selves were the same. Would you like to go?"

Analyzing his own response, Mayne said slowly, "I'd be interested to know if it could be done, but not in going to see that world. Why should I, when it's just like this one?"

"That's rationalizing. You don't really want to experiment for yourself, do you?"

He nodded. "You're right. The resistance is there." He set his jaw and pulled out his rifkey. "An analog...a duplicate..." He traced the pattern. Nothing happened. "Apparently we can force our actions but not our wills."

"Jonno must be the nearest analog you can accept. Try for one more distant – one only a little like you."

That attempt failed also.

"It begins to look as if your contact with Jonno was a freak accident. Ignorance of what you were doing must have played a key part in it; though it seems that once the worlds have been linked, and you've accepted it, the resistance vanishes."

Ithleen considered for a moment, then pulled out her own rifkey. "I think I'd like to meet an analog of myself; let me try." She patterned her rifkey, but had no more success than Mayne had had. "Let's try for analogs of each other, or of anyone else we know."

When these attempts had also failed, Mayne said wryly, "I didn't mind trying those – I suppose I already knew I wouldn't really be trying, whatever I told myself."

Ithleen nodded. "We'll never be able to duplicate the conditions of your contact with Jonno. One must be ignorant of the possibility of success, in order to be really willing to try; now that we know contact is attainable, we can't will ourselves genuinely enough to bypass the resistance."

"I feel both relief and faint regret."

"So do I."

"Well, even with all the nearest universes subtracted, we still have an infinity of others to investigate. I'll start in again as soon as I've got a few tools and instruments made. I may as well get to work on that."

"And I'd like to get started on your books."

"I'll give you my code for ordering supplies. Does your computer have a built-in scanner? You'll have to work from hardcopy in using any of our data. And better keep all the wexter data on your incompatible equipment. No sense making it available to anyone here."

Both were soon immersed in their work again – the multiverse and its puzzles a briefly postponed pleasure.

***

Ithleen spent the rest of the weekend reading summaries of the state of physics in the ISC world, with a concentration on astrophysics. On Monday, Van and Davith, who were accustomed to Mayne's equal oblivion to the world while he worked, managed to shut off her reader at midday and haul her out to the kitchen with them and the plennor for a meal, to ensure that she ate at least once a day. Plennor Mayne himself was busying himself reading while he ate.

As the kitchen processor was withdrawing their food choices from storage and flash-cooking them, Van made a remark about the perks of working for a plennor — or at least for this plennor — and Ithleen asked how she and Davith had come to do so.

"Chance," Van responded. "Blissful chance, as it turned out, but we didn't know that at the time. You see, when someone becomes a plennor or laudor and gets ner own lab, ne can also choose ner own staff, on any grounds ne wants. A lot take along their old associates; others interview the year's graduating scientists and technicians, and invite them to join ner staff."

Davith put in, "Nobody refuses. Quite aside from the prestige, it lets you work at the cutting edge of your field."

Van resumed. "Maybe no one refuses, but some try hard to be picky. After all, some of the big shots are petty tyrants that nobody wants to work with, however prestigious they may be. Sometimes they make out whole lists of qualifications they want in their assistants, but we were warned that what they really want are 'people meek enough to put up with a lavishly spoiled genius,' if I remember my instructor's crack correctly."

"Our plennor," Davith remarked, "just sent word he needed two new assistants with clean habits who were willing to work hard —"

Mayne cut in, tacitly admitting he had been listening. "I did put intelligence first among my requirements. And got it."

The two techs glowed at the compliment. Van went on, "We heard all sorts of stories about why the two previous assistants had left. Some said Plennor Mayne worked them to death. Others said he was impossibly...er..."

"Vain and demanding, I believe was the phrase," Mayne said blandly. "One of my other assistants told me, while he was drunk and disgruntled, that that was what another assistant had said."

"Did you fire him?" asked Van.

"Of course not. He was a perfectly competent worker, never drunk or hungover during work hours."

"You didn't mind his spreading that insult?" Davith's tone held a touch of indignance-on-behalf-of.

Mayne shrugged. "I've heard worse opinions about me."

"So how come there was the opening for us?" Van asked.

"They both chose later to apply for positions supervising the commercializing of the TKM."

"And you recommended them both?" This time Davith's tone merely anticipated an affirmative.

"They were capable of handling the job."

Davith shook his head over such indifference to personal relationships, and summed up his own experience to Ithleen. "What we found when we'd worked here a while, was that we are expected to work hard, even overtime occasionally; but Plennor Mayne always gives us time off to make up for it, and accepts it if we say we can't stay that day; and he always makes sure we get public credit for our help in the work. We like working here."

"And we like our plennor, too," said Van.

Flustered by this comment as he had not been by the reminder of criticism,

Mayne quickly changed the subject. He asked Ithleen if she had found the equipment and supplies adequate.

"Yes, thank you. The only thing lacking is enough hours in a day."

Van said, "I don't know how the wexters expected you to work in your own world if you lack all this information about the galaxies and such."

Ithleen looked guilty, and then confessed, "I've no idea whether any of this will be useful or not, Van. It just fascinates me, and I've been gorging myself on it. I'm especially fascinated by what your astronomers call 'the hapsar mystery.' It's not in my out-of-date Geode texts."

"What's a hapsar?" asked Van. "I took an astronomy option in first year at college, and the word sounds vaguely familiar, but..."

"Half the mystery seems to be that no one knows exactly what it is," said Ithleen, laughing. "It seems that either old records are wrong, or some stars and galaxies are moving or fading out or getting obscured by dust. At any rate, the astronomers keep having to update their charts. There doesn't seem to be any pattern in these events, and nothing catastrophic is occurring among the still-visible neighbours of the vanished objects, so it doesn't seem to be any sort of widespread destruction; but it's certainly puzzling, and I'd like to learn more about it. Later, of course. What I must get down to, first, is a systematic comparison of your physics observations with ours. Of course, there can't be any glaring differences: after all, both our universes fall within the narrow parameters that permit life to exist. On the other hand, there do seem to be major differences in life's ability to tap into psi forces —"

Mayne nodded, remembering Robinaire's descriptions of the psi in Zar Haughn's world and Aresette, widely different.

" — and it appears that those forces are the elemental ones of all the universes. Of course, we've sampled only Earths, and mostly human ones at that; but the variation could indicate a general difference in the accessibility to the psi force; and that suggests that happenstance universes, including divergent ones, are more likely than divergent ones alone. The wexters, of course, are very interested in the amount of psi use in various universes, and their probes brought back a lot of data on it. So far, I haven't spotted anything my intuition calls significant, by either my standards or theirs."

She grinned again. "Unless my interest in hapsars indicates that my intuition is tying them into psi, somehow." Her smile faded. "Something about that sounded almost right. Almost." Her eyes defocused. "Not connected... Important to the wexter queries? Investigatable by psi? Or am I just wishing I could find a way and an excuse to study them? Whatever the reason, my intuition seems very interested in them."

Van said, "You talked about psi forces just now. Do you know what they are?"

"Well, if my theory's right, psi is the tappable part of what I've called the fluxate, which is the non-corporeal substance, energy, condition, existence, that makes up not only the finer levels of infra-sub-particles and of space itself, but also the multiverse. It contains the universes, and it fills the universes, and it is the universes, and it forms the infinitesimal, infinite barrier between universes. I named the extent that it forms the diaphane — 'dia' for 'through, between, made from' and 'phane' for 'to appear, to be like, to manifest itself.'

"The fluxate comprises everything. Although quanta of space, energy, and matter are derived from it, it is not quantized itself. Every part of the diaphane is not merely the same as every other, it is every other part. When you tap into the fluxate, by the use of psi, you can have action at a distance in space or time, because there is no distance in the diaphane. Every 'part' is completely entangled with every other one — and yet can also be completely separate, simultaneously. Interaction with consciousness depends on observer focus. The amount of the fluxate seems to be infinite; but how much a sapient can draw from it by natural talent apparently varies from one universe to another."

"Wow," said Van. "And when we use the TKM or the TPA, we're actually immersed in this diaphane?"

"Not immersed. The wexters tell me that can be fatal. But the energy is available everywhere in the multiverse, if you have either the natural talent or the psionics knowledge. It's like the difference between drowning in an ocean and merely scooping up a bit of its water."

Half-aloud, Davith said, "All the energy of all the universes. It's mind-blowing."

"It might be!" punned Van.

There was a moment's contemplative silence, then Mayne, who had already discussed all this with Ithleen, returned to present concerns. "The wexters aren't expecting instant results from your studies, I trust?"

"No. I made sure they know that a human needs to do a lot of just sitting-and-thinking, or even going off to do other things to clear ner head. So before I get back into their data mass, I'll visit a few other universes myself."

Mayne raised an eyebrow at this calm announcement. "Do the wexters accept that as a necessary part of clearing a human's head?"

Ithleen laughed. "I can't say I convinced them it was. In fact, they disapprove rather pointedly of their pet theorist taking any risks. But since they feel so strongly about not forcing conformity on others, and letting individuals make their own choices about actions as well as opinions, they can't insist on my following their nervous wishes. They've left my rifkey with me, so I'm free to go to any other world I please."

"You really want to? In spite of your sheltered life in Geode?" Mayne said.

"I'm aching to go. As I told you, I'd have gone exploring for the wexters myself if I'd had enough experience and knowledge to do any good. But I don't need to know much just to take a quick look at some worlds for my own satisfaction."

"I might point out that you don't know enough to know how much you do need to know. But since I agree with the wexters' principle of free choice of action, and share your craving to see other worlds, it would be hypocritical for me to try to discourage you. I haven't much experience yet myself, but wouldn't it be better for you to come along with me on a trip or two rather than striking out on your own, even just to 'take a quick look'? As we've already found out, the unexpected has a way of happening."

"I'll be glad to have your guidance, if I won't be in the way."

"Far from it—as you've already proved by rescuing us from the execution squad in Ocerat. I'll be pleased to have back-up on the next worlds."

Davith said eagerly, "May we come, too?"

"Not yet. The rifkeys offer built-in protection to the user, but not to anyone being taken along. So until I've gained more experience myself, I'd rather not have the extra responsibility of an unprotected person along."

Davith's face fell, but he asked sturdily, "What do we do while you're gone, then?"

"You continue to cover for us. Don't worry, I'll leave enough work to keep you busy."

"When are you going, Plennor?" Van asked.

"Tomorrow." Mayne turned back to Ithleen. "I've had Van and Davith making a few copies of a miniature laser I've designed. It has a variable intensity that will work either as a light or, briefly, as a burning tool or weapon. That's for emergency use only, because there was no way to store a long-use charge in it without making its size awkward. At full strength, its power pack will drain within a few minutes."

Van remarked, "We put them inside flashlights, so they'd look casual. Davith and I had to go around privately buying up the flashlights one at a time, so Supply wouldn't wonder why the plennor suddenly had a yen for them."

Mayne went on, "I've also had them make a few miniaturized

instruments. I hope to get better ones later from the wexters; but it will take them a while to design something humans can use."

With wistful humour, Van said, "Don't use up all the adventures before we get to go!"

"I don't intend to be adventurous at all, Van. We're just going to take a brief look at a few more worlds."

"I hope," said Van, "that those don't turn out to be famous last words."

***

Simao had put cautious surveillance on Mayne's lab and apartment, but the building was recent enough to have been provided routinely with the built-in bug-scramblers that were standard protection in ISC property, commercial and government offices elsewhere, and in the homes of celebrities and public figures.

There were, of course, ways to defeat the scramblers, if one had access to the right equipment; but, as Simao pointed out to Polminander, a physics plennor could find anything Simao could plant without full scale backup from Security, if he were suspicious enough to look. And since the project was still unofficial until they got enough data to justify legitimate Security interference, Simao could not risk alerting the plennor, who could simply order Security to track down the violator of his privacy, and to put on additional safeguards.

This left only long-distance electronic surveillance: movement-actuated cameras covering the doors of the building, and whatever could be picked up through the windows of the little-used auxiliary rooms. "No way I can get interior sound at this stage," said Simao apologetically. "All the walls and windows are fitted with standard sound blocker/scramblers, and since the building's air conditioned, they don't normally open any of the windows. And, of course, the rooms are all fitted up with the latest in anti-bugging devices, to make sure no Company can steal a process by hearing work being discussed before it's published, or seeing what goes on in the main lab."

He waved down Polminander's attempt to complain. "If we can justify more elaborate installations later, I'll see what I can do; but I'm stretching things as far as I can go now on the basis of that false-alarm 'missing' report, by saying that rumours of it may have reached the public, who might come around gawking or trying to play pranks like more false alarms of various disasters... or anti-science terrorists who might attempt to make an attack under cover of the gawkers."

He had promptly noted and reported that a woman was now occupying one of the extra rooms in the living quarters. "Well," said Polminander with satisfaction, "I certainly managed to jolt our stiff plennor out of his self-sufficient habits."

Then Simao brought him a video of the woman. She was tall, casually dressed, and had brown hair: obviously not the short, fashionable teenager with her light auburn hair and elegant clothes. Polminander was furious at himself for having jumped to the conclusion that his "agent" had infiltrated the enemy's inner defences.

The tape showed the woman coming out of the building with Sartyov, apparently for the explicit purpose of looking at the weather, for they were regarding the sky, and Sartyov was saying something about the city being hotter than the Compound because of the buildings, air conditioner exhausts, traffic, and shoals of warm bodies. He should have ordered video surveillance earlier.

The unknown woman's deep-set grey eyes had a serious, rather wondering look, but when she laughed at Sartyov's comment that everyone always wanted whatever weather it wasn't the season for, the smile lines fell naturally into position.

Sartyov pointed to some condensation trails overhead, talking about cirrus levels, and offering to get a poster on cloud types, earning an enthusiastic thank you. The technician made a few more remarks — that the neighbour's cats weren't hanging around for once, and that the plennor was very strict about not letting them into the lab to shed hair around the equipment, though she'd seen him petting them outdoors — then the two women went back into the building. The stranger, Polminander noticed, moved with the grace of a dancer.

Polminander could not categorize her. In spite of the hint of naivety in her first expression, she held herself with an air of competence and self-assurance: she could not be some unsuccessful relative come to sponge off the plennor. Her clothes were unfashionable but well-cut and of good material, speaking neither of poverty nor of a sudden splurge, but rather of adequate means and independent mind.

Nor did she fit the more likely guess of a pick-up, professional or amateur: nothing about her suggested glamour or allurement. Her clothes were quiet, loose, and casual; her posture was equally unprovocative; and her face bore no make-up.

True, it was a social era in which allurement was popularly limited: while most women and perhaps half the male population wore provocative clothes and make-up to parties, few of either group wore them on more casual occasions; but he got the impression that this woman went further — that she deliberately played down her natural sensuality.

Finally, Polminander shrugged and turned off the tape. "Whatever she is, her moving in with the plennor is an extremely uncharacteristic piece of behaviour on his part. It must be significant. Find out who she is, where he ran into her, and how long he's known her."

***

By Tuesday morning, Simao was ready to rip out his neatly groomed hair. He had taken the risk of briefly using Security agents. One had tried to pump Vandrai Sartyov at a restaurant on Monday evening in a necessarily casual way, but had got nowhere. Yes, the plennor had a guest; it was none of her business who or why, and certainly no one else's. People over sixteen could legally live where and with whom they chose, and whatever the moral pressures of the reactionary majority in society nowadays, a plennor did whatever ne pleased, and no one ever questioned nem.

Anyone trying to harass one of them answered to Security for threatening a natural resource. And in case the questioner was a reporter, ne was reminded that unless ne got permission from the subject, only public actions, or matters that bore on the carrying out of public duties, could be publicly commented on, for any citizen. A plennor's duties were in no way affected by ner social life, so unless the social activities occurred in public, they were not fair game.

Another agent had got into the lab by the pretence of checking on fire safety, long enough to surreptitiously lift a set of fingerprints and to hear a name: Ithleen. Simao had personally run the prints through the ident computer, and tried the name as first, middle, last, and nick name. All he got was No Data No Data.

He cautiously contacted wider fields of security. No region had anything on the prints or name. They appeared on no birth certificate, no identity card, no driver's or pilot's or boating licence, no credit or debit cards, no membership or subscription lists, no criminal record, no school record. The woman might not exist, for all the trace he could find of her.

He tried to work from the other end: when and how had she become a part of Mayne's life? According to all he could find out, Mayne had not been farther from his lab than the city of Neithon in the past year; and nowhere in the area could Simao find an Ithleen. Nor could he find any association with the name anywhere in the plennor's history.

When he reported his failure to Polminander, the administrator was both disappointed and pleased. "If he's covered his tracks, she must be important. Keep trying, and keep up the surveillance."

***

Polminander called Haldis Gythstrom and arranged to "casually" meet her grand-niece Tuesday afternoon. As he chatted with Robinaire, he skillfully elicited from her the fact that she had recently met the plennor, and asked her what her visit had been like.

"He showed me around his lab. It was just as dwerpy dull as Aunt Haldis's."

"But surely you found him interesting? Our most famous plennor..."

"Oh, yes."

"What happened after your tour?"

"Plennor Mayne took me home," said Robinaire, smoothly skipping everything that had to do with the multiverse.

"What did he talk about while you were there?"

"The machines, mostly."

"What did he say about them?"

Robinaire recited her tour of the lab.

"Did he show you every piece of apparatus in the lab?"

"Everything there was in the big middle room, I think. Bor-ing!"

"Was there anything or any place they didn't show you?"

"Not in that room," sighed Robinaire, in weary remembrance. "At least we didn't go into the smaller labs and offices and storerooms."

"They kept you out of those?"

"No, I think they would have made me look at them, too; but there wasn't time before I — left."

"You should go back for a longer visit, then, and see everything."

"I've seen more than enough," said Robinaire. "But I will go back," she added complacently. "The plennor said I could come and talk to him. But I've had other things to do. There were two parties, and some shopping, and my Theatre Workshop day. I'm going to go to a drama school in the autumn. I'm taking lessons, and I've had parts in four commercials. Now that I'm off school for the summer I've been able to work full time..."

Shutting out her ramblings, Polminander thought that if the plennor wanted to talk to her then she had made progress. But he had an uneasy hunch he had missed something in her account of her visit to the lab. Was the girl being evasive? If so, why? She had not seemed concerned over his questions about the lab. Perhaps it was just that she had got on with the plennor a little better than she cared to discuss with a near-stranger... No, Mayne had not followed up the acquaintance — seemed to be occupied with another one, in fact. Hmm. Perhaps he could strike a spark there? "Do you know Ithleen?"

No flicker in her eyes. "Who?"

"The woman who's staying with Plennor Mayne now."

"Staying with the plennor?"

Yes, definitely a flicker. At least the plennor interested her, if the lab and the work did not.

"Yes, she's been there for three days now."

"Why should she be there?"

Had there been a shade of emphasis on "there"? If so, what was its significance? She hadn't seemed to recognize the woman's name, so presumably did not know her and expect her to be elsewhere. Maybe it was just jealousy that someone else had been invited there. He picked up that theme.

"He must have invited her, Robinaire."

"Why would he do that?"

"Perhaps he's — fond of her and wants her around."

"Why would he want an old woman around?"

"She's only about twenty-five, Robinaire. What made you think she was old?"

"Tw- " Robinaire stopped herself. Ithleen was part of the multiverse, and not to be discussed. "I — just thought so."

Maybe just hoped so, and trying to pump me in turn, decided Polminander. So no gold in this vein yet. But at least he had her in position to produce some ore. "Why don't you go and make her acquaintance, Robinaire, and see what she's like?"

"I could go and see, couldn't I?" muttered Robinaire.

"I hear she's an interesting person. You could tell me all about her next time I visit."

"I don't know," said Robinaire, wrestling with the problem. If Ithleen were now part of real life instead of the multiverse, could she be talked about?

"Anyway, you want to see Plennor Mayne again, don't you?"

"Sure."

"Don't wait too long. He might get interested in other... things, and forget about you. You should stay longer, too, and really get to know him."

"Maybe I will."

You will, my little recording machine, thought Polminander, satisfied with the feelings he had stirred up. And this time, stay long enough to learn something!

***

A little later that afternoon, Ithleen and Mayne stood ready to leave. Each had, besides ner rifkey, one of the miniature flashlight-lasers and assorted small tools and recording instruments.

"We'll be using Geode as a base, since we needn't worry about appearing in front of visitors there," Mayne told his assistants. "We won't stay away more than a week, and if we have any trouble we may return sooner. But we probably won't have any difficulties. We have a back-up rifkey, and we intend only to observe, anyway. At the least sign of hostility, we can slip away."

"Good luck," said Davith.

"Take care of yourselves," added Van. "We want you back again. Quite aside from the problem of being asked where the bodies are, if you don't return."

"We'll be careful. Ithleen, how about you choose a world?"

"Ready for your first trip into the multiverse?"

Ithleen gave him a big smile. Then she took out her rifkey and pressed the random-choice selection on it. For the two scientists, the lab faded and vanished.

Chapter 10

Struggle

Ithleen and Mayne stood at the edge of a public square, facing a glassy-looking hemisphere, remarkably featureless, about four stories high and the same in width. Some distance in front of it stood a pedestal bearing a plaque.

Ithleen's eyes were wide with wonder, her lips parted as though she wanted to speak but wasn't sure what to say.

"Your first time off-world can leave you at a loss for words," Mayne said pleasantly.

"Not just off-world but into an entirely different universe!" Ithleen said, her voice echoing the excitement that she was attempting, but failing to contain. "So different from my home world. The dome here looks almost - decorative. There are so many pedestrians crossing through the square; each intent on their own various errands." They were ignoring the dominating structure with the indifference of familiarity. Their clothes were so varied that no over-all style could be discerned. The rule appeared to be individuality.

"This is probably a major city," Mayne mused, "in a world with global communications, and a society in the throes of change. I don't think we'll be noticeable, so we can try mingling a bit."

One man was seated on a bench and idly looked at the structure. He was in his early fifties, still trim and healthy, though his pensive face and slightly stooped posture suggested a scholar rather than an athlete. His dress was khaki walking shorts and a crimson sweater, with equally bright knee socks above loafers. His mild interest indicated that the odd structure was a permissible object of curiosity in the society, so Mayne said, "Shall we be tourists and do a little gaping?"

"Is that what tourists do?"

"Of course, you wouldn't have any in Geode, would you?" Mayne led the way out into the open and across to the pedestal.

The plaque read, "The Old Psi Lab. No admission without authorization. DANGER: Do not approach beyond the fence."

Thus directed, they noticed that what had appeared from a distance to be a band of metal circling the base of the hemisphere was in fact a smooth-surfaced free-standing wall.

The man from the bench rose and walked over to them. He looked earnest but not assertive, "If you're interested, I can tell you its history," he offered tentatively, as he pushed back a lock of hair that promptly fell back over his forehead.

"Please do," Ithleen said.

His voice immediately gained confidence, and an experienced lecturer's ease. "You may remember that it was built during the Waiting War Years, when psi was still a new idea. Tradition says a family named Gabrick got us started in psi - on both sides - but we've never been able to trace them down in any records, so maybe it was a code-name or a distorted memory of a catch-phrase the early experimenters used. Anyway, they sold somebody high up in the military on its possibilities, and the government poured so much money into the project that we're still paying for it. Apparently the crash-priority paid off, from the military point of view: it seems the psionicists gained quite a control over the psi processes."

"Apparently?" Mayne said.

"Well, yes, the old lab itself is proof that they did , but we really don't know what they actually found out. We're just beginning to re-learn the basics."

"All their processes were lost?" Ithleen said.

"Yes and no. Your history books will have told you about the accident that blew everything up. Unless you've read the recent ones that are beginning to tell the whole story? No? Well, it wasn't the way you were taught in school. It seems that what happened was that the psionicists found themselves in telepathic communication with their counterparts on the Other Side."

He shoved his hair back again. "Well, you may have heard how scientists hate to have restrictions on information flow. First thing you knew, they were exchanging interesting bits of information; next thing, they were deciding to refuse to work on the whole operation. Thanks to their trading of information, someone among them realized that both sides had committed their whole resources to the psi struggle, and... well, in the end, the scientists made a sort of suicide pact, to permanently seal up the labs from inside, by psionic means."

"No dissidents?" Mayne asked.

"There were only a few key personnel on either side who really understood enough to matter. On our side, they arranged for the rest of the staff to be out on a fire drill, along with most of the military guards. Then they sealed the place psionically, and killed their personal guards. And when they were sure the other side had also acted, killed themselves as well. On the other side, they blew the place up, with themselves in it: we don't know whether destroying everything was intentional, or a miscalculation."

"So all that remains is this sealed hemisphere," Mayne said.

"Sphere, actually. Naturally, the military tried to get in, and they soon found the barrier surrounded the place, including underground. They wasted most of the rest of our resources trying to get in."

He paused as if expecting indignant mutterings. When none came, he went on. "Well, from there your history books are pretty accurate: the loss of their potential war toys made both sides suddenly start re-figuring their costs, and eventually relations thawed out into trade, and after nearly a century of peace it seems safe enough to have another go at psionics; and those of us who are trying to scratch up an understanding of the basics again, on a tiny budget, sometimes come here and sigh at the old lab. Maybe hoping some crazy kind of leakage will touch us with inspiration — since none of the Gabricks seem to have survived — to start over."

"You're a psionicist yourself?" Mayne asked.

"One of the few — if I can call myself one - with no concrete results in the study. My name's Ronsil Hadroubef, by the way. Ronce for short."

Mayne introduced himself and Ithleen. "We find both the story and the ideas of psionics very interesting. You say they sealed the lab psionically. What do you mean by that?"

"I'm not quite sure myself. As near as we can figure from our attempts to get in, there's an invisible barrier that permeates the place from its outer wall to at least two-thirds of the way to the centre. No one's ever got further."

"What sort of barrier?"

"A kind of emotional resistance. The further you go, the worse it gets. We've mapped out a route that far in, with the codes to the door locks figured out; but at the furthest point anyone has ever got, from any side, there's always been some set-up that requires more than one person to get past it; but by that point, no one has been able to trust a companion enough to co-operate. If they're not driven out, they turn on each other. We've been able to rescue some, and to bring out the bodies of the others, by sending in two or three very co-operative people who are very determined not to try to get all the way in. Sometimes we've even lost some of them."

Ithleen asked, "Do you keep trying just for that challenge, or is there a practical reason?"

"It was never confirmed, but one of the junior staff who — ah — had an emotional relationship with one of the key scientists, and maintained he'd been told some of the plans, said they intended to leave some information at the centre of the building, where peaceful people could get to it in later years. This has encouraged us to believe there is a way to get through the barrier."

"If the budget for psi investigations now is small, perhaps people don't really want it," Ithleen suggested.

"Well, they don't, I suppose. They still associate it with the old war days. But I've a hunch that psi is the key to interstellar travel, and we need that to get our world flourishing again. The crafts we sent to closer planets before all the money went to the war just aren't practical for the longer distances. So if there's any hope of psi getting us there, I'll keep after it for the rest of my life."

"I'm with you there!" agreed Ithleen. "And in any case, the intellectual challenge..." She glanced at Mayne.

"What credentials do you need to be a serious investigator?" Mayne asked.

"I don't know what credentials one could have, except interest. You're interested?"

"We are indeed. I've dabbled a bit in psionics," Mayne said.

"Any success?"

"Some ideas about amplifying natural psi mechanically."

Ronce instantly invited them to his home for a discussion. They had soon littered his study with pages of diagrams and equations, as Mayne gave him a lead into the line he had taken for his first amplifier; and it was settled that Mayne and Ithleen might make at least a preliminary sortie into the Old Psi Lab whenever they chose.

"There's no way to prepare you for it. All I can tell you is that your own emotions are turned against you; and the more people there are in a group, the more likely they are to turn on one another."

"Perhaps one of the emotions exploited has been guilt over the war-aims of the original psi efforts," Mayne said.

"You may be right. Certainly a pair of my current crop of young students got further in than anybody did earlier. But they swore they'd never make another try. Every time I've tried it, I've become more reluctant. I just do rescues, now. I'm pretty good at that, so I guess I've really given up wanting to go right in, myself. I'd still like to see it cracked, though."

"Well, perhaps we will be the ones that get through. I can assure you we have not inherited any guilt over that war."

Ronce gave his visitors an early lunch of sandwiches, then took them back to the Old Psi Lab and unlocked the gate in the added wall, pointing out that its snap lock opened from inside by a simple knob. The building sat solidly in front of them, with a small door visible now that they were inside the fence.

"I'll see you in, and past the first interior door. Here's your copy of the map: you'll see the door combinations marked on it. This is how you operate the outer one." As he worked on the entrance door, he went on, "I think you'll begin feeling the psychic defences even before we're in."

"A feeling of reluctance? The thought it might be better to try at some later time?" Ithleen said.

"That's it. You're in the outer fringes."

Ignoring the sensation, the three stepped through the door into a reception room, from which corridors led in three directions. Mayne glanced at the map of the building. "We should take the inward one. I have the feeling if we do so we'll get lost, and that there's really a shorter way from one of the halls parallel to the outer walls."

"It's easy to pick out the misdirections here," Ronce said. "It gets more confusing, or rather, people get more confused as they go in."

At the end of the short corridor, Ronce instructed Mayne to operate the lock of the next door while he checked him on it. Mayne thought with irritation that he did not need to practice in order to handle a simple electronic lock, then caught at the thought. Artificial irritation, he realized.

"Most of the locks open this way," said Ronce, in a carefully neutral voice, well aware of the pressures already on them. "The combinations are all marked on your map, as far in as we've got. What may be beyond that, we don't know."

Mayne suppressed the impulse to say impatiently, that he'd told them all this before.

"This is as far as I'll come. We've found that relative strangers are distrusting of each other by the end of the next corridor. I'm already feeling I don't want to let you go on just in case you do solve what I haven't! If I go any further, I wouldn't care if you ever got back. If you're not out by tomorrow, a friend and I will try to come look for you; but you know we can't guarantee to reach you in time."

"We understand," Mayne assured him, still holding his impatience in check.

Putting deliberate warmth in her voice, Ithleen said, "And thank you, Ronce, for all your help."

"Good luck," he said, and hurried out.

Mayne and Ithleen walked slowly along the next stretch of corridor.

Ithleen glanced nervously over her shoulder, then caught herself. "The fear is starting," she reported.

"Yes, I feel it. Diffuse, so far."

"We have one advantage, besides our lack of guilt over their war,"

Ithleen remarked, determinedly cheerful. "We know we can always get out by transplacement, if things get too bad to stand."

Mayne started to answer, then cut himself short, not wanting to lessen her optimism and confidence.

But the same thought had occurred to Ithleen. "No, we can't, of course. The presence of other psi interferes with the rifkeys' operation."

"Not all psi. It has to be strong, and focused on us; and it might just confuse the setting, as it did that time I got Robin off the missile."

"Or it could stop the rifkeys from working at all, as it did on that world with the broadcast power. This place is saturated with psi, of unidentified varieties; and right now it is focused on us," she added, rather sharply. "With the defences in here set to turn tools against their users, we'd better avoid using any but the simplest and most necessary tools, especially psi ones."

"You don't have to belabour the point," Mayne grumbled, then quickly apologized, reminding himself to fight irritation.

They activated the lock for another door, then consulted the map. "Apparently there's something particularly bad ahead," Mayne pointed out. "But we can make a detour through these offices here."

"That's a relief," admitted Ithleen.

"Then it's a delusion. We go straight on."

"Are you sure? Maybe we — No, you're right. I want to take the detour, so it's wrong."

They pressed on. Nervousness increased, and a sense of revulsion began to develop. Stuck in this grim, drab building, full of cobwebs and dirt, when they could be out in the fresh air and sunshine!

"Considering," said Ithleen, "that I grew up in an underground city, this sudden passion for the great outdoors is quite an achievement of the old psionicists."

Mayne brushed the back of his hand across his forehead. "The hall seems to have become narrower and lower as we go along. Hope it's not going to close down to a crawl space." He tried to keep his voice casual, but he found himself cringing.

"Claustrophobia is starting," diagnosed Ithleen. "I have an advantage here. The sensation of being enclosed seems quite natural to me."

"Take the lead, then," Mayne said, and added, "Where you go, I will," rude belligerence breaking through his normal calm courtesy.

They went on, fighting the urges to turn aside, to turn back, or at least to stop and wait a while. But eventually Ithleen's steps began to falter. "So tired," she gasped.

"Keep on. Remember, your sensations aren't real."

"You'll have to take the lead again. The claustrophobia's let up, so you needn't be afraid any more."

"Then just make sure you keep up with me. You're not going to drop back on the excuse of resting, when we know it takes at least two to get through!"

"Don't order me around!"

They both caught back their next words.

"Sorry," said Ithleen. "Irritation seems to have built up considerably. At least anger seems to counteract the weariness, or else that effect has been reduced in this stretch."

"The effects seem to keep changing. Catches us off guard that way."

"I can figure that — Sorry. Let's carry on."

The next door refused to respond to its lock control.

"We'll have to go back and try another route," said Ithleen.

"Don't jump to conclusions! Sorry. Remember, whatever seems right is likely to be wrong. It may be a simple time-lapse-variant lock." He took a small instrument out of his pocket. "Let's see if the circuit's live... Yes. Ah! Here's the right sequence..."

"Don't!" cried Ithleen. "You might set off a booby-trap!"

"Your reaction is fear, not reason." Artificially conjured arrogance enabled him to ignore her warning, and he pressed the sequence, though a pang of apprehension struck through him as he did so. The door swung open.

Ithleen's fingers dug into his arm. "What is it?" she gasped.

For there was something in the corridor beyond the door. Something that was coming towards them.

Chapter 11

Barrier

Mayne clamped down on his nerves, which were screaming at him to run. "It's imaginary, Ithleen. There's nothing there."

"There is! There is!" she breathed hard.

"I'm going on. Will you stick by me, or are you going to run away?" He was dismayed to hear the contempt in his voice.

"Please don't go! Don't desert me!"

He clenched his teeth and stepped into the new corridor. The vague, menacing "Something" pounced, and he flung himself down to dodge it. Ithleen instantly sprang in beside him. "What is it?" She crouched over him, hands half-raised, in guard position.

"It's nothing, purely conjured fear," he said, trying to believe it. He picked himself up. "Come on."

As they faltered their way along the hallway, the unseen menace hung about them, reaching... reaching... Gradually Ithleen dragged to a halt. "Come ba —" She cut herself off, and instead forced out the words, "You go on. I can't."

"Yes, you can!" he insisted roughly. "You have to. It needs two." Taking her hand, he yanked her on down the hall. She stumbled after him. They made it through another door.

"How far are we?" she asked.

He pointed on the map. "About halfway. See? We're here."

"Is that all? And it's going to get worse, we should stop and rest."

"No. We won't stop."

"You're a bully!" She caught herself and apologized.

Soon he had to pull her again. There was a certain savage satisfaction in shoving her shoulder or yanking her arm. And perfectly justified, of course!

She snarled at him, "Don't push me around!"

"I'll do as I please!"

He parried her karate blow just in time and swung one of his own. She slid away from it, came in with another, and did not quite escape his second blow. She staggered back and collapsed in a heap.

His fury, and satisfaction at having a target for it, momentarily vanished. He flung himself down beside her. "Ithleen! Are you hurt?"

"Of course I'm hurt, you idiot! No, no, not really. Just bruised." Her own anger faded against his solicitude. "My fault, anyway."

He hated to say it, but he asked, "Do you want to go back? If I were really to hurt you..."

She managed to smile at him. "I know you won't."

"I don't know it! And we don't need to go on." Now that he had faced the idea of going back, it beat urgently at him.

"No. We'll go on. All we have to do is keep our induced fear focused on the other person's safety, and our anger against the resistance."

"Easy to say..."

"You'll manage," she said.

Her faith in him pushed back the shadows for a moment. He helped her up and they continued.

And at last they reached the barrier that had stopped all their predecessors.

The wide corridor floor ended in a gap, some nine meters long. It was spanned by a catwalk barely twenty centimeters wide; and five meters of the catwalk hung downward in two sections, like an inverted drawbridge. They could see no ground below the gap.

There seemed to be a fogginess in the corridor, swirling gently above the gap, and blending with a growing stench.

"What's down there?" whispered Ithleen.

"I don't know, and it doesn't matter." Mayne tried to speak firmly, but found his voice shook. He had visions of layer after layer of evilness: of unnameable slimy beasts, of a row of pointed stakes, of a pocket of molten lava, of a pool full of piranhas, of an endless fall into space... one image crowding out another and all utterly real. He could feel each terror waiting there.

Ithleen's white face told him she was seeing her own supply of horrors, conjured from evolved instincts, her world's legends and shock stories, and her own childhood fears. "We have to cross that?"

He wanted to say no; that they could go back; that they should go back. What was the sense of going on? It wasn't their battle. There was plenty of knowledge to be sought elsewhere. And what did the needs and yearnings of the people of this one Earth matter? He had only promised to try to help, and he had certainly tried. So they wanted a way into the far reaches of space? So did Ithleen, and she had to do without. If he couldn't even give it to her, why torture himself trying to give it to these strangers? Because he couldn't, he thought vaguely. He did not quite understand what he meant by that, or why his lack should seem so important; but he drew on the deep, stubborn strength of his will, and said instead, "There's a lever here beside the wall. Let's see what it does."

He pressed it down slowly. Servo motors hummed, and the inverted drawbridge lifted to complete the catwalk. But there was no way to lock the lever; as soon as he released it, the bridge fell with a jerk.

The first wave of guilt came then. *How could he have done such a thing?* he felt, unaware that he had not the faintest idea what the thing was. How could he live with himself? Better to die here, to throw himself into that terrible pit, than to live in such shame! He must run away before anyone knew! He found himself actually turned away, straining towards the return route.

He almost tripped over Ithleen, who had sunk to her knees, hands over her face. "Oh, please, I didn't mean to! I know I deserve to be thrown down there, but please don't!"

With difficulty, he said, "No one's going to throw you down. You're not guilty, Ithleen! We had no part in this war, or anything else!" he added defiantly, crushing down exaggerated memories of small wrongs he had done. Even things he had merely wished for - like the death of a sadistic teacher - seemed suddenly unbearably evil and shameful.

"Pull yourself together!" he snapped, as much to himself as to Ithleen's bowed head. "The only way to get across is for one person to hold this lever down while the other crosses."

But how could you trust anyone to hold the lever while you crossed a twenty-centimeter wide bridge over nameless horrors? He turned his thoughts away: to whatever was down there.

Let Ithleen go, he thought cunningly. Then if anyone lets go of the lever, it'll be me, safe here. Let her find out what's down...

A genuine horror, at his own induced betrayal, hit him. "Ithleen! Hold down the lever: I'm going across."

"You'll abandon me here," she sobbed; "at the mercy of - of that, down there!"

"There — is — nothing — down — there!" he ground out. "And there must be a lever on the other side. I can hold it down and you can come after me."

"You're planning some trick!"

"No!"

"How can I trust you?"

"Ithleen, I am trusting you," he snarled, while his mind shrieked, not to trust her!

He saw the effort with which she gathered her control. With a violent shove, she thrust the lever down and croaked, "Hurry!"

He stepped out onto the catwalk. Fear, fury, guilt, and suspicion lashed at him in confusion. He set his mind to chant, "I can trust her..." He reached the bridge section. One step, two, three. It was holding firm. Suddenly the realization hit him: even if he could trust Ithleen, how could he trust the builders of the trap?

He hesitated. Was that a tremor in the bridge?

Could he turn, on this narrow walk? Twenty centimeters - a handspan. Could he fling himself back if the bridge fell? Only three paces so far; he might make it back. But if he went on...

He set his jaw and continued.

The pit yawned beneath him, pulling. He kept his eyes on the far end of the catwalk, and forced his feet to keep moving.

He was past the central crack. At least he was now facing the nearest safety. Illusion of safety! If the bridge fell open, he could never cling to its smooth surface, let alone climb it!

Three-quarters. What was it that had been in the pit — ? Had been? It was rising up, coming after him! His head twisted to look — and his foot slipped.

In a lithe twist, he came down crosswise on the bridge, precariously balanced. Slowly he squirmed until he was lying along its length. Pray Ithleen was not watching, or kept a tight control on herself. If she instinctively moved to offer help, the lever would snap up. In his intensity of concentration, even the emotions faded to a background clamour in his mind. Carefully he raised himself to a crouch, to a stand, and walked on.

He was well along the rigid part of the catwalk before he realized he was off the bridge. He looked back. Ithleen had curled herself down over the first lever, in a position that would take deliberate untangling to leave: a sudden fright could not send her running.

He pushed down the second lever and called back to Ithleen, "Ready, come across."

She lifted her head, then unwound herself and stood up and came to the catwalk, her steps faltering as she reached it. She stopped, and looked down once. Then she ran across.

Amazement momentarily flooded out all other emotions in Mayne. "How could you run that narrow bridge?"

Ithleen tossed her head. "Narrow? Twenty centimeters? I do high-wire work for recreation, remember?" Then memory of horror crossed her face. "After I got up, I suddenly thought, what if your call was a hallucination, and I'd let go too soon, let you fall? I wanted to run the other way, so I ran this way, instead."

"If I had gone down, the gap would have been there, and you'd have fallen, too."

"I know. It seemed - appropriate."

"Ithleen, do you notice we've been using the past tense? The induced emotions seem to be gone."

"You're right. Do you think that gap was the last barrier?"

He shook his head. "Look. Even though we've released both levers, the bridge is staying up now: retreat is still being encouraged."

"I wonder if that gap is even real?" Ithleen mused.

"It doesn't matter. The belief itself could be deadly. But since we've held out against all we've been urged to feel and believe so far, the attack may take a new form beyond here."

They moved on slowly, real fatigue dragging at them now. No new form of attack appeared to develop, except the tension of expecting one, and the worry that something too subtle to detect was working on them. Their map showed the route through the remaining corridors, and nothing urged them to deviate from the most straightforward way. That too was worrisome. With no evident danger, their stretched nerves began to relax, while logic kept telling them they must stay alert.

Since the door-lock codes were no longer known, Mayne had to work them out slowly with his instruments, probing electronically. Each use of a tool was a tense moment; but no dangerous malfunction occurred.

Finally they reached the door to the room they were seeking, marked as the one alleged to contain the cache. Here even Mayne's instruments failed to find a way to unlock the door.

"Must be a psionic lock, needing some specific thought to operate it. It could be anything!" he muttered.

Ithleen shook her head. "People are rarely random when they select a code. Is there anything they might logically have chosen?"

"An equation or name known only to the group?"

"No, they're supposed to have left papers for a later generation. That means they meant people to get in eventually. So the code should be something hard for the wrong people, their own generation, to figure out, but easy for later people, " she said.

"Then it'll have to have an emotional component."

"How about the opposite of everything we've been through: peace, trust, goodwill – everything war-minded people wouldn't feel?"

"And probably a simple 'open' command with it," he agreed. "Let's try it."

The reduction in the psi pressure around them had already begun to relax them from their tightly wound state of resistance. Now they faced the door and deliberately lowered their defences yet more, releasing even the tension that had been engendered by their expectation of further attack, putting their minds on the trust and co-operation that had enabled them to win through, on the joy they would bring to the yearning new psionicists if they succeeded, on the pleasure of helping other people, the consciousness that they themselves would gain nothing from the papers they sought.

Then Mayne ordered, "Open!" and the door lock clicked. They exchanged pleased smiles, pushed the door open, and stepped in.

And staggered, at the blast of sheer hate that hit them. In their unresisting and trusting state of mind, the shock was almost overwhelming. They found themselves cowering back towards the door. Hate and returning fear surged through them as the malevolence blazed at them.

Mayne crushed down his evoked response. "Artificial!" he gasped. "Nothing - alive - to hate!" Hatred and anger were emotions humans used to make themselves persevere in spite of fear; but here the defensive emotions would be even more crippling than the fear.

Across the room stood a jury-rigged control panel, with a large knife-switch centred on it. The psionists' final preparation, probably wired up during the minutes of the fire drill.

It was ten steps across the room. Mayne took the first.

The rage tore at him like the Avenging Vultures of old myth. He twisted, turning away, then forced himself back, and took the second step.

Physical pain knifed into him on the third step. The fear told him it would get worse; and the hatred said that something would enjoy his pain.

Four steps. Not real, he told himself, trying to forget what he had said earlier about belief in injury. Five steps. Six.

The hatred lashed at him, and fear said: *I may already be injured irreparably, and if not I will be. I must stop, go back. I am whole,* he told himself.

Seven steps.

On the eighth step he knew he had lost. Nothing was worth this deliberate acceptance of pain. He turned back, towards release, and felt the instant promise of an easing.

Ithleen, white, swaying, blind with pain, halfway across the room, took another step.

Mayne twisted back and took the ninth step. He fell to his knees. Ordered himself to crawl. He tried to hurl his body forward. The intense effort moved it only into a slow lean; but he finally fell against the panel.

He could not force his hand up to the switch.

Killing hatred poured through him, ripped at him, tore along his nerves, tried to drive him back, paralyzed his arm muscles.

"Ithleen!"

A sound more gasp than word answered him faintly.

"Think against — it with me! Think of — whatever you love — science — adventure..."

He forced his own thoughts onto things that had given him pleasure in his life. The sheer joy of intellectual work; the peace of flying a plane, cut off from the problems of dealing with people; the fun of rock climbing with his parents; canoeing alone at dawn; the day he found a previously unknown fossil while on a field trip with his mother; doing experiments in his father's lab; the pleasure of working with the TKM, doing easily what was so laborious without it; relaxing with a light novel...

His arm moved; his fingers contracted. The switch went over.

Instantly, the pressure vanished, and both humans collapsed.

Eventually Mayne shoved himself up and reached to Ithleen.

"All right!" she assured him. "You?"

"Yes."

"Wexters — are right. Humans aren't — rational."

Accepting a hand, Ithleen pulled herself up. "Let's see what we get for this striving."

There was a drawer under the control panel. In it they found a thick, bound sheaf of papers, containing, as predicted, incomprehensible notations.

"Well, here's Ronce's lifework ready for him."

"Let's ask him to make us a copy to take back with us," Ithleen suggested. "Since the wexters already know so much psionics, they may be able to figure out what's here; and I'll have data from another universe to compare to what we know."

The walk out was short. There was no trace of any of the horrors; the Old Psi Lab had become simply an empty building.

"The conjured horrors are fading from my memory, like a dream. For you, too?" Mayne said.

"All except the last one — that I'd failed you. That was a rational fear."

"But I wouldn't have fallen. The traps were all emotional ones, for people who couldn't trust or co-operate."

"I know." Ithleen smiled wanly. "It's just taking me a while to believe what I know!" She added, "I see there's more to this adventuring than the excitement of physical danger."

As they finally emerged, Ithleen expressed surprise at finding it was night. "It's taken us the whole day!"

"Did it feel shorter?" asked Mayne drily.

"Far longer! But I assumed that was subjective."

Mayne located the gate in the protective fence, turned the knob, and held the heavy gate open for Ithleen. Wearily, the two explorers walked through the dusk to Ronce's home, nearby.

He greeted them with relief and approval. "You got out again on your own. Good work. How far in did you get?"

Mayne held out the papers.

Ronce was so overcome he could scarcely reach for them. Then he clutched them to his breast and began babbling about the colleagues he must inform of the great event.

"Can you hold off announcing it for a few hours?" Mayne requested.

"But why? It's a tremendous event. Not just to scientists, but to the whole world. It may be the beginning of our reach to the stars!"

"We'd like to leave before you break the news; and we'd like to have you make us some copies first, if you will." He was not sure what methods of copying this world used, so he did not know how long it would take.

"Leave!" Ronce batted the hair off his forehead, even though for once it had not fallen. "You can't do that! Everyone who's interested in psi will want to talk to you, not to mention reporters."

"That's exactly why we want to leave before they know. When we've gone, just tell them that a party under your direction obtained the papers."

"But it was you, not I!"

"You made it possible. If you want to be very upright and modest, you can say you weren't among those who reached the final point. But don't identify us, please."

"After what you've done for me, I can't refuse any request you make; but I wish it weren't this one."

"But you'll do it?"

"Very well. But I shall make it very clear it wasn't I who got in. In science, only absolute honesty makes progress."

"That belief assures me we're leaving the data in good hands," Mayne said.

Ronce made them photocopies of the papers, then asked, "Won't you even tell me where you're going to hole up? I hate to lose touch."

"Perhaps we'll contact you again some day. Especially if your people achieve advanced psionics," said Mayne. If they did, this world could safely be told about the multiverse. Especially as it seemed to have come through its crisis of global war and achieved a lasting peace.

"Tomorrow I shall wonder if I've been talking to the mythological Lorebringers this whole time."

"It's already tomorrow. And I think we'll leave while it's still night."

"Then all I can say is, my deepest thanks."

"Thanks for the copies; and goodbye."

"Goodbye, Lorebringer."

As they walked quietly out of sight, away from Ronce's door, Mayne said, "I think we'd better take this information home, and report to the wexters."

***

On Mayne's world, they walked from the corridor into the main lab, stopped short in the doorway. Half a dozen pieces of apparatus were missing. Two had been encased in cabinets securely bolted to the floor. Their stands had been sliced through to dismount them.

"We have been raided," said Mayne quietly.

"Haughn?"

"At a guess. Only psionic equipment removed." Mayne crossed to the desk. "Manuals gone, too. He's moved some disks but left them. Probably decided they wouldn't fit his readers."

"So what are you going to do?"

"In sequence: make a report to the wexters on everything we've seen, including this; get some sleep; print out some new spec sheets; get Van and Davith started on building replacement equipment. And then figure out some way to get at this man Haughn."

CHAPTER 12

Tools

Around mid-morning, Mayne called his two technicians to let them know he and Ithleen had returned. For the benefit of eavesdroppers, he casually mentioned that there was work to be done, if they cared to come in on a day off. They agreed with an eagerness that they explained when they arrived: the raid had occurred sometime during Thursday night; the assistants had discovered the loss on Friday and spent that day and the weekend worrying about it.

"We figured it must be extra-universal; so we didn't call Security," reported Davith.

"Good. I'd like to get rid of those two cut-off stands and the lopped-off workbench from the earlier raid, just in case we should have any curious visitors."

Ithleen suggested, "The best way to get rid of them without any trace would be to take them to Geode. You could also make the immits for your replacement TKM there."

"Good ideas. Then we've got to get hold of Robinaire. She's the only one who's seen Haughn's world or any of its people. Van, will you phone her and see if you can persuade her to come here?"

"Oh, she'll come. She was here while you were away."

"What did she want?"

Van and Davith exchanged a glance, and Van murmured, "Nothing in particular. I think she finds us a novelty in a somewhat dull existence."

"I shouldn't think she'd find this lab any more interesting than her great-aunt's. All to the good, however. Ask her to come right away, if she can."

Van turned reluctantly to a phone. Mayne and Davith emptied the workbench drawers and cabinets, then began unfastening the equipment stands. Ithleen continued scanning Ronce's psi papers into a computer and putting the results onto two large-capacity disks: one for themselves and one for Jonno, whose equipment matched Mayne's.

When Van told Robinaire that Mayne was back, the girl agreed to come to the lab immediately. When she arrived, Van met her at the door. Robinaire was wearing a fluffy, black-polka-dotted white dress, which Van considered inappropriate for wear in a work environment, but which, she grudgingly admitted, did look quite good on Robinaire. Van glanced with a mixture of approval and despair at Ithleen who, as usual, was in a loose, pocket-strewn, plain green pantsuit, and wondered whether she really had succeeded in finding a companion for the plennor. Well, there hadn't been many options after all.

Robinaire asked Van, "Why did Ithleen come back, too?

"The wexters want her on hand. So don't complain to the plennor about the arrangements."

"Wouldn't do much good to complain, would it?" said Robinaire grumpily. "Not if those wexters put her there, and he hasn't objected. But," Robinaire's voice sounded more cheerful, "she's only a multiverse person, anyway, like those game characters, so she won't be around forever."

Mayne had been recounting the trip to his assistants, with occasional comments from Ithleen. As he turned to greet Robinaire, the two technicians went on with the discussion.

As Van and Davith continued vicariously sharing Ithleen's experiences, Mayne began talking to Robinaire about her own interests, knowing that would relax her. She told him about her ambition to become an actress. Her good memory and her good looks had given her a start, even if only in advertising jobs; but the legal requirements of school had hampered her availability. She had enrolled in an elite drama school, though she would have to wait until the autumn term to start there. She mentioned, and cynically dismissed, the possibility of getting assistance with contacts from her show-business father, saying she could make it on her own.

Under Mayne's attention she was relaxed and happy until he casually asked, "Think you could have a go at identifying Zar Haughn's world for me, Robinaire?"

"You want me to go there!"

"Only for a moment, Robinaire. Nothing could hurt you."

"No!" She looked as if she might rise and run. "You can't make me!"

"Of course not. And we wouldn't, even if we could."

She relaxed a little.

"But we'd very much like you to do it for us." He gave her his sudden, warm smile, and took both her hands. "Won't you do it for us, Robinaire? I'd be right with you, every moment, and it would take only a few seconds. You'd never see Haughn, or any of his people. We could land on another continent of his world, if you wanted."

Under the full force of his personality, Robinaire wavered; but her fear was a strong counter-force. "I can't!"

Mayne continued to talk gently and coaxingly to her. Van and Davith began to look on in fascination at this unfamiliar side to their normally reticent plennor. Ithleen was already acquainted with his persuasiveness and showed no interest in watching this wooing of the will.

"A couple of the others could come, too, Robinaire. Ithleen has a rifkey now, so there could be three of us to protect you. We have laserguns; and we could get other weapons, too, if it would make you feel safer."

Robinaire looked at Ithleen and stopped wavering. "No."

Mayne recognized defeat for the present. "All right, Robinaire." He released her hands and turned away.

"Plennor Mayne, you're not mad at me, are you?"

"No, of course not, Robinaire. I'm just disappointed. And I have to think of some other way to get there." He turned to the others. "We may as well get on with other things. I'm going to visit Jonno again, today." To Van and Davith: "I'll take one of you with me, if you still want to try a transplacement."

"Do we!" Davith pulled out a coin to toss, then paused. "If Ithleen comes too, you could take us both."

Mayne hesitated, then said, "I think it would be wise to get those stands out of sight first; and the sooner we get the replacement immits the better. If one of you would like to get those jobs done, you'll also find it a more interesting trip to Geode than seeing a near-duplicate lab on Jonno's world."

"Right." Davith gave the new decision to his coin, which bestowed the Geode trip on him, and the trip to Jonno's lab on Van.

Mayne came back to Robinaire, with another idea. "You don't mind just talking or thinking about Haughn's world, do you?"

"I guess not."

Mayne took his wexcorder out of his pocket. "This is a kind of recorder, for thoughts as well as words. Now, I want you to go over in your mind everything about your visit there. You have such a good memory, Robinaire. Say it aloud if you like, but think as well of everything you saw or felt, and particularly whatever you noticed or were told about Zar Haughn. The wexters may be able to locate him if they know enough about his personality. You really do want to help us, don't you?"

"Oh, yes, I do. Just not…"

"You don't have to go back. Now, think. This place vanished and the other began to appear. What was it like?"

She touched the recorder he was holding out, then cupped it in both of her hands and began to speak towards it. "It was a big room, with bright lights, and lots of little lights in machines…"

Mayne took her through her descriptions twice, gently and with a warm interest so that she would not feel harassed. Finally he thanked her gravely, and added a few mental comments of his own to the recording, then put it away.

"It's a long shot," he said to the others. "They might be able to work from her memories. Now shall we…" He hesitated, realizing that if they all transplaced out immediately, an abandoned Robinaire might be even less amenable if another attempt had to be made to persuade her to go to Haughn's world. "Shall we get back to work?"

A quiet bustle began of work that held little interest to an onlooker. Mayne attentively answered the questions Robinaire asked at first, careful not to let her feel excluded: when sufficiently motivated, he could allow for other people's feelings; it was part of the courtesy that had been drilled into him — nuisance and distraction from work though it was.

As he expected, Robinaire soon grew bored and restless, and finally took her leave. The others promptly packed up their work, and Mayne and Ithleen took out their rifkeys.

Van and Davith waved excited good-byes; then Ithleen operated her rifkey – taking Davith with her – and a moment later Mayne took himself and Van to Jonno's world.

They materialized in the living quarters and made their way cautiously into the lab section. They found Jonno in the main room, alone as usual.

"Jonnan, just the man I want to see!" Jonno exclaimed.

Mayne quirked an eyebrow, but before asking questions said with automatic courtesy, "This is one of my assistants, Vandrai Sartyov."

"I'm just along for the ride," admitted Van. "Hello, Plennor Mayne. How odd to call someone else that!"

"How do you do, Ms Sartyov. The whole multiverse business is odd, but stimulating. Spen has been back, Jonnan."

"Ne's really getting bold. What did ne want?"

"Ne gave me a wexcorder and asked me to report on any of my discoveries that I cared to discuss. I can't imagine why. The wexters are obviously far ahead of our little knowledge of psionics, and they know what you've done, which is ahead of me, too."

"They want to know all they can find out about any universe that has psionics; and you've invented a few things I haven't."

"Gadgets," Jonno insisted.

"Ithleen says they love gadgets," Mayne said. "Then they make them into toys, so finding out about gadgets is a self-indulgence."

Jonno grinned. "Then I have a strong feeling of fellowship towards them. I'd make these gadgets myself even if my ISC didn't need them to keep the Regions happy. Speaking of the wexter gadgets, the preliminary check I made on the analyzer's summary seems merely to confirm your guess that the recorder is an undifferentiated solid. But one should never disdain to do an experiment merely because theory says there's nothing to be found there."

Mayne smiled. "My feelings exactly."

Van asked, "Don't you have any full-time assistants, Plennor?"

"No, I prefer to work alone. When I need one for something specific,

I get one from the general pool. And anything that needs team efforts, I farm out to other labs. I imagine Jonnan does the same?"

Mayne nodded. "Yes, I'd rather have the crowds working somewhere else. But I find it useful to have a couple of assistants on hand for small things, and I prefer them to be ones I'm familiar with; so I get permanent ones."

Van went on, "Then I guess Davith and I don't have analogs here. I feel sort of relieved, somehow, but just a tinge disappointed, too."

Mayne said, "So far as Jonno and I have been able to check, there are no analogs of anyone else from my world on his." Van would have pursued the matter further, but Mayne, who regarded his assistants as extensions of himself, cut her off by turning back to Jonno.

"I've got a disc full of cryptic psi data here for you to puzzle over." He explained the circumstances of its acquisition from Ronce's world. "I've got a set of the papers for the wexters, too, and one for Ithleen and me to work on if we get the time. Among the lot of us, we might eventually decipher the notation. No doubt the wexters will figure it out quickly, since they probably already know everything this people had found out; but I don't suppose they'll give us any help on cracking the notation. They're in no hurry for us to learn more advanced psionics."

"They don't seem to mind giving us the products of their knowledge, though. Spen said they were willing to work on those tools you want. I told nem what I had in mind as useful capabilities, and ne said ne thought such things would be simple to incorporate in a pair of tools. My designs are what I want to show you."

"What did you suggest the wexters make for us?" Mayne asked.

"The first is an electromagnetic detector, generator, calibrator, and general manipulator, and the other's a psionic projector." Jonno opened a fingerprint-locked drawer and took out a fold-up computer, which also required his fingerprint to unlock it without scrambling its contents. "I'm not trusting any of this to my online computers," he told them. When he turned on the little computer he also had to enter passwords at three levels.

"I've drawn it as it would be with immits." He called up the first 3-D image and rotated it slowly for full viewing. "I told Spen the functions I wanted to include."

"You've chosen a long, narrow casing for the tools," Mayne remarked, leaning in closer to the computer.

"Yes, I decided that the most inconspicuous guise for them on most occasions would be to incorporate them into a functioning pen or pencil."

"Precisely what functions did you ask for?"

"My first thought was for a set of meters, covering the whole electromagnetic spectrum, and then for an EM generator, too, so you can manipulate as well as measure. And I threw in a sound generator, though I don't know if that will really be useful. I found, after a little juggling, that I could get them all into the same pen if I accepted fairly severe limitations on a range of about twelve meters."

"I presume all their devices will be fully psionic?" Mayne asked.

"Yes, including the readouts. You'll see a mental image of the types of meters you're accustomed to using, projected wherever you're looking, bright or dark depending on the background you see it against."

"Good. That will let us be unobtrusive if necessary," Mayne said. "Do we use a dot code to operate the tools?"

"No. All you need to do is picture the multiverse symbol as you order the particular operation you want the tool to perform. The lasers remain on a manual switch, and their recharging will be automatic."

Mayne considered a side issue. "I wonder if the lasers will then be less protected against analysis."

"I had the same thought, but Spen said they'll be made so that any attempt to probe them will cause the psionic energy patterns to collapse into random atomic matter."

Mayne nodded. "Let's get back to the pentools, the — we really do need names for them."

Van, who had been trying out various combinations of the operative words on a small notepad, suggested, "For the EM generator-calibrator et cetera, how about gennor?"

Mayne shrugged. "It's your device, your choice."

Jonno, compensating for his analog's insufficient courtesy towards his assistant, asked her, "What would you suggest for the other tool? The psi projector?"

"Is psiproje too hard to say?"

Before Mayne could say it was, Jonno declared, "That will do nicely, thank you." Van beamed proudly.

Mayne sighed, accepting Jonno's decision again. "So what does this... psiproje do?"

"It affects neural patterns at a basic level. It can't read or transmit thoughts, but it can nudge feelings and stimulate some basic physiological responses in the person it's aimed at, such as making them more tired than they should be. And even knock them out.

"I've given the wexters a number of different exterior designs, so the pens will look casual and draw even less attention in a search," Jonno said. "They'll also be different colours and textures, so you can tell them apart at a glance or touch."

"That's well thought of. I'm grateful for all this, Jonno. You've not only saved me a lot of work, you've done this faster than I could have."

"The tools aren't made yet, remember. They all depend on the wexters' translating of my ideas into their terms. And don't forget, my designs don't always work."

"That's because you work under pressure to keep producing something. I have the time to think things through before trying to make them work; and even so, my first models don't always do all or exactly what I want them to."

Jonno gave him a wry smile and a lifted eyebrow. "I'm not convinced, but thanks for the encouragement." He returned to the matter in hand. "I talked to Spen about the rifkey problem as well. I suggested they be made to fit into personal jewelry: ring, watch, lapel pin, and gave them a variety of samples. Spen said the rifkeys are already near the practical limit - especially since they have to have room for our fingers to differentiate among the dots; but ne's going to keep my samples on hand in case we want something that will fit into them, sometime."

"I trust you chose cheap and simple jewellery, that won't tempt thieves?"

"Yes, of course, though I suppose there's nothing that's proof against the pettiest or most desperate of thieves. But at least the wexters' safety devices should prevent the tools' use by anyone not instructed on them."

Mayne nodded and stood up. "Now, much as I'd like to stay longer and talk, I'd better get back. Someone, presumably Haughn, raided my lab for more psionic machines. I want to cover up their loss, since this man Polminander seems to be snooping around for some reason, and I don't want him to have anything to augment his curiosity."

"Surely you can keep Polminander's personnel out?"

"I could, but that would let him know I'm aware of him and convince him I've got something to hide. I'm leaving the place relatively open to him in hopes he'll either tip his hand as to what he wants, or decide I don't have it and go away."

"Perhaps your ISC isn't as nearly perfect as my envy painted it."

"Nothing ever is. Come on, Van, we've got work to do. Thanks again, Jonno."

"Good luck, Jonnan."

Chapter 13

Exile

"Add a Karilly oscillator to the supply list, Van... Oh, good afternoon, Spen."

The two assistants jumped and turned. Mayne saved the file of the design modification he was working on, set the computer to standby, and gave his attention to the wexter.

"We have been considering your report on the ruler Zar Haughn," Spen said, "and also the impressions reported by Robinaire. Our conclusion is that the man represents a potential danger to other universes; we would like to see him restricted to his own."

"And you want me to do the restricting."

"You are the only agent we have."

"Have you found his world?"

"The information was not sufficient. We have never worked with second-hand personality information; however, there is a slim possibility that I might be able to draw out sufficient information from Robinaire's mind in a personal interview."

"Davith, see if you can get hold of her, will you?"

"Yes, sir." Davith went away to use his office phone.

The wexter went on, "According to your report, Haughn is dependent upon limited-intelligence psychics as part of his transplacement procedure. If they are removed from his world, he would be confined there, at least for the present."

"How many psychics does he have? A mass evacuation, carried out by ones or twos, doesn't sound practical."

"As yet we have no data on their number; but we can handle their removal ourselves once you have planted identifying devices on them for us. Since they are living under a tyrant, persuasion should not be difficult."

"People sometimes prefer the hardship they know to the strain of facing the unknown."

"But their future will not be unknown to them, since they have precognitives, telepaths, and clairvoyants among them, they will gain at least some idea of what awaits them, when you contact them."

"What will you do with them?"

"We are searching for a suitable human world, where the attitude of the population towards the simple-minded is kindly and loving, but where the technology is relatively unadvanced, so that the necessary amplifiers to use the teleporters for transplacement cannot be built. Since our caltor, our personality-searching device, was designed to seek out individuals rather than populations, it has taken time to modify it enough to search out population-sized numbers of suitable individuals."

"Is it ready now?"

"We have already used it, and have found a number of worlds which seem to have such populations; and we have been analyzing them for the best choices. But we will need a scout to visit each of the remaining possibilities. It is merely a matter of carrying instruments into the worlds, and waiting while they make their readings in various spots of each world. We wish to make very sure of our preliminary data, especially the lack of technology. Our robot probes cannot carry out this final task as the instruments which will do it depend on a psionic linkage with the judgement faculty of a living being."

Mayne nodded. "Speaking of instruments, do you have any of Jonno's tools made yet? Or the large-capacity rifkey?"

"We have given priority to the tools, but even they are not ready, for we realized that we needed to incorporate further safety devices into them and your lasers and, most importantly, the rifkeys."

"My lasers? Did I design something dangerous?"

"The danger is not primarily in your design but in our addition. Although we trust you with as powerful a weapon as a self-charging laser, the possibility of accidental or forcible loss exists, either on other worlds, or through raids like Haughn's, or even here in daily living on your own Earth."

Mayne thought, parenthetically, that he was seeing so little of his own world lately that it hardly needed to be counted. Still, there was the mysterious Polminander prying about...

Spen was continuing, "So we must consider the possible results if other people were to obtain possession of the laserguns. Not only could the weapons be turned on you, but if you had a lasergun lost or stolen while you were among the people of a technologically unadvanced society, a power-craving person there could do great harm to ner own people with such a perpetual-energy weapon. We would not wish to be responsible for such a thing."

"You're right. I should have thought about that. You've come up with an answer that's better than leaving the laserguns at home?"

"Yes, of course. We would not wish you to face dangers unprotected."

Mayne smiled. "Even an expendable should be preserved as long as possible. So what are you making for us?"

"A slightly more complex version of the fusing device we planned for the pentools. In addition to randomizing its internal structure if a probe attempt is made, it will also accept a mental command to randomize. Furthermore, it will restrict the life of the charger to one eighth of a year, so that if all other precautions fail, unauthorized use will at least be limited to that period. We considered a shorter term, but Jonno argued for the need to retain laserguns in storage, against possible loss or destruction of the ones you are using."

"We should have spare pentools, too."

"We cannot mass produce them, as we can simple rechargers. Remember, they will be affecting the minds of sentients; we cannot risk damage because of malfunction."

Ne went back to the lasers. "We also considered requiring a mental command for the recharging, but again Jonno's argument prevailed, that if you needed to use the laser as a weapon, you might not be able to spare the attention to order recharging; also, that you might need to entrust the weapon to an ally who might be too psi-deficient to operate it mentally.

Since these tools will protect our agent and will not lead anyone to us, we agreed to permit this degree of risk in their design."

"It sounds like a good compromise. What's the range of the mental command for randomizing?"

"About twenty-four meters, twice the range of the pentools' operation."

"Are you putting the same probing restrictions and duration into the pentools?"

"Yes. Although they do not have as great a potential for harmful use, it seems practical to limit even that risk. We are also adding yet one more safeguard to the rifkeys."

Mayne raised an eyebrow. "I thought they were already protected against prying."

"They are; but we have finally acknowledged that we cannot assume we are the only beings of superior psychic ability in the multiverse; so it is conceivable that even our dot-code precaution might be circumvented somehow; or someone you trust with the information might prove corruptible."

"So what change are you making?"

"A physical protection, designed to prevent their use by unauthorized persons even if they learn how to operate them. The new rifkeys are attunable to you as individuals; only you and those you personally designate to the rifkey will be able to use them. If they leave your possession for more than one hour, the essential parts will randomize and fuse, rendering them unusable."

"Not much leeway."

"There was much argument over the time limit; so the decision was taken for a safety margin, to allow for accidental separations."

Mayne considered the matter, then said, "Whether the rifkey is fused or simply stolen, I'd be just as stuck, myself; so the fusing is a good idea."

Spen continued, "I suggest you exchange your personal rifkeys now. I myself will be your safety measure on the scouting trip." Mayne caught a trace of both nervousness and pride in Spen's announcement: for a wexter, ne was being very daring by staying in close contact with an agent who would be active in other universes, however harmless those universes seemed to be.

"Fine. Van, will you ask Ithleen to come, please?"

During the break in the conversation, Davith reported back from his phone call: "Sorry, Plennor; Robinaire isn't home. I left a message for her to come out here as soon as possible."

"Thanks, Davith." Mayne turned back to Spen. "You haven't increased the anti-probing protection in the small rifkeys, have you? If so, I won't be able to make even the simple repairs I did before. I am, of course, expendable, but it would be a waste if I got stranded unnecessarily; and if Ithleen should decide to look at any more worlds..."

"Ithleen is not expendable," Spen stated firmly; "but we cannot refuse her free choice. We can only hope her incomprehensible craving for 'adventure' has been satisfied, or that our precautions will prove sufficient to protect her. We also wish to preserve our explorer, of course, if we can. So we have limited the anti-probing reaction in both sizes of rifkey to the deeper levels, which we believe to be beyond your current ability to probe, in any case. You need not fear to make any repairs of which you are capable."

"That seems reasonable." And it also, Mayne thought, enabled the wexters to continue testing how much of the shallower, non-threatening parts of their devices a human could figure out. This particular human was his world's top psionicist; though that world was an infinitesimal sample, at least he was guaranteed safe-to-the-wexters by their selection device, so he was a good starting point. The risk of testing more advanced worlds' psionicists could wait until the wexters had finished assessing him.

Mayne put speculation aside as he got out the photocopies of the Old Psi Lab papers, and turned back to Spen. "This is the information from Ronce's world that I told you about in my report. Of course, there probably won't be anything new to you in it..."

"Nevertheless, we are pleased to have it. It will be another outside view."

Ithleen came from her office, and Spen produced the new rifkeys, removing the old ones she and Mayne laid out on a work bench. Spen explained to Ithleen the changes ne had already told Mayne. As the humans picked up the new rifkeys, Spen announced, "I am now activating the attunements. You must keep the rifkeys within reaching distance of you from now on, or at least be within reaching distance once each hour. Each rifkey has been marked with an initial so that there is no chance of confusing them, should you have occasion to use the other person's."

"Do you mean within literal arm's reach?" asked Ithleen.

"Not quite. But they must remain available to you. If you cease to have access to them, they will sense the break in contact and begin count-down. It will be cancelled if you return to contact within the hour."

Mayne asked, "When do you want your scouting trip done?"

"The preliminary analysis should be completed by now. We estimate the scouting will take less than an eighth of a day, so I will check and come back for you about mid-afternoon." The wexter left.

Mayne asked, "Ithleen, are you interested in going along on this scouting trip?"

She considered. "No, I think I'll stay. I've finished programming my computer to do an analysis of a mass of the data the wexters have given me so far."

Mayne nodded to a hovering Davith, who already had his coin out, and who, with a cheer, won the toss. Mayne told him, "Get some lunch, and be ready when Spen comes back."

"You bet I will!"

***

Spen reappeared as promised around fourteen-thirty, and confirmed the wexters' readiness for the final scouting. Mayne and Davith were waiting, and vanished with nem, taken along by Spen.

Van, having watched them off, returned to work on the replacement psionic machines, laboriously using a non-psionic micromanipulator to connect the new core packet of immits to their macro circuitry. Ithleen had already started her analysis, stopping the run occasionally to debug the program she had devised.

They were still at these tasks when Robinaire turned up, an hour or so later. She was dressed professionally this time, as if she had just come from an interview: a white-and-navy flower-and-trellis-printed blouse and fitted navy slacks. "Davith said Plennor Mayne wanted to see me."

Remembering that Robinaire's co-operation was necessary, Van consciously made her voice friendly. "He does, but he's not here just now. I expect he'll be back fairly soon."

"I'll wait, then." Robinaire sat down to watch Van work; but obviously found it boring, for she soon began wandering restlessly around the lab. She seemed distracted, and answered only absently when Van tried to make conversation. Finally Robinaire drifted into Ithleen's room and watched her for a while, her expression resentful and mistrusting.

Eventually noticing her presence, Ithleen looked up. "Hello, Robinaire. You look rather unhappy. Anything wrong?"

"No," said Robinaire unconvincingly. "Ithleen, will you show me how these rifkeys work?"

"Yes, of course. But didn't you see Plennor Mayne use his while you were trying to get free of all those worlds you went to?"

"I wasn't really paying attention to what he did. Anyway, he said the thing wasn't working properly then. I'd ask him now, but... You know he wants to take me to Haughn's world..."

"He'd never trick you, Robinaire."

"Well, anyway, I'd rather ask you."

"Are you thinking you might go eventually? He'd very much like you to."

"Well, I'm thinking about it," said Robinaire.

Ithleen smiled and took out her rifkey. "It's very simple. You just give the rifkey directions in your mind, while you touch it: if you don't care where you go, you just place your hand over the dots; if you want to go to a specific place, you touch out a pattern." She paused, as a way to ease Robinaire into acquiescence occurred to her.

"Why don't you put your hand on it while I run through the pattern, and will us to go somewhere that you choose, so you'll know it's safe?"

Robinaire considered the suggestion, looking half eager, half fearful. "Will the rifkey work for me if you're operating it?"

Van came quietly to the doorway of Ithleen's office, watching with interest to see if Robinaire could be persuaded to help.

Ithleen said, "We've never tried sharing orders to a rifkey. But I'll direct it to obey your command. That should work."

Robinaire hesitated another long minute then, with abrupt determination, said, "Okay. I will!"

Ithleen patterned the rifkey, then held it out towards Robinaire. "Now, you touch it and – "

Robinaire slapped her fingers across the rifkey. "Take her away from us!" she cried.

Ithleen vanished.

Van, after a startled moment of silence, cried, "Robinaire! What a horrible thing to do!" She looked expectantly at Ithleen's chair; but the seconds passed and the scientist did not return.

Alarm hit Van. "Robinaire, what have you done?"

"I sent her away!" Robinaire was triumphant. "She doesn't belong here. She's not a real person, only a game-world sort of thing!"

"But she's not coming back!" Van cried, her alarm growing.

"I hope she doesn't ever come back!"

"Oh, you'll catch it when the plennor gets home!"

Robinaire whirled and ran out of the lab, leaving Van to stare at the empty chair.

***

It was another hour before Mayne and Davith returned, to find a distraught Van huddled tense and unmoving on a chair, all her energy poured into simply waiting.

"Hey, Van, we found a world!" announced Davith as they appeared.

Mayne was a quicker observer. "What's wrong?"

She sprang up and ran to him. "Plennor Mayne, she hasn't come back!"

"Who hasn't? Report coherently, Van!"

The command steadied her. "It's Ithleen. Robinaire asked to see how the rifkey worked, and when Ithleen showed her, Robinaire used it to make Ithleen disappear. And she hasn't returned!"

Mayne controlled his shock, his sensation that the multiverse had suddenly fallen into that deadly diaphane. "What exactly did Robinaire do? Did either say anything?"

Growing calmer now that the plennor was there to take charge, Van went over the episode in detail.

"So Robinaire activated the random mode of Ithleen's rifkey and directed it to take her away. But if Ithleen was holding the rifkey, it would have prevented her from landing in any danger, and would have taken her home if anything started to hurt her. No," he corrected himself, "it would take her home only if she were touching the end of it at the time. How was she holding it, Van?"

"I — I'm not sure. I think her fingers were on the sides. She was holding it out to Robinaire, coaxing her to try a transplacement, hoping to get her comfortable with the idea of using it, so she might decide to go to Haughn's world for you."

Davith suggested, "Maybe Ithleen stayed away to worry Robinaire."

Mayne shook his head. "I doubt if she would do that, especially as she'd know the rest of us would be far more worried. She must have run into difficulties after she materialized somewhere. Something serious, or she'd have come back by now. I'd better find her quickly." Mayne traced the pattern on his own rifkey, and faded out.

The seconds and the minutes passed. Van and Davith looked at each other. "Not him, too!" cried Van. "Is there something wrong with these new rifkeys?"

"We went to a dozen universes safely," argued Davith. "And got back without any trouble."

"But the wexter was directing you. Maybe we've lost them both now!"

CHAPTER 14

Limbo

The minutes dragged through an hour and more. Van and Davith were torn by their helplessness. There was nothing they could do themselves, no one on their own Earth to whom they could appeal for aid, and no way to contact anyone elsewhere: even the wexters' recorder, slow as that might be as communication, was with Mayne. After fruitless speculation, review of their non-resources, and plain worry, they gradually fell silent. Their normal departure hour had passed without remark or even notice; they clung desperately to their vigil.

And finally Mayne reappeared. Alone. Their cries of relief blended into anxious inquiries: "What's happened?" "Where's Ithleen?"

"I can't get her," said Mayne heavily. "I've seen her innumerable times; but every time I transplace into the world where she is, she's transplaced out. Since it takes a bit longer to materialize than to fade out, I get only a glimpse of her. Sometimes I thought I was catching up, so I kept on; but I never did. I don't know how many universes we've been through, but I don't dare go any further."

"Why not, Plennor?" Davith asked, brow creased with puzzlement as well as worry.

"The first universes were ordinary, civilized ones. Then we began to appear in ones that had reverted to savagery; then devastated ones; then ones that had never had life; then ones with alien forms of life; then ones with horrors like things out of some old book on the occult; and finally - non-worlds. I don't know how to describe them. They were simply - places - of nothingness. With a sensation of emptiness, loss, alienness. And it was getting worse."

"You had to leave her in that?" cried Van.

"It seemed to be my arrival that set off her rifkey each time. I didn't dare pursue any further," he repeated.

Van turned to the practical. "What are we going to do, Plennor?"

"Something is malfunctioning in her rifkey and possibly in mine. But since the rifkeys are psionic, there's just a chance a change of operator might affect the functioning. So I want each of you, to try one trip to her. If you can reach her, try to bring her back. If you can't bring her, come back promptly yourselves. Now, you understand how to operate the rifkey?"

"Yes, Plennor."

He made each of them go over the operation, and drilled the pattern into them by hypnotic command.

Each in turn, faces set with concentration, transplaced out, and shortly after, returned, to find Mayne pacing in agitated suspense. "It's just as you described, Plennor: she vanishes."

At the second return, Mayne broke off his pacing to make another brief report into the wexters' recorder, then picked up the rifkey again. "I'm going to talk to Jonno. Perhaps another mind on this will help somehow. Meanwhile, see if you can get hold of Robinaire."

He found Jonno in his kitchen, so engrossed in a book that he had forgotten to finish his supper.

"Jonnan," With a single look at his analog, Jonno snapped his book shut and shoved his dishes into the automatic high-temperature sterilizer/sorter. "What's wrong?"

"Ithleen is lost in the multiverse, and I can't get her out. I've tried everything I can think of; but maybe I'm too concerned to think straight. So I'm hoping you might see more reason in the pattern than I do."

"Tell me the pattern, then."

"According to Van, it was Robinaire who effected the first transplacement. She pressed the random control on Ithleen's rifkey, and Van heard her say, 'Take Ithleen away from here.' Of course, the rifkey operated on the thought impulse before the words, so Ithleen was moved before she could even think of an objection. She had just ordered the rifkey to obey Robinaire's command, hoping that if Robinaire did a few transplacements, she'd get over her fear and take me to Haughn's world.

But Robinaire somehow sent Ithleen off alone; and now, for some reason, Ithleen's unable to get back."

"Can she move around to other places?"

"Yes and no. She may have had some volition in staying or moving at first, but since I've been trying to get to her, she's been moved out of each universe as I came into it, gradually being forced in one direction, if I can call it that, and now she apparently has no control over her movement."

"Sounds like a combined malfunction of your rifkeys."

"That's what I think, too. We've no other rifkey to try, but I sent my assistants, in case a change of operator might help. These new rifkeys are personally attuned; since that's the only change, the fault might be there. But Van and Davith had no better luck than I did."

"Have you reported to the wexters?"

"Yes, several times; but there's no telling when they'll pick up the recordings. And I may have made Ithleen's situation desperate." He described his pursuit, and the limbo into which Ithleen had been driven. "I can't just leave her in that place and hope the wexters will be able to do something eventually!"

"No, we can't. Nothing occurs to me immediately, Jonnan. Let's go to your world, so I can talk to the witness. Always best to go to the original sources."

Mayne managed a wan smile of acknowledgement at Jonno's attempt to lighten the mood, and took them to his own lab.

The technicians reported no success in contacting Robinaire.

Jonno, sounding for once very like Mayne, said to Van, "I'd like you to describe to me everything that took place this afternoon - before the transplacement, during it, and after."

Van went through her story again, carefully and in detail. Jonno stood thinking about it; then he said, "Wait a minute. Jonnan, you quoted Robinaire's words as 'Take Ithleen away from here;' but Van, you've just given them as 'Take Ithleen away from us.' Which is it?"

"From us," said Van without hesitation. "Is it important?"

"I'm trying to figure out what the rifkey was set to do. Remember, Jonnan, how your rifkey malfunctioned because it was pre-set?"

"Yes, but only for the one transplacement. It resumed proper operation after that. This one keeps on malfunctioning."

"Perhaps not. Maybe it's simply continuing to function on the same command."

"How do you mean?"

"To take Ithleen away from here would be a simple command, promptly completed. Even if the mental set included 'and keep her away', it should only prevent her return to this Earth. But if the word was 'us,' it indicates a broader idea, of keeping her out of contact with everyone Robinaire thought of as being in her 'us' group: those associated either with this immediate place, or with Robinaire's whole Earth. What the rifkey has done — and is continuing to do — is to remove Ithleen not only from this universe but from any other that you people have been to, so that you can't reach her by willing yourself to a known place rather than to her."

Mayne exclaimed, "And every new universe she's in becomes one I've been to the instant I materialize there! It fits... appallingly. Jonno, you're not part of our group here, or even of this Earth. Maybe you can reach her."

"Except for two things. First, I don't actually know Ithleen."

Mayne moved uncomfortably. "But you did see her. Spen said that was the essential thing, so vital that the wexters won't allow us to see them at all. You do remember seeing her, don't you?"

"Vividly. But the other problem may be worse. I'm your analog. Will the rifkey let me near her, any more than it will you?"

Davith spoke into the tense silence. "If it just has to be someone from outside our Earth, who knows Ithleen, can't we get someone from Geode?"

Mayne shook his head. "They're terrified to go Outside. They couldn't will a transplacement. Ithleen said that after she got a rifkey, she offered to give her two fellow pilots a trip to see an undamaged world, but even they refused."

Van said to Jonno, "If the rifkey has absorbed Robinaire's attitude — her definition of 'us' — maybe it will let you go to Ithleen, because Robinaire talked about you as just another part of the multiverse, not one of us."

"Ms Sartyov could be right," Jonno said. "But if I'm not outside Robinaire's 'us' concept, my attempt to reach Ithleen could push her yet further into this limbo. Is there any safety margin? Do we dare risk it?"

"Do we dare not try?" cried Mayne. "That limbo isn't meant for humans. We've got to get her out of it."

Jonno nodded. "I'll try then."

Mayne taught him the transplacing pattern, then cautioned, "You should be able to return immediately whether you succeed or fail; but if something we haven't thought of delays you, remember you must be back within an hour, or the rifkey will fuse."

"I'll remember." Jonno traced the pattern and disappeared.

***

The whiteness of transplacement faded into the greyness of the new scene. There was a sense of unreality, of wrongness, of a cold that was not merely physical, which struck Jonno even in his moment of materializing. He saw Ithleen, sitting huddled in on herself, on a featureless plane surface, visible through a heavy twilight.

"Ithleen!"

She sprang to her feet. "Plennor Mayne! You got thr– Oh! It's not –"

"It is, actually, though the wrong one. I'm Jonno."

"Any Plennor Mayne is the right one at this moment!" declared Ithleen, with a shaky laugh. She came to him with her two-handed greeting. Her hands were icy, and trembling.

"You're in shock!" he realized. "Let's get out of this." He transplaced back to Mayne's lab – and found himself materializing alone.

"Did you see her?"

"Yes and spoke to her. She wasn't shifted away from me, but I can't bring her back. She's in a state of shock. Get blankets ready, and a flask of hot, sweet tea."

Van and Davith ran to obey his orders.

"It's as bad as you said, Jonnan. I could feel it even in a single minute there. How long has she endured that?"

"It must be at least fifteen minutes since I broke off pursuit, when we had slipped into a deep limbo universe."

"There's psychic pressure there that's probably cumulative. And knowing you can't get out would build the strain fast."

"How is she?"

"Depressed, but holding control of herself, so far."

"If you can't bring her back, can you at least get her out of that limbo universe?"

"I'll see." He transplaced back.

Ithleen was huddled against the cold again, but this time she was looking up. As he appeared, she rose and reached towards him. "Jonno! I've never been so glad to see anyone in my whole life!" Her voice was not quite steady, but she smiled and added, "I knew you'd come back, of course, but thinking it was over, and then seeing you go..."

"I know. Let's see if I can at least get you out of this set of universes." He tried a random transplacement, but again found himself alone. He returned hurriedly. "Your rifkey is maintaining a hold on you. Mine can't touch you at all till yours is turned off somehow. Well, let's see if I can move it away from you."

She handed it to him, and he concentrated on the intent, while operating his own rifkey. All that happened was a deepening of the twilight around them. "It won't let go of you," he realized. "And it will move only deeper into these limbo universes, taking you with it. Try walking away from it."

"I've already tried that. I can't move more than half a metre from anything I have here. It's as if every point in this universe is equivalent to, or contained in, this little bubble around me. Everything I put down simply moves with me in my bubble no matter what direction I walk in."

"Try walking away while I hold the rifkey."

The result was as she had described: she walked, but the distance between them stayed the same. Jonno tried it the opposite way, but he too could not move beyond the limit, no matter how long he walked.

"When you went back without me, the first time, I tried in desperation to turn my laser on the rifkey; but I got only the feeblest glow out of it. Energy seems to be absorbed here, possibly in proportion to its strength, because my own energy doesn't seem to be lost as quickly."

"But it is going?" Jonno asked in renewed alarm.

"Yes. It's tiring even to stand, now."

"Your rifkey must be far stronger than your laser; why isn't — oh, of course, it's not self-contained."

"I thought the laser wasn't either."

"Not quite the same set-up. The rifkey draws in full power as it needs it;

the laser fires from its storage cell, just using a wexter gimmick to bring in a steady small trickle of power to recharge that cell. The drain here must be able to pull the charge out as fast as it builds up. But there's no hope of the rifkey's running down: it doesn't store energy. And somehow it must be able to obtain power even in this energy sink. Wexter fail-safe design for a vital tool."

"The rifkey won't open, either. When I found my laser so feeble, I wanted to try it on the circuitry, hoping that would be more susceptible; but the rifkey wouldn't respond."

"It's still carrying out its previous order. It can't do anything else until that's completed."

"But its order was just to take me away." Ithleen's eyes widened as she suddenly realized the implications. "Indefinitely! It can't finish that!"

"We'll find a way to get you out of here!" Jonno promised fiercely.

"What else can we try?"

"I don't know." His hair-rumpling motion was not Jonno's usual absent gesture of puzzled thought but a fierce reaction of frustrated effort. "I don't seem to be thinking very well, somehow."

"Creative thought takes energy, too. I've noticed my own thinking deteriorating into simple, primitive emotionalizing."

"Yes, I can feel that, too, very strongly. Try to concentrate on useful emotions, like hope."

Ithleen nodded. "And on my belief that Pl- that the two of you will think of a solution."

"I'll go back for a minute, and confer with Jonnan again. Maybe he's thought of something, now that he's been out of these limbo universes for a while." He pressed her hands. "I'll be back."

"Yes, of course," she said to both intentions, and smiled at him. "It's not quite so bad, now that I've been able to talk to someone. I may be free of the Geodan agoraphobia, but I find I have a related weakness. I can't stand a complete absence of people. When I realized here that I was completely cut off..." She shuddered.

"Ithleen —"

"I'm all right now. Go back for your consultation."

"I'll be back," he said again, and patterned a transplacement.

In Mayne's lab again, he reported what he had learned. "Can you think of anything else to try?"

Mayne shook his head. "If her moves were a straight line regression, I could transplace to the next universe and block it, then to hers, and perhaps blow the rifkey; but with infinity to choose from at every point, it could simply dodge the blocked universe. If we had another rifkey, she and I could try a synchronous transplacement to the same new universe, with you there as a marker; but we can't wait till we can ask the wexters for another rifkey."

"You could deposit me in the new – No, of course, that would mean you'd been to it."

Mayne resumed the pacing Jonno's arrival had interrupted. "And every wrong move we make puts her into a worse limbo universe. If we could move her to a universe where the physical or psionic laws were different, perhaps her rifkey would lose its hold; but we've no way to choose among universes we haven't been to. Perhaps even the wexters can't choose circumstances. Have you any more ideas, yourself?"

"No thoughts at all, except that I can't leave her there alone. I've got to get back to her."

"But if we get a solution while you're away, we won't be able to apply it."

"Then I'll do ten minute stints till we can think of something. There won't be many of them. She's been moved deeper into limbo three times since you last saw her."

"Then go to her. But keep checking here."

"Right." Jonno set a ten-minute count-down on his watch, took the blankets and flask of tea Van and Davith had brought, and transplaced back.

"Anything?" asked Ithleen hopefully.

"Not yet." He wrapped the blankets around her and sat holding her as she drank some of the tea. "But we'll keep working on it; and meanwhile I'll stay with you, just going back now and then to find out what the others have thought of; but I'll always come back, until we can get you away."

"Jonno, I'm so thankful for your presence. I can face the thought of dying, but being cut off from everyone who cares about me is more than I can bear. It makes me want death to hurry..."

"No!" Jonno's arms tightened about her. "Fight it! You're not cut off. We care about you, and we're going to get you out of here."

"I can believe that as long as I can touch you. I can even begin to take an interest in things again, to wonder about this place, this situation. I can see why I'm being held from transplacing back, but why can no one else get to me? Plennor Mayne — Jonnan — tried over and over; and I had a glimpse of Davith and Van once each, the last two times I shifted before you came."

He told her what they had figured out about the circumstances.

"So Robinaire wasn't just confused in giving the order then. But why should she dislike me so much that she wants to get rid of me?"

"You've been distracting Jonnan's attention from her."

"What?"

"You've lived in an ivory tower. I think Jonnan has too since he got his plennorate. His ISC has a soft touch. I've had to continue working at holding my position, so I've had to learn to be more observant of people's attitudes and relationships. I admit I'm not good at it, but I do notice some things, such as Jonnan's strong concern about Robinaire, an attitude he didn't display towards his assistants. So Robinaire would resent losing his attention, and resent your sharing his multiverse activities with him instead of her."

"Yes, of course; I should have thought of it. I thought of her as a child he had briefly had responsibility for, but who was now safely returned home, and so out of the multiverse and our lives."

"She is not as naive and uninvolved as you think she is, Ithleen, though certainly childish, with this malicious act... Are you any warmer?" He snuggled her more comfortably against him.

"Yes, thank you, a little. But you must be getting cold yourself, by now. I don't need both these blankets. Put one over your shoulders."

"You keep them on. I can thaw out when I go back to keep in touch with the others."

Wanting to keep talking, Ithleen broke a pause with, "I wish I had some instruments with me. This is an intriguing place. If I can ever get free of it, I'd like to come back and investigate it."

"You have courage, Ithleen."

She laughed. "No. Curiosity! The curse of the scientist!"

"Well, we'll plan to come back, then. We'd need rather specialized instruments, I think..."

"Psionic, I presume; there are certainly psychic effects here. When I could no longer ignore them, I tried to analyze them. It's the emptiness you sense first, a feeling that there's nothing else but yourself. Like standing alone in a vast, anechoic chamber, where there's no sound except what you make yourself. Even that fades instantly. And there's nothing to see or touch or smell or taste. No movement except your own, and that doesn't take you anywhere... You can't imagine what a difference it makes to have someone else here."

"I can begin to."

"And then you feel that you've lost the whole universe — the whole multiverse — and everything that was in your life, every person and every thing that ever mattered to you... You're alone and lost forever, beyond all human touch. And then you feel alienness, wrongness, entrapment about you, and seeping into you. But mostly it's being alone, cast out, unwanted, thrown to the — the — to that alienness, which will consume you, separating you forever from all hope and love and warmth..."

"Easy, Ithleen, you're reconjuring it. You're not alone now; I'm here. Whatever there is, I'm between you and it."

She sighed heavily and laid her head against his shoulder. "I know that's impossible, but I feel it's true."

This time she let the silence last, taking comfort from touch instead of words, until Jonno's timer buzzed. Instinctively, she clutched at him, then deliberately pushed herself away. "Time for your break. Make it a long one. Since you're our transportation, we can't afford to have you go numb here."

"I'll make it short, Ithleen." Impulsively succumbing to the emotional pressures, he tilted her head up and kissed her gently. "See you in a few minutes." He transplaced out.

***

"You're late!" cried Mayne.

Jonno glanced at his watch. "No, it's just ten — oh, my watch must be running slow as power seeps out of its battery." He moved to stand over the portable heater the technicians had brought. "Have you thought of anything?"

Mayne resumed his pacing. "We've been trying to get hold of Robinaire, on the long chance she could cancel the instructions she gave the rifkey, if she were willing to, and if she would go with you, and if the rifkey would allow even her near Ithleen. But we can't contact her. Somehow, we've got to destroy Ithleen's rifkey."

"How? Lasers and explosives are useless in that energy sink."

"If energy drain is proportional to strength, how about using something less violent? Vibration, corrosives?"

"Against a wexter tool? And there isn't time. Ithleen won't last long enough! Remember she's in an even deeper limbo now than when you last saw her. It began biting into me even in the short time I was there."

"And a physical attack won't damage a wexter tool, either even if you retained enough strength there to try to smash it."

"The harder I tried, the faster I'd lose strength."

Mayne muttered, "No way to pour excess energy into the rifkey, or drain energy out of it. Can we block the connection between Ithleen and the rifkey? Or confuse its recognition of her, or of me and my staff?"

"How?" demanded Jonno again. "We don't understand its workings." He snarled, "Why didn't the wexters give you a means to summon them in an emergency?"

"They're not in the rescue business. I'm expendable, and they didn't expect Ithleen to be in danger. There's no way we can transplace to the wexters, or even communicate with them directly."

"They don't monitor your reports steadily?"

Mayne shook his head. "Sporadic pickups, safer for them than establishing a predictable routine. Any other ideas, even wild ones? Ones you think won't work? They might suggest some other possibility."

"Nothing. It's difficult to think creatively there. Mental energy is dampened, too. We regress into a state where emotion is intensified and rational thought is slowed."

His voice unsteady, Mayne said, "Ithleen..."

"Is already weak. If she isn't moved soon..."

Mayne shouted, "Why won't the emergency override work? She's certainly being harmed!"

"Because the other mode's still in operation. No other psionic control can touch her until the operating one completes its order."

"But its order is to keep her out of contact with us. That can't be completed until she, or this world, has ceased to exist!"

"And we can't deceive the rifkey," said Jonno grimly. "Since its psionic senses reach into other universes, it won't shut off on any false information we could give it about this world. I don't know if the wexters could block its senses, but we can't wait around in the hope that they can."

His control slipping, Mayne exclaimed uselessly, "There's got to be some way to destroy that rifkey!"

"Keep working on it, Jonnan. I'll go back to her now." Jonno re-set his timer, and took back the rifkey. The assistants had brought a large packet of sandwiches and another blanket. Jonno bundled them under his arm.

Davith said awkwardly, "Tell her we're trying..."

Van cut through his floundering. "Give her our love," she said simply.

Jonno nodded. "It's what she needs most right now."

He transplaced back and told Ithleen all that had been said. Huddled against him again, she said as steadily as she could, "Well, finding out what won't work is a step towards finding out what will. And there's still the hope of using Robinaire."

Jonno hesitated. He had no faith in Robinaire, but did not want to say so. "It may take a while to find her, Ithleen. She's either hiding out in shame, which I doubt, or out enjoying herself somewhere!"

Ithleen laughed. "Don't be so fierce, Jonno. She couldn't have known this would happen."

"She's a self-centred little brat, and if it were my lab, I'd never let her set foot in it again! Why Jonnan cares about her is beyond me."

"She's a child. And she has a talent for making people want to look after her."

"I never felt it."

"Didn't even you find something for her to do so she wouldn't be bored, while she was in your world?"

"Oh, that. That was just to get her out of the way." Jonno continued, "It wouldn't take much logic to see that Robinaire is too selfish and too young to be trusted in this multiverse business."

"But part of his method of keeping her quiet about it was to let her come to talk to us."

"I would rather have risked her talking to a skeptical world than have her hanging around my lab. Look what's happened to you because of his choice!"

"You haven't his patience, Jonno. Though your being here proves you have equal kindness."

"I'm here because there's someone worth saving."

"You're very good for my morale. I know you're suffering yourself, by now..."

"It's worth it."

"Your flattery is... outrageous... but most kind..." Her voice was failing, and Jonno looked at her with renewed concern.

"Why don't you try to get some sleep, Ithleen, and conserve your energy?"

"I'm... a little afraid... to let go..."

He touched her hand and her cheek. She was icy again, in spite of the blankets and his arms. He was shivering himself, and a numbness of will was creeping through him. There must be something he could do, he thought fiercely. But by now he could think only of superficialities and emotions. Logical thought seemed paralyzed.

He was startled when his alarm sounded. He had slipped into a complete daze of non-thinking; the limbo universe must now be draining his energy proportionately faster than it was taking Ithleen's already depleted store.

He lifted his cheek from the top of her head, and carefully laid her down. She barely stirred.

He transplaced back to Mayne's lab and collapsed into a chair. "Anything?" he croaked.

"A desperate idea," said Mayne. "If we can't separate Ithleen from her rifkey, and can't destroy it, we've got to make it sense her as dead, so it will register completion and shut off."

"How?"

"Use hypnosis to cut off her vital functions. The brain can survive up to four minutes' deprivation of oxygen without damage. The rifkeys are set to react instantly to body malfunction, and activate the emergency homing mode. If you stop her heart and breath, the rifkey should register death within a minute or two at most, conclude its command is complete, and shut off, letting you transplace her away from it and revive her."

"Won't the rifkey check her for brain activity? I can't stop that."

"The rifkeys are set to react instantly to anything affecting body functions. Brain damage would be far too late for them to respond."

"You're right. But what if the rifkey is capable of picking up my pre-damage command to her to revive after I've moved her back here? If it grabbed her away from here again..."

"The rifkeys can sense into other universes but they can't act there. Even if hers tried to resume operation, I don't think it could reach her. And once it's off, it should need a new command to start again. Anyway, we've got to try something."

Jonno nodded grimly to that and, taking back the rifkey, transplaced.

Mayne had barely had time to resume his pacing when Jonno reappeared. "Too late. She's unconscious, and I can't rouse her."

CHAPTER 15

Desperation

Mayne thought frantically, then grabbed the rifkey and transplaced himself and Jonno to the presence of Geode's chief medical officer, Ciath, in a lounge much like Ithleen's, but decorated in blue and cream.

Before her startled look could fade back into her usual serenity, Mayne was saying, "Ithleen is trapped in a place that's draining the life energy out of her, held by a device that won't let go until it gets a zero life reading from her. Have you anything that can temporarily suspend her vital functions? Can you completely stop her life," he stressed, "and then restart it, after we bring her to you?"

Worried, Ciath looked into space, as though running drug capabilities through her mind. "Yes, I can stop her, and revive her if you can get her to me fast enough."

"If the device lets go, we can have her here in seconds."

"Come with me." She put down the script she had been reading, led the way to the dispensary, which neighboured her living quarters, and carefully loaded a hypodermic, after consulting a chart for Ithleen's body weight and sensitivity factors. "This is a self-operating microsprayer: just place it against the vein on the wrist, this way."

"Is the drug instant?"

"No. This would normally take up to twenty minutes to work; it will probably be much faster if she's as weak as you say, but I can't estimate the difference without examining her. There are faster drugs, but they would do too much damage. You must get her to me immediately after her functions stop, so I can revive her and this will have no after-effects."

Jonno took the hypo and transplaced.

Ithleen lay inertly as he had last seen her. Briefly pulling away the blankets, he applied the drug to her arm as instructed. He checked that she had not re-pocketed her rifkey, so that it would not be carried along to detect her revival.

Patterning his own rifkey, he very carefully instructed it to move himself and Ithleen's body to Geode medical centre the moment the other rifkey switched off. Over and over, he stressed it was not to move him until it could take Ithleen as well, no matter how much harm was being done to him.

Then he sat, holding Ithleen tightly against him, and waited.

As the minutes passed, he slumped and fell over, but still maintained his hold on both the rifkey and Ithleen. He was near unconsciousness himself when normal lighting suddenly flashed against his eyelids, and calm, competent hands touched him, as others tried to pull Ithleen away from him.

He resisted unthinkingly, but lost the struggle immediately. He was lifted onto a stretcher and wheeled away. But Mayne was gripping his shoulder as they moved, and saying, "You did it, Jonno! She's here!" He relaxed and blacked out.

***

Ciath called Mayne the next morning to tell him that Jonno had been checked out and was waiting to see him.

"And Ithleen?" He knew she had been successfully revived the previous evening. He had not left until Ciath assured him not only of that, but also that she was sure there were no after-effects, side effects, or doubts of Ithleen's continued health, and he had seen Ithleen himself, in comfortable sleep; but she had been kept under observation, and he wanted the final verdict.

"She's just awakened, and my staff is giving her a final check now. It's routine. Our monitors say she's all right."

Jonno's first question on awakening had also been for Ithleen — As the two plennors, together again, now waited more calmly to see Ithleen, Jonno said, "We've been very lucky, Jonnan. We could have lost her."

"I know. I was afraid we had."

"Can't you keep that child of yours out of this multiverse business?"

"You mean Robinaire? I need her. She's the only one who can find Haughn's world for us."

"In that case, Jonnan, let me give you some advice..."

"Yes?" Mayne tried to speak neutrally but heard in his own voice the anti-enthusiasm commonly accorded to unsolicited advice.

"Pay her sufficient attention to keep her happy, or she's liable to do more damage."

"It's a nuisance having to worry about people's feelings. Why can't everyone be self-sufficient and independent?"

"Because not everyone is a Jonnan Mayne. Even I, though I feel much as you do, realize I have to consider people's emotions and relationships occasionally. Your girl is used to being the centre of interest. If you want her around, you've got to give her the attention she craves."

Mayne sighed. "I suppose you're right."

A medical aide looked in to tell them Ithleen was now officially released, though under orders to rest for a day, and was awaiting them.

They found her looking pale and worn, but alert and smiling a welcome. Mindful of her orders, she stayed in her chair, but lifted a hand to each of them. As the two men crossed to her, she said, "I don't know how you did it, but I know I have you to thank for my life."

"Jonnan figured out a way to make your rifkey think you were dead, so it would release you."

"And Jonno carried out the procedure." Mayne explained what they had done.

"And by now it will have fused, of course," added Ithleen. She sighed and continued; "I don't remember much of it, but I do remember how much it meant to have you there, Jonno. The comfort of your presence was so deep that I still feel it."

Jonno, who was still holding her hand, said, "I'm glad."

She turned to Mayne, who had begun restlessly moving about the room. "Have there been any new developments while I was away, Ple— I guess I'll have to call you Jonnan now, with two Plennor Maynes."

"You could have done that long ago."

Ithleen smiled. "Has anything else happened? Haughn? The wexters?"

"No."

"What are we going to do next, then?"

"I suppose the first thing is to take Jonno back to his own world."

Jonno interrupted, "If I'm not imposing, I'd rather like to stay a while. We can learn more about each other's work. And, to tell the truth, I want to get in on this multiverse exploring. I've been restless ever since I learned about it."

Mayne hesitated, feeling the same brush of reluctance he had felt before about including Jonno in his multiverse adventures. A wave of shame said sharply to him that he had been glad enough of Jonno's help when he needed it! He assumed his feeling was a part of the natural antipathy towards analogs, and since he liked Jonno as well as being grateful to him, he was determined to shake off any such traces of rejection. Still, he said, "Can you afford the time away? You said your ISC is always pressing for new gimmicks."

"Yes, but I haven't taken any vacation in years. They may make a fuss about the suddenness of my decision to take one, but they can't do much except grumble if I say I need one now to protect my health."

"From the sample of the multiverse you've had so far, you're more likely to lose your health," Mayne said, in grim jest.

"If we can persuade the wexters to give me a rifkey too, we might all be a bit safer."

"I suppose you're right," agreed Mayne. "Well, I'd still better take you home just now, so you can make arrangements to cover for your absence. You say your ISC's fussier than mine, and even I had a visit from Security when I assumed I didn't need to bother with any explanation."

"So I give them a plausible explanation, before they even wonder. Won't take me long to send a message to Admin, leaving the bureaucrats to stew, unable to find me to ask questions." Jonno looked pleased at the prospect. "You can bring me back in a few minutes. Don't forget to ask the wexters about the rifkey."

"Right. Ithleen needs a replacement one, too." Mayne took out his wexcorder and put in the requests.

"Should we not go back to your world, Jonnan?" suggested Ithleen. "Van and Davith must be worried. Or did you go back to tell them we were safely here?"

"Yes, after the medics swore you were both all right, I went back. They were still waiting at the lab."

"They've had rather a lot of anxious waits, poor kids. What do we do then, stay here, return, or go elsewhere?"

"If by 'elsewhere' you are hinting you want to do some more sampling," Mayne warned.

Ithleen laughed. "Not this time."

"Do your medics want you to stay here today?"

"No, they've released me."

"Then I suggest I take Jonno to his world and then to mine, and return to take you back to mine as well."

"And then what?" asked Jonno.

"If my assistants have succeeded in locating Robinaire, I'll have another go at trying to persuade her to help us with Haughn's world. Perhaps she'll be contrite, and I may be able to build on that."

"See you shortly, Ithleen."

When Mayne returned for Ithleen, he found her chatting with a cheerful and energetic man of sixty, with bright dark eyes below thick white eyebrows, who waved his hands about as he spoke. Mayne remembered seeing him briefly on an earlier visit: Ithleen had been shooing him away from investigating the "outside material" — Mayne himself — after the rescue from Ocerat. The man was saying, "Ithleen, where do you find these superb specimens?"

"You've heard my lectures on the multiverse, Karby."

"I know, I know; I'm being rhetorical. Their charts are fantastic, Ithleen. Do you know they match and vary in the most inexplicable ways? Not like family resemblances at all. Absolutely identical in some spots, and simply random variations in others. I can't find a pattern at all. Analogs, you called them? I shall write a monograph on them. If only I had material to work on..."

"Well, you can at least meet one right now. Plennor Jonnan Mayne, our chief geneticist, Karby."

Karby turned and peered at Mayne. "You're chart number one. I've been most eager to meet you. I wonder if you would..."

"Karby!" said Ithleen. "It happens there are more important things in the multiverse needing attention."

"More important than genetic knowledge?" said Karby blankly.

"Yes. It is possible that unless we look after the other matters, someday there won't be any Geode or its store of knowledge; so contain your craving for information."

Karby sighed. "I know better than to question your judgement, Ithleen. But I wish…" He sighed again and subsided, then bounced back with an eager invitation to the visitor. "Perhaps you'd like to see our labs?"

"Another time," said Mayne politely.

"Yes, I know," interrupted Karby gloomily, "you have to save the universe. I mean the multiverse."

Ithleen laughed. "Not that melodramatic, Karby. Just stop a potential conqueror, and possibly a species of psychics, if they show up."

"Oh, is that all?" returned Karby spiritedly. "Then I'll expect to see you back next week."

***

"You have a hint of satisfaction in your look, Captain. Have you dug up something useful on one of Mayne's assistants?" Polminander steepled his hands and waited patiently.

"No. They're as clean as I expected," replied Simao.

"Then what is it you've got?"

"The plennor has been ordering large quantities of technical supplies — and he's so impatient for them that he sent the order in to Supply on the weekend, asking for delivery first thing Monday. For a plennor, they managed it! I got a man in on a delivery trip: he says there are a number of bare spots on workbenches and floor in the main lab where marks show there have recently been major pieces of equipment. He managed a quick look in the auxiliary rooms — nothing piled up or shifted recently to make room for anything else. The tentative conclusion is that apparatus has been moved out of the lab entirely — unrecorded by the door cameras."

"And now the plennor wants supplies — like someone who's sold his demonstration models and wants to re-stock. The question is, what could he have sold? Robinaire described the apparatus to me; it all sounded like stuff he's already published. If he had something new, something that would be an advantage to buy before publication..."

"A new item could be concealed among a batch of old ones."

"So it could, Captain. Did your man count the number of missing items?"

"Yes. And noted their locations."

"Good. What have you got from your surveillance lately?"

"The plennor and the woman Ithleen appear to have been absent five days. They returned Saturday night, or, to be precise, early yesterday morning. Lights came on briefly in the lab, then in the living quarters. Sunday was busier than a weekday: Sartyov and Kamalua went in before noon, and stayed until well into the night. The Filyk girl visited there during the afternoon, staying about half an hour. She looked upset when she left; perhaps Mayne got rid of her, to clear the way for some of his undercover activities, because around an hour later, there seems to have been a bit of a flap: Mayne kept pacing back and forth, and the technicians were bustling about, carrying what looked like something bundled up in blankets. There appeared to be someone else there, too, though the cameras never got a clear view of him."

"Why not?"

"The main lab room has clerestory windows: too high up to get a good angle on faces. Our only level views are glimpses through the surrounding offices, when their doors into the big room are open."

"So what was all the excitement about?"

"Couldn't tell. It died down in the small hours. The assistants went home, then back in as usual this morning, where they calmly opened up for the delivery people."

"And the plennor?"

"Is a plennor, so his living quarters have one-way windows to protect his privacy. All we can say is that the central hall light was left on all night."

"Well, perhaps the Filyk girl noticed something before she left yesterday. See what you can get out of her."

***

When Mayne brought Ithleen back to his lab later that morning, she was received with warm concern by the two technicians, who then reported that Robinaire was still not responding to calls.

"Better call her yourself," advised Jonno. "I suggest you tell her that her foolish prank has kept you too busy to see her, but now that Ithleen is safely back, you hope she'll come out here again. That will let her know she hasn't done irreparable harm, promise her your attention, and warn her that she'll lose it again if she tries any more tricks. And don't mention Haughn."

"I'd better not mention what she did, or name Ithleen either, to be safe," Mayne said. "I'll have to leave a message, and she might have company when she plays it back."

After further thought, he put through a message he hoped was both innocuous and reassuring: "Sorry I missed you yesterday. If you're not busy, we'd *all* enjoy having you visit today." He stressed the "all" just a little, hoping Robinaire could read it as assurance of Ithleen's safety, and hence her own re-acceptance.

In a few minutes a nervous Robinaire called back to say she would come out in an hour or so.

The two plennors spent part of the interval attempting to duplicate Robinaire's feat of transplacing someone else without going along; but no matter how firmly one ordered the rifkey to accept the other's command, the rifkey would not send the first off unaccompanied.

They appealed to the theorist for ideas. "I can't think of any physical reason against it," she mused, "and it can't be something our rifkeys are incapable of, since Robinaire used mine. It could be that Robinaire has some unusual psi talent..."

"But?" Jonno prompted, hearing the doubt in her voice.

"But I'm remembering how Jonnan's freak contact with you couldn't be repeated. That transplacement didn't involve special psi talent, because Jonnan himself tried to repeat it, and couldn't. So we come back to the psionic laws, and perhaps rifkey response to those laws."

"But how could it be rifkey response?" Mayne asked. "The wexters didn't expect my analog contact; and their exhaustive briefing on the rifkeys didn't include anything about unaccompanied transplacement."

"I don't think they deliberately built them in, but they didn't specifically prohibit them. I think the wexters may have built better than they realized."

"That would explain why the rifkeys were able to make those transplacements, but not why they can't continue to."

"Do you have the proverb, 'One burn, sure learn'?"

"Something like it. You're not saying that applies somehow to the rifkeys? That they've learned from the one disastrous trip?"

"Not directly, but through their users. Remember, the rifkeys pick up subconscious wishes, such as not wanting to go to complete duplicates of ourselves or our worlds. As long as we believed it was impossible to get to an analogous world, we didn't fear it, and the transplacement remained possible; but the instant we knew it was possible, it ceased to be."

"Yes, we've accepted that paradox; but how does it apply in this new case? We're not afraid of anything in this case, surely?" Mayne protested.

"How secure would you feel if you knew someone could slip in a command to your rifkey to move you somewhere you didn't want to go?"

"But we'd have to give permission first, as you did."

"You may feel confident; but it would appear that your subconscious is not quite so sure, especially after I did just that! Unlike the wexters, who use their tools as adjuncts, we are completely dependent on our rifkeys. You don't need to be a Geodan to fear being stranded in a foreign universe, or trapped in a limbo!"

"But we accept the wexters moving us around," Mayne argued.

"Can't my subconscious make a distinction between people I trust and those I don't?"

"That depends on whether the fear has been generated by logic or has developed out of primitive instincts. Consider Geodans. I know that if I wear the proper protective clothing, or am sealed in my plane, I can go out onto or over the surface of my planet. My seals failed once, and I got a dose of radiation, so I worry a bit that it could happen again; but it doesn't stop me from going out, because my fear is rational. But Ciath, who knows just as well as I that our protective seals are normally adequate, and who is the calmest person I've ever known, couldn't force herself to go out, no matter how she tried to persuade herself, because her fear is tied into basic instincts."

Jonno commented, "But some people do overcome phobias, under stress of another need, such as rescuing their children; or they gradually teach themselves to face their fears."

"People do, but the rifkeys can't," she said. "The wexters have made that the most basic part of the rifkeys' programming, so they can guarantee that the rifkeys will never deposit us in flame or vacuum, et cetera. If the basic order could be modified, the guarantee would fail."

"But if the fluxate energy is the basis for everything in the universes, does that imply there's some great psi Overmind that provided the interaction that formed those universes?"

Ithleen laughed. "That's metaphysics and out of my field. We can imagine all sorts of things, and my world had religions and philosophies that did: a universal consciousness that created the world; cycles of pure thought, pure energy, pure matter, and more variations that I've long since forgotten. Perhaps the origin of the universes simply took far longer than we can imagine, or some unknown factor can precipitate a cascade of fluxate interactions, as an event singularity. Or perhaps thought exists independently of matter, and evolved, or devolved, into the diaphane fluxate, which gave rise to the multiverse, which can eventually produce life, which can rise to thought again. I rather like that one myself."

"Intuitively?"

She shrugged. "Not enough data to say. I may just like the idea of ongoing cycles, and the thought of being part of something even vaster than the multiverse. Perhaps some day we can persuade the wexters to probe the diaphane for actual data, and hope to get beyond hypotheses; but in the meantime, I think we'll have to limit our speculation to the things that affect us directly."

She lifted her wexcorder from a pocket. "I've been recording our conversation, so perhaps we can at least get confirmation from the wexters on my hunch about the rifkeys being able to learn from one another. We do know that they can sense both into the subconscious and into other universes; it seems reasonable to assume they can share information. But don't count on the wexters knowing. Remember, they build psi devices mostly by instinct; it's only recently that they've bothered with theory."

Jonno put in, "And chose you as a short-cut to correct conclusions. So, unless conflicting evidence comes up, we might as well accept your hunch — about the rifkeys at least — as a working hypothesis."

"Then let's get to work on something more productive," Mayne suggested.

The two plennors turned their attention to Jonnan's new designs for his TPA, and soon had a desk littered with diagrams and equations. Van and Davith resumed building frames for the prospective equipment, and Ithleen retired to her office to check on what her computer program had done so far with the wexter data.

They were interrupted some time later by the arrival of the wexter, and gathered again to confer.

"We have been reviewing your reports," Spen said. "The limbo universes you describe are of great interest. We would like to send some probes to one, if you will supply guidance."

"I will," said Jonno quickly. "Ithleen has to rest."

"The guidance is not required immediately. I will let you know when we are ready."

"Have you brought us more rifkeys?" Jonnan asked.

The wexter caused two to appear. Ithleen and Jonno picked them up and the wexter activated their attunement. Jonno saw that his was labeled "J 2".

Spen went on, "Although we have not had time for consideration, Ithleen's hypothesis about the unaccompanied transplacement seems reasonable to us. Still, we would like to examine the person who accomplished the transplacement, to check the alternative hypothesis that she has extraordinary psi ability. She is the same one who contains the information about Haughn's world, is she not?"

"Yes; and she's on her way here now."

"Report in the recorder when she is here, and I will return." The wexter vanished.

The others dispersed to their assorted tasks again until Robinaire arrived. She slipped in nervously without sounding the doorbell, and stood hesitantly just inside the main room, looking very little-girlish in a peasant blouse and skirt; but as Mayne looked up with an absent, "Oh, hello, Robinaire," she ran to him and seized his hand.

"I'm sorry! Honest I am! Are you mad at me?"

Focusing his attention on her, he said, "It's Ithleen you should apologize to. You nearly killed her."

"Ithleen, I am truly sorry for - what I did," Robinaire said. "I wasn't trying to hurt you. I just wanted you gone." Then lowering her voice so only Ithleen could hear, "I suppose I was feeling a bit - jealous..."

"Thank you," Ithleen said, patting her gently on the shoulder. "We'll forget about it if you promise never to try anything like that again."

"Oh, I do!"

"And if you'll help us now," Mayne said.

She turned pale. "Zar Haughn's world?"

"If necessary. But perhaps not. We're going to try something else. A wexter is going to come to talk to you. Ne speaks telepathically, so ne may be able to find in your mind the information on Haughn's world. And if ne's successful, there won't be any need for you to go to Haughn's world."

"What does telepathy feel like?"

"With the wexter, it seems like ordinary conversation: none of the effort that's required in using our psi machines. You just talk as you would to anyone else; and when ne replies you'll think you're hearing it. As for nem looking into your mind, I suspect there won't be any sensation at all. Now, if you're ready, I'll let nem know." Without giving her time for hesitation, he reported her presence into his wexcorder.

Within a few minutes the wexter materialized in front of them. Robinaire huddled back against Jonnan, and he gave her the security of his arm. "This is Spen, Robinaire."

"Greeting," said the wexter. "You radiate a strange combination of fear and happiness. The fear is directed at me and is unjustified."

Robinaire giggled and relaxed. "It is just like talking."

"Please think now of the occasion of your transplacement to the world of Zar Haughn, and especially of the Zar himself."

"Tell you about it?"

"Visualizing it in your thoughts will be better."

"Okay."

There was silence for a few minutes. The others had gathered around and waited eagerly; but finally Spen said, "Regrettably, the experiment has failed. Try now to think of the occasion on which you transplaced Ithleen without accompanying her."

"Why?" cried Robinaire. "I said I'm sorry!"

"Easy, Robinaire." Mayne tightened his arm around her reassuringly. "Ne just wants to know something of the processes involved."

"But I don't know them."

"That's all right. Just think through what happened. What you thought then."

Robinaire shot a glance at Ithleen, who was looking elsewhere. "Do I have to? Won't you all get mad at me again?"

"We won't know anything you're thinking, Robinaire. It'll be just you and Spen; and ne doesn't care anything about it except how." It occurred to Mayne that he might be stretching the truth here; the wexters did care if something happened to the consultant they had taken such effort to obtain; but since they apparently tried to behave logically, they wouldn't hold grudges.

Still huddling close against Mayne, Robinaire finally agreed to have Spen look over her memories of the transplacement. After a few more minutes, Spen said, "No unusual psi abilities seem to have been involved in the transplacement. There appears to have been a combination of hope and a belief in the uselessness of the attempt, which together may have contributed to the effectiveness of the action. Are humans prone to perform actions which are merely expressions of emotion?"

"It varies with the human," said Ithleen, "but if you generalize and ask if we act irrationally, the answer is yes."

"Even you scientists?"

She laughed. "Yes, again."

"Then Haughn must be assumed to be even more unpredictable. It is disappointing to have achieved nothing towards locating his world. If you have any better success at this, please inform us immediately."

"In case we do," said Mayne hastily on what sounded like an exit line, "have you completed any of the new tools?"

"I will bring some by midafternoon." This time Spen did fade out.

"Robinaire," said Mayne gently.

She shuddered. "You want me to go!"

"You have promised to help, remember, to make up for what you did."

"I'm afraid!" She clung to him.

"Robinaire, I'll look after you. It'll be just a few seconds. Nothing will happen to you. Now, it wasn't really as bad there as most of the other places we went to that time, was it?"

"I know it wasn't, but I'm afraid! It's going to hurt!"

"It couldn't possibly hurt, Robinaire. You've just built it up into something frightening by thinking about it. It'll be over so fast you'll hardly notice it. You could think of something pleasant you're going to do afterwards. Perhaps find a pleasant world for you to visit. Or, if you don't like transplacing, perhaps there's something here on this Earth we could plan to do when we come back; and you could think of that the whole time. Think, now, there must be something you'd like that we could arrange."

He felt her trembling stop as she suddenly looked at him in the thrill of an emotional blank cheque. "We could go anywhere here? You'd take me?"

"If you take me to Haughn's world first, yes."

"You promise?"

"I promise."

It took her three attempts to speak, but she finally did. "I'll go, then."

"Good girl, Robinaire. We'll go this afternoon then, as soon as we have the wexters' tools, and get it over with. Do you want to wait here till then?"

"No, I'll come back," said Robinaire. "I don't want to just wait."

"All right; be here by fifteen-thirty."

Jonno and the technicians murmured words of approval, then drifted away to resume their work. Ithleen had already gone back to her office.

"There's a girl who was in my class," said Robinaire. "Her name's Charadine Lagaronde, and her parents are terrifically wealthy."

"Yes?" said Mayne politely, his mind half back on his design work.

"Her parents are having a huge party for all the important people from the Regions who are here in Neithon."

He nodded. "The unofficial ambassadors of the Regions, and representatives of companies, here to deal with ISC."

"For them, and for big shots in ISC and Neithon. And Charadine's allowed to have all of us from her year there."

"I'm sure you'll enjoy it very much. Is it soon?" He said.

"A week from tomorrow. You said anywhere."

"Pardon?"

"You said you'd take me anywhere. Will you escort me to the party?"

"What?" he yelped. "A party? A formal party?"

"Yes," she whispered, cowed, then, fiercely, "You promised!"

"So I did," he said, appalled. What had he let himself in for? His mind shot back down the years to the last time or so he had endured the boredom of a purely social gathering, and he winced.

The "aunt" with whom he had lived had come from an ambassadorial family, and the "uncle" from an ambitious business milieu. The uncle's incompetence had reduced them to their shabby-genteel existence, but both foster parents had remained convinced of the value of social graces in achieving a place for oneself in the world, so the boy entrusted to their care had been thoroughly grounded in social behaviour. Further, he had had to serve as a mentor and practice guest/escort/stranger in Aunt Derrim's protocol training classes.

With the semi-exception of occasional conferences of professional societies, and ceremonies bestowing awards on him, he had attended no formal social functions since his late teens. And now he was trapped into an elaborate one by the bond of his own word.

"But Robinaire," he protested, "why should you want me to go with you?"

"You're Plennor Mayne," she said simply.

A practical thought occurred to him. "Surely you must already have an escort?"

"I did have, but he's taken a job in Bruza Region, and he's had to go off sooner than he expected."

"But there must be any number of others who would be pleased to take his place."

"The rest of the class is mostly paired up already. Anyway, I want you. And you promised. And," she whispered, trembling again, "I will go to Zar Haughn's world for you."

Mayne suddenly realized that however irrational her fear, it was intense, and that she was offering a very real sacrifice for the sake of her party.

"All right, Robinaire." He drew a deep breath. "We'll go to your party."

***

As promised, Spen delivered the pentools a little before fifteen hundred hours. The two plennors tested them eagerly and found them exactly to Jonno's specifications. The wexter had brought three sets, tacitly accepting both Jonno's enlistment as another agent for them, and Ithleen's right to continue sharing in the explorations.

Robinaire arrived back shortly after Spen departed again. The girl was pale and nervous, but determined. For once, she was not fashionably dressed, but wearing slightly scruffy slacks and blouse.

Mayne greeted her with his warm smile, and a bit of her tension dissolved. "We'll go right away, Robinaire. It won't be so bad, really, you know. Just in and out. You'll scarcely even see the place."

Robinaire said nothing. Her hands were clenched.

Mayne took out his rifkey, glancing at the others, who had now gathered around, then back at Robinaire. "Can you bear to land near Zar Haughn's lab or palace, or whatever it is? Not in it, just near enough for me to take a quick look? If not, we'll go to another continent, but I'll be going back later, to scout the place, and it would save me time it I could go straight to it when I return."

Now that the moment was upon her, Robinaire spoke out of the blankness of despair. "It doesn't matter."

"Good girl." He smiled at her again, but for once she did not respond. She had the look of one who awaits the knife of sacrifice. Mayne was touched, and vowed silently that she would enjoy her party whatever he suffered from it.

"Hold the rifkey, then, and think of Zar Haughn's world. Of the building you were in. Think of being outside that building, under cover, just near enough to see it. Can you hold that thought?"

"Yes." She repeated his words.

"Now think of our going there." He led her finger through the pattern. Nothing happened. He said gently, "Let's try again, Robinaire," and prompted her through the procedure again. There was still no result.

He consulted Jonno and Ithleen by glance.

"She can't will it," said Ithleen.

Robinaire gave them such a look of despair that even Jonno was moved to say, "We believe you're trying, Robinaire. We can control our actions, but we can't force ourselves to want something."

Mayne turned back to Robinaire. "How about trying to send me there alone, the way you sent Ithleen off?"

Holding the rifkey himself this time, Mayne again led Robinaire through the pattern; and again they achieved nothing.

Still gently, Mayne said, "Come now, Robinaire, you can't mind if I go. Just

think of Zar Haughn's world. Anywhere on it, and will me to be there. If you can do this, you don't have to go at all."

He glanced at Ithleen. "You said we can accept passive transplacement."

Ithleen nodded, and he turned back to Robinaire. "Suppose we try it this way, Robinaire: put your hand on the rifkey and think about Zar Haughn's building. You don't have to will anything, and the rifkey won't operate; it will just, I hope, set itself. Then while you hold the thought, I'll do the willing."

That method also failed. Robinaire, near tears, cried, "I do want to help!"

Jonno said, "How about trying hypnosis, to remove her fear?"

Mayne hesitated. "That can be dangerous to the subject. It can interfere with necessary caution."

"Not if you're very careful to specify only one particular fear, and especially if you make the command valid for only a limited time."

Mayne considered, then nodded decisively. "Robinaire? Are you willing?"

"Oh, yes. Then I can get it over with!"

Mayne tranced her and told her that, until the transplacement was completed, she would cease to fear the trip to the Zar's world.

"Now," he told her as, alert again but relaxed, she waited for instructions, "think of wanting us to go to Haughn's world, within sight of his headquarters." She nodded.

He held the rifkey within her reach. "Keep thinking of the grounds outside Zar Haughn's headquarters. Now put your fingers here." He shifted his own to the end of the rifkey to make room for her. "Now think of us going there while you touch the dots I showed you with your other hand."

Frowning with concentration but no longer looking anxious, Robinaire followed his instructions.

And finally, they faded from sight.

Twenty seconds later Mayne's crumpled body reappeared, alone, on the lab floor.

CHAPTER 16

Interrogation

"Jonnan!" Ithleen cried and dropped to her knees beside him. With quick hands she examined him. "Unconscious. No visible wounds. I'll take him to the medics." She took his rifkey from his hand and slipped it into his pocket.

"Where's Robinaire?" asked Davith.

The others suddenly realized that she had not returned.

"We'll have to get her back," Jonno said. He sighed, took out his rifkey, and traced the pattern. Nothing happened.

"Check it," said Ithleen as she pulled out her own rifkey. "Follow me to Geode." She touched out the pattern, and she and Mayne vanished.

Jonno took her suggestion and arrived at her location in Ciath's office as the medical officer was coming across to look at the patient. He tried again to transplace to wherever Robinaire was, and again got nowhere.

"I'll keep trying," he said; "but it looks as if we'll have to wait to see if Jonnan can tell us anything."

Ciath summoned a robot gurney, and moved Mayne into the adjacent hospital. Ithleen and Jonno sat in silence in a waiting room, taking turns, periodically, to make vain attempts to transplace to Robinaire. Finally the chief medic came back out to them.

"Cee, what's happened to him?" demanded Ithleen.

"Neuro-shock," said Ciath. "Only a stunning dose. He should come out of it in two or three hours. Did a piece of equipment blow up?"

"We don't know what happened. He went to the world of an enemy, and immediately reappeared unconscious, brought back by the emergency homing mode of his rifkey because he was hurt."

"Immediately? Must have been a weapon, then. I've only a few accident cases in the records; but the effect seems to be the same."

Jonno put in, "Ithleen, didn't Jonnan tell us that Haughn's men used some kind of stunning pistol the first time they appeared?"

"Yes, and there was no permanent harm." She breathed a sigh of relief, then quickly added, "Can there be cumulative damage?"

Ciath considered. "Not from stunning-power shocks, unless they are very close together and prolonged or many."

"Jonno, would you like to go back and tell Van and Davith that he's going to be all right? I'll wait here till he recovers."

Jonno nodded. "I'll come back and see if he can tell us anything."

Ciath told Ithleen, "We can't hasten his recovery; but we can ease the pain of coming out of it."

"When will he be able to talk to us coherently?"

"As I said, it'll be two or three hours before he's conscious again, but I'll want him to rest before you bother him with any questions or problems."

"I hate to say this, but it's urgent we talk to him as soon as possible, even if he isn't fully recovered. There may be another life at stake, someone who matters a lot to him."

Ciath hesitated, then said, "I'll call you as soon as he's conscious."

Eventually her call came, and Ithleen and Jonno entered the treatment room to find Mayne conscious but still enclosed by the diagnostic and care machines.

"Jonnan, what happened?" Ithleen demanded.

"I was about to ask you the same question." He spoke with some difficulty.

Jonno asked, "Do you remember transplacing to Haughn's world with Robinaire?"

"Yes. We saw..." Mayne broke off remembering, "Robinaire! Is she all right?"

"We don't know. She didn't reappear."

Mayne tried to sit up, but was held down by the machines. "Didn't you go after her?" he cried incredulously.

"I tried to, but my rifkey wouldn't take me to her," Jonno said. "We've continued to try, but we can't get to her."

"Ciath says you were stunned by a neuro-shock weapon," Ithleen said. "Haughn's men?"

"The rifkey wouldn't have put us down where hostile people could see us."

Jonno suggested, "Maybe it got confused because Robinaire was helping you to operate it."

Mayne shook his head. "In a wexter device the danger avoidance would override all other considerations."

Ciath stepped forward and released him from the medical machines, then helped him to sit up. "You're to take it easy," she ordered.

Mayne thanked her and then ignored her. "Haughn's men could have come upon us immediately after we completed materializing. But it seems coincidental, which is always suspect. Besides, it was too fast. If they had been close enough to beam us down before I had more than a glimpse of the place, surely they were close enough for the rifkey to refuse to operate."

"As mine does now," agreed Jonno. "It's clearly too dangerous to transplace to Robinaire and so it won't allow us to. Jonnan, you could transplace to the world now and not only to Robinaire, but we risk the same thing happening if we try before we know what happened the last time."

"A mechanical trap of some sort?" suggested Ithleen.

Jonno deduced, "You must have been holding the rifkey in our standard manner, with a finger on the emergency homing end; so it automatically snatched you home the instant you were hurt. It couldn't take Robinaire along because you weren't conscious long enough to will it."

Mayne nodded to that, but objected, "A trap would be even greater coincidence. Haughn can't have traps set on every square meter within sight of his building. Even if he was worried about being traced after his second raid, he'd have no idea where or when we'd show up."

"Psychics!" cried Ithleen. "Precogs!"

Mayne said slowly, "Then he'll know of every attempt we make to get into his universe."

Jonno immediately turned to the practical. "Can human psychics be jammed?"

Mayne shook his head in uncertainty. "I don't know enough about them. My work has been almost entirely in pure psionics and machine-augmented psi."

"Our psi amplifiers: could we try to work out a reverse effect, and shield ourselves with it?"

"We can try to jury-rig something. But how do we project its effect across universes?"

"I'll ask the wexters if they can," said Ithleen, taking out her recorder.

When she re-pocketed her recorder, signalling the end of her concentration, Mayne reached for his rifkey. "Let's get back and collect up my data so we can start work on that shield."

Ciath made a protesting gesture. Ithleen said, "No use, Cee, the matter's urgent."

"Listen, sib, if you people don't take better care of yourselves, I'm going to have to expand my hospital!"

Ithleen smiled. "We'll do our best to stay whole, I promise. Be seeing you."

"I expect you will!" was Ciath's parting shot.

Van and Davith were still at the lab, though by now it was mid evening. Ithleen quickly told them the current situation, while Mayne called up the data on his original amplifier that might be helpful for the shield.

Jonno and Ithleen joined him on linked computers, and they began going over those bits of theory, scant and rather vague as they were. As they set up, Jonno asked Ithleen, "What was that Ciath called you?"

"Called? Oh, sib. Cee's one of my socilings."

"That's an explanation?"

"Sorry. She's a sociological sibling: we were brought up in the same family. We also happen to be genetic cousins; but of course, I think of her as a big sister. She's seven years older and has always mothered me, even after she graduated from the family." Ithleen grinned. "I love her in spite of her frequent attempts to practice matchmaking on me!"

"I'd like to hear some of your background, when we have time."

"And I more of yours and Jonnan's."

As Mayne had earlier told Ithleen, he had worked largely by inspired guess and an experimenter's feel for the right design when it came to psi;

and Jonno's experience had been similar. No one on the ISC worlds really had any clear idea of psionic theory.

"That's all that's been hypothesized so far," Mayne concluded, and said to Ithleen, "I know your world doesn't have psionics, but you told me your own work related to it, that the diaphane fluxate is psi energy, or the source of it. Can you tie our hypotheses into that?"

She nodded, but with doubt in her expression. "My equations are for basic theory, not practical applications. Remember, no one in Geode believed psi was real, until the wexter came, and even then we didn't hope to use it ourselves, until you brought your TKM data to us. You've found a way to tap into the fluxate, so you know far more about practical application than I do."

"Nevertheless, can you give us a crash course in psi theory? We've discussed its ideas, but now we need specifics."

"You'll have to be ready to accept some ideas that physics considers impossible, because we're dealing with a different reality."

Mayne shrugged.

Ithleen plunged in. "I've had to invent terms and notation; if I translate them into familiar physics terms, they're going to sound like infinite velocities, reverse energy, action at a distance, and other forbidden concepts, so be ready to suspend judgement, remembering it's only how they appear when looked at from a conventional viewpoint - just as light from a moving star can appear superluminal due to its angle of approach, even though it isn't really exceeding the speed of light."

"Caveat noted."

Switching to her own computer, which was programmed to handle her new terms, she began showing them definitions, then equations, explaining as she went along. The plennors, jotting the terms into computers prepped to accept graphics by stylus, pressed her closely with questions and challenges, and helped her to translate their own work into her terms. After much work by all three, Mayne said, "Well, if psi energy really works the way these equations say, it looks as if it would be possible to reverse the effect. But that wouldn't be sufficient; it would merely damp out the psi ability of a user of the machine. What we want is to project a dampening field throughout a surrounding area."

Jonno nodded. "And simple interference wouldn't work, either. We need something unnoticeable; otherwise we advertise our presence, and we're back where we started. We seem to require a device which affects psi and psionics, yet isn't psionic itself, or can shield itself against its own effect."

Mayne caught at that idea. "Perhaps we can make it along the lines of our augmented lasers, so that it psionically accumulates energy while its broadcast is shut off, storing it inside the shield around its field generator."

"Can we make a shield?"

"With the understanding Ithleen has given us, I think we could, eventually; but since we need it now, we'll have to ask the wexters. Their whole lives are based on psi and psionics, so they're bound to have efficient shields. Since it's within our near-future level of technology and we need it to get at the threat they want stopped, I think they should be willing to give us the information."

"More likely the device without the information," Ithleen said. "Maybe they'll even have something ready-made which they can lend us."

Mayne answered, "I presume that most of their devices are designed to mesh with their own natural psi, so we couldn't use them. Remember, everything they've given us so far they've had to make specifically for us; and it takes them a while to figure out something simple enough for us to operate, with our low-psi minds. So even if we have to ask them for the component parts, as with our pentools, it'll probably be faster if we work out a general design ourselves. Ithleen, when you reported our problem to the wexters, did you stress its urgency?"

"Yes. I expect Spen will show up as soon as the wexters happen to pick up the recording. That could be soon. They'll be wanting to know whether you've located Haughn's world."

"Then let's get busy with what designing we can do ourselves. I think we may as well go back to Geode; we'll probably have to use a TKM, if only to test what we get from the wexters, and we haven't finished replacing the one Haughn stole from here."

Ithleen explained to Jonno, "Our engineers have already constructed a second one for Geode; and in gratitude for building us the first one, they have given Mayne first priority on both our equipment and their services."

"We may well need their help," said Jonnan. "Very few devices work right in their first model. Even with wexter parts, we'll probably have to do a lot of testing, second-guessing, and adjusting."

"What about us, Plennor?" Davith asked. "You can take us along."

Mayne shook his head. "As you just heard, there'll be plenty of help; and I still need you two here to keep up appearances, in case that man Polminander is still interested in us. You carry on here as usual, while we're gone. If I need you for anything, I'll come here for you, or phone a message to your recorders if it's after work hours."

The technicians reluctantly agreed; and the three scientists transplaced back to Geode.

When Spen came, ne dashed their hopes of a ready-made solution, and confirmed their estimate of the rest of the situation. "We have no method of projecting a general psychic disruption into a universe. Our principles approve defence but not offence; so our research has been biased. And, with your psi-limited minds, you could not operate any of our portable shield devices. Our purely psionic ones are not portable. To modify any of them would take longer than making something new for you. Can you supply us with exact specification of your needs?"

"Yes, we've been working on that. We need either information or working parts to provide energy, shielding, and the actual disruption activity," said Mayne, proffering their detailed notes.

"The energy accumulator we have already adapted for you: we will scale-up the one we constructed for your lasers. The shielding we can design without much delay, applying what we have learned while modifying other items for your use. The disruptor function, however, will require much effort, as it is not the sort of thing we have ever considered making — we use, modify, and shield psi energy; we have never had occasion to nullify it completely. But since this situation is ultimately linked with a possible need for defence, I will likely be able to get high priority on the matter. I cannot estimate a time for you; but I will inform you of our progress."

***

Robinaire had regained consciousness to find herself strapped into a reclining chair, and with a number of electrodes attached to her head and body. Through the dwindling haze of pain she heard Porduc — the sneering man from before — phoning Haughn to say she was awake. By the time she had fully recovered, the Zar had arrived.

He wasted no time. "I want information. You are attached to a machine that will tell me if you lie. If you refuse to answer we will use this other machine, which applies a stimulus directly to the nerves. Since it doesn't immediately damage the body, it can go on as long as we wish. Do you understand?"

"Yes," said Robinaire, too frightened even to protest.

Haughn stood over the controls and readouts of his polygraph, to calibrate it. "What's your name?"

"Robinaire Filyk."

"You're an operator for a psionic machine?"

"No, I'm not a machine operator."

"What are you, then?"

"I'm — I'm an actress."

"Then what were you doing running a psionic machine the first time we took you?"

"I wasn't running it. It was being shown to me. I was just visiting the lab."

Porduc said, "We don't need the polygraph to say that's a lie. She came here deliberately this time."

"Yes, but she doesn't have to be a psionics operator. An actress would be a good choice if some group in that world wanted to send a spy here to find out something about us. Who are you working for?"

"Well, I'm not really working yet. I'm just between schools, actually."

Haughn rephrased his query: "Who sent you here?"

"Plennor Mayne."

"And who is Plennor Mayne?"

"Why he's one of the most famous men in the world!"

"*What* is he?"

"He's a scientist. He knows everything."

Haughn snorted. "And who does he work for?"

"The ISC. The International Science Complex."

"And who runs that?"

"A group of scientists who are just called the Council."

"How did you get into this world?"

"I don't know how it's done. I'm not a scientist."

"Porduc, give her intensity twenty for five seconds."

Porduc flicked on a switch. Robinaire cried out and twisted in the chair.

"How did you get here?"

"Please, I don't understand it..."

"Thirty."

Robinaire screamed and writhed.

"Cut!" snapped Haughn. "I said five seconds."

"I'm sorry, I didn't hear you," defended Porduc.

Haughn turned back to Robinaire and his polygraph. "What means did you use to come to this world?"

"A thing called a rifkey. I don't understand it!"

The room phone rang. At Haughn's gesture, Porduc went over and switched it on, revealing the features of a severe-looking woman. After a brief conversation, Porduc turned and called back, "The keepers say the precogs are onto something, but very confused."

Haughn considered, then said, "Tell them I'll come there. It'll give this girl some time to think about the consequences of stubbornness." He glanced at his watch, said, "I'll be back in twenty minutes," and left.

Porduc, also looking at his watch, scurried back across to the nerve stimulator. "Twenty minutes. Say fifteen to be safe, that's a thousand seconds." He adjusted controls. "If I start at ten, that's... one notch more every thirty seconds..." He set more dials and switches, then looked up to grin at her and, with a flourish, flick the on-switch.

"Oh, please don't! I don't know anymore."

Porduc laughed. "I'm not asking you anything!" He hovered near her, watching as she writhed, and listening to her pleas as they turned to screams, and eventually to weak moans.

"Porduc! Turn that thing off!" Haughn had returned before his estimated time. "You're wasting her."

Porduc instantly obeyed, but whined petulantly, "Well, she isn't important."

"Anything to which I am giving attention is important; and I will not have the effectiveness of this method lessened by the stupidity of a sadistic fool! Give her a restorative injection. I will deal with you later. And if your interference has delayed my questioning. I *will* remember it."

The threat was spoken in a quiet, almost conversational tone; but Porduc's remnant of excitement wilted, and again he scurried to obey. Robinaire shrank from his nearness as Porduc touched the injector against her arm. She moaned, "Oh, I'm glad you're going to die!"

Porduc's attempt at a sneering laugh came out as a nervous giggle. "Wishing won't make it so," he said, and returned to his post at the nerve machine.

Haughn was regarding Robinaire with puzzled interest, but said only, "Are you ready to tell us about this rifkey?"

"I don't understand it. I don't know any science."

"How do you operate it? What did you do when you came here?"

"I just touched the rifkey and thought about this place."

"So it's psionic. Do you have to use human psychics as well, the way we do, or does your rifkey work on its own?"

"On its own."

"Do you use psychics for anything?"

"No."

"Everything's machines?"

"Yes."

"But you had no equipment with you, and no time to get rid of any. So you were able to come here without bringing even a control unit with you?"

"I don't remember anything about arriving except seeing a big building in front of me. I didn't bring anything along."

"How did you expect to get back?"

"Plennor Mayne would take me."

"So, he can send you without coming himself, but he has to come in order to fetch you back."

Since the plennor was neither captive nor rescuing her, Robinaire accepted Haughn's assumption. She was sure he would come for her, but she was worried about how long it might take him.

Haughn switched to another angle. "Why did Mayne send you here?"

"So he could find your world."

"How could he send you if he didn't know where the world is?"

Robinaire reached back to a memory of the plennor's explanation, and quoted, "We can go back deliberately to any one we've visited before, even if it was by chance the first time."

"So he could return you here, and then track you down?"

It amounted to that, so Robinaire said, "Yes."

Porduc, with a touch of his blustering manner back, put in, "Maybe we'd better get rid of her again, quick."

"Not so fast. We know now that this man Mayne's ability to move or trace between universes is limited." He spoke to Robinaire again. "How did you get back to your own world from Aresette?"

"Plennor Mayne came for me."

"Why? What use are you to him?"

"I don't know that I'm any *use*," said Robinaire.

"Then why would he bother fetching you back?"

"Because he's kind, and I think he likes me, too."

"Good! Either one is a weakness. Is he the one who built those experimental machines I took from that lab?"

"Yes."

"Then he *is* brilliant. I could use that mind; and with his weaknesses. We can bait a trap with her. But — how powerful a force does he have behind him? This ISC, how large an organization is it?"

"I don't know. It doesn't have the size or population of a Region, but everyone thinks of it as if it were actually a Region."

"So your ISC is small but powerful. Does its Council control the scientific resources of your world?"

Robinaire thought for a moment. "I suppose it does. Most new discoveries come from ISC, and its threat to cut off a Region from the distribution list gives it a lot of bargaining power."

"Possibly a covert dictatorship," Haughn interpreted. "Is Mayne one of the leaders of this Council?"

"No. He just works for it," Robinaire answered in the present tense, as she had been asked. Mayne was no longer on the council.

"Probably run by people with less brain power but more sense. Have they ordered him to look for me, or is it merely a private feud because I took his equipment?"

"They don't give him orders. He can do whatever he likes, as long as ISC gets the results of it."

"A semi-freelance agent with a large staff?"

She counted. "No, there's four."

"Only four?" he repeated, incredulously. "Nobody does modern research with only a handful of people."

"He can give orders to other labs to do what he wants, or get more to come into his, if he wants."

"I see. And could he also call up a large force to invade this world?"

Robinaire remembered the plennor's wish to avoid inter-world invasions in either direction. "He doesn't want to do that."

"But he could, if the ISC wanted it? There are armed forces available in your world?"

"The Regions have armies; and," remembering school lessons again, "they'd all like the ISC to join with them in a war if they dared to start one."

"Which confirms that the ISC already has the top power," Haughn deduced. "So whether it comes into this matter depends on its policy, or on Mayne's decision to continue to keep this secret, as he seems to be doing. Probably hoping to gain some advantage over them, to reach a position of greater power for himself."

He turned to Porduc. "Take her over to a cell in the Admin block for the rest of the night. Put a clairvoyant and a precog near her, with orders to watch her constantly. Four guards, with stunners and handguns, also on shift."

He glanced at Robinaire and added, "Female guards. And line up a team of psi technicians for tomorrow. I want a full set of tests made on this girl."

"What for? She can't be psychic. She's not mentally deficient," Porduc said.

"That's the way I thought when we first saw her. But she's not of our universe. In her world, psi powers may *not* be restricted to the mentally limited."

Porduc shrugged. "Okay, I'll have the techs here in the morning. What if this guy Mayne shows up in the meanwhile?"

"According to the precogs just now, he'll make an attempt tomorrow night, but he'll flee back to his own universe without accomplishing anything. But we're also going to have some other kind of trouble, but the psychics can't seem to sort out what it will be. Maybe it's that foolish Resistance movement again."

"Why don't you wipe them out?"

"It gives the discontented a harmless way to let off steam. We'll keep at the precogs; perhaps they'll get a clearer idea as the time gets nearer."

***

The next morning Robinaire was brought back to the psi lab for the tests. Haughn told her, "Some of the tests are passive; others require you to make an effort. Every time you fail one of the active tests, Porduc will turn on the nerve stimulator."

"Oh, please don't. I can't do any psychic stuff."

"How do you know? Have you ever been tested?"

"Well, no, but..."

The tests were exhaustive and exhausting. As the hours went by, Robinaire's tormenters were required with increasing frequency to give her restoratives and respites. The testing went on remorselessly through most of the day.

***

The technicians' report disappointed Haughn. They had found Robinaire's memory talent; but that was of no use in his quest for improved transplacing methods, nor even of use in his present ones. On nearly everything else she was rated no better than average. They did find a small and erratic talent in precognition, but it was entirely uncontrollable, and operable only in matters pertaining to herself.

"So she's quite useless," said Porduc, with the satisfaction of one who had guessed right.

"As I said before, we'll keep her as bait. Perhaps Mayne has figured out a way to detect the stunner trap we rigged the last time and that's why it's taken him so long to make this attempt. We know Mayne is going to try to come here this evening but will be frightened off by something before we can get him so there's no use setting up another stunner trap. We must rely instead on his desire to get to the girl."

"What about the trouble later tonight? Will that be him again?"

"No, the precogs are sure they don't see him coming again tonight. The psychics seem to think the trouble will be serious, so if it's those ridiculous Resistance people, they must have got aid from one of the unallied countries, maybe several if the matter's really serious; one alone's too small to worry about."

He considered for a moment. "I suppose I'd better have a couple of the current Resistance leaders locked up, then thrown out again, to make their followers think we've turned them. It won't kill off the movement, but it should interfere with their immediate plans, and might keep them disorganized long enough for us to deal with this outworlder Mayne."

"Shall I take the girl back to her cell now?"

"No. I presume this Resistance attack will be against the Admin building. If they should get in, they'd probably try to take away anyone they found in the cells. We can lock the girl in an office here. But I want her to stay under constant guard. Put two female guards in the room with her and two male guards outside. Stunners and pistols for all of them. And I want our best clairvoyant and precog with the guards outside the girl's door."

"Xabis and Grellor?"

"Yes. Wait, I don't want the precog's attention exclusively on the girl. Put Xabis with the guards and take Grellor to your office, with a keeper, and check on him every hour to see if he's come up with anything clearer on the night's trouble."

"You want me here all night, then?"

"You're to patrol the building. I'll give you half a dozen Zarsmen. I shall take charge in Admin myself. That's the likeliest focus of attack. But they might aim a diversionary attack here. Each of us will have a telepath constantly at hand so we can communicate. And keep yours in touch with Xabis. If anything so much as a sneeze disturbs her, send me word by the telepath, call out your Zarsman patrol, and go investigate immediately."

"Why so much fuss over the girl? Even if any Resistance fools get in here, they won't know she's of any importance to you."

"If they see guards, they'll guess."

"Then why not just put the guards inside with her?"

"I want a defence in depth. I don't expect Mayne to get in tonight, but I'm not taking any chances. Psychics are never dependable, even when they're sure of something, which is rare enough! So keep alert for anything."

CHAPTER 17

Foray

Early on Tuesday morning, as Robinaire was undergoing the beginning of Haughn's psi tests, on another world Ithleen and the plennors were working with components supplied by the wexters. They worked all day and in the end had come up with a plan as well as a means to carry it out.

Ithleen outlined her plan to them, "Haughn can prepare his traps only where his precogs tell him there'll be an invasion attempt. If we could overload his precogs, he couldn't cover all the ground."

"And you've got a way to do that?" Mayne asked.

"A risky one. Can you build a time-delay on-switch into your disruptor?"

"Of course."

"Then we make a long series of random, abortive landings, setting our rifkeys for instant transplacement back home each time, so Haughn gets no chance to stun us. Somewhere through the series, we drop off the disruptor, set it to turn on and blank out its area to psi at a later time. After we seem to give up, we transplace back into the dead area around the disruptor."

"I'll have to place it at the first jump that puts me in an obscure corner or unused room," Mayne said. "There should be a lot of offices and storerooms not in use at night."

"Is it night there?" Jonno asked. "We don't know what time zone Haughn's in."

Mayne considered. "I got a brief glance when Robinaire and I transplaced to his world. It was late afternoon here and Haughn's world had a noon-high sun, putting him three or four hours behind us."

Ithleen said, "And if we've outmaneuvered his precogs, he shouldn't see any reason for alarm tonight."

The others concurred, so at around four hundred hours on Wednesday, they put their plan into effect.

The disruptor had been fitted into a backpack which Mayne carried by its straps, instead of wearing it, for quick release. Mayne took each of the others on their first trip, who immediately began to randomly transplace in and out of Haughn's world, in and around his headquarters. The random program had been worked out by a computer. It was nerve-wracking work, particularly until Mayne had dropped off the disruptor; but all went well as far as they could tell.

***

The three of them transplaced together to the location of the disruptor. Mayne took the disruptor in the backpack with them so it could continue to cover their movements.

After walking through various hallways, they eventually found themselves surveying a large laboratory room. In among a crowded grouping of smaller apparatus, Mayne spotted his own stolen equipment, partly dismantled, the cores lying together in a small group on a countertop.

Taped to each piece of equipment and on top of the core pile was a sheet of notepaper imprinted with the words, "From the lab of Dr Perine Cazl" plus a stack of Mayne's manuals, neatly squared up and topped by another sheet of paper addressed to "Haughn."

Mayne spoke in a low tone, as he stuffed the printouts and manuals into an outside pocket of his backpack, and reshouldered the pack. "There's too much of my equipment here to transplace in one trip; but if there's time after we find Robinaire, I'll try to come back here and fuse these cores. Also bits of the auxiliary parts. That might confuse the analyzers."

"Good idea," Ithleen said.

"Let's keep going."

Peering into a corridor on the far side of the group of lab rooms, they saw two guards and a psychic, sitting facing a closed door. The guards were bored but wakeful, and were keeping the psychic awake by pokes and pinches whenever she dozed off.

The three scientists drew back, and Mayne murmured, "Do you think it could be Robinaire? The fact we couldn't transplace to her suggests she may have guards with her steadily."

Ithleen said, "Haughn may have learned from her that you rescued her before. If so, he could guess you'd come for her again."

Mayne considered the situation. "We can't rush the guards, they may have an alarm system, and they're too alert for us to reach them before they could use it. The only hope I see is to knock them out with your psiproje, Jonno."

"It'll be tricky, swinging from one to another, so they all doze off at the same time and don't notice the others falling over. And you'll have to turn off the disruptor before the psiproje will work, which means that if there's a clairvoyant alert anywhere in the building, ne'll spot us."

"The psychic that's here may be the only one awake at this hour."

"If she's a telepath, she could yell into someone's dreams."

They didn't have any other options, so Jonno took out his psiproje and, holding in his mind the multiverse symbol and the effect he wanted, he willed the projector on as he nodded to Mayne, who turned off the disruptor. The three scientists held their breaths. The guards and the psychic yawned, stirred uneasily, then gently slumped off their chairs.

Mayne switched the disruptor on again and they rushed forward. The door was locked mechanically, and a quick search of the guards' pockets produced no key that would operate the lock.

"What are you up to, out there?" called a woman's voice from inside the room, as they vainly tried the keys the guards happened to have.

Mayne answered instantly, pitching his voice to urgency. "Don't be alarmed, but there's a fire in the lab. We've got to get you out, in case it spreads. Can you unlock the door?"

"No!" There was alarm in her voice. "Is it bad?"

"Not yet, but we can't get it under control."

Another woman's voice joined the first at the door. "There's a telepath somewhere keeping tabs on the clairvoyant out there. Just make sure she understands the situation, and Zar Haughn will bring the key. Have you pulled the alarm? I don't hear it."

"We've called in, and got everybody else out. No need for a racket. But we haven't time to wait. Stand back. We're going to cut the door open."

Mayne signalled to Jonno and Ithleen. Jonno readied his psiproje while Mayne kept his hand on the disruptor switch; Ithleen began to cut the lock with her laser.

They realized from the remark about the psychics that an alarm had already been given, by the clairvoyant's very unconsciousness. Whether they had minutes or seconds left they could not tell. Time had been spent talking to the inner guards; time was being used by the cutting of the lock. There was no way they could hurry.

Ithleen worked carefully, not letting haste require repeat effort, and wasting no photon, knowing her power was limited until the disruptor was turned off again.

Finally she was through. As she crouched out of the line of fire Jonnan turned off the disruptor and kicked the door inward.

As soon as Jonno could see the guards and keep his aim away from Robinaire, he fired the invisible beam at the guards. The two women crumpled before they could lift their stunners.

Mayne switched the disruptor back on to blank their area to telepathic probing while Ithleen crossed to where Robinaire was now sitting up, only half-awake, on a cot. As Ithleen spoke to her, taking out her rifkey, Robinaire cried, "No!" and tried to scramble away. "Please! Not again! I can't do those things!"

"Robinaire! It's..."

"No!" Dazed and confused, Robinaire struggled. "I won't go back to that room!"

Running steps came to an abrupt halt outside the room. The would-be rescuers whirled to see Porduc grab a guard's stun pistol, swing it up at them, and pull the trigger.

CHAPTER 18

Information

Nothing happened. Startled, Porduc bent his cropped head over the stunner's bulky pack and began to check it. A guard who had arrived with him raised his pistol, and the three scientists dived for cover behind the furniture of the room, Ithleen pulling Robinaire down with her. Mayne lased the light fixture in the office, and Jonno drove the guard back with a quick flash from his own laser.

Porduc, turning away from the pack, was again trying to beam them down; and the guard was firing blindly into the dimness of the room.

"Let's transplace out, fast!" cried Jonno.

"We can't," said Mayne. "The disruptor is blocking off that stunner. If I turn off the disruptor, we'll be unconscious before we can transplace."

"Ithleen, are you ready with Robinaire?"

"Yes. She's all right now she's heard your voice."

"Jonno, will you take along that psychic out there with you?"

At his affirmative, Mayne continued, "I'm going to try to burn that stunner's power pack. Be ready."

Mayne raised himself from cover and fired his laser at the pack of the only stunner in use. At the same time Jonno fired again at the guard, throwing off his aim as he shot at Mayne.

It took a moment for the laser to burn into the vitals of the power pack. In that moment Porduc leaned over it again in angry frustration at its non-operation; smoke poured out, then suddenly the pack exploded in a searing gout of light, heat, and kinetic energy. Porduc was lifted and smashed against the corridor wall, his neck snapping as he hit head first.

Swirls of smoke and bits of wall and ceiling filled the air, and pyrotechnics flamed and roared up from the pack.

"Go!" yelled Mayne above the racket, and switched off the disruptor. He and Jonno leaped out into the hall, wasting no glance behind. Justifying their trust, Ithleen also squandered no time checking on their safety, but whisked herself and Robinaire back to Mayne's lab.

The guard, half-dazed by the explosion, and trying to shoot at both plennors at once, fell to a swinging chop of Mayne's hand. Voices could be heard approaching the corridor, but they came from the far end away from the labs: Mayne sprinted the other way in the direction of his stolen equipment.

Jonno, pausing on a quick thought, grabbed the second stunner and its pack, then crouched by the clairvoyant's unconscious body. Counting seconds, to give Mayne all the time he dared, Jonno waited until the approaching guards burst into the corridor, then startled them back with a laser beam turned high enough to hurt. They recovered and began to return fire from their doorway. Some of the bullets came uncomfortably close; as Jonno's count reached three minutes, he activated his rifkey and vanished with the psychic and the stunner.

Reaching the main lab, Mayne saw the psychic and his keeper timidly peering into the room from their doorway. Neither were armed, so Mayne ignored them. Still at a run, he crossed to where his own apparatus lay spread on a workbench. He aimed the recharged laser at the pile of cores, fusing the immit-holding structures into featureless lumps. Then he turned his attention to the various frameworks and destroyed random connections there.

By the time he had finished, he could hear the pack of guards pounding up the long corridor towards him. He jammed his laser into a pocket and yanked out his rifkey.

There was a sudden tug at his sleeve. He whirled, startled, for his ears had told him that the guards were not yet quite to the lab.

It was the psychic, his face slightly animated in an urgency that contrasted with his non-descript appearance, receding hair of indeterminate shade, clothes which had lost whatever colour they had had through innumerable washings: institutional garb.

"Come, too!" he cried.

"Come, then!" Mayne pressed the homing control of his rifkey. The guards' bullets slashed through his fading image as he and the psychic dematerialized.

He met the anxious faces of the others as he appeared in his lab. They had known it would take him time to destroy his equipment, but had felt the wait drawing out painfully.

"Jonnan! You made it!"

"With a bonus," he answered. "He volunteered to come."

"Wonderful world. Wouldn't tell," said the psychic.

"That must be the world the wexters have picked out," deduced Jonno. "The precogs must have seen it, and risked keeping Haughn in ignorance. We'd better send another message to the wexters."

Ithleen told Mayne, "We've already reported to them about the first psychic. Considering the intensity of their interest in the matter, I expect Spen will arrive any minute."

"So might Haughn," said Mayne grimly. "He seems to have been away while we were there; but when he learns what we've done, he may come to try to recapture his psychics or to take vengeance. He has this universe located, but presumably not either of yours yet. We'll go to Geode. No need to dodge questions there." He glanced at his watch, "Nearly six-thirty. Take everyone, will you? I want to call Van and Davith and tell them to keep clear of this lab until further notice."

While Ithleen and Jonno relayed the other three people and the psionic equipment and printouts to Geode, Mayne made his calls, taking time to be sure the abruptly-awakened technicians understood his orders. Confident that they would obey, and cautiously oblique, he did not give a full explanation, adding only, "Robinaire is with us again. We're all leaving to avoid other company. I'll probably contact you in a week or so."

Mayne followed his colleagues to Geode. As he dropped his backpack in Ithleen's lounge, he finally had time to turn to Robinaire and ask, "Are you all right? I can't say how sorry I am."

"Is Porduc really dead?" she demanded.

"The man with the stunner?" Mayne pushed aside the vivid, unpleasant memory. "Yes, he must have been killed instantly."

"Oh, I'm glad! He was the one who — who —" She clung to him, shaking.

The clairvoyant, Xabis, whom Jonno had put on the sofa, was beginning to stir, and soon sat up. Her face, a milky brown shade with a gentle beauty, was barely lined, but her black hair had sprinkles of grey in it. Her clothes, like those of the other psychic, were a drab shirt and pants; their only individuality was a flower drawn in pencil on the lapel by an unskilled hand. She took in her new environment with her psychic sense, and said only one word, with deep satisfaction: "Safe!"

"Haughn's psychics are obviously willing enough to leave him," Jonno remarked. "That may help us get the rest of them for the wexters."

Spen appeared then. "You have two. I will examine their minds."

The others waited in silence while ne communicated with the Kinnasooran psychics, then returned to general broadcast again: "You have brought back Haughn's chief clairvoyant as well as his only reasonably dependable precog! This is excellent progress. We will examine them at greater length, and then send them to the world we have chosen for them. I will return with whatever further information we learn. "

All three vanished.

"Well," said Mayne into the sudden feeling of let-down. "Robinaire, do you feel you could tell us all that happened to you?"

"I — I guess so."

She was still in the shelter of his arm, and he led her to the sofa and made sure she was comfortable. "Let's get this recorded for ourselves, too," he suggested.

For once she was not quite letter-perfect. She hesitated now and then, and her voice grew unsteady as she told of the use of the pain machine in her questioning, and especially of Porduc's unauthorized use of it.

She continued her story until she reached Haughn's demand for a description of Mayne. "Do I have to tell you what I said, and what he said?"

"No, don't bother."

Jonno remarked, "It might be worth hearing his opinion of you. To help judge what he's liable to do about you."

Robinaire sighed and repeated Haughn's summary.

"So, he drastically misinterpreted Robinaire's description and underestimates you," Jonno said.

"Well, we don't dare count on that, so I can't see that it's useful. Go on, Robinaire."

As she concluded, Mayne said guiltily, "Robinaire, if I'd had the least idea what would happen, I'd never have asked you to go!"

Robinaire sighed, pleased with his deep concern over her. "I'm glad it's over at last. It's been awful, knowing something dreadful would happen if I went."

Ithleen looked at her and said, "But you went anyway, in spite of your precognition. You have certainly atoned for your mischief, Robinaire."

"More than atoned," agreed Mayne warmly. "You think Haughn's right, then, Ithleen? Erratic precognition?"

"It seems to have been amply demonstrated: she foretold Porduc's death, and she told us she would be hurt in Haughn's world."

Jonno said, "I think we can assume Haughn's test results are accurate, since his people appear to be experts in such testing. So Robinaire's memory is also a psi talent?"

Ithleen nodded. "It might be regarded as the reverse of precognition: an ability to re-see and re-hear things exactly as they happened. Normally, we remember only the gist of things, and our memories are actually coloured by our own feelings at the time of the happening and of the remembering. Under hypnosis, we can 'relive' scenes; but Robinaire can do it without that. We are also able to deduce some of the things that will probably happen in the future; a precog can sort out the probabilities with a precision far beyond our normal level. In Robinaire's case, it seems to need the drive of strong emotion to operate."

"What's the use of it?" cried Robinaire. "I can't stop anything. It was no use sending Ithleen away, or refusing to go to Haughn's world!"

"Wait a minute," said Jonno. "You transplaced Ithleen because of a precognition? What was it?"

Robinaire looked surprised, then confused. "I don't know. I can't see what's going to happen. I just... feel... When something bad is going to happen, or stop happening, I feel..." She struggled to express what she did not understand.

"But you foresaw Porduc's death," prodded Jonno.

"I didn't see it. I just knew he'd die and stop hurting me."

"Don't forget," put in Mayne, "she was under the extreme emotional pressure of — of torture, that time."

Concerned, Ithleen said, "Does this mean I'm a potential danger to the rest of you? If so, I'd better — move out of your lives."

"No!" said Jonno.

"Certainly not," Mayne agreed, and pointed out, "As Robinaire implied, you can't dodge an accurate precognition. If there really is a danger, it might as easily be caused by your absence as your presence. In any case, we wouldn't think of letting you give up the multiverse to try to protect us."

"Suppose it's a personal danger to Robinaire?" suggested Ithleen. "Her precognitions seem to be tied to herself."

"We'll just have to take good care of her."

"Speaking of that," said Jonno, "how are we going to protect her from Haughn? He knows she's good bait: he may come after her."

Mayne said slowly, "If we've captured Haughn's best clairvoyant, as the wexter says, it should take Haughn some time to locate this universe. Remember, the first time Robinaire was in his world, he complained that even his best clairvoyant had sent him on false trails when he was hunting for a universe with psionics. In fact, I get the impression that all he can do in a deliberate hunt is to detect transplacing activity, and trace points of origin. So Robinaire should be safe in Geode for the moment, especially if we're careful never to transplace directly between here and Haughn's world."

Ithleen said, "And now that we've got his best precog, we may be able to get into his world, and keep him busy there."

"I see one problem with the idea of keeping Robinaire here," said Jonno.

"For how long?" put in Robinaire quickly. "Friday is party day."

"I won't let you miss your party," Mayne assured her. "But if you want to stay out of Haughn's clutches, and be a help to us, I think you'd better stay here before and after. Will you?"

Robinaire yielded instantly to his look. "Okay."

Mayne asked her, "Have you any appointments in the next few days?"

"A couple."

"They you'd better record a message for each saying you've gone out of town and will contact them when you return. We'll take the recording back to your world and send it to the people concerned."

"Can't I go back myself? I want to get some clothes, and other things."

Ithleen assured her, "We can supply most of your necessities here."

"But I have a lot of things to do there before the party, such as the final fitting for my dress. If it's all right for me to go back for the party, why can't I go back long enough today to catch up on things?"

Mayne said, "By Friday we hope to have Haughn too busy to think about you. If he should find you today, you might never get to your party."

"Oh."

Again Ithleen reassured her. "You can get a dress here instead. My clothing quota is well underused." She had another thought. "Ciath and her husband are in a drama group that loves putting on costume plays. Their designers would probably be happy to make you as fancy a dress as you want."

"Oh!" said Robinaire, in quite a different tone. "Maybe I can wear something really out-of-this-world!"

"I'll ask Cee about it. Perhaps you'd like to stay with her and Leoshem while you're here? Or you could have an apartment on your own; but you might find that boring."

"I'll take the drama people."

Ithleen cautioned, "Don't expect to meet professionals. Arts and sports have to be hobbies here, things we do in our spare time. So the quality of our drama probably won't be up to your standards, and the attitude will be quite different." She looked at her watch. "It's past seven , Cee will be awake." She went to the phone, and soon called Robinaire over to accept Ciath's prompt invitation.

Since Mayne had been to Robinaire's apartment block, seeing her home from her first inadvertent expedition into the multiverse, he undertook the tricky task of getting her there unobserved by his own world. He managed to transplace them to the landing of the emergency stairs at her level, and they reached her apartment without being seen.

Robinaire hurriedly packed a suitcase while Mayne programmed her phone to send her messages to her friends, at a later hour, when it would be too late for them to call back for explanations; then Jonnan transplaced them back to Geode, with a mild sigh of relief at getting her safely beyond Haughn's immediate reach.

Mayne programmed her phone to send her messages to her friends, at a later hour, when it would be too late for them to call back for explanations; then Mayne transplaced them back to Geode, with a mild sigh of relief at getting her safely beyond Haughn's immediate reach.

They found Jonno and Ithleen looking over the stunner and power pack that Jonno had brought back from Haughn's world. Mayne nodded approval at it. "You had more presence of mind there than I did, Jonno."

"I want to know how it works," said Jonno simply.

"I'm curious myself, but didn't think of grabbing a sample."

"What's our plan of attack on Haughn?"

"We'll need information before we can make one. Perhaps the wexters will have some data for us from the two psychics soon."

"How about this Resistance group on Haughn's world? I know Haughn seems to think they're a joke, but they might at least be able to tell us more than the psychics can about Haughn's organization. Think we could we contact them?"

Ithleen suggested, "The wexters' caltor? On such a well-subdued world, it must take a definite type of strong personality to lead such a movement."

"That's an idea. We'll ask Spen the next time ne comes. Meanwhile, let's all get some rest."

***

In the evening the group gathered again in Ithleen's study.

Spen had brought information pieced together mostly from the psychics' subconscious memories of comments heard, or lessons given to them as children. There were about forty of the psychics, living in a dormitory section somewhere in the set of buildings that formed Haughn's headquarters.

A service staff of keepers looked after the psychics, and guards prevented unauthorized passage in or out of their quarters. The psychics worked under threat of pain, and all hated not only their guards and keepers but also Haughn, who had personally supervised the testing of their psi powers and their training to obedience.

The psychics differed widely in their abilities, and in their intelligence, ranging from the capacity of a particularly bright child down to incoherent, with no direct correlation between the two abilities. The precogs could sometimes locate a trouble-spot fairly closely in time but had greater difficulty with space; and they often failed completely or gave warnings for what proved to be trifles.

There was less of a striking difference between the rescued clairvoyant and the ones still in Kinnasoor than they initially thought. Her talent was stronger than theirs, particularly for detection of transplacing psionics; but given enough transplacements - especially ones involving their own universe - her fellow clairvoyants could locate the other universe eventually. The telepaths could then communicate the knowledge to the teleporters, and also to instruments made by Haughn's corps of scientists, led by the caustic but bright Doctor Perine Cazl.

Kinnasoor appeared to be a highly industrialized empire, comprising the entire western hemisphere of its world and half of the east. The clairvoyants were aware of an undercurrent of unrest among a small part of the population; occasionally the telepaths had been taken out to track down particular sources of rebellion. The psychics did not see Haughn often, but they paid attention to whatever scraps they heard about him. Though of his history they knew only school-taught basics: he had inherited the nominal monarchy of a dominant nation, taken over genuine control of it, and expanded it into an empire.

The wexter agents were surprised to learn that he allowed full freedom to the press, and nearly as much to education, apparently so sure of his grip on the empire that he was indifferent to criticism, short of urgings to rebellion.

He employed or subsidized many scientists, mostly engaged in directed research into technology; but fairly large numbers were allowed to follow their own interests in basic science to keep the wellsprings of knowledge flowing.

He was able to use his psychics to monitor those to whom he had delegated the maintenance of the laws he had set out. The penalty for abusing a position of appointed power, like that of lying in a court case, was death; and the threat of exposure by the psychics hung over all concerned, so that the psychics rarely had to be actually used to maintain honesty.

On the matter of locating Resistance personnel, Spen had said that the caltor could not in itself achieve this end; but ne thought that a combination of the device and the ability and knowledge of the clairvoyant Xabis might suffice.

"If that can be done," Mayne decided, "one or more of us can go in to make contact, and get further information. I think the Resistance movement will be the best bet, if we can make them our allies. Provided we can get to them in the first place: Haughn may be keeping an eye on them."

Ithleen considered, then said, "I think not. He's contemptuous of them, and he knows he can round them up whenever he wants to. According to Robinaire, he uses them as an occasional training exercise for his bodyguards. He had used the psychics for more important things; and now he uses them for inter-universe ventures, as well as watching for us. He'll have to limit his watch for us to immediate threats in or near his headquarters."

"We'll try then, as soon as Spen is ready." Mayne glanced at his analog. "It won't take all of us just to make contact, get information, and start the planning. Do you want to have a look at Haughn's stunner, and see if there's any hope of making a defence against it?"

Jonno nodded. "I've an idea that might work."

"At least, you can analyze the stunner, and give the information to Ciath, in case we need her services again after a stunning. You can join us later."

"Right."

Ithleen said, "I trust your 'us' includes me? If the first days are merely reconnaissance, even the wexters can't object to my going along; and you might have need of contact or supervision in more than one place at a time."

"Glad to have you."

Robinaire said, "You're going away?"

"Yes, for a few days. But don't worry. I'll come back for your party."

Robinaire smiled, her eyes distant. "The costumers are making me a divine dress."

"I hope you enjoy the event very much," said Ithleen. "Both of you."

Spen appeared. "We are ready with our probe and the clairvoyant."

Mayne said, "We'd better work from my world; we want to keep this one hidden from Haughn's clairvoyants, even if we have taken away his best one." He turned to Jonno. "Are you going to work on the stunner analysis here or on your own world?"

"Here. I can do faster and better work on the parts I can have others make." Jonno added, "Are you sure it's safe to take her to that party?"

"I think we can risk one evening, especially in a public setting. Haughn seems to be worried about attracting the attention of any powerful organization on my world, and he appears to think the ISC is one."

Mayne transplaced himself and Ithleen to his lab. Spen and Xabis joined them and, a moment later, the caltor appeared. It was a large, rectilinear object, free-standing on the floor, and completely enclosed in featureless panels: with the wexters' psionic operation, there was no need for read-outs or physical controls.

Xabis, guided either by Spen or her own ability, crossed to the caltor as Mayne brought her a chair. The psychic was still in her drab clothes, but she was now wearing a brightly enamelled flower brooch. The wexters, Mayne thought, were already offering comfort to the individuality-starved psychics.

There was silence then for many minutes. The two scientists were excluded from the wexter's link with Xabis and the caltor, so could not sense anything happening. They curbed their impatience and waited.

At last the wexter said, "We have contact with two people, together, whom Xabis identifies fairly certainly as Resistance members. They have leadership traits in their personalities, so are probably people of some importance in the movement. Xabis senses restraint and open defiance of Zar Haughn; it seems likely they are captives."

Mayne decided, "If they're prisoners, we'd better transplace them here. Spen, I think as soon as you've directed us to these Resistance people, you'd better take Xabis and your equipment away from here. The less they see when we bring them here, the less Haughn can get out of them if he should recapture them."

"I would prefer to leave in any case," Spen said. "When you are ready to make the raid on the psychics, report and return, and we will supply the marking devices. We will check the recorders frequently."

Using Mayne's rough sketched map of Haughn's headquarters, Xabis was able to point out the Admin wing, and tell them that the holding cells were in its basement.

A few seconds later Mayne and Ithleen stood in a harshly lit concrete corridor. A brief exploration brought them into a long room lined with barred cells.

CHAPTER 19

Resistance

The two nearest cells were occupied by a woman of about thirty and a man in his late forties. The woman was tall and slim, with dark hair pulled back in a severe style which emphasized the beautiful bone structure of her face. She was dressed in a smart royal blue skirt suit. The man was of medium height, with thin fair hair and a small moustache. His posture and greyish brown clothes echoed this nondescript appearance so well that the outworlders guessed he cultivated the look for anonymity.

The two prisoners looked up as the door opened, but neither said anything. The man turned away again; the woman watched the newcomers.

After a quick glance showed that the other cells were empty, Jonnan addressed the prisoners. "Are you Resistance personnel?"

"As if you didn't know!" responded the woman.

"Ignore them, Sandriam," advised the man.

Jonnan said, "We don't know. We're not Kinnasoorans. We're looking for a couple of people who are defying Zar Haughn."

Sandriam stood up from her cot. "I've heard what happens to those in his power who defy Zar Haughn. But while I still have free will, I do defy him!" Her voice rang.

Jonnan nodded. "We'd like you to come with us. Will you?"

"What kind of game is this?" demanded the man. "You can force us to go anywhere you want."

"We are also against Zar Haughn, and we wish to show you something that may aid in your fight against him. Will you come?"

Sandriam suddenly crossed to the front of her cell and gave Jonnan a long, searching look, then said, "Yes, I will come. Erlin, let's see what he wants."

Erlin came forward more slowly, looked them over, and finally said, "Well, why not? There's no way we can fight, anyway." He looked at his cell's lock. "If you're not the Zar's people, how did you get a key to - "

Jonnan nodded to Ithleen, and each transplaced the nearest prisoner to Jonnan's lab. As the involuntary exclamations died, he said, "You are now in another universe. If you decide to go back we'll bring you, but we hope that you'll agree to help us. I believe we have a common cause."

"And what's that?" demanded Erlin.

"We want to curtail Haughn's power."

"We want to destroy him!" said Sandriam.

"What you do to a dictator of your own world is an internal matter," replied Jonnan. "Our concern is to stop his expansion outside his world."

"So it's true!" cried Sandriam. "There have been rumours that he uses those psychics in some diabolical machine to go to another world."

"I understand it's only a psychic amplifier, not a 'diabolical machine'; but he is crossing to other universes, and we want to stop him."

"Then we'll help you," Sandriam said.

Erlin demanded, "What can you do? Can you give us the means of going to other universes?"

Jonnan shook his head. "Our own devices are borrowed. And we can't even lend them: they'll break down irreversibly if they leave our possession."

"Then what can you do?" Erlin repeated. "And what is it you want us to do?"

"We want to raid Haughn's headquarters, and we need a set of distractions organized to prevent his psychics' spotting us before we get in there. We got in today because he wasn't expecting outside interest in his local prisoners, and because his organization of the psychics is in temporary confusion. We can't expect either condition to last or be adequate for a major raid."

"Why don't you use your own people for your distraction?"

"Because we may need all of those that are here for the raid."

"Two! What can two people do?"

"By use of our transplacing ability, we can remove the psychics. I think their absence would ease your own problems somewhat."

Sandriam caught her breath. "Ease them! It would half eliminate them! People are afraid to join us because they think those psychics can spot them anywhere in the world."

Ithleen said, "Why did he have you imprisoned?"

"Our spies say there was something going on in his headquarters last night. The Zarsmen swooped down on us with no warning using a clairvoyant to point out the leaders of our local cell."

Jonnan commented, "Then you should be pleased to hear that we took away Xabis, Haughn's best clairvoyant, last night. Also his best precog, Grellor. That's why were able to get to you."

"Now, we can operate, and recruit!" Sandriam said.

"We concentrate on winning converts to the cause of freedom, while waiting for any chance to make a genuine difference by an attack. And only core members would be involved in that. The rest are just spreading the word, which leaves them fairly safe. Zar Haughn is so sure of himself that he doesn't care what people say."

"Do you two want to go back to your world, then?" Jonnan asked.

Sandriam raised her chin. "I certainly do. With two of the best psychics gone, we might even have a chance to make a real strike! And if you can take away more of them ... if Haughn now also has to worry about raids from off-world, he's going to be too busy to pay attention to us. This could be our chance."

"Erlin, let's get back and see what we can organize to help them, before Haughn gets interested in us again."

"We're not asking for anything elaborate, just enough of a distraction to enable us to get to the psychics with, say, an hour's grace before the guards close in on us."

"Even so, it can't be done overnight. And you'll need to be with us, to share the planning." When Mayne agreed, Sandriam said, "Take us back, then."

"Where do you want to go, in relation to where you were, direction and distance?"

Erlin was able to supply close enough directions for them to appear near an insurance office building. "I'll contact the people we need and tell them to report to you here. I'll come in again myself tomorrow."

Inside, Sandriam considered their appearance and decided their clothes were enough like Kinnasooran styles to pass. "Erlin will arrange for identity cards for you, along with incidental things like club membership cards, credit cards, money, transport passes, and other odds and ends to make you look like citizens."

She began to coach them on details of Kinnasoor, with particular attention to how best to avoid drawing attention to themselves. She also told them about the power structure of the empire.

"Until Haughn, the position of Zar was a limited monarchy that was unfortunately quite corrupt. When Haughn began taking over power, he had popular support. He cleared out many nests of corruption - but only so he could organize the government as he wanted."

"How does he maintain his authority?"

"By the Zarsmen - his private police, and the general fear of the psychics he's rounded up, and by powerful weapons made by a group of military researchers. Some people work for him voluntarily, others out of fear; and a few churn out things he can bestow on us as his bountiful gift - medicines, electronic devices, crop improvements. Hardly anyone is willing to fight for the freedom to rule ourselves.

"On a raid, we always lose some of our personnel, Haughn just kills a few of the leaders his psychics pick out. It's a price we're willing to pay if we're to get our freedom back."

Jonnan said, "Well, if we can take away the psychics, it should put things on a different basis here."

"If you can take away the psychics, there'll be a period of confusion and disorder, and we'll have a chance to strike a real blow, before they detect us."

Ithleen said, "Haughn probably won't be paying much attention to you right now; he'll be too annoyed at us — and even if he has no wish to get you back again — he may still be irked that we took you."

"What do you think he'll do?" Sandriam asked.

"Look for us," Jonnan answered. "When he doesn't find us at my lab, he might damage the place, if he's there in person and has a temper; but I don't think he'll venture any further into that world, knowing we could be hiding out in any other universe."

Sandriam looked surprised, so he explained further: "Haughn knows nothing about my world except that it has inter-universe transplacement; and he's worried about being traced back to his own world by a superior technology, so he won't let his men stay there any longer than he has to, unless he's sure we're there or that he can match our technology."

Ithleen added, "He'll certainly want to get his psychics back. Thinking they're still with us, he'll come after us."

Jonnan nodded. "Whatever he wants to do, he can't devote all his resources to us. As you pointed out earlier, he has to keep a lot of his psychics' attention on running his empire. I think his best compromise would be to put some precogs on a stand-by watch for any attack from out-world, and some clairvoyants to searching for any transplacing we may be doing, both concentrating on events connected with his headquarters. And that, along with the loss of his best psychics, gives us a fair chance to slip in and out of his world."

Sandriam smiled at him. "Well now we just have to wait. The cell leaders will be in charge of the synchronous raids and ensuring that the various plans are not likely to interfere with yours. For the rest, as I say, it's just waiting."

***

Early the next day, a young man named Nasrock, of surly good looks and a settled expression of suspicion, arrived with a sketched map of Haughn's headquarters which Sandriam's group had put together. Nasrock hung on his leader's words, glowered at Jonnan, looked appraisingly once at Ithleen, and agreed without enthusiasm to be a guide when Jonnan said he wanted to survey the place in person.

"Let your assistant do the scouting," said Sandriam. "A leader has to learn to stay at the control centre."

"I haven't got an assistant with me," said Jonnan.

Sandriam gestured.

"Ithleen? She's not an assistant."

"Whatever you call her, it's better that she go."

"I'm quite willing, Jonnan."

"I'd prefer to see the place myself."

"There'll be people coming today whose plans you should hear, and one or two you should meet," said Sandriam firmly. "You'll have to stay."

Jonnan shrugged. "All right, then."

Nasrock, scowling more than ever over the stranger's usurpation of his leader's attention, led Ithleen out.

Sandriam dealt competently with the several men and women who reported in to her in person. Their reactions to Jonnan varied; some accepted him simply on Sandriam's tacit recommendation; others looked at him with habitual suspicion of any newcomer; others again were interested that this stranger was so completely in their leader's confidence; but none exhibited Nasrock's personal resentment. Sandriam did not explain Jonnan or his projected part in the plan to any of them.

A young man arrived, and was briefly introduced to Jonnan as Erlin's son, Fledger, who refused to deliver his message in front of a stranger. She returned to Jonnan with excitement in her eyes.

"Erlin has managed to track down a young psychic that the Zarsmen missed. We heard of him some time ago, but delayed getting hold of him till we had an immediate use for him, for fear of leading the Zarsmen to him. He's very limited, but Erlin thinks he'll be able to pinpoint the location of the other psychics for you."

"Are there many undiscovered psychics in the population?"

"This is the only one we've heard of so far that Zar Haughn hasn't sieved out. Everybody's got a bit of talent, but not enough to be useful, even with Haughn's boosting machines. It's because ones with over-standard ability are so rare that we wanted to save this one for some special effort."

When Ithleen and Nasrock returned, the two scientists began pouring over the set of partial plans of Haughn's headquarters.

"He'd want the psychics handy to the labs where he tests prisoners," mused Jonnan, selecting one sheet of the maps.

"His lab complex is an annex to the Admin one," Ithleen pointed out. "I think it's a good bet the psychics are kept there in the central building, perhaps close to these connecting passages you see on the first and second floors."

"And it's only a guess he needs them close; he might have fast horizontal transport as well as vertical. Still, we might as well start Sandriam's psychic searching that area first." Jonnan said. "What about a way in for us?"

Sandriam answered, "There's a guard who's one of our converts. He can take the three of us in with him under the guise of a pair of guards smuggling in a couple of prostitutes. Then we can work our way from there."

Jonnan asked, "When do you plan to use your psychic?"

"Tonight, in the post-midnight hours. He'll be taken to the vicinity by a man who has been told that our ultimate purpose is to try to broadcast thoughts of rebellion in to the psychics - in case he's caught. We'll get word during the morning if the attempt succeeds."

Sandriam sent Nasrock off to carry word of which part of the building was to be probed first. He went, with continued reluctance to leave his leader, and a final glare at Jonnan.

Once he was gone, Jonnan mentioned, "Tomorrow I'll have to go back to my own world for half a day; but I've arranged for the third member of our team to take over here for me. He's a sort of distant cousin of mine, with a similar name. Like Ithleen, he can make any necessary decision that comes up."

"Why do you have to go?"

"I have an obligation that has to be taken care of on that exact day. It has an indirect bearing on the problem of Haughn; but it's a part of my world, which we're still trying not to describe."

"I suppose it must be important," said Sandriam, suppressing her curiosity with a visible effort. "How long will you be gone?"

"I'll leave in the afternoon, and return...say, about mid-morning on Saturday." He had no idea how long through the night the ambassadorial party was likely to run, and thought he had better allow himself a few more hours of sleep than the time zone shift would give him.

Back in the region containing both the Zar's palace and the Resistance base, they found things had run smoothly for the others, so well that Erlin was feeling a bit of superstitious worry. He regarded the unexpectedness of Jonnan's planned absence as a relief, something to break that smooth run of good luck and let them start a new run without catastrophe.

***

Nasrock came in the next morning, bearing, with no apparent pleasure, the news of success in the mission. With a fair degree of confidence, the psychics' quarters were marked on the sketch plan, roughly where Ithleen had predicted.

Early that afternoon Jonno appeared in Sandriam's apartment, where he was introduced to the Kinnasoorans and brought up to date on the situation.

"So we're still in a holding state, waiting for the assorted parts of the Resistance machine to get up to load," Jonno summarized what he had been told. "And nothing's expected to happen for another few days."

"That's right. How has your own work been going?" Mayne said.

"Some progress. You might like to take a look while you're back. I made notes, of course."

"Perhaps I'll go back right away, then, to have time to look at it."

"I'll be interested in hearing your ideas on it," Jonno said. "You might be able to catch incipient mistakes."

"You're way ahead of me on this one, Jonno." Jonnan took his leave and transplaced out.

Ithleen was amused, as the day wore on, by Sandriam's reaction to Jonno. Having been told of a relationship, she had expected some similarities; but she was taken aback by sudden flashes of identical personality, followed by ones at complete variance.

***

In the evening the blow fell. Nasrock brought Erlin the news: "The Zarsmen have got Fledger."

After a flash of shock and alarm, Erlin asked heavily, "What happened?"

"They tracked down the psychic. Somebody must have noticed our use of him last night. Fledger was looking after him. They took them both."

Erlin mumbled, "I should never have let him go."

Sandriam said, "Erlin, they'll keep the psychic, but perhaps they'll let Fledger go. They'll soon know he isn't one of the leaders and doesn't know much."

"When they find out he's related to me, they'll think he knows a lot. And you know the Zar's methods of asking questions..."

They both fell silent.

Ithleen spoke briskly. "Then we'll have to get him out of their hands."

Erlin snarled, "Do you think we wouldn't, if we could?"

Ithleen said gently, "Of course you would. What I meant was that I will go for the boy."

"How?" demanded Sandriam.

"I've met Fledger, so I can home in on him. By going to another world, I can transplace back to where he is, provided he's alone at some time. Then I can reverse my path and bring him here."

Jonno said, "What if the precogs warn Haughn?"

"They've probably been told to watch for something more important than a rescue attempt of a minor Resistance person."

"They may have been told to watch for any transplacement from outworld into headquarters," Jonno demurred.

"Perhaps; but I think there's a good chance I can get away with it, before they can co-ordinate the matter, and get the psychics' warning localized and translated into orders to put guards in the prison. Remember, Haughn has only second-class precogs and clairvoyants now, so they might not notice me in time."

"All right, the risk is fairly reasonable; we'll go," Jonno said.

"It would be foolish to risk two, and since I've met Fledger, I'm the logical one to go."

"It's just possible they've left the psychic with Fledger for the moment; if so, I can transplace him out for the wexters to collect at the same time as you bring Fledger."

"Highly unlikely that the Zarsmen would put him in the cells even temporarily; they'd take him to the psychics' quarters."

"I'll come anyway," said Jonno steadily. "I can follow you on my own, if necessary."

"As you wish, then."

They wasted no more words. Ithleen transplaced them to Jonnan's lab, then back to Fledger in Kinnasoor, to the cells where she had first seen the Resistance leaders.

Ithleen went straight to the youth. "Fledger, I can get you out of this, if you'll come with me. Are you willing?"

"Sure, but how?"

Ithleen transplaced the two of them away.

Jonno checked the other cells, but found no trace of the psychic, or any other prisoners. He had made the mistake of not taking out his own rifkey immediately on arrival. He reached for it as he heard the corridor door swing open, but the stun blast caught him before he touched it.

Chapter 20

Misdirection

"You've done very well, Geeling," said Haughn, "capturing one of these elusive outworlders on the basis of a precog's jumbled report. Now, let's see what we can find out about this man." Haughn moved to a table and surveyed the objects lying there. "This is everything he had on him?"

"We searched him to the skin, sir," said the technician Geeling.

Haughn looked first for identity. "Jonno Mayne. Mayne! Could this be the same man the girl called Plennor Mayne? Yes! It's a title. What luck! To take him by chance, in exchange for a worthless Resistance prisoner!"

"If he came personally to get the prisoner, maybe the kid was more important than we thought."

"Unlikely. This fool goes around rescuing useless people. And whether his motive is altruism or arrogant refusal to be beaten even in trifles, it has delivered him into our hands; and I'm perfectly happy to make the exchange, however important the boy may be to that farcical Resistance movement."

He glanced over at Jonno's unconscious body. "He has two of my best psychics very well hidden out somewhere. I risked sending a pair of clairvoyants to his world to search for them, but couldn't find a trace. But he'll tell us where to find them before we're through...and a lot of other things, too."

Haughn returned to looking through the items on the table. "A neat little laser. Self-contained, so it can't have much power, but it might please Doctor Cazl to have it. What's this round blue stone? A weapon of some sort? We'll want that analyzed. And this flat green object: it looks like a solid chunk of some synthetic material. He must have some reason for carrying those things."

"The flat one's a game board," Geeling said. "See the other side?"

"I saw it. But I can't picture this earnest do-gooder being so fond of games that he carries one around with him, especially when he's on one of his foolish rescue missions. It could be a signalling device, or even part of his transplacing equipment. A remote control, perhaps. Until it's been analyzed, it stays classed as suspicious."

He put the rifkey down and mused over the remaining items. "What else has he got? A very intricate pocket computer, I see. Doesn't look any more advanced than ours, but it might be able to handle more than we can with this size. Or perhaps this is his transplacer control. If the other objects prove innocuous, I'll let Perine check out the computer, too."

"Look at the notebook there," suggested Geeling impatiently. "It's in code."

Haughn leafed through it. "Nothing so dramatic. Merely abbreviated self-reminders, I think, with some technical jottings. See, here's a list of supplies, checked off: a note to see - someone's initial - about... I'd say it's an assistant to do a computer project... also checked off... Hmm. This appears to say, 'Make instruments for limbo.' I wonder what that means. Not checked off. I don't think there's anything useful here."

He tossed the book down on the table, and pushed aside the other personal items: including the innocent-looking pen set.

He picked up the two unidentified objects he had first separated out. "These are the only things whose purpose is not obvious. That girl he sent here spoke of touching Mayne's transplacing device. I assumed that meant it's some large, freestanding object, which stays in his universe, the way ours does, while he takes only the control with him. But Perine said that according to his manuals, he's got something called immits that are beyond nanotechnology, which he used in those pieces of equipment she got so little out of before he came and fused them."

Reminiscent anger distracted him. "Why Perine Cazl left both the apparatus and the manuals out where anyone could find them..."

"Scientists aren't very practical," said Geeling, with the superiority of a dangerous errand runner. "She probably thought no one would dare break into your labs."

Haughn shrugged off his annoyance. "However, we now have the author of the vanished papers to question."

"There aren't any places to attach cables," Geeling pointed out. "Or any switches to push."

"If his grasp of psionics is better than ours, he might not need either. Everything could work psionically. Whoever was with him today seems to have abandoned him. It would seem his subordinates are not as altruistic as he is!"

He smiled briefly, then went on thinking aloud. "That may also mean that they're harmless now that they've lost their leader. But that's no reason to put off learning all we can about his transplacing methods."

He handed the rifkey and recorder to Geeling. "Take these objects over to Doctor Cazl's own lab and tell her to drop everything else and analyze them. But she still can't have any of the psychics until this Outworlder problem is dealt with."

Haughn picked up Jonno's laser and computer, then put them back down on the table. "No, if I give these to her now she might find an excuse to play with them instead of tackling the other objects. Get things rolling on those, then keep an eye on Mayne. Call me as soon as he's awake."

***

Jonno regained consciousness strapped into a reclining chair in Haughn's psi lab/interrogation room. He heard Haughn being notified. By the time Jonno had recovered from the aftereffects of his stunning, Haughn had arrived.

He came to stand beside Jonno. "I am Zar Haughn. You have caused me a certain amount of inconvenience, Plennor Mayne, which you will now proceed to make up for, starting with information."

He gestured at the machine overhead, from which a long, flat antenna, wedge-shaped in cross-section, aimed its broad side at Jonno. "Let me explain this neural stimulator. It produces sensations directly in the nerves, none of them pleasant. Up to intensity ten, it is merely discomfort. By twenty it is pain; at thirty it is strong pain. By eighty there is permanent damage to the nerves; ninety causes sufficient degeneration with death eventually resulting; and I have calibrated intensity hundred to a point where it kills immediately."

He moved to the controls of a second machine, off to the side. "You will notice that you're hooked up to a polygraph. It is not necessary for you to answer verbally for me to tell from your physical and mental reactions when a question has been significant to you. Nevertheless, you will answer all questions, or Geeling will turn on the nerve stimulator."

"Won't that interfere with your polygraph readings?" asked Jonno with interest, though his nerves had tightened at the threat.

"It's programmed to handle it," Haughn assured him. "You will save both of us time and yourself pain by telling the truth immediately. Now, you are Plennor Jonno Mayne? You work for an organization known as ISC, which controls the science resources of your world?"

Jonno gave an affirmative to each, qualifying the last one with, "Not all, but it has the best."

"Did the ISC send you here, or did you come because I took apparatus from your lab?"

Jonno suddenly realized that Haughn had assumed he was Jonnan Mayne. Of course, Haughn had no idea there were two ISC worlds. Was there any advantage in that? Well, every bit of ignorance or misinformation was a disadvantage to Haughn; might as well play up to this one. "I suppose you could say I came because of your theft."

"Are you quite sure it was not orders from your superiors?"

Jonno remembered that Haughn was worried over the possibility that the world he had raided had superior technology. Apparently he also thought in terms of an aggressive ruling organization, and the thought appeared to be more of a deterrent than a provocation, so it was worth building up. But Haughn could detect any outright lie. Jonno searched hurriedly for a misleading truth. Well, in this multiverse venture, he supposed he could rate Jonnan as senior personnel; and Jonnan had asked him to come to this world to fill in. Feeling his way carefully, Jonno said, "Not really orders; but it was suggested to me."

Haughn slipped in a more important question. "Where are the psychics you stole from me?"

"I haven't the faintest idea," said Jonno cheerfully. That was true in a literal sense.

Haughn glanced at Geeling, who was hovering nervously over the stimulator controls. "Start him at twenty and take it up to thirty, slowly. Now, where are the psychics?"

"I don't — know."

"Forty."

"I — don't — have — them."

"What did you do with them? Fifty!"

"Sir, I don't think he can talk, at that intensity."

"I know; turn it up and hold for five seconds. What did you do with the psychics?"

Since he was working as an agent for the wexters, Jonno was able to say, "I — handed them — over to — higher authority."

"Don't stall! What has the ISC done with them?"

"I understand they're — in another universe — but I've no idea — which one."

"Why has the ISC put them in another universe?"

Jonno drew on his stamina and steadied his breathing.

"I'm not in the Council's confidence. I suppose they had no use for them." Each statement was true, on its own.

"Then why did you think the Council wanted them?"

"I didn't."

"Then why did you take them?"

"They wanted to come along. I don't think they like you, Zar Haughn."

"How could they know..." Haughn cut off his question. Of course a precog and a clairvoyant would recognize the opportunity. He dropped that subject and went to the one that interested him even more. "Your actress and spy told me you don't use psychics with your transplacer. A fact confirmed by observation when you rescued her. Which of the items you were carrying is the control device for that apparatus?"

Fishing for information, Jonno taunted, "You must have had it for two or three hours by now. Don't tell me you haven't even got it identified!" He could see that the rifkey was not among the scatter of his possessions on the nearby table; but had it been far enough away from him, for long enough, to fuse?

"I know it is one or both of two objects," Haughn said evenly; "and my experts can analyze anything psionic, so you gain nothing by resistance."

"They obviously haven't figured this out!"

"Not in two hours; but they will. Now stop stalling. Which item is the control, the little sphere or the flat rectangular block?"

It was safe, then. "The block."

"And how does it work?"

"I wish I knew!"

"Didn't you make it?"

"No. It was issued by higher authority."

"Why was it given to you?"

"Field tests of the new small model." It was hard to think flexibly with the pressure of the steady pain beating through him, but he must do so if he hoped to convince Haughn that an ISC world was too dangerous to attack.

His only hope of beating Haughn's polygraph was to hold steadily in his mind a firm belief in the ruthless technology that Haughn seemed to find plausible, and to tell, as far as he could, truths whose interpretation managed to build up the fabrication. Above all, he must somehow, in spite of the pain and the twists of the questioning, remain consistent. If Haughn once caught him out, he would know the polygraph was untrustworthy.

"How long has your world had inter-universe transplacement?"

"I've only recently found out it existed. But apparently it's not a new invention."

"How could it be hidden from you, when you're working in psionics?"

"Someone must have struck a more productive line of research long before I started in the field. I once thought I was in the forefront of psionics; it was a shock to find I was only repeating others' work." He let the bitterness of this truth come through.

"Why is your Council so secretive?"

"I wouldn't know. I suppose all rulers are." Again he let Haughn make the mental connection between the two unrelated statements, and added three more for Haughn's mind-set to tie in: "I've heard about a couple of devastated worlds, but only as stories. I suppose the Council likes to keep a good image."

"What sort of weaponry does your world possess?"

"I've no idea. We've had the ability to destroy a world for over half a century." Only a few of the Regions were still interested in offensive weapons. But they kept quiet about anything they were working on.

"How is your Council able to suppress knowledge of discoveries?"

Jonno visualized the sort of Council Haughn believed in, and imagined how it would adjust the actual situation. "Whatever we discover, we have to submit to the Council for permission to publish." The word "permission" was stretching things, but the Council was the authority behind the editors who assigned priority to articles and books, and the editors could reject a manuscript that was badly written or that lacked evidence of honest research.

"If the Council decided to keep a new discovery under wraps, there are three things it could do." Well, it could. "Kill off the researchers; destroy their minds; or trust them to keep quiet while doing further work on the project. People with families are vulnerable to threats."

Haughn nodded. "Yes, I've kept some of my would-be heirs in line that way. So, your Council has kept the knowledge of transplacement to itself until recently?"

"I can't say how many people were entrusted with the knowledge, since I wasn't." Even if all the wexters knew about it, Jonno had no idea what the wexter population was. "There's obviously been activity in the field."

"And you claim you don't understand how it works?"

"It's way beyond what little I've done in psionics."

"What's the other thing you were carrying, the one like a round stone?"

"A recorder." Jonno could see no harm in this information. Since neither he nor Mayne could analyze it, he doubted that Haughn's people could.

"How do you use it?"

He risked another half-lie. "Hold it in your closed hand and talk towards it." As long as Haughn did not know it could pick up unvoiced thoughts, and record without being touched, there was a chance he might happen to bring it near enough for Jonno to report into it anything he learned here.

"And how do you play back what's been recorded?"

"I don't know. It's for reporting to higher authority. I haven't been able to find any controls on it. My guess is that it needs some kind of reader, which I wasn't given." A wexter, to be precise.

"You expect me to believe you can't make any of these gadgets? Your name was on those immit-device articles. Do you admit to being able to make that equipment? Or did you lay claim to someone else's work?"

Stung by this reminder of Mayne's suggestion that he use his analog's work to buy time for multiverse exploration, and the temptation of it, Jonno snapped, "I've made the telepathy amplifier. I'm still working on the others."

Haughn looked over the remainder of Jonno's possessions. "What about these two things?" He picked up the laser and computer.

"Waste of time to make off-the-shelf equipment myself." Only the computer was made commercially; but the statement itself was true.

Haughn put down the computer, but weighed options on the other item. "A laser flashlight mass-produced for the citizens would be good public relations." He handed the laser to Geeling. "Send it over to Admin, Geeling, and tell them to put it in a safe."

"Why not keep it here? We've got safes."

"I want to be sure it's also well out of Mayne's reach."

"But he can't reach it. He's strapped down."

"We *are* going to have to release him, to get work out of him," Haughn pointed out.

Flushing, Geeling hurried over to the door and called a guard for the errand.

Reluctantly but firmly, Jonno sent the mental order to the recharger unit in the laser to fuse the system, hoping that if Haughn noticed a spike on his polygraph record he would take it for Jonno's concern over losing the device or over the idea of working for the Zar.

Haughn returned his attention to Jonno. "Your manuals mentioned devices called image circuits or immits, which my psionicist, Doctor Cazl, says must be something at the nuclear level, based also on the fact that she could not analyze them in the time she had. Your equipment supports the idea it involved something beyond our normal tools."

Geeling returned. "On its way."

The Zar continued, "Unfortunately, your articles dealt only with advanced equipment, not with the making of these immits themselves; and they seem to be essential to the equipment."

He left the polygraph and came to face Jonno. "I have psi boosters and linkages of my own, but they are bulky; and working through psychics is a clumsy process anyway. I want your immits, to make more compact machines; and I want their applications so that I can do away with my need to use psychics, for transplacement. You are going to explain your image circuits in great detail, and then help me to build a more efficient transplacing system."

"No."

"Geeling, turn up the stimulator, slowly."

"How far?" Geeling wetted his lips nervously.

"Why, until he agrees," said Haughn pleasantly.

Geeling began to call out, "Twenty...twenty-five...thirty...thirty-five." He swallowed, and resumed, "Forty...forty-five...fifty..."

"Cut, for a bit." Haughn waited patiently until Jonno could focus his attention on the outer world again, then said, "Remember, permanent damage at eighty. No survival after ninety."

"You won't get – work from a – dead body."

"If I get none from a live body, it might as well be dead. Start in where you left off, Geeling. Fifty, was it not?"

Geeling flipped the switch back on. "...Fifty-five...sixty..." he said hoarsely. "Sixty-fi— Sir, the EEG pattern says he's unconscious."

"All right, turn the machine off."

"Are you going to kill him, sir?"

"As he said, he'd be useless dead. This machine is our fastest means of breaking people, but it's not the only one."

CHAPTER 21

Party

Mayne called for Robinaire at Ciath's quarters in an odd combination of moods: he was annoyed at having to break off his Resistance project, but pleased to leave the boredom of its inactivity.

He knew his appearance at this party would be a sensation among those who followed the social news. There would be reporters trying to find out why he had gone, and a flood of new invitations for the clerks to deal with. He wondered with wry amusement whether the senders of the new invitations would hate him or his hostess of this night more when they received the standard refusals.

Robinaire was spectacular in a gown of rich ecru satin, boldly patterned in leaves of russet, gold, and black, which the costumers in Ciath's drama group had designed to look flattering on Robinaire and to emphasize the beautiful light auburn colour of her hair, which had been carefully touched up so that no mousiness showed. Cubic zirconia gems flashed more brilliantly than diamonds at her throat and ears. Her hair had been swept up into a smooth, sophisticated style, which she had the poise to carry off. The total effect was enough to focus even Mayne's attention on her, and win an honest, "She is indeed," to Ciath's proud, "Isn't she lovely?"

Ciath hugged Robinaire, and said, "I hope the party lives up to your expectations."

"It's already starting to," said Robinaire, glowing from Mayne's compliment.

Since they could not transplace directly to the party, they went to Mayne's home. From there he drove to the express gravity tunnel between the ISC Compound and Neithon, entered one of the carrier cars, and sat back for the five minute pendulum swing into the city.

Robinaire had, of course, informed their hosts in advance of her change of escort, and Soltain Lagaronde had instantly leaked the news to the press.

The time at the party passed swiftly. Robinaire chose to spend most of the time dancing, which enabled Mayne to dodge many of the celebrity-hunters. Not until this evening had he ever thought it was possible that anyone could actually enjoy a formal party.

But Robinaire's enjoyment was obvious, unquestionable and contagious. He began to perceive that there were a variety of pleasant emotions possible in social life, after all. Not enough, by any means, to convert him to a general liking for it — his long years of discomfort and resentment had burned too deeply for that — he conceded the possibility of occasional, qualified enjoyment. He met Robinaire's blissful smile with an honest one of his own.

***

Ithleen had delivered Fledger safely to Erlin, who sent him to a safer location. Jonno had not followed Ithleen to the Resistance apartment, but she was not immediately worried. If he had found the psychic, he might be waiting in Mayne's world, in case the wexters were monitoring the recorders just now, and would come immediately to collect the youth. That would minimize transplacements, and avoid having to bring the psychic back to Haughn's world or stash him in Geode.

But as several minutes passed, Ithleen became uneasy. She keyed in a transplacement to Jonno. There was no response. Growing more alarmed, she transplaced to Mayne's lab, then to her own study. There was no indication that Jonno had been to either.

Her worry mounting, she thought of seeking Mayne's help, but by this hour he would be at Robinaire's party, and she could not transplace straight into the midst of that. She had no idea where the party was; so there was no way she could get a message to him. She went back to the apartment where Sandriam and Erlin waited.

"It looks as if Haughn's got Jonno," Ithleen told them, keeping emotion out of her voice. "I can't get through to him by transplacement. Sandriam, can you get hold of that guard of yours?"

"Do you mean to waste our means of entry to try to rescue one person?"

"My using your guard doesn't mean he can't be used again," argued Ithleen. "He'll have no part in my activities after I'm in, so no suspicion should fall on him."

"But what possible hope have you of doing anything single-handedly? It's sheer foolhardiness to go in there!"

"We don't abandon our friends when they're in trouble," said Ithleen evenly. "If you won't help, I'll have to find a way in on my own."

Erlin said, "Sandriam, she brought Fledger back, and, as she says, her going in tonight doesn't mean it can't be done again."

"Unless they catch her. No one can withstand the Zar's questioning."

"That's the chance we all face, when any of us are picked up. We'll warn Yarley of the added risk of being seen with her. He can make his own choice."

"Very well. See if you can get hold of him. I've got a dress for her." While Erlin phoned, Sandriam took Ithleen to another room, where she produced a short, sleek, shimmery, fire-red slip-dress, slit up the side of the left thigh. Ithleen took off her quiet sea-green suit and white blouse and, with a grimace of distaste, slid into the proclamatory vermilion dress so she could look the part. Sandriam got out make-up of matching brightness and asked, "Do you know how to use this?" Ithleen nodded. "Good. Skip the subtleties; just emphasize your eyes and mouth. Be lavish."

Ithleen ignored this last advice and applied the vivid colours in a few light, deft touches. Sandriam, her look of settled doubt changing to one of surprise, agreed it would suffice. Ithleen then noticed with concern, "It's got no pockets, how can I carry my tools?"

"Here's a purse."

Ithleen put her pentools into the black clutch purse, among a few odds and ends Sandriam considered it appropriate for her to have. Her laser would not fit in, even if she left out everything else, so she had to leave it. After a moment's hesitation, she gave the mental order that destroyed its charger; in case she failed to survive her rescue attempt.

Her thin rifkey could be fitted into the little bag, but Ithleen was concerned over the possibility of losing the whole purse, and the rifkey was vital for rescuing Jonno. She finally taped it to her thigh with the dress covering it.

As Ithleen walked about the room, getting used to the high-heeled black shoes, Sandriam surveyed her critically. "You're more convincing than I expected."

As they returned to the livingroom, Erlin announced, "Yarley's on his way to pick her up." He gave a small exclamation as he caught sight of Ithleen. "You've transformed her, Sandriam."

"Yes," said Sandriam, sounding neither pleased nor proud.

Finally Yarley — a sturdy young man with a cheerful countenance and militarily cropped dark hair — arrived, and was briefly introduced. Ithleen said, "Let's go. There's need to hurry."

"That's a pity," said Yarley. "However - "

"I'll take you by car," offered Erlin, "so you won't run into competition from any other off-duty guards. You can walk the last bit."

There was no difficulty about their entrance to the guards' section of the sprawling Admin building. They passed the stand-by staff's room with nothing but a few unsuspicious, ribald comments.

A few hall lengths farther in, he paused. "This is as far as I can take you without rousing suspicion. You said you wanted to go to the labs, so you'll have to go along that way. I'm willing to risk coming along, but you've a little more chance alone. You can claim to be on your way to some higher-up who's sent out for a, uh, for a woman."

"Thanks. I'll manage from here. I've memorized the route, from our maps and your description."

"If anyone challenges you, say you're going to see Rofe Barlo; he's one of the live-in researchers. Runs the tech corps. He's got enough pull that maybe nobody will want to stop you."

Ithleen repeated the name, and her thanks.

She had several narrow escapes from observation, but had reached the laboratory annex before she was actually challenged. Three guards turned into her corridor when she was at a doorless stretch.

"Well, well, what have we here?" demanded one cheerfully, as all three looked her over with approval and anticipation. "Looking for a man, dolly?"

"His name's Barlo," responded Ithleen, giving him a neutral smile.

The leader of the guards gave a hoot of delight. "Zar Haughn's roped him in to work on a special project that's got the whole place jumping tonight. So come on with us."

"That's what you say," countered Ithleen, thinking fast. "How do I know it's true? I'd better go check with him first."

"Listen, these research types have got clout. We wouldn't dare pull a fast one on him; and you won't be able to see him tonight. So come on."

Ithleen made an attempt to slip by.

"No, you don't!" Half playfully, half seriously, they grabbed at her.

Her hands moved, and the nearest man doubled up and collapsed, and the second staggered; but they were men trained in combat methods, and after the initial surprise, they swarmed over her with greater reach and weight. Battered and dazed, she sagged captive in their grip.

***

The party lasted into the small hours, and so did Robinaire's infectious enjoyment. Mayne was expecting boredom to claim him any minute as the novelty of the situation wore off; but Robinaire kept them active. She chose who they would or would not talk to with a high-handed ruthlessness that it would never have occurred to him to employ. She watched him with a quick eye for lack of interest in a conversation and instantly rescued him with a request for more dancing. In her own milieu, he recognized, Robinaire was entirely competent.

As they took their leave, Robinaire said, "Let's drive back on the road instead of taking the express."

A couple of hours before dawn, under a clear, mid-August sky, they drove along the little-used road. A full moon was well down towards the western horizon, but to the east, stars still stood sharp against black.

"What a lovely night," said Robinaire. "Look at how many stars you can see, away from the city."

"Less light pollution. At this hour, we're seeing stars we normally think of as belonging to a later season."

"What do you mean?"

"We usually consider the ones we see early in the night as being the seasonal ones. And because we turn towards morning in the same direction as we're moving on our orbit, we get a preview, in the late night, of what we'll be seeing in the evening, later in the year. These in the east are the ones we call the winter constellations."

"Uh, I see," said Robinaire, in the tone of one who does not. "There must be millions of them."

"About six thousand visible to the naked eye, counting both hemispheres." He said.

"Is that true?" she cried incredulously. "Only thousands?"

"Yes. And there are far more than millions of them, even in our own vicinity, too far away to see by eye. But science can show them to you in a telescope."

"Oh, who cares about that? It's second-hand."

"Some of us find it exciting." He thought of Ithleen, who found even second-hand stars fascinating, and wondered how she and Jonno were doing with the Resistance people. Presumably all sound asleep at this hour.

It had been an interesting break, but he was eager to rejoin them. Not only to get on with the "containment" of Haughn, but simply to resume the pleasure of working with them. There had been occasions during the evening when he would have liked to point out amusing or interesting things to them, and had been conscious of their absence.

He shook his head ruefully. That was what happened when you let people into your life: you became dependent on them. Already it was unthinkable not to have the companionship of Ithleen and Jonno; he even missed the lively chatter of Van and Davith; and, he glanced at Robinaire, snuggled warmly against his side – even Robinaire had somehow become established as a part of his life, that he had so carefully kept uncluttered. All since that distant evening, only three and a half weeks ago, when the wexter had first appeared. But for all the complications, he could not unwish any of it.

He drove into the garage of his own building. Reaching for his rifkey, he turned to smile at her in the dim automatic lighting. "Well, has it lived up to your expectations?"

"Umm," said Robinaire, "So far it's been perfect."

"So far?" Surprised, he paused. "There's more?"

And at that moment Haughn's men struck.

CHAPTER 22

Coercion

Ithleen twisted her wrists against the cord that held them. Her captors had dropped their playfulness when her karate blows had revealed her to be other than she seemed. She had expressed the intent of seeing a researcher involved in the sudden flurry of unscheduled work of the night; she had crippled a trained guard; under her disguise they had felt the spring-steel muscles of an athlete in top condition; they had brains enough to know the matter had better be reported immediately.

But the injured guard needed attention, and they were not sure a single man could control her, so they shoved her into a storage area that could be locked with a bolt, and tied her with heavy twine from packages there. They helped the injured man towards a medical station, summoning reinforcements by pocket intercom as they went.

Ithleen knew she would have only a few minutes. She squirmed onto her knees with her hands still behind her back and looked around her in the light from the hallway that came over the partition walls surrounding her. Her purse was lying nearby, where the guards had tossed it down after checking it to be sure she carried no weapon.

It was one of Jonno's pentools she was after, the gennor. She nudged it aside from the other spilled items and twisted around till her bound hands could touch it. She set it mentally on fairly low-powered infra-red and used the warmth to guide her hands in setting it against the cords, then raised its intensity to high.

She gasped as the beam burned a slash across her wrists and back, but held the tool steady, forcing her attention away from the pain with the wry thought that Ciath would have much to say this time! Finally — after bare seconds, actually — the twine charred and parted. In another moment she had freed her feet as well, and scooped up the spilled contents of her purse.

A quick look selected a tall crate standing against one of the partition walls. It was four meters to the top of the wall, but only half that from the top of the crate. She scrambled up, crouched, and launched herself, the purse clenched in her teeth to free her hands. In a moment she was balanced on the ten-centimeter-wide partition. She moved lightly along the wall top, as far as the storage area ran, then came down to continue moving on the corridor's floors once again.

It was soon clear that there was an organized search for her going on. Sheltering inside a room, she heard the voices of two Zarsmen officers she had dodged, as they conferred out in the hallway. "We'll start in Block M and move out. Make sure all your men have body-heat detectors, and passkeys for their areas."

"What do the psychics say about all this trouble?"

"They're wonkier than ever. The precogs seem to think something big's going to happen, but keep saying, 'Not yet.' The clairvoyants say there's an outworlder here, but it's the one the Zar has in the psi lab they point out."

"Maybe they consider him more important than this intruder, if there really is one."

"Well, I've heard that the prisoner's the leader of the outworlders."

After they moved away, Ithleen cautiously continued on her way. Somehow she had to get past the line of search, without exposing herself to the psychics by using her rifkey, and do it before the psychics started checking for her presence again.

She wondered why they had concentrated their attention on Jonno. Had the precogs seen him doing something that would be important to the psychics? Or was he deliberately concentrating his thoughts on their haven world, to distract them from someone arriving to rescue him?

She heard quick footsteps and dodged into the nearest open door, an office. The chance of anyone happening to come into this particular office at night seemed safely small.

But to her surprise as well as alarm, the footsteps stopped at the door. Standing behind it, she readied herself. Then a voice said softly, "Ithleen?" Sandriam's Zarsman pushed open the door and stepped in.

"Yarley! How did you find me?"

"I knew where you were heading, so I grabbed a detector and came along the hallways."

"You're taking a risk. Remember I'm here to help one of my own people, not the Resistance."

He looked at her, then away. "Well, I'm not here for them either. I'm here to help you."

"Thank you. What can we do?"

"Can you get into that equipment locker? They usually have one side without shelves."

She opened. "Yes, I can squeeze in."

"Then just stay there till the search line gets this far. We'll see if we can get it past you."

Subjectively, it was a long wait. At last, there were sounds. Ithleen, watching through a small hole in the cabinet door where something had once been attached, saw Yarley swing his infra-red detector around the room as another guard stepped into the doorway. The two men looked at each other and said, "What are you doing here?"

Ithleen noticed that Yarley had placed himself between the door and her cabinet.

"Looks as if we've both been sent to the same corridor," said Yarley. "I'm not surprised. The officer who assigned me was half blotto. Well, you carry on. I'll go back and see where I'm really supposed to be, before I get in trouble for not being there."

He casually flicked off the room light, and shepherded the other man out and on to the next office, where he left him. As his steps faded down the hall, Ithleen waited a little longer before risking any sound herself. When she was sure the searcher was beyond earshot, she tried to open the door of her metal cabinet.

There was no way to open it from inside.

***

When he saw Geeling and a pair of guards bring in Robinaire, lax and crumpled in her party finery, Jonno recognized defeat. He did not know whether he could rebuild Mayne's psionic apparatus or not, but he would have to try. From Mayne's instructions and his own work on the analyzer,

Jonno had begun building a TKM. Perhaps he could do enough with that to keep Haughn patient, till rescue came.

Geeling was reporting, "No trouble at all. She arrived at the lab within an hour of the best prediction, and we just beamed down the driver and grabbed her. She got a peripheral dose of the stunner, but we were on the driver's side, so he absorbed most of it. She should come around soon."

"No one saw you?"

"Not even our targets," boasted Geeling, strapping Robinaire into another of the reclining chairs. In unconscious tribute to the Geodan costume designers' skill, he straightened Robinaire's gown.

"The psychics are sleepy and clumsy tonight, sir, very erratic. We took the best remaining precog to Mayne's world on the earlier trip to pick out a time and place to catch the girl when she wasn't in a crowd, and we had to press him hard to get even one chance. Now all he'll say to questions is 'world, world'. The other psychics don't make much sense either."

Haughn stroked his beard. "They've made a poor showing today. One or more outworlders got in long enough to injure a guard. It looks as if they all fled back to their own world. There are guards at all entrances, and patrolling the buildings, but I'm having the clairvoyants make periodic scans through the interior looking for any large scale-invasion, as well."

It was nearly two hours before Robinaire was conscious and usable. Haughn waved Geeling to his post at the stimulator, and crossed to stand in front of Jonno, who roused from a deliberate, trance-induced doze.

"Plennor Mayne, you are a good enough liar to defeat the immediate visual check of the polygraph, but not to defeat its recordings. You could not control quite all of your emotional response to the subject of your transplacer. It's apparent your claim of ignorance is false."

"It may be true that you didn't invent it, but I think you understand it. You are going to explain every part of the one I have, and build me another working model to prove your words."

"I can't."

"Geeling, focus the stimulator on the girl."

Jonno said forcefully, "I cannot build that thing!"

"Start the girl at intensity ten."

Geeling worked the controls and Robinaire squirmed. Haughn turned to her. "You remember how bad this can get. If you don't want to go through it again, persuade your friend to obey me."

Robinaire looked at Jonno. "It — gets awful!"

"I know, Robinaire. I've felt it. But I can't do what they want. I don't know how."

"Fifteen," said Haughn.

Robinaire cried out and twisted in the straps. Jonno winced.

"Twenty."

"Listen, Haughn, I'll make whatever I can for you; but I haven't the least idea how to make that device."

"Thirty."

Robinaire screamed. Jonno was despairingly silent.

"Continue upward, Geeling."

Geeling hesitated, then obeyed. "Thirty-five... forty..." Again he had to stiffen his resolve, but went on. "Forty-five... fif – She's unconscious, sir."

"Off, then. Either we have mistaken the degree of his concern for this girl, or else he is telling the truth... and that I do not believe. You claim that when some person or team invented this device, your Council clamped secrecy on it. But you want me to believe further that you have not even studied it?"

Jonno remembered Mayne's early difficulties. "I can't get it open." With the rifkey fused, that was now a true statement about both devices.

Haughn made a scoffing sound. "Nothing would be sealed that well unless it were either absolutely foolproof or in such copious supply that ones that failed could be discarded. How many were you given?"

"Just the one."

"Are we to believe, then, that these things are perfect?"

"Your own scientists must have tried to open it. How far did they get?"

Haughn refused to be drawn, and kept up his pressure. "The girl is recovering. We can start the stimulator again and hold her just below her point of collapse for hours, if we wish. Or we can take her up to the point of destruction."

"I can't tell you what I don't know. I've already agreed to tell you what I do know."

"There are more things we can do to the girl. For instance, mutilation. No doubt you consider her very pretty?"

"I consider her a nuisance!" said Jonno feelingly.

Haughn went quickly to his polygraph, and summoned back the reading on Jonno's last statement. He frowned at it, then returned to face Jonno again. "Yet it disturbed you to see her in pain."

"It would disturb me to see even you in pain; but right now I'd cheerfully put you there!"

"I'm going to give you time to think about the matter," Haughn told him. Noticing that Robinaire was conscious again and had been listening, he turned to her. "See how persuasive you can be. Geeling, bring the polygraph record." He left the room, followed shortly by his assistant.

"Robinaire," said Jonno, "if I could stop him from hurting you, I would."

How was he going to get them out of this? Even with the pain machine turned off, he seemed unable to think of anything promising. If Haughn got precise-immit technique to combine with his own technology in psionics, his already skilled staff might leap ahead of the ISC worlds. Yet how could he refuse Haughn the information, with Mayne's Robinaire at stake? Haughn could actually get all the data he needed by raiding any technical library on Mayne's world, if it ever occurred to him that the information was not kept secret.

Robinaire said into the silence, "I'm sorry I'm a nuisance."

"Nuisance?"

"You told Zar Haughn I was."

Jonno's sense of fairness was stirred. Robinaire had never asked to become involved in the multiverse. Quite the opposite. "Well, I suppose I was unjust. It's not your fault Haughn brought you here." He smiled at her.

She was instantly reminded of the other Plennor Mayne. "Do you know what happened to—"

He cut her off. "I heard them say they stunned your escort and left him at the lab. You had returned from the party?"

"Yes. I thought we were safe again."

"A pity you couldn't have gone straight to and from the party. Apparently they didn't want to risk a public abduction."

"Oh, is that what happened? I thought that was where they'd attack us. When they didn't, I thought I must have been wrong this time."

"You thought — Robinaire, did you precog this?"

"Yes. At least, that Haughn would find me and hurt me again, today."

"Why didn't you tell us?" he cried. "We could have kept you safe on another world."

"I wanted to go to the party."

"Even knowing it would lead to this? Knowing, this time, about Haughn and his machine?"

"Yes," said Robinaire, and a little smile shaped her lips. "It was worth it."

***

Mayne came back to consciousness through a confusion of images: kaleidoscopic impressions of the party; the vivid touch sensation of Robinaire curled into his side on the drive home. As his thoughts focused to a realization of what had happened, he also became aware that Robinaire was gone.

As he forced his cramped, unresponsive, aching body to move, he puzzled over why Haughn should have taken Robinaire, and not him. A hostage for the return of the psychics? Or had he decided that her own talents might be useful after all?

He lurched into his quarters, and transplaced to Sandriam's apartment to consult with Jonno and Ithleen.

Both weren't in their rooms. Worried, he knocked on Sandriam's door in vain till he heard her voice from the livingroom: "Is there news? I must have fallen asleep."

He walked down the hall and joined her. "Where are Jonno and Ithleen?"

"They transplaced into the Zar's headquarters to rescue one of our people. Ithleen brought him back, but Jonno was apparently caught. We managed to get Ithleen in after she found she couldn't transplace again. Yarley, the guard who helped us, called to say she was being searched for, but still had a chance, because everything's in an uproar there."

"What's happening?"

"The psychics are in confusion, half the Zarsmen are hunting for an invading force they think got in from off-world once and might come back. And the other half are guarding against any attempt to break in from this world. If we could only have known ahead of time, we might have had a chance to act before they organized their defence."

"Sandriam, can you fake a mobilization of force? Enough to concentrate the psychics' attention on the idea of danger from this world?"

"Yes provided we don't have to carry through with it. We're not prepared for anything but a short raid."

"That's all I need. I'm going to have to try to transplace in to Haughn's headquarters. My only chance of success is to have everyone's attention focused on this world. How long do you need to get your raid started?"

Sandriam considered. "It's a question of how many people I can get hold of without notice. Give me two hours. But remember, we can't keep up the pretence of a full-scale attack for long. The psychics will realize it's phony."

"Time your action for exactly two hours from now, then."

"You're really going in, alone?"

"I'll have Ithleen's help and Jonno's as soon as we can get to him. That's all we expected to have."

"Be careful."

"Of course, Sandriam." She pulled out her phone as he transplaced back to his lab. He told the wexcorder that he urgently needed the markers for the psychics, and began to wait.

The wexters, alerted by the alarm, were prompt in sending Spen with the markers. Ne explained, "They are microscopic implants. Touch this instrument to the skin of the subject and the implant will be injected. Their signal duration is brief, but we will be monitoring, and will act promptly on your signal."

Mayne nodded, pocketed the instrument, and looked at his watch. Not yet time. What was happening to the others? He found himself tense again, and again exerted control to relax. He suddenly realized that, unusually, the wexter had lingered. "Is there something else?"

"It is important to remove the psychics; but it is also important that you should bring back the theorist. It was never our intent or expectation that she should participate in the risks of actual exploring, let alone fighting an enemy. We only stress that she should not be considered expendable."

"I don't consider any of my group expendable, though we all realize we may be killed."

"You humans are of great psychological interest."

"Well, human instincts seem to include a liking for excitement," Mayne said absently, his attention on the task ahead. His alarm buzzed. "Time to go."

***

"Have you decided to co-operate?" Haughn asked Jonno.

"I've already told you I'll try to make J — my own equipment. The transplacing device is beyond me."

Haughn regarded him broodingly. "It's possible your ISC has conditioned you to believe that. I can break that conditioning in time; you will build the simplest of your experimental machines immediately, explaining every step, especially your image circuits."

"I'll have to start with the slowest part: making immits physically — You do have nanotech facilities? — I need the manually shaped ones to build a crude psi amplifier that will boost my own ability, so that I can make more precise one that others can use. Unless I can use your own psi boosters?" Jonno did not want to hurry things, but he did want to look co-operative; and he would not mind having a look at Haughn's equipment, if he could.

"No. I want to see every stage of your work."

"Then I'll need micromanipulating equipment, in a top-quality clean-room; calibrating lasers; variable-field adjustors with simultaneous-dimension tensing..." He continued listing equipment and supplies, then concluded, "And kindly return my computer, at least for the duration: I work better with familiar tools."

Haughn nodded, and as Geeling released Jonno, the Zar waved at the table: "Help yourself."

Jonno took advantage of the permission to pocket his other possessions, too. Most of them he cared little about, but he did not want to draw attention to the fact that he was repossessing the pentools.

Haughn said to Geeling, "Have a telepath brought here." He turned back to Jonno. "The girl will stay at the focus of the nerve stimulator beam. If you try to stall, or make faulty apparatus, the stimulator will be turned on. The telepath will keep you in circuit with her feelings, so you'll know exactly what she's going through."

The beginning of an idea came to Jonno.

***

Ithleen wished uselessly for her watch. She had no idea how long she had been trapped in the equipment locker. Since she was too close to its door, she had to use the gennor on low power trying to fatigue the metal around the latch. There was a risk of the gennor's psionic power being detected by a psychic, but what choice did she have. Again she turned off her gennor and pressed on the circle of metal. This time there was a sharp crack. The door opened.

She found a pile of lab coats there that would cover her clothes as well as a box of tissues to wipe away the makeup. She put her tools and rifkey into its pockets, wincing as she ripped off the tape that had held the rifkey to her leg.

As she reached for the door, she heard a soft sound. She whipped out her psiproje. She mentally set it for instant unconsciousness, and waited for another sound.

A voice said quietly, "Ithleen?"

"Jonnan! I nearly beamed you out!"

He filled her in quickly finishing with, "Sandriam's faking attacks to distract the psychics, and I gambled on transplacing in. Do you know where the others are?"

"Yes. Jonno's in Haughn's private psi lab, and I suppose Robinaire too."

"Let's go."

They found the corridor empty at the moment. As they began walking along it, Mayne told her, "We've got to make our try for the psychics, too. Spen brought me the markers."

After a few minutes, Mayne said, "I recognize this area. We're near Haughn's lab."

"People have ignored us so far. Do you think we can walk straight in?"

"If he has guards posted, we'll have to use our psiprojes on them —"

An alarm signal began yelping, and an intercom system called out, "Full alert! Full alert! Outworlder invasion attempt!"

Mayne said, "The clairvoyants must have spotted us."

Chapter 23

Counterattack

Jonno had refused the technical personnel Haughn had offered him, pointing out that he was accustomed to working alone, and would only be slowed by assistants. Haughn was, of course, recording everything.

Jonno was now in a clean-room, surrounded by a number of automatic sound cameras, and under orders to describe his every action and the reason for it. With him, along with Haughn, were Geeling — wielding one of the bulky stunners — a telepath, and two Zarsmen, all keeping carefully out of his way, but watching him alertly. Like himself, they were all wearing spotless, non-static, lint-free gowns and caps; even their shoes were covered with socks of the same material. To the consternation of the guards, their guns had had their surfaces vacuum-cleaned before they were allowed into the room.

Jonno said, "I am now applying the controls of the micromanipulator, and will be simultaneously concentrating on my intent. I'll have nothing to say for a while. Your instruments will have to be content with the machine read-outs."

And now it was time to see if his idea would work.

From the start, Jonno had been faintly aware of the telepath's mental presence — a thin film of sleepy boredom — and beyond that, Robinaire's emotions. She too was bored and uncomfortable, and worried as well.

He began to form the immits, giving himself longer rests than he needed between each effort. In these intervals, he began cautiously directing thoughts towards the telepath herself.

First he concentrated on awareness of her as an individual rather than as the tool she was considered here - learning that her name was Dielle —

and on the emotions of friendliness and the sympathy of shared captivity. When he felt her attention sharpen and a trickle of similar feelings returned, he began to repeat in simple series the ideas of the psychics escaping to a new and peaceful world and of himself being the agent of that escape.

Eventually he got a definite response, and sorted out the knowledge that the precogs had seen an escape attempt and that the clairvoyants believed that the promised land of the vision existed. It had caused unrest and uncertainty among the psychics, whose reaction had been to draw in on themselves and resist the pressures to supply information, as well as causing genuine confusion in what they did perceive. Slowly and simply, Jonno went over the concept that in order for him to help the psychics, they must first help him.

As he repeated these ideas during his rest intervals, Dielle began to accept them; and she demanded what help he wanted.

A report from the psychics, Jonno explained, that an invasion in force was about to take place at the further side of the Admin building. So alarming a report that Haughn would be drawn to investigate it himself, and to concentrate his guards there, away from the labs.

Dielle grasped the intent, but protested: they were punished for every mistake. Jonno concentrated again on the bliss of escape to the peaceful world, where no one would ever hurt them again — at the cost of a risk now.

There was a hiatus, during which Jonno presumed a slow conference was going on between his telepath and one or more other psychics.

At last came the decision. A longer pause followed, presumably for the plan itself to be disseminated among those who were needed to implement it. And then, finally, the room phone rang, and a wildly gesturing keeper on its screen babbled his report to Zar Haughn.

Haughn reacted quickly. He punched a new connection on the phone. "A large-scale outworlder invasion is predicted, for some time within the next three hours. Put a pair of guards on every key point in the Admin building, and bring every other guard to Area Y, third floor Central. I'll be there in five minutes. Once we're in position, sound the general alarm to alert all the non-combatant staff, then shut it off and wait."

He cut the connection and turned to Geeling. "Give your stunner to this guard, and get out two more for us. I'll join you out in the psi lab." To Jonno, who had deliberately paused and looked up as if surprised by the disturbance, Haughn said, "Keep working. Don't forget the girl is still under the nerve stimulator. If you try any tricks, you get stunned." Then he went out through the room's airlock.

Jonno went back to work, as directed, but paused after a couple of minutes to ply his computer. He casually took out his psiproje-pen and used it to scribble down a notation of the computer's reading, gambling that the guards would not think to wonder why he needed the figure in sight instead of in the computer's memory.

He laid the pen down on the workbench, its working end pointing at the guard with the stunner, and turned back to the micromanipulator. With both hands on its controls and his gaze ostentatiously on its image screen, he mentally switched on the psiproje after presetting the mode to low intensity.

The guard yawned, hefted the load of the stunner pack, cast a guilty look at his fellow, and sat down.

The other guard said, "Get up, Frintoc. If the Zar comes back..."

"He's too busy." Frintoc yawned again. "This thing's too heavy to stand around with. I can beam the prisoner just as fast, sitting."

Jonno increased the intensity. Frintoc squirmed out of the pack's carrying straps and leaned back on the pack. His head gradually lolled. The alert guard shook the other's shoulder, snapping out his name again. Jonno slammed the psiproje's intensity to high; and both guards collapsed.

Jonno snatched up his psiproje and computer and took out his gennor. A long sweep of the cameras made hash of their digital recordings. A few quick adjustments of the micromanipulator controls set it to destructive activity on the work he had started.

"Come on," he told Dielle, and led her out through the airlock. Directing her to wait, he crossed to the interrogation/psi room door and beamed down the technician, then released a momentarily alarmed Robinaire.

"We don't have a rifkey," he told her; "so we've only two choices. To get out of the building and try to stay ahead of the Zarsmen till Jonnan or Ithleen can get to us, or to try to use one of Haughn's teleporters. But they seem to need amplifying equipment, and we know nothing about that. So

I think we'd better try to find a way out, hoping the psychics will continue to aid us by misleading Haughn's searchers."

To Dielle he said, "If you come with us we'll try to get you safely out of this world today. Then we'll come back for the others."

They moved towards a main corridor door; but before they could reach it, there was a double thump outside it, and a moment later it opened.

Reaching for the psiproje, he stopped. "You're a bit ahead of schedule, aren't you?" he greeted, as Mayne and Ithleen pulled a pair of unconscious guards into the room and shoved them behind bulky apparatus.

"My day off got interrupted," returned Mayne, with a matching display of casualness.

"Jonno, are you all right?" asked Ithleen, coming over to him.

"Fine, as long as you don't need any mountains climbed or oceans swum at the moment." He smiled at her.

"We've got to try to get to the psychics," Mayne told him. "There's a full-scale alert going on. I don't know whether that will help us or hinder us."

"It's meant to help," said Jonno. "I'll explain as we go."

"Better tell me now, then you can take Robinaire back home for me. I need Ithleen as a guide, so I can't risk her not being able to get back."

"And we need me because I'm in touch with the psychics," Jonno said. "You'll have to take her yourself while Ithleen and I start for their quarters. You can home on us before we get there. You'll be able to return: the psychics are working with us now."

Mayne turned to Robinaire. "Let's go."

He took her back to her own apartment. "I think it's safe for you to be home now. With the psychics no longer working against us, so Haughn won't be able to come after you any more."

She was too exhausted to pay much attention when he transplaced back.

"Let's hear about the psychics, Jonno," he requested as he matched steps with the others.

Jonno explained their co-operation, ending with, "We can communicate with them through Dielle. They're willing to try to distract or confuse their guards and keepers for us."

"We're almost there," cautioned Ithleen.

They stopped, and Jonno asked Dielle to think through a picture of approaching and entering the psychics' area.

"One entrance to the area," he reported from her visualizing. "Two Zarsmen on guard."

"Can Dielle get the other psychics to cause a small distraction so we won't be noticed when we go in? Nothing to get the guards excited and phoning Haughn..."

"How about a spreading squabble?" At Mayne's nod, Jonno instructed Dielle, who eventually reported understanding and agreement.

The psychics elaborated their noise and confusion, and the outworlders finally got all the guards unconscious.

"Tell the psychics to come to me, Dielle," said Mayne. "I'll touch them with this instrument, which temporarily marks them, and soon our allies will take the marked ones to the good world. Here, you're first, so you won't get overlooked."

Ithleen went to the other rooms and took care of the remaining guards and keepers. As she returned she said, "Jonno, have Dielle get a clairvoyant to check if there are any other psychics in the back rooms who haven't come out."

By the time Mayne had applied the markers to the remaining psychics, Jonno had fetched the only one who had not come forward, a sleepy youth who had dozed off in spite of the excitement, and who was now frantic not to miss the promised exodus. As Mayne touched the wexter instrument to this last one, and Ithleen reported their success into her wexcorder, Jonno said, "That's it, then, except for the three Zar Haughn has with him. Shall we go while we can, and come back when the alert's over, or shall we try to find the Zar?"

"You won't have far to look," said a voice from the doorway. Holding a stunner on them was Zar Haughn.

CHAPTER 24

Imprisonment

“Hands on top of your heads!” They reluctantly obeyed.

Haughn gave Mayne a smirk then addressed Jonno. “I see your older brother has arrived to try to rescue you. How did you get away from my guards?”

They could see that Dielle, as well as the three psychics that had been with Haughn, were in the hall.

Do they know that we’re trying to get you people away? Jonno asked Dielle, audible in Mayne and Ithleen’s minds through the shared connection as well.

Everyone knows that you will help us all escape to a safe world, she told him. *I’ve informed these last three about your companion.*

Jonno directed her, *Ask the telepath to make contact with me.*

“So you decline to answer?” said Haughn. “You’ll change your mind!”

Jonno felt the new contact, and a quicker mind than Dielle’s said, *I’m Ancelen. You’re going to help us?*

Yes. But we need help ourselves, first.

“No sudden moves,” ordered Haughn. “By the way, where’s the teenager?”

As the three prisoners stepped towards Haughn, Mayne answered, to pull the Zar’s attention away from Jonno. “We put her into another universe to get her out of the way.”

“Bringing us back to the question of just what you were hoping to - ”

At that moment Dielle and the other psychics vanished, leaving only the three in the outer hallway who had been with Haughn.

There were cries of astonishment and alarm from the half dozen

Zarsmen, and a tendency to crouch defensively, with raised weapons, against an unseen enemy.

A word of startled fury escaped Haughn, then he said, "So that's why you're here. Well, you'll soon be begging for a chance to persuade your superiors to send them back!"

To his guards, he said, "Take them back to the psi lab. And move those three psychics to the outer hall, well clear of the entrance." He backed partly out of the archway, keeping his weapon steady.

Jonno told Ancelen the other psychics were safe. He added quickly, *Tell Zar Haughn the invasion has started.*

"Sir!" called a guard from the outer hallway. "The psychics are babbling about the attack! We're losing!"

Haughn began, "Contact the – "

And suddenly there were soldiers, as if conjured, in the very room with them, in a set of little flashes like showers of falling light-sparks; and all of the earlier inhabitants of the room and hall found themselves unable to move. The soldiers wore flexible, metallic-looking clothing that resembled stylized partial armour, ornately finished. On their heads were helmets with transparent face shields; and each wore a communication headset. There was a look of polish, both literal and metaphoric, about them.

The squad commander, a tall, strongly built man with aquiline features, glanced about unhurriedly, assessing the scene, then murmured inaudibly into his microphone. After a pause, he flipped up his faceplate: "Okay, bring in the three who aren't in uniform, and take all the guards to the pens. Orinx out."

Other soldiers appeared in the archway, carrying the paralyzed psychics, two women and a man, whom they set down and re-balanced on their feet beside the rest of the group.

The flashes returned, this time encompassing their vision. The visual impression of light-sparks faded to reveal a room of ample size, but bare of all furnishing, except for the buttons and slots of a very limited food dispenser in one corner and an enclosed lavatory in another. The walls, floor, and ceiling were made of a substance which looked like blocks of brown stone, but which was warm and resilient to the touch. In lieu of windows, the outer wall had several scattered blocks missing.

The prisoners' paralysis had vanished; the unknown soldiers were gone along with all of Haughn's Zarsmen. Aiming his pistol, Haughn said, "Your troops seem to have made a little mistake."

"That group wasn't ours," Mayne told him. "Since you can't use our transplacing devices yourself, we're your only hope of getting out of this world again."

"Perhaps I don't need to get out. If your troops have taken over my world, perhaps I can gather allies here. However," He clipped his pistol to his belt. "I'll reserve my decision until I know more of the situation."

The two plennors and Ithleen drew apart to confer. Mayne said to them, "We have to get these psychics out. Ithleen, I'd like you to take Jonno back first to get a new rifkey. Then come back here to help with the psychics."

Ithleen took out her rifkey and traced its pattern. Nothing happened. She repeated the motion, carefully, then pressed the homing end, and finally tried the random mode. She looked at Mayne. "Try yours."

Mayne's rifkey was equally unresponsive. Jonno, turned to block Haughn's view of his actions, had taken out his pentools, and now reported, "No response here, either. All psionic tools appear to be dead."

"Even my watch has stopped," Mayne observed. He looked at Jonno. "Can the clairvoyant tell us anything?"

Mental communication was clearer than verbal with the psychics, so Jonno put the query through Ancelen, the younger of the two female psychics. She was short and thin, with a short mop of curly dark hair, and a livelier expression than most of the psychics. It was hard to judge their ages: Ancelen looked like a teenager, but was probably physically in her twenties.

Ithleen peered through the window holes. "We're in a tall building, at one corner of what looks like a hexagon of very large, square-built towers, arranged around an open area. There's a series of thick cables joining the towers at the top, with an assortment of pennants hanging from every meter of the cables' length."

Jonno, relaying information, said, "It's a games arena. The clairvoyant, Connerisk, gets an overwhelming impression of competitive violence as entertainment. Or at least this part of it."

Connerisk, a husky, fair-haired youth with the face of a little boy, who was probably in his late teens, looked eagerly around for approval, and Jonno sent him a compliment by way of Ancelen, as well as a direct smile of thanks.

"Can the psychics tell us anything else?" Mayne asked.

After a long pause, Jonno reported, "Only that we are going to be in danger and will have to make choices."

Ithleen grinned. "That's become standard operating procedure!"

"I think they mean something specific, but can't pin it down. Wait a minute: Connerisk has something more..."

The clairvoyant, Connerisk, had wandered over to peer out the window Jonno reported. "He says he gets the impression of a hunger for sensation... even if it's personally fatal... a willingness to gamble on one's survival for the sheer excitement of facing danger... a strong liking for gambling in any form... an individual, arrogant belief in one's own superiority as a survivor, with a sadistic contempt for the less fit..."

"Here comes someone," Ancelen said aloud.

A section of the wall opposite the window gaps disappeared and Orinx, the raid leader, stepped in, followed by two other soldiers.

Haughn pulled out his stun pistol and attempted to fire at the officer, who looked at him. Orinx remarked, "All your electronic and psionic weapons were blown as you came through our world's psionic barrier. By the way, the barrier's effect on unshielded gadgets is quite permanent. So you might as well dump them; or keep them to barter for favour with a possible patron."

He glanced over the group. "Now, I want to sort you out. I got the impression you people are two opposing camps. Am I right?"

"I am the Zar of Kinnasoor, the empire which comprises most of my world," Haughn informed him. "These three are my subjects, and those three are my prisoners."

Orinx laughed. "Prisoners don't have prisoners. However, I'll be glad to give you separate cells, to keep everybody safe and sound till tomorrow."

"What's to happen then?" Mayne asked.

"That's for Chancellor Ulfri to decide. Since it was her team that spotted you people hopping around that universe and sent us to bring back a sample, she gets first say. She's got a reputation for coming up with special ideas. Or, you'll just be part of the Games. You aren't likely to survive, either way."

Haughn demanded, "What's happened to my men?"

"They've been recruited. They told us they were mercenaries that you picked up in another world to be your personal guard. They'll be given places in the Games; the survivors will be accepted into the army." He looked around at all of them. "I'm Major Orinx. Now, who gives orders on your side?"

Mayne answered, "No one gives orders. We're just a group of friends, and that includes these other three. Although they come from the Zar's world, they prefer to stick with us now."

"Is that so..." The officer's amused voice trailed off as he looked at the faces of the psychics. Orinx grinned. "Well, we've plenty of cells. Since whose side these three are on is disputed, we'll put them by themselves. And you — what did you call yourself? Zar? You can have a cell of your own."

He gestured to the Kinnasoorans. "Come on, now, you four." He walked out of the cell, and Haughn, with a shrug, picked up his useless stunner and followed.

Jonno advised the psychics to go with the soldiers.

Stay in contact with me, Jonno, directed Ancelen. *We'll try to get all of us free.*

The wall resolidified behind them.

"Just in case he was lying about what's affected our tools, or how permanent the damage is," said Mayne, "check them occasionally, especially if we get moved to another location." He tested one of his own pentools as he spoke, then shook his head.

They examined their cell, but could find nothing promising. There was no trace of the temporary door. And though Ithleen thought she might squeeze through one of the window-gaps, the ten-story drop to the beginning of the battlements and ledges made that a worthless effort. The roof was even further away, and no grip could be obtained on the edges of the "stones": their outer surfaces went soft under the pressure of fingers, which slid without purchase; the feeling was like thick velvet over a smooth, seamless, vertical wall.

"We may have to work with Haughn to get out of this," Mayne said. "Since there seems to be nothing we can do for the moment, we might as well rest. I think we'll need our strength tomorrow."

CHAPTER 25

Entertainment

The room to which the three wexter agents were brought the following day continued the theme of stone they had seen in their cell and in the outer walls of the towers, but this time it counterfeited showier material: the light and dark green of malachite, the deep blue of lapis lazuli, the rosy sprays of rhodochrosite, the swirls of white marble, and the opulent magenta of sugilite.

The room was well filled with a variety of people. There were quite a few soldiers, in their bright, pseudo-metallic uniforms. A fair number of spectators with an air of importance, garbed in rich, colourful clothes, circulated near the front of the room. A larger number of people, brightly but less sumptuously dressed, along with what seemed to be a camera crew, filled most of the rest of the space.

On a dais at one end of the room was what could only be called a throne, in polished ebony inlaid with platinum, its interior well cushioned in red plush. It was occupied by a woman in her late thirties who was dressed in an ankle-length white satin sheath dress; its neck, cuffs, and skirt slit were edged with lapis lazuli cabochons shot through with pyrite. Black star sapphires flashed on each hand. Her hair was dyed three colours: various locks of black, white, and blue were woven into an elaborate pagoda-shaped coiffure, sprinkled with tiny silver reflectors from which dangled white and blue diamonds.

She was just over medium height, but held herself regally tall, and wore spike-heeled, platform sandals to increase the effect, which her high hairstyle completed. Her expression and gestures were those of a sensual rather than an athletic or intellectual person; and her figure was both still slim enough and sufficiently curved to look good in her sheath dress.

Standing on one side of her was Major Orinx, now dressed in a red and gold uniform which included one of the pseudo-metallic cloth capes they saw on the male aristocrats. On the other side was Zar Haughn. Though still in his preferred casual wear, the Zar had been permitted to add a cape of rank, in cobalt blue.

"So you've chosen your side," observed Mayne to Haughn.

"Since I was fortunate enough to be offered a choice between designing destruction and suffering it, I have been able to establish myself by demonstrating my ingenuity."

"Doing what?"

"As I've just said: inventing interesting ways to destroy you, for the benefit of Chancellor Ulfri." He inclined his head towards the enthroned woman. "And the amusement of her people."

"So you share their tastes after all," Mayne said.

"I dislike their tastes. But I accept whatever is necessary for my own survival."

Chancellor Ulfri, addressed the prisoners. "Major Orinx and Zar Haughn inform me that you three represent yourselves as a group of friends; and Zar Haughn tells me you come from a culture where friends seem to go into danger to help one another. Is that true?"

Mayne shrugged. "Yes."

"I'm delighted to hear it. I always like to add a special show when it's my turn to hold the Games. So if it goes well I shall create a new Advisor position for Zar Haughn."

She resettled herself and made a signal to the man who appeared to be in charge of the camera crew. Before the Chancellor began speaking, the three prisoners suddenly found themselves in a similar state of paralysis as they had been in yesterday.

"Citizens of Guradcruze: welcome to our fifty-third performance of the World Games. We are going to have what I have been assured will be a very special show to conclude the Games, involving outworlders of an unusual culture. This show has been arranged for us by another outworlder, a guest who promises us great entertainment."

She paused to gesture at Haughn, who made the suggestion of a bow towards the audience, playing the role of visiting royalty who had consented to be an aloof advisor. His cool self-assurance seemed to impress the local audience.

Ulfri continued. "Zar Haughn is visiting us from an Earth where he is the main ruler. He has brought with him these three prisoners, who not only joined in a rebellion against his empire but also made a personal attack on him. I am sure you will appreciate that he has thought up something truly special for them!"

Happy laughter saluted this remark as she paused for the reaction: "And now, my people, it is time for us to begin. To those of you who are at the arena in person, and to those of you who watch from your homes or places of work or recreation, I wish happy viewing. I hereby declare the Fifty-Third Guradcruzan World Games — open!"

A fanfare of music was piped in from somewhere, while Ulfri smiled to the cameras. All of the audience except the guards and a few officials hurried away, moving towards the inner side of the tower complex.

The three prisoners, their partial paralysis reduced enough to allow them to walk slowly, were taken out after Ulfri's small party, onto a spacious balcony that sat among the assorted battlements of the lower part of the building. The towers' entire array of ledges, walkways, arches, and balconies, was now adorned with richly dressed people.

On her private balcony, Ulfri again had a raised and regal-looking chair. The rest of her party took assorted other chairs and benches, or stood on a lower level against the broad railing. There was some jostling for position; its aim seemed to be for the best views rather than the most comfortable or prestigious seats.

The competitions in the arena were straightforward. Singly, or in hordes that filled the huge courtyard, people sought to kill other people, with a variety of weapons from bare hands or short knives to laser pistols and sonic projectors. They fought on foot, on horseback, and on motorcycles. Sometimes both sides were armed alike and matched in numbers; at other times the weapons were varied or the numbers uneven; but the battles all appeared to be willing ones. They were interspersed, however, with more wretched scenes, where obviously unwilling victims, with little or no weaponry, were hunted down by gradual maiming, or were secured to stakes and toyed with until ner life was extinguished.

The Guradcruzans in the Chancellor's party watched with excitement, often laying quick bets on the outcome of a competition, or on how long a victim would last. Zar Haughn looked on without expression, though he made an occasional comment on the tactics used by one side or another in the competitions.

In one of the intermissions for clearing and cleaning up the arena, Ulfri looked over her prisoners. "You don't seem to be enjoying the Games. Is it because you think you're to be put down there yourselves? Don't worry; we have something better in store. All this." she waved a jewelled hand at the arena, "is merely physical. My specials always feature psychological aspects; arena stuff is too crude for that. So enjoy this part of the Games."

"Your entertainment doesn't suit our taste, Chancellor," said Mayne evenly.

Ulfri looked surprised. "Are you serious? Do you find no excitement in watching this? I know otherworld cultures are different, indeed, we have been unable to find any like our own; but surely an enjoyment of battle is not cultural but biological."

Ithleen answered, "The tendency to use violence may be universal, but the enjoyment of it as entertainment is not."

"No, you're wrong," said Ulfri, "The love of drama is innate!"

"Violence, even if it's only acted, eventually loses its drama and becomes dull horror. It has to be continually increased to retain its impact; and finally you run out of excesses to add. People just become desensitized," said Mayne.

"Hmm. You may have a point there," mused Ulfri, stroking the gems on her neckline. "It's true I've always found it best to climax my Games with something small-scale and intense, because people are sated with sheer physical spectacle by that point. Yes, I suppose it's a more concentrated form of drama I give them: intimate scenes of psychological stress and individual danger. But they'd feel cheated if they didn't get the big show first; so that also satisfies some natural craving."

"Perhaps in your people it does. Human nature needn't be the same in every universe. And you may breed for the kind of people who enjoy your culture. Most self-destructive species must finish themselves off fairly quickly. I doubt yours will last long," Ithleen finished judiciously.

"Is that a veiled threat? Zar Haughn has told me that your world is run by a ruthless technocracy, so powerful it overcame his world in a single night's attack. But he thinks our weapons are superior."

"Theirs may be superior, Chancellor," Haughn amended. "Their attack was so quick and devastating that I had no chance to see their weapons before your soldiers brought us here. I can estimate superiority only on the basis of their non-military technology, since that's all I've seen."

"And their world really attacked yours in a full-scale conquest simply in retaliation for a few trifling raids you made?"

"Or perhaps for even less reason than that: perhaps the very knowledge of our existence was enough to set them on us," said Haughn.

Ulfri shook her head, setting her diamonds shimmering. "I find it hard to picture these philosophy-spouting, violence-rejecting people as representatives of a world that conquers on sight."

"I underestimated them, too, and suffered considerable loss and damage at their hands even before the conquest."

Ulfri considered the prisoners again. "It's true they don't appear fearful. Have they such confidence in themselves that they think they'll survive?"

Haughn shrugged. "Perhaps they expect their superiors to attack this world before you get around to killing them.".

Ulfri smiled. "If they do, they won't carry it out in a single attack. These people had no shields against our barrier. All of their first attackers will find themselves helpless."

"You're assuming they don't have the technology to detect your barrier and counteract it before they come in. Remember, this group wasn't planning to come here," Haughn said.

"I only hope they're good enough to provide a battle. I can't believe they will be, when I consider these samples." She smoothed her gown and turned back to the arena. "Well, we may be able to form a more valid opinion after we have tested these three to destruction."

CHAPTER 26

Assessment

After the arena part of the Games, the wexter agents found themselves in a large, multi-storied room, filled with assorted constructions and pieces of equipment. There were several electronic boards and a large number of cameras throughout the room. The prisoners' partial paralysis was increased while they stood waiting.

Chancellor Ulfri, with Zar Haughn and Major Orinx were also there in close attendance.Ulfri said, "You are going to undergo a series of tests. How many, of course, depends on how many you survive."

"And if you run out of tests before you run out of prisoners, what then?" asked Mayne.

"I would declare an extension of the Games, and we would hold you over for the second day, while my advisors scrambled to think up another set of tests that would cap even this lot. I hope you last long enough to get them worried that they might just have to do that!"

"We'll do our best to worry them," promised Mayne drily.

"I do hope Zar Haughn is right about your being close friends who will be concerned for one another. I've become known for my psychological specials and would hate to have one fall flat. The extra kick in this show is to come from the strain on your trust and the eventual decay of your altruism. Well, let's begin."

"High above you," pointed out Ulfri, "you'll see a large container. It is full of hydrochloric acid. The bottom of the container has been designed so that different spots on it will be eaten through at different rates, so that, if nothing prevents it, you will find yourself eventually dodging a steady rain of acid."

She smiled. "It's there as an incentive for you to take action. You can see, over to the side, an even larger container on a crane arm, which we can swing out — it is acid-proof and will protect you completely. All you have to do to arrange for this protection is to let one of your number leave the circle."

"And what will make that difficult?" asked Mayne.

"The rest of your circle has now been blocked by a high cylindrical force field. The passage of one body-mass out through this gap marked by the coloured lights will affect three automatic triggers. One will enclose the acid container, eliminating that danger; one will close the gap in the force field, so no one else can get out; the third," She smiled again in anticipation, "the third will turn on two nerve-stimulator beams, aimed at the two who have been left in the circle. Zar Haughn tells me he has made you familiar with the effects of these stimulators."

Sapphires flashing, Ulfri made a one-handed gesture of presentation. "One of you must abandon the others to intense pain for a period of time. Or else all three of you stay. Oh, and you may notice that the first drops have started. See the effect on the floor of your circle!"

Mayne caught his analog's eye. "Jonno?"

"Ready. Who hits?"

Mayne hesitated only a moment before accepting responsibility. "I will." He turned and beckoned Ithleen with a motion of his head. She came quickly to his side.

"We've a solution," he told her.

"That's fast," she smiled. "What is it?"

"This." He slammed a blow into her midriff. As she doubled up, Jonno caught her and slung her through the gap.

The three switches closed. The outer covering swung over, blocking off the rain of acid; the gap markers winked out; and the two plennors collapsed, writhing, on the floor.

Ithleen was spared seeing the beginning of their agony. When she was able to unfold herself and draw air back into her lungs, she began to crawl back towards the circle.

Ulfri, delighted, ordered, "Cut the force field. Hold the beams tight on the two men. See what she does."

Major Orinx said, "Five to one she can't do anything, even if you give her a chance."

"Taken!" cried Ulfri. "Listen, woman. If you get them out of the circle, they're yours. We'll turn off the beams."

Ithleen had reached them. Kneeling, she tried to get a grip on, Jonno, the nearer man; but as her arm entered the beam she became unable to control her spasmodically twitching hand. She pulled back, gasping, then made a flashing grab. The result was the same.

"Ten to one!" cried Orinx.

Ulfri hesitated, saw Ithleen begin to reposition herself purposefully, and said, "Done!"

Ithleen placed herself on her back, legs doubled up, feet against Jonno's body. The agony in her feet did not matter; her leg muscles still worked. She shoved, followed the body, and shoved again. There was a scattering of cheers and curses among the technicians, who had also been making bets, as she got the first man over the line. Her feet still too cramped to use, crawled back for Mayne.

"Concede?" asked Ulfri, as Ithleen began to move Mayne with the same method and determination.

Orinx threw up his hands in exaggerated defeat. "Concede."

"Cut the beams," ordered Ulfri. "Let them all rest. They'll need to be steady for the next one."

There was an unhurried bustle of activity among the onlookers as bets were paid off, equipment was pulled away and dismantled, and most of the cameras were moved over to a new area of the big room, where technicians made final adjustments and last-minute checks to a new array of equipment.

The paralysis was left off of the prisoners, though a set of guards watched them, keeping well back. The guards were scarcely needed at the moment; the wexter agents were not capable of any attempt to attack or try for freedom, as their muscles slowly unknotted from their ordeal.

Ithleen sat between the two plennors, who lay where she had shoved them, gathering their strength. There was no aid she could offer except her caring presence: she put a hand on each man.

"Ithleen," Mayne managed to croak, touching her hand, "did I hurt you?"

"Of course not," she assured him quickly. "You're much too expert to misjudge a blow. But it was a dirty trick to give me no say on who went out!"

Jonno, taking her other hand, and speaking with equal difficulty, said, "We counted your vote. We simply outvoted you, two to one."

"I want a recount," said Ithleen with deliberate levity. "I didn't hear the voting. You've been doing too much associating with telepaths lately."

"Jonno, are you still in touch with Ancelen?" asked Mayne, his voice steadying under his will.

Jonno forced his attention onto his contact with the telepath. "She withdrew her attention when the pain started, but I can still feel her presence."

"Do they know what's going on, that we can't help them yet, but haven't forgotten them?"

Jonno checked. "Yes. From what they've learned of this place, they're horrified by the possibility of remaining. They feel we're their only hope of getting away - and they want to know if there's any way they can help us."

"Not yet; but tell her to keep tuned in whenever there isn't too much pain, in case we have to move fast to get away. Can she link the others to you, too, if we should have to give instructions to everyone at once?"

"Yes; if she has a few moments' notice."

Ulfri came over to them, walking gracefully in spite of her long, narrow skirt and high heels. "We're ready for you now; and you appear to be sitting up and taking notice again." This was not literally true, as the plennors had remained lying down, to get all the rest they could; but all three now obeyed Ulfri's gesture, and got up.

Ulfri told them, "This one's very simple. You'll sit in these three compartments and dismantle the set of electronic equipment you'll find in each. Zar Haughn tells me you have the requisite knowledge."

"And what's the catch this time?" Jonno asked.

"Each set is connected to sources of lethal radiation aimed into the compartments. If you don't get the set apart in time, the shielding in your own compartment will be drawn away, exposing you to the radiation.

If you make a mistake in the dismantling, the shields in the other two compartments will be pulled back, finishing off the other two people. Again, any one of you may escape by simply leaving the compartment. But if you do so before all the sets are dismantled, the two people remaining will be irradiated. And since you'll each be enclosed separately this time, there'll be no chance to repeat your spectacular gesture of self-sacrifice."

Closed into the compartments, the three scientists began to examine the complex circuits in front of them. Mayne said, "Jonno, check with me to see if we have duplicates. Starting at the upper left corner..."

They quickly established that the sets were different. "Individual work, then," Jonno muttered, his attention already on the work. "Well, unless our hands are still unsteady, it's just a question of whether we can trace out the circuits correctly and in time."

"Haughn's had a part in this, so look out for tricks. Make sure you know what you're doing before you touch anything."

Within seconds, their attention focused wholly on the circuits, the plennors had almost forgotten the danger. After careful study, they began to manipulate and disconnect, pausing many times for more study, then operating again.

Finally Mayne sat back and relaxed tense muscles as he looked around. He was not surprised to see that Jonno had beaten him; the younger plennor was more adept at this sort of work, and completely forgot his self-doubts whenever he became absorbed. Mayne was surprised, however, to see that Ithleen was also sitting back already. "All done?" he asked her, "or just taking a break?"

"Neither," said Ithleen quietly. "I haven't analyzed a circuit since my student days. I don't dare touch it."

They had forgotten she was purely a theorist. No amount of intelligence could substitute for practical experience; she could not work on the circuit without more risk to the other two than she would chance.

But if she left it untouched her own survival would be brief. And if either plennor left his compartment to try to get a look at her circuit board and help her, she and the other plennor would both be irradiated. The only choice appeared to be between one survival and two, and the two would be achieved only by waiting helplessly for Ithleen's destruction.

A few seconds went by as the two plennors surveyed the situation, rejecting the option of passively accepting their own safety at the price of Ithleen's life. Then Mayne said, "Jonno – Ancelen?"

"Of course!" cried Jonno. "Ithleen, ready?"

Ithleen was a shade behind the pair of analogs in sharing the thought. "Ready? Oh. Yes." But then she hesitated. "It's riskier than just waiting."

"We choose to take the risk," said Mayne.

Jonno added, "Why not? We could lose in the next test, anyway."

"All right," Ithleen agreed. She leaned forward and directed her gaze onto the circuits.

Ancelen's contact came, established itself, and brought in Jonno to share Ithleen's perceptions. On an added thought, he had Ancelen link in Connerisk as well: the clairvoyant's talent helped Jonno be sure of his deductions about the deliberately confused connections, without elaborate checking. The shortcut was risky but necessary: time was much shorter now.

As seconds slipped by, Jonno studied the pattern of circuitry; then he directed Ithleen, and she picked up the tools supplied and began manipulating the components. She worked with control and precision, and with complete faith in Jonno's directions; she was the only one of the three scientists who was not tense and perspiring.

And finally her set too was disconnected. Jonno and the psychics withdrew; and the three wexter agents sat back, becoming aware of the sudden swell of talk in their immediate audience, as more bets were paid off and pleasure or disgruntlement expressed.

The guards took the three agents out and held them under the paralysing control again while technicians cleared away the compartments and prepared the next trial.

Ulfri turned to one of her technical staff, all her gems flashing with her movement. "Extylin, do we have audience reactions yet on the first event?"

"Yes, Chancellor. It was very popular, but unexpectedly, there was a strong swing of sympathy to the prisoners, starting when the men threw the woman out, and mounting when she went back in for them."

Ulfri frowned, then shrugged. "Well, they weren't able to do anything so ostentatiously gallant this time. Interest should return to the gauging of their various survival chances."

"Yes, Chancellor. And I think we'll have a good reaction on this second performance. The suspense when the woman took so long to start working was excellent. How was she inhibited?"

"I've no idea. She can't have been frightened: she worked confidently enough once she started." Ulfri rubbed her cuff jewels pensively.

"One of my crew did overhear her say something about it being less risky to wait. Perhaps she misunderstood the situation, and the others had to urge her to work. Or perhaps she was trying to sacrifice herself for the others, in her turn."

"Perhaps. I trust none of their conversation is picked up by the audio?"

"No, ma'am. Would you like us to include that, this time?"

"Certainly not. We've already had one surge of sympathy for them; we don't want to risk another by letting the audience see things from their point of view. And that includes the audience here, too - seeing the audience reaction affects the viewers. Make sure any technicians near enough to hear the subjects talking are wearing earphones and listening to instructions instead."

Major Orinx interposed, "Seeing that these people are different from the usual run, don't you think there might be some added suspense if we heard them offering to make their sacrifices for each other?"

"No. There's more suspense in wondering if they will, or whether this is the time they'll break. And speculating on their motivations gives people something to do during the breaks - not everyone pays attention to the commercials! Besides, how could their deaths be a satisfying conclusion, if people began to identify with them? No, I want the audio kept on the betting and speculation going on here, as usual. Never give up the long game for the short gain."

Ulfri turned to Zar Haughn, who was watching the proceedings with his usual impassivity. "Well, you appear to be right on one aspect of these people at least. They are foolishly loyal to one another. And they also seem to be good survivors, even if they do spout ridiculous philosophy. I'm pleased with them, and with your scenarios. How long do you think they'll last?"

"I'm not a betting man, Chancellor. I will say only that enough chances will defeat even the most competent survivor; and that their tendency to be self-sacrificing is likely to hasten their end."

"Well, this next test will give them full opportunity to indulge in their penchant for self-sacrifice. Let's see which one they decide it's to be."

CHAPTER 27

Choice

Three cranes had deposited the prisoners on a small platform in the centre of the area which was covered with unmarked sand. One of the cranes withdrew; the other two dangled thin ropes down to the platform.

Ulfri addressed her prisoners: "The area around you contains a large number of pressure-sensitive mines. This time we will allow two of you to come out: each of those ropes will support one person. If you refuse to leave, the nerve stimulator beams will be used to drive all of you out through the mine field. You have thirty seconds to make your choice of who shall be left."

Jonno said quietly to the other two, "I'm the only one with a hope of telling where the mines are. There isn't time for Ancelen to adjust to working in a different mind. And if I tried to lead you, they could force us to separate."

The other two nodded slowly. Each touched his hand briefly; then Ithleen and Mayne took hold of the ropes and were drawn up and back, into the charge of the guards again. They stood watching Jonno with outward calmness, except that Ithleen's hand was tight on Mayne's arm.

While the other two were being removed, Jonno had had Ancelen link him with Connerisk again, and explained to the clairvoyant that he needed to know where objects were buried under the sand.

He heard Connerisk's voice now: *I can't see everything. It's hard work being aware of hidden things, especially if they aren't near me. And I feel dizzy, seeing something through someone else's eyes.*

Ancelen herself cut in to remind Connerisk that the wexter agents were their only hope of escape. Still protesting the difficulty and doubt of success, he finally agreed to try. His decision was just in time; although the mental exchange had taken barely more time than the removal of the other two agents, there was a stirring of impatience among the spectators when Jonno appeared to be delaying his start; and Ulfri's hand had stilled from its pleased stroking of her sleeve.

Jonno looked at the area immediately around him. Connerisk told him, *I think there... and maybe there... perhaps nothing there.*

Unconsciously holding his breath, Jonno stepped into the clear spot and looked again. Connerisk took him another step, another, another. Warming up to the task, the clairvoyant began to perform almost enthusiastically. But suddenly, after nearly a dozen steps, he said, *No clear spots on any side.*

Jonno stepped carefully backward, then waited a few moments while Connerisk found a safe continuation through the buried maze. They went on, one pace at a time. But three-quarters of the way to safety, Connerisk began to tire and falter.

Jonno told him to take a minute's rest, and stood still until he saw Ulfri, her toe tapping impatiently. To give the viewers something to see while he coaxed Connerisk, Jonno made a half-step forward, then pulled back before he touched the ground. *Let's try again, Connerisk.*

I can't. I'm tired.

Sorry, but they won't let me wait any longer.

Ancelen cut in: *Connerisk, you help him or I'll link you to someone in pain.*

All right, all right! But I can't see properly when I'm tired.

Just do your best, Jonno told him.

That spot, said Connerisk, and Jonno stepped towards it.

Wait, no! I meant that's a bad spot, Connerisk corrected, and Jonno fought to recover his balance without completing the step.

Where's a good one? Jonno asked, keeping his mind calm, though his heartbeat had accelerated briefly over the narrow escape.

This way. No, maybe this – I tell you, I can't see them!

Keep trying. Take it slowly. Find any safe spot, even if it doesn't lead on. As long as I keep moving, and occasionally try a new spot, they may remain patient. I can step back again if we hit another dead end. That's good. Now another one...

More and more slowly he approached the edge of the area. Finally Connerisk said, *I can't see at all. I just can't, Ancelen!*

Jonno estimated the remaining distance. He made the decision. *Okay, Connerisk, thanks.* He jumped.

He did not quite make it to the edge, but there was no explosion, and one more step took him clear.

There was the usual small tumult as Jonno was brought to join the other two. Ithleen managed to unlock her fingers from Mayne's arm – hampered more by her own tension than the partial-paralysing effect which, at half strength, kept them from sudden moves – and reached out to touch Jonno, oblivious of the cameras zooming in to catch this display of emotion, until Ulfri's snapped command zoomed them out again.

Technicians moved about, setting up new apparatus, and the camera operators hurriedly concentrated on this activity. After a few minutes, Ulfri strolled over to the prisoners, nodding the cameras back in to catch her outline of the next ordeal, making sure that the focus was on her.

"Two of you will be secured against the wall there, with a laser pointed at each. Every ten seconds a computer will send a 'fire' or a 'don't fire' signal to one of the lasers in turn. The choice of which signal it sends will be random, except that there will never be two 'fire' signals in a row, and it will always alternate between the two lasers and their targets. You follow me so far?"

"Yes."

"The third person will have a button to press, which will inhibit the next signal from the computer. But the inhibitor button will take twenty seconds to recycle. So if you press it just before a 'fire' signal, it will stop that; the next signal will be a safe one; and the button will be ready for use again. But if you press it before a 'don't fire' signal, the next signal could be a 'fire' one, and the button would not work again in time to stop it."

She paused to let them appreciate the danger, one hand absently playing with the lapis lazuli gems on her neckline as she smiled at them; then she resumed: "Now the bursts will not be of lethal power, and the lasers are programmed to swing about a little, so the hits will be scattered; some may even miss; but cumulatively, they will destroy their targets, if few enough of them are inhibited. Of course, you can always press the button every second time, thus ensuring the safety of one of your friends by sacrificing the other. Or you can try to outguess the program in an effort to save them both. I leave you to calculate the odds against your doing so."

Mayne asked, "How long does this go on for?"

"Ah, that you won't know. We have set a time limit, to make it fair to those who are wagering on the outcome. But it will be long enough to do permanent damage, if your guessing is poor. Now, who wants to be the one who guesses which choice-moments are going to be the harmful ones?" She eyed Jonno. "Perhaps you'd like revenge on your friends for so readily abandoning you the last time."

To the other two, Jonno said, "I'm the logical one."

They nodded, and Ulfri said, "What, you all agree? Do you really think you can trust him to try to stop the laser blasts?"

"Don't worry," said Ithleen, "your fun won't be cut short."

"I believe you do trust him," said Ulfri, marvelling. "Well, over you go, then, and get into position."

Under Orinx's direction, the guards secured Ithleen and Mayne against the wall by metal bands about their waists. Ulfri, smiling at them again, said, "You can try a little dodging if you like. If you think you can lean out of the line of fire instead of into it."

Jonno was led to a console with a light and a button. Ulfri told him, "Within every ten seconds, after that light has been turned on, you must make your guess and decide whether to press the button or not. When the light goes off, the computer's program is completed, and we will release whatever is left of your two companions."

Jonno had already appealed to Ancelen again: *Please ask Rexede to tell me when there's going to be a 'fire' signal.*

I'll link her to you.

Rexede, you understand the situation?

Yes, the precog Rexede replied, *Ancelen has been showing us what's happening.*

Are you ready to predict for me?

I can't. It's a random program. It's not even on tape. The computer generates the random number each time.

But it's a yes-no situation, each time. It's not as if you had to pick from a wide field of choices.

But it's random. There's nothing leading up to the choices. The probabilities are equal every time. There's no way I can tell what's coming.

You can't get anything at all? Shaken, Jonno looked at the other two agents, who were depending on him, confident that he had already arranged for the psychics' help. He had let them accept the danger, and had not had sense enough to check first that he could give them the protection he thought he could.

I could only guess, same as you, Rexede told him, pleading for understanding and forgiveness.

Jonno thought desperately. *Ancelen, has the computer got any sort of a read-out that Connerisk could watch for me?*

Yes, it has; there's a camera focused on it. But Connerisk's exhausted. He can't even see the readout. In fact, he's half asleep.

Then how do you know about the readout?

Same way I could tell Rexede about the computer operations: there's a man watching it to be sure everything's working properly. I can see what's in his mind.

Ancelen! Jonno yelled mentally, then quickly apologized. *Please tell me every reading.* He couldn't know what the next reading would be, but he could know what the current one was, with a very small margin of error.

Okay. It says the first is going to be no-fire.

The guards finished securing Ithleen and Mayne, and moved away. The light went on.

Ancelen passed along the readout information to him at each ten second interval. *No... no... fire!*

Jonno pressed the button and held his breath as the double ten seconds ticked by. There was no flash.

No... no... no... no... now! She continued instructing him at each interval, *no... no... He's stopped watching!*

The blast struck the wall beside Ithleen's head, raising blisters on her ear. The monitor returned to watching his readout, and Ancelen resumed calling. But again the man's attention wandered, and the second missed yes-call burned Mayne's thigh. Another struck his shoulder before the monitor returned to duty. Minutes later a long yawn and stretch permitted a blast to touch Ithleen's neck, for another visible scorch. Two more missed calls were missed shots as well, as the bored monitor again looked elsewhere. Another shot caught Ithleen's side as he looked at his watch.

And then, finally, the light went off.

"The luck of these people is incredible!" said Ulfri to Zar Haughn, shaking her head in disbelief.

"It can't last. Anyway, the next test is purely physical skill. Luck can't affect it."

"Extylin, how are the audience ratings?"

"Best we've ever had, Chancellor." He consulted notes. "People are pleased with the ingenuity of the situations and the apparent emotional involvement of the subjects. Intrigued at the way they try to save one another instead of concentrating on their own survival. Wondering how long they'll do that, and amazed that they've survived so long. Bets are at an all-time high."

Ulfri turned back to her prisoners, considered them a moment, then said, "We'll let the other man be the active person this time." She signalled the guards, who took Ithleen and Jonno to the new area.

Ulfri explained to Mayne: "You'll be at the other end of a laser this time. There are two light-sensitive screens up there. A spot will appear alternately on each screen, at some random position. Your task is to sight your laser on that light spot by the time the laser fires, so that its beam hits the spot. The delay time between appearances of the spot is just long enough for average reaction time of shifting to the new aiming spot. Of course, reaction time falls off with fatigue."

"What's the danger this time?"

"Your two companions have been placed in air-tight compartments. As they breathe, they are using up the air that's already in there. Each time you succeed in hitting your target, the person connected to that one gets another puff of oxygen, and some carbon dioxide is absorbed from the compartment. Now, just as in the previous test, it's possible to concentrate on one of the targets, and give yourself a better chance to save one. It's up to you."

Mayne knew that his reaction time was faster than average; but it would unquestionably slow as the effort dragged on. He could only hope that the trial's length was also based on average figures and that he might last out.

Ithleen and Jonno, to whom Ulfri's words had been relayed by speakers, immediately sat down in their compartments, deliberately relaxing, and began controlled, even breathing. Jonno, using self-hypnosis, was able to slow his respiration below normal.

The test began, and at first went well; but as time piled up, eventually Mayne began missing. Obviously the time had been calculated to last beyond average ability. Gambling that Jonno had succeeded in stretching out his air supply, Mayne began favouring Ithleen; but soon both of the victims began to slump.

Willing himself to speed and accuracy, Mayne peered through blurring eyes at the screens. He could not see the light spots.

It took him several frantic seconds to realize the lights really were not there; the test was concluded; and the compartments had been re-opened to the air.

"You have done so well," Ulfri told them, "that we shall have to keep two of you over till tomorrow for a new series!" She was so pleased with the success of her latest special presentation that she spoke in triumph, postponing concern over the need to find a second climax, to top the one she was planning for this day.

"Two?" exclaimed Mayne, looking again to reassure himself he had seen both of the others emerge.

"Two," said Ulfri; "for in our final test, neither luck nor skill can serve you. You will have no control over the danger. Only a choice as to which one it will strike." She looked them over with a smile. "We'll let the woman be the chooser this time."

As Orinx and the guards took charge of the two plennors, Ulfri led Ithleen and Zar Haughn up a dozen steep steps onto an unrailed platform. Extending out, from a few centimeters beneath it, was a metal-walled enclosure, about two meters wide and five long. At the far end, dividing it into two compartments, was a short partition with a heavy metal door currently projecting straight out from its end. The guards were securing one of the plennors in each compartment, bound to the end wall of the enclosure by, as before, a flexible metal band around the waist: again Ulfri was leaving her prisoners enough freedom to squirm and cringe, if they would oblige her.

Ulfri directed Ithleen's attention to a control console in a glassed-in booth at another level above and a little behind the catwalk. "From there, well out of your reach, I am going to start a force beam moving out along the pen. We have arranged for it to be made visible; you will see it as an arc of light moving out from its base under this platform. From up here, you can watch it all the way to the far end. And you can watch the expressions of your friends, too, as they await your choice. The beam is harmlessly diverted by metal; but what it does to flesh and bone...well, you'll have the chance to see."

Gems flashed as she pointed to a large switch on a console mounted beside them on the catwalk. "You may push that switch in either direction. When you do, the metal door will be slammed in front of whichever compartment you have chosen, left or right as you move the switch, protecting the man behind it and condemning the other. Of course, if you make no choice, the door stays open, and both die."

"What —" Ithleen began, "What's this dial?"

"That will show the beam's progress. You must make your choice before the needle touches the red zone. After that it's too late."

Ulfri complacently smoothed her dress and added, "Now, you will be set loose from the partial-paralysis, so you can make your choice at the last minute and move fast enough to implement it; but don't get any foolish notion of trying to storm up and turn off my controls: the door will be locked."

Dutifully followed by Zar Haughn, Ulfri turned and mounted to the control booth. When both were inside, she made a show of turning a key and shoving over a bolt.

Ithleen stood alone on the catwalk, with the meter and switch beside her.

Haughn chose a vantage point in a corner of the booth to watch the unfolding of his planned climax. Ulfri stood poised over her two simple controls. With a graceful wave of a jewelled hand, she signalled for the removal of the partial-paralysis from the three prisoners; then she set a dial and pushed the on-switch.

The needle on Ithleen's console quivered and began to move. Below her feet, she saw the arc of light come out and begin to slide forward, centimeter by centimeter... a decimeter... another... a meter...

The needle crept towards the red. Ithleen looked out at the two men, each standing quietly, awaiting her choice, making no attempt to influence her decision as to which one she must kill. The beam swept forward along the enclosure, a quarter, halfway, three-quarters... The needle moved smoothly up, five widths away from the red area... four... three...

Ithleen slapped over the switch.

CHAPTER 28

Escape

The door slammed across in front of Mayne. At the same instant Ithleen ran out along the narrow wall top and flung herself down in front of Jonno.

"Ithleen!" He tried uselessly to pull her behind him.

Ulfri cursed and slapped at her control board. The beam stopped, and then withdrew.

Zar Haughn, turning to look at her, raised his eyebrows. "Why?"

"Because there'd be only one of them left!" snarled Ulfri. "I need at least two to run a second series."

"You could run this scenario again, with the woman chained to her place on the catwalk," suggested the Zar.

"I never do the same thing twice," said Ulfri haughtily. She added in a matter-of-fact tone, "Aside from the aesthetics of the matter, doing it twice would make it look as if I'd been defeated in my first attempt. I prefer to have it appear that I have allowed them to survive in order to hold them over for a yet better test. A repeat would also be anti-climactic, after the woman's stunt..." She opened the control room door and called down to Orinx, "Major, unfasten them and take them all out."

Within the enclosure, the three prisoners had watched the withdrawal of the force beam with as much surprise as thankfulness. Then Ithleen stirred and said, "I'm all right, Jonno. The beam didn't touch me, honestly! You don't have to hold me up."

"I happen to like holding you."

"I — know. When Ancelen linked our minds, she joined the emotional levels first. Yours was a flood of warm protectiveness."

"I felt your emotions, too. Under an intense curiosity as to how the linkage would feel, there was a sort of shy eagerness for it. You do care, don't you, Ithleen?"

"I – yes – but –"

His arms tightened about her, and his head bent towards her; but at that moment the guards finished pulling the walls and partition clear and applied the paralysis again.

Major Orinx, who was happy over winning his latest bet – he had switched sides halfway through the trials and started betting on the prisoners – pulled Ithleen and Jonno gently apart, then herded the three prisoners over to Ulfri, who had descended from her position at the control board accompanied by Haughn.

For the benefit of her audience, Ulfri was looking extremely pleased and, after nodding in the cameras, said cheerfully to Orinx, "A fine performance. We have got excellent spectacle out of these subjects. The best we have ever had! And now we are to have a bonus. A second day's special entertainment for the Games! It's unprecedented. Put them in a cell to rest up for their performance tomorrow. Zar Haughn, you have until tomorrow morning to think up a few more activities for them. And your new ideas must be even more dramatic!"

As the sound camera was turned elsewhere, she added, "And this time one of your schemes had better turn out to be foolproof, if you wish to retain your new status here!"

"It's easy enough to ensure that, if you drop your requirement that each test has to provide at least a nominal chance for them to survive."

"There's no drama without that."

Orinx asked, "Shall I take them back to the army tower, Chancellor?"

"No," said Ulfri thoughtfully. "Shunting them back and forth would suggest routine, and I want to keep up the feeling of drama and suspense. Put them in one of the cells here. And put guards on duty at the cell, too. Make a big display of it."

With due ostentation, a large escort of guards took the three prisoners a short distance along a corridor to their new cell. One of the guards touched a control set in the corridor wall, and a space appeared in the pseudo-stone.

The prisoners were taken through and the paralysis released as the guards left. The door vanished.

The cell was a duplicate of their previous one; nevertheless, they explored it carefully — and just as vainly, it turned out.

Mayne asked, "Have you told the psychics how much we appreciate their help?"

"Yes," Jonno said. "Any ideas on escape?"

He shook his head. "We'll just have to think over everything that's happened since we've arrived and see if we can find a weakness."

They settled down to grim reverie. Time moved inexorably forward.

When Ancelen reported that Connerisk was recovered, Jonno asked the psychics to do a survey of the tower complex, linking him in so he could assess it. He relayed information to the other agents as he made the survey: "The towers are connected only on the first two levels; outside exits are on the ground floor only. Lots of ways out to the ledges and balconies, but they're all inside, around the arena. There are guards at all the outer exits and at all the tower junctions."

Mayne suggested, "Have a look through the power and research towers."

Jonno soon reported, "The labs are very well equipped; I think we could find good enough equipment to improvise anything we know how to, if we could get at it. The power/industrial tower is heavily guarded at the entrances, but its night staff is skeletal. I think it's largely automated, anyway, so there probably aren't many people there even in the day."

"I don't suppose there's any way we could locate the Guradcruzan version of transplacing equipment," Mayne muttered.

"We'd have to be able to recognize it. What we really need is a way to repair our own rifkeys," Jonno said.

Mayne shook his head in doubt. "Even if we could, would they blow again as we passed through the barrier?"

Ithleen said, "Remember, they're wexter tools. I think their fail-safe design would complete the move they had started before the break-down affected them — like a glide after your engine cuts out. But they might not break at all; the barrier might work only on incoming machinery."

"But in either case," said Jonno, "we wouldn't be able to get back unless and until the wexters find us a means. And we have six people to move with only two rifkeys. And three of those people are beyond our physical reach right now."

"Do the psychics know all that?" Mayne asked.

"Yes; Ancelen's linked with me, and understands we'll have to get ourselves out first, and then find a way to come back for them."

The discussion about the rifkeys reminded Ithleen about Mayne's advice to recheck their own equipment; she took hers out and tried it, running through the modes and touching out the pattern several times. She continued idly holding the device, thinking of the time Mayne's rifkey had failed and he had been able to patch it up after she showed him the mental symbol for opening it. The rifkey came apart in her hands. She looked at it with surprise, then exclaimed, "It's not entirely dead!"

Mayne pulled out his own rifkey and tried it for both transplacement and opening. The second command worked. In a moment, both plennors were huddled over the two rifkeys.

Finally Jonno said, "You can see a lot of fusing in each rifkey."

Ithleen said eagerly, "If the damage is tiny, then he must also have been right in saying their control was designed to break rather than destroy, so they could copy any new weapons brought in."

Ithleen said unabashedly hopeful. "Knowing the wexters, my hunch is that they designed the rifkeys so that any attack on them would blow a different component."

"So we could cannibalize one to repair the other!" cried Jonno. He peered at the two rifkeys. "It looks to me as if the destroyed parts are not quite in the same spot. What do you think, Jonnan? Can we trade a portion over?"

"Depends on how extensive the damage is. If it overlaps in the least, the changeover would be no use: we have to move a whole module, to be sure of including all the sub-immit-level circuits..."

"And if we can get you two into a lab," said Ithleen, pulling herself down from excited hope to practicality. "Any ideas on getting us out of this cell?"

"The door is created by a touch to the wall: no keys needed," Mayne mused. "Any way we could persuade or trick the guards into doing that?"

Ithleen said, "What we need is a way to get them to press the spot without noticing what they're — Jonnan! Is it possible to plant a hypnotic suggestion by telepathy?"

The two plennors looked at her in surprise, then at each other in consideration. "I've never heard of telehypnosis," said Mayne; "but then, my Earth has never had telepaths good enough to try it. In this case, the telepath would have to relay the suggestions..."

"No," Jonno corrected; "she can make a direct link."

"Right. Have a go."

"You'd better be the one: it might need your self-confidence. I'll ask Ancelen to move over to your mind."

There was silence for a while as Ancelen and Mayne grew accustomed to the new partnership.

Ithleen suddenly stood up and said, "I'm hungry!"

Mayne said, "Sorry, I had to practice and Jonno might have recognized the touch of Ancelen's mind."

Ithleen, looking amazed, sat down again. "I had no idea."

"It'll take more than a simple suggestion to control the guards; but at least I know they can be reached without their awareness." He sat back and concentrated. The others kept tensely quiet.

The seconds became minutes... And then, abruptly, the door appeared. Mayne relaxed, and led the others out. The four guards stood on either side of the door, two of them chatting desultorily, all of them oblivious of the prisoners. He touched the door closed again, against the possible passing-by of someone other than these four who had not been ordered not to see it.

"Which way, Jonno?" he murmured.

"This way. Get Connerisk to check ahead of us so we won't run into anyone."

They made their way to a room with micromanipulating apparatus. All three entered the sealed chamber.

Asking the psychics to keep watch for them, the plennors minutely studied the transplacing devices; Ithleen periodically renewed her contact with the rifkey . Their verdict, finally, was that one whole rifkey could be made from the two, provided their skill was sufficient for them to disconnect the modules without further damage, and to reconnect them correctly.

Without needing to confer, the plennors chose Ithleen's rifkey to repair.

As they worked, Mayne commented, "Since Ithleen can take only one person with her when she transplaces, I think it should be you, Jonno."

"Why?"

"Because you're our best gadgeteer. The rifkey might blow again on the way out and need repeat repair before any further use."

"You're the expert among us on the rifkey," Jonno said. "Besides, it'll definitely blow on any attempt at a return transplacement without shielding; and our only hope of getting that is the wexters' technology."

"However small the chance that your technical expertise will make a difference, it is a possibility; so logic says you should go," argued Mayne.

"Wexter-type logic!" snorted Jonno. "Even if we accept the need for technical ability as valid, there's no advantage to my going over your going."

"There is to Ithleen."

***

By the lab clocks, it was past three before they completed their task. They were still arguing over which one should accompany Ithleen.

As they called her over to take back her rifkey, Ithleen said, "I've been thinking about the barrier. We need to wreck the defence-field system before transplacing out. Using Connerisk, you could select a key part of its power supply or control that's vulnerable to laser fire."

"Yes, but we can't get through to the power area, remember?"

"Yes, I know; but I can get to the other tower: I can walk the cable that holds all those pennants."

He hesitated only a moment. "Jonno, repair my laser. There are lots of standard components stored here. I'll get Connerisk to survey the power equipment with me."

Both tasks took time. Ithleen went out to have a look at the cable. It was rough, and would have unexpected bumps where some of the pennants had wrapped around it, invisible in the dark. It would be cold to her bare feet; and broken strands could startle her by their sudden stabs. There was little wind, but it came in odd gusts and eddies around the towers.

In this plan, she could take no one along with her; and if she failed at any point, there was no hope for those left behind; but if she succeeded, she could bring all of the others out. It was a better hope than that the wexters

311

might show up in time, with some sort of shielding immediately available. She returned to the plennors and waited quietly until they completed their work.

Mayne told her, "I've selected the spot. Connerisk says it's definitely where power is fed to the barrier. Ancelen will show you an image of it and its location. You'll have to make your way up two stories from where you get into the tower."

Ancelen made a temporary switch of mind contact to show Ithleen what Mayne had marked out to her in her image of the power supply. When Ithleen was sure she could find the place, Ancelen returned to Mayne. Jonno handed Ithleen the laser; and the plennors walked with her to the doorway of a balcony.

He said, "Jonno, you'll want to see her off," and turned away abruptly; but catching Ithleen's gesture as he moved, he turned back to touch her outstretched hands. "It's silly to say take care of yourself, when we're sending you into this." He smiled suddenly. "The wexters may never forgive me for this."

Her hands tightened on his; but matching his light tone, she said, "I'll tell them you apologize for using their walking calculator." She and Jonno went out onto the balcony.

Ithleen took off her high-heeled shoes and tucked them out of sight in a corner. She asked Jonno, "What are you two going to do?"

"Oddly enough, we're going back to our cell. If you succeed in blowing the power supply of the defence system, there's going to be a furious search for the saboteurs; and if we seem helplessly sealed in the cell, we should escape suspicion."

"What if the Guradcruzans ask where I am?"

"We'll claim someone came and took you out. Don't worry about us; we'll be all right. It's you on that untested cable, in the dark; and with a jury-rigged rifkey..."

"The cable's easy," Ithleen lied quickly. "And anything you and Jonnan have put together will work."

"Ithleen..." He gathered her into his arms and kissed her lingeringly.

She clung to him, then pushed herself away. "I must go."

He gave her a hand to climb up the crenelations to the pennant-cable, and watched her step out onto it with confident poise. Trying not to think of the long drop below her, he watched the white blur of her lab coat fade into the darkness, then went back in to join Mayne.

As they made their way back to the cell, Mayne remarked, "I've asked Ancelen to keep in contact with Ithleen, and to tell us when she transplaces."

"Why not link directly?"

"It might be a distraction to Ithleen at a moment when she needs all her attention elsewhere."

The guards continued to look through the prisoners, and obligingly closed the door after them, still oblivious to the whole matter.

The plennors sat down and waited. Time stretched. Neither would voice a doubt; conversation ceased. By force of will, Mayne refrained from calling Ancelen's attention back to his own questions; but he wished he had asked for more than a final report.

But at last Ancelen came through: *She's shooting at the machinery. Huge sparks, thick smoke. Alarm whistles screeching. Yells. People running. Machinery collapsing. She says, "Give them my love".* Taking Ithleen's words literally, Ancelen accompanied the thought with a flash of emotion to Mayne, causing him to startle.

Jonno cried, "What's wrong?"

"Nothing." Mayne assured.

Gone! said Ancelen.

"She made it, Jonno! Blasted the power unit and transplaced out!"

"But what shocked you?"

"Ancelen transmitted a moment of pure emotion... meant for you. There wasn't time to switch her over. It... startled me. At least Ithleen's safely out of here."

Neither spoke about the chances of the transplacement having been completed safely. They settled down to wait again.

***

Ithleen materialized in her study, and let out the breath she had been holding. Even after a successful transplacement, there was no guarantee the rifkey would not break down again, or take her elsewhere than she intended; but she did not hesitate. Obeying Mayne's orders, she directed herself first to the cell holding the psychics. Again the rifkey worked. Surely it was only her overwrought imagination that made the transplacement feel different, somehow unsteady, its luminous whiteness dimmed?

Rexede and Connerisk were asleep. Ithleen told Ancelen, "I must take you one at a time."

Yes, I see. Take the others while I tell your friends. They want to know about you. Ancelen had the mischievous grin of a child who has just got away with playing a prank on her elders.

Ithleen did not pause to ask what was amusing her, but transplaced the other two in turn. She had no need to wake them; they were eager at all levels of their minds to go away from Guradcruze.

The repaired rifkey held up. But was the white instant duller, and longer than usual, each time? Or was it a sensation the rifkey gave her through its psi connection, its way of warning her that it was not operating at optimum efficiency?

Just let it hold up long enough, she willed, and returned a third time, for Ancelen.

They're very happy, the telepath told her. *Would you like me to link you?*

"No, don't take the time. I'll be with them in a minute." Ithleen transplaced Ancelen out. At last she was able to direct herself to the plennors.

The rifkey did not work.

CHAPTER 29

Confusion

Ithleen crushed down a moment's incipient panic. She tried to reach each of the plennors, separately, and failed again. To test the person-seeking mode of her rifkey, she transplaced, via Mayne's lab, to Ciath.

Ithleen found Ciath, with her husband Leoshem and other actors, in the Geode theatre, giving a new play a read-through.

"Ithleen! At last!" Ciath's calm was not exactly broken, but it was a bit ruffled around the edges. She put her pages on a table and crossed to her friend. "Where are the others? Jonnan never brought Robinaire back. What's happened?"

"Robinaire's safe at home. The two plennors are in danger." Ithleen made another attempt to reach them.

"You're hurt!" cried Ciath, as a turn of Ithleen's head revealed the laser burn on her neck. "Come to the —"

"No time! I've got to get to the plennors. And I've got some people to look after, as well, at home." Ithleen tossed the last words behind her as she ran out: rather than risk the rifkey's breakdown by overuse, she was going back to her quarters through the travel tunnels instead of double-transplacing there.

While she was on her way, Ancelen's query came to her: *What's wrong?*

Ithleen answered, *I can't get to the others. The rifkey works; there must be hostile people with them. When you last contacted them, could you tell if they were still in the cell?*

Yes. Ancelen showed a memory view of the cell, including some soldiers. A corporal was saying, *"Zar Haughn was right — one of them's got loose, somehow."* Your friends were saying, *"Why did you take her away? What have you done with her? Bring her back!" They were still arguing when you brought me here and I lost contact.*

"What will they do to them!" Ithleen muttered. She could go back to some other place in the building; but with a single lasergun she could scarcely fight her way through an army. The wisest, if hardest, thing to do was to stay out of that universe so that she could transplace in directly to them as soon as she got a chance. She refused to think about the possibility that they might be killed out of hand in revenge for the power damage.

If they had had the chance to argue, the corporal might have considered the plennors' claim that someone else had taken the missing person away.

The cell guards would swear that no one had either come or gone. But the only alternative was transplacement, the Guradcruzans had been positive their barrier had destroyed all the prisoners' tools. So confusion must have reigned for at least a while - and Ulfri would want to have her fun in the killing of them, and would not be kind to anyone who deprived her of that pleasure. So the plennors were probably still alive; but that did not mean they were either safe or unhurt.

Back in her study, Ithleen began willing the rifkey at fifteen second intervals.

Ancelen offered timid encouragement. *They're very clever; they'll find a way to stay safe.*

"If only the guards will leave them alone, just for a minute!" Again Ithleen willed the transplacement.

And suddenly her study faded... whiteness... and she was there, in the cell. She almost staggered with relief, and Jonno caught her. "You're safe!" she cried.

"Until the soldiers get back with orders. Take him out, fast!" Mayne ordered. Ithleen obeyed, then flashed back and brought Mayne.

With the plennors finally safe, Ithleen sank down in shaky reaction on one of her armchairs. "It's been quite a day," she said with deliberate understatement.

"It has!" agreed Jonno more emphatically.

Mayne took out his wexcorder and considered it. "Jonno, do you think there's any chance this thing survived the defence barrier?"

"Everything we could test was broken. Still, we've nothing to lose by trying."

After Mayne had made the attempt, he and Ithleen were patched up again by Ciath's medical team. "Laser burns!" Ciath scolded. "You have rough playmates."

"They meant to be rougher," Ithleen told her.

After a brief discussion, they decided to remain in Geode until Spen contacted them again. In addition to the inadvisability of using the repaired rifkey unnecessarily, there was the advantage of not having to conceal the presence of the three psychics here. Further, Geode was a world Zar Haughn had never heard of; so even if he had retained his position with his new allies, he could not lead them to this location. The three agents had reason to hope that the damage Ithleen had done to the Guradcruzan equipment had rendered it unable to trace her transplacements from that world; and neither Haughn's nor the Guardcruzans' method of universe-crossing it seemed had a person-seeking mode.

It was unlikely that the Guradcruzans would launch a retaliatory attack on Mayne's world while their defence barrier was damaged; and they would probably hesitate to do so anyway, after Haughn's warnings about the ISC world, and the supporting evidence of the amount of damage that had been done by just three of its alleged inhabitants. But it was possible that Ulfri would send raiders to try to recapture her lost prisoners; so it seemed wise to minimize their multiverse activity until they were all re-equipped.

An apartment had already been set aside for the plennors' use whenever they were in Geode, which the Geodans hoped would be often. Ithleen arranged temporary quarters for the psychics as well.

They were all thankful to get a full night's sleep.

***

The next morning the small group regathered in Ithleen's study. The psychics had been offered a tour of Geode, but preferred to stay with the only familiar people in their rapidly shifting lives, while they awaited their transplacement to the promised haven world. The scientists had scarcely resumed discussion of the situation when Spen appeared.

"We have received your report," ne announced.

"Then the recorders still work!"

"The originals on which they were based were designed to be sent into extreme environments in probes. These are merely modified to record thoughts instead of only exterior conditions. We left them sturdy." They thought they caught the faint glint of humour, as if Spen appreciated that the adjective was an understatement.

Jonno had a sudden thought. "Then the one Haughn took from me is still functional. But he's unlikely to be able to analyze it, even if he happened to be carrying it when he was taken to Ulfri's world, or gets them to take him back to his own."

"It is to be hoped that he does have the recorder," said Spen. "Even if he never uses it deliberately while investigating it, some of his more intense thoughts may be recorded while he has it with him. This will provide us with some small amount of information on him."

Remembering more, Jonno said, "Actually, I think Haughn sent the recorder to that scientist, Cazl — the one who was privileged enough to talk back to him. She wouldn't have been able to figure it out, but there wasn't time enough for her to realize that and send it back to him. But if he does get home, he might easily go to see if she's made progress."

Mayne asked Spen, "Do you still consider Haughn a danger?"

"That is uncertain," Spen said. "He is no longer in a position of direct power. But he has allied himself with people whose ability to move about the multiverse is rather greater than his was. They appear to be largely inwardly directed, but they do make hostile contact with other universes. It is probable that the victims in their non-competitive arena activities are mostly captives from other worlds."

"You want another containment!" cried Jonno.

"It would seem advisable."

"Any idea how?" demanded Mayne. "There's no small collection of power to remove, in this case. Presumably their transplacing devices are known and exist all over the planet. The other city-fortresses must have defence barriers, too. Or, if the whole system is interlinked, they'll soon have it repaired; then we won't be able to get in and out till we have shielding."

Ithleen said, "Spen, do you know how their barrier works? Could you distort it to become a barrier to them?"

"If feasible, that is an excellent idea. I will see if we can act upon it, after one of you guides a probe to the Guradcruze world for us. We have one standing by to home on you instantly; you need not stay longer than it takes to operate your rifkey. Make several random transplacements both going and returning, to defeat any tracing."

"I'll do it," said Mayne quickly, holding out his hand to Ithleen for her rifkey before she could volunteer.

Jonno asked, "Do you have replacement rifkeys and pentools for us?"

"We have no spares at this time; I will take the remains of the cannibalized rifkey for restructuring. It would be best if we examined the repaired one also, after Jonnan returns. Extensive makeshift repairs such as you have described might not be permanent. Give me the old pentools, as well; perhaps we can repair them also, or at least re-use the undamaged parts, to reduce construction time." The agents laid out the tools on a workbench, and they vanished.

Ithleen reluctantly handed her rifkey to Mayne. "If this is untrustworthy..."

"I'll specify an uninhabited area between the fortresses," Mayne assured her. "If there's a breakdown, I can wait till you get new rifkeys."

He activated the random mode on the rifkey, and followed instructions through the set of transplacements, before and after a directed hop to Guradcruze, noticing, as Ithleen had, that the rifkey's action seemed indefinably less sure. Back with the others, he was thankful to hand over the rifkey and see it vanish into Spen's care. "Did your probe find the place?"

"We may presume so." Spen's confidence was reasonable. "If not, I will return later for another try, when I bring new rifkeys. Meanwhile, I will take these last three psychics to the haven world. Do you wish to be moved to another world, or will you wait here?"

Jonno said, "Here."

Mayne nodded. "And there may be reporters hanging around my lab, after that party the other day."

"I will come here, then, when I have further information." The wexter vanished, taking the psychics, who were so interested in the promised new world and reunion with the rest of their group that they forgot even to say goodbye.

The wexter returned that afternoon, bringing a single pair of the pentools, and no rifkeys. "You were extremely fortunate that the one you repaired did not fail. It must be completely rebuilt before it is safe. However, we have no missions for you until we have worked out the details of distorting the defence barrier of Guradcruze. Our probes are collecting data on it now."

"Will the Guradcruzans notice them?" asked Jonno.

"The probes are virtually undetectable. From the damage to your tools, we have already made several guesses as to what technology the Guradcruzans have employed for their barrier, and can test for all these possibilities. I will bring the new rifkeys as soon as we have completed them and our device to distort the Guradcruzan barrier."

Chapter 30

Catastrophe

Mayne was alone in Ithleen's study when the wexter returned. Spen caused a rifkey and three pairs of pentools to appear on Ithleen's desk.

"Just one rifkey?" cried Mayne, in dismay, then, in quick comprehension, "Oh, of course, they have to be attuned."

"I will deliver the other two later. I am pleased to find you alone. I have something to discuss with you. We have completed the device to seal in Ulfri's world."

"Good," said Mayne, with cautious relief, but also with a touch of weariness. "The sooner we get it done the better."

"Regrettably," said the wexter, "the process of placing the parts of the device is dangerous. In fact, a number of our scientists refused to work on the device in protest against even an agent being asked to deliver it."

"They consider this worse than going to unknown universes, then?"

"Yes. The risk there is of injury or death. In this case..." Spen hesitated. "Let me explain the situation first. The sealing device consists of a number of parts which must be placed at widely scattered points on the world. They do not need to be triggered. When enough are interacting with the defence barrier, the blockage effect will be initiated."

"Like attaining a critical mass," murmured Mayne.

"At that point, the inhabitants will not be able to switch off their barrier, for it will be interlocked with our own modifying equipment, and no longer dependent on their power. It will block passage into or out of that world until its people become advanced enough to overcome the effect. Even then, it will take a vast, co-operative effort. So long as they continue to be competitive and to concentrate on entertainment, they are unlikely to free themselves."

"Can they get to other worlds in their own universe?" Mayne asked.

"Eventually. They should have time to grow before they encounter any other peoples. If they fail to mature, they will probably destroy themselves first, anyway."

"You said that when your device reached critical concentration, it would block passage. Is that the danger? That I'd be caught on the world as I placed the final one?"

"If you worked on that world itself you would."

"And the alternative...?"

"You could work from outside that universe."

"From here?"

"No. From the diaphane. The area between universes which we called no-space until we adopted Ithleen's word, diaphane. She has told you what she has deduced and intuited about that... place?"

"Yes." Mayne smiled involuntarily as he remembered their long discussions. "An indefinable 'volume' of basic energy, out of which the very space of a universe is formed, and which separates the universes, and in some sense contains them."

"The separations are both infinitesimal and infinite," Spen said. "We have no adequate words to describe this diaphane, and Ithleen's description is mathematical. We discovered that it was possible to break a transplacement in the middle so that we hovered within this infinite-infinitesimal otherness briefly and then cancelled the transplacement and returned to our reality promptly. Lingering within the diaphane proved fatal." Spen spoke the statement flatly.

Mayne thought about how brave the timid wexters really were, saying nothing of how the explorers' unnatural deaths must have racked the rest of the telepathically connected population.

"What else did you discover about the diaphane itself?" Mayne asked.

"That nothing material can exist in such a place. If you undertake this project, you will be changed into a state of quasi-existence, suspended in a place of non-existence, placing virtual objects that will become real again only after they materialize in the Guradcruzan world. The danger is that you may not be able to resume existence when you have completed the work."

"In other words, I die. Nothing new about that danger." Mayne shrugged.

"Having no real existence, you could not."

"You mean it would be something like that limbo Ithleen got into."

"Much worse. She was at least in a place, however alien; and she would have died had she stayed there. So far as we can estimate you would continue for the duration of the universes 'around' you. As an immaterial consciousness. Our psychonomic theorists say that the state would be one of inexpressibly intense need to be rematerialized."

"I'd simply go mad."

"Very likely. But that would not close you off from the sensation. No catatonia could be deep enough to do so, for you would 'exist' as pure consciousness... entirely and eternally craving contact with existence..."

"I can see why some of your people refused to contribute towards the project. How likely am I to become trapped?"

"Your safety would depend upon your own willpower. You are the strongest-willed sentient we have ever discovered, so some of us think you could withstand the diaphane."

Spen paused a moment, as if gathering nemself to face ner people's shared memories, then plunged into a direct account. "Our first explorers, who made no attempt to stay, returned safely. We then sent volunteers at staggered time intervals, prepared to linger long enough to make observations. The later arrivals reported, from their mental contact with the earlier ones, that there was a growing 'pull' to discard one's ties to normal existence and become a completely disembodied consciousness. The others were able to drag one of them back and out of the diaphane. The others were lost, leaving us only memories of the beginning of their torment."

"Will I have an escort of minds to pull me back?"

"No. Our minds are not close enough to a human's. If you choose to take the risk, I will take you there, give you the virtual devices, and place you at the Guradcruze universe, then retreat to a holding spot not quite in the diaphane, where others will cluster near my point of entry to maintain mental contact with me to be sure I did not slip fully into the otherness.

Once you mentally set the autoguide switches that would take the devices into Guradcruze, you would have to will yourself to come back to me. We believe that the basic energy in the diaphane is pure psi; in any case, it seems to allow actions to be performed by direct will. Once you return, I would bring you out and back to here."

Mayne marvelled this time at Spen's personal courage. Even with a backup team, ne was facing the ultimate horror of being cut off forever from the tight mental linkage of the wexters. Mayne had just rediscovered how precious even human-level companionship was. He turned his thoughts firmly to practical considerations. "So the main difficulty is getting back."

"You would be a form of this psi energy yourself while you are there, feeling the constant pull to blend into the greater whole, but unable to dissolve so completely that your consciousness would cease. You would remain aware of your situation as long as it lasted; and it would last forever."

There was a pause, as both of them thought about that, then Spen went on: "We believe your willpower is strong enough to carry out this task and return."

Ne added, "The only other factor is time. The longer you stay, the likelier is your entrapment. We have considered using more than one agent, to shorten the time period slightly; but there are so many unknowns that we might merely increase the number of persons lost into non-existence, if something beyond our knowledge goes wrong. You must make your own decisions; but we ask you earnestly not to permit Ithleen to participate in this work."

"I promise that. In fact, I won't let anyone else risk it. But you'll have to avoid letting the others know there is danger if we're to keep them out of it."

"I do not understand you humans. Are you saying that you people are somehow attracted to danger?"

"No, I'm saying Jonno and Ithleen wouldn't let me face this risk alone, especially if they thought added numbers might reduce my own danger."

"This we can grasp. But you," puzzled the wexter, "you would consider going into this danger even though you are not lessening danger for someone else?"

"I am lessening danger. If the Guradcruzans continue collecting offworlders for their torture-entertainment, my friends and I are likely to be their first target. Zar Haughn could direct them to my world."

"Do you consider your own world already in danger from them?"

"She might start raiding my Earth for more victims. So sealing the Guradcruzans in is important to me both personally and for my world's sake."

He refrained from mentioning one more reason for volunteering: if he refused to do something the wexters needed an agent for, his value to them dropped drastically, and the likelihood of their shutting him out of the multiverse — away from Ithleen — rose in corresponding degree. He dismissed the hope that gratitude for his taking this risk would increase their valuation of him: when it came to protecting oneself or one's world, even humans discarded other emotions; certainly wexters would. He did add, however, "All things considered, it seems worth the gamble."

"We are pleased," the wexter said formally, then added, "But at this moment, I wish I did not know you personally."

"I understand." Mayne smiled ruefully. "Attachments are wretched things. But once you accept them, there *are* compensations."

"I have discovered that, with or without compensations, attachments appear to be irrevocable." For the first time since Mayne had known the wexter, ne made a movement. Something, which might have been an arm, lifted under the shimmering silver covering and reached out, still shielded, to touch him lightly. "Should our acquaintance end with this project, I would like you to know I have received pleasure as well as knowledge from the association."

"I can say the same, Spen." Mayne said. After a pause, he asked, "Are you typical of your people?"

In almost whimsical philosophizing, Spen remarked, "Every person feels that ne is the standard of what ner people should be like, if only to make ner world a more familiar and comfortable place. So I may say that I am, representative of my people, except for my disapproved tendency towards recklessness, which seems to have been reinforced by my association with you humans."

Becoming formal again, ne added, "We will prepare for the project, and I will return for you early this evening." Ne faded out.

***

Ithleen and Jonno phoned from a nearby public lounge to invite Mayne to join them.

"You've seen Spen?" Jonno asked as his analog joined them.

"Yes. And," Mayne remarked as he handed Ithleen and Jonno their replacement pentools, "so far, it seems we're still in business. And so is Spen"

Jonno smiled. "Is ne going to bring us more rifkeys?"

Mayne nodded. "Yours are coming."

Ithleen asked, "Did Spen have anything to say about the projected sealing off of Ulfri's world?"

"Yes. It turns out it'll be quite simple, from our viewpoint. The wexters have prepared a set of devices that will react with that world's barrier as soon as they're delivered to the world. They're making all the arrangements." He carefully said nothing about the diaphane; he knew that Ithleen had heard earlier about the wexters' disastrous attempt to probe that alienness. "It needs only one person, so I'll do it myself this evening."

To Mayne's surprise, the wexter materialized amid the group in the lounge. Spen delivered the other two rifkeys to Ithleen and Jonno and attuned them.

Spen announced to everyone, "Our project is waiting."

Mayne stood up. "I'm ready." He glanced at his analog. "Take care of things, Jonno." He crossed to the wexter and tuned to look at Ithleen, saying nothing. He and Spen vanished.

As the minutes passed, the casual conversations gradually died. Although they had no idea when to expect Mayne back, they began to react as if he were overdue. Jonno was restless, wondering, in retrospect, why his analog had asked him to take care of things, when there was nothing to do until Mayne's return. There was an uncomfortable flavour of last-message about it.

Suddenly the wexter appeared. Alone.

"Ulfri's world is sealed in," ne told them. "But we have lost Jonnan."

Chapter 31

Persuasion

"What do you mean, lost?" demanded Jonno sharply. Ithleen stared at the wexter, unable to grasp the concept.

Spen put into their minds the entire conversation ne had held with Jonnan when he accepted the mission, complete with their emotional overtones. Ne concluded, "He successfully completed the task; but he has not returned. The likelihood of his doing so drops constantly with time; therefore we must now assume he will not return."

"Spen!" cried Ithleen. Comprehension had flooded her, and with it, horror. "You let him go into the diaphane, knowing what it was like, what it could do to him?"

"He went of his own free choice, understanding the risk," said the wexter. "And he was accepted as an expendable agent from the beginning." But with ner words, ne projected to her ner own regret and sense of loss, and added, "He worked quickly; he should have been able to return. Some other factor has invalidated our calculations."

Ithleen came across to nem. "If you can't get him back, send me to him."

"You! Even if it is possible, I would not be allowed to! What purpose would be served by putting another person into that state of suffering?"

"Company," said Ithleen, "so that he would no longer be alone in the agony."

"I would not dare try!"

Jonno said, "Can you send another person in to him? I'm another expendable."

"This has not been considered. I must ask."

Ithleen said, "Jonno, the multiverse needs you, and so does your own world. Besides,"

she shaped a smile: "I asked first."

"They won't let you, Ithleen. They consider you to be much more valuable. Jonnan and I have merely re-invented a few things they already knew about," said Jonno. "If it can be done, I'll do it."

The wexter said, "I will consult..." and vanished.

Jonno put an arm around Ithleen's shoulders. "They'll never let you go, Ithleen; so it has to be me."

Ithleen pulled out her new rifkey and patterned it. The instrument, obeying its fundamental injunction of safety, refused to operate.

"Spen said only the wexters can make this transplacement, Ithleen, and they won't."

"They've let me go into danger before..."

"That's different from sending you themselves into certain — loss."

Ithleen cried, "I don't want you to go! I want to go myself! We can't leave Jonnan there without trying to help him! Oh, they must let me —"

"They can get more explorers, so maybe they'll let me go. I won't let him suffer alone, Ithleen."

Spen reappeared. "It is possible to send another human into the same location in the diaphane; but this in itself would achieve nothing; there would be only momentary contact before the unanchored mind drifted off again. The other would have to return promptly or become equally entrapped and cut off from both return and the first mind."

They stared at nem in appalled and agonized silence.

"However, *some*," ne emphasized, "of our theorists think there is one special case that might have a small hope of holding contact for long enough to have some effect..."

"What is it?" cried Jonno quickly.

"Because you are his analog, your mind might be able to bond with his for a few moments. If, in that brief time, your mind could mesh with his and restore a sense of direction and the will to return, you could both return."

Before Jonno could speak, the wexter went on starkly: "But, there are three other possible outcomes. If it took too long, you might both be lost, either locked together or drifted apart again, probably the latter; or you might not be able to guide him into willing his return, and return without him; or it might take you so long to direct him that you could not get back out yourself. It would depend entirely on you," ne stressed. "We can provide the initial and final impulses for the passages in and out, but only your own determination can bring you back to our reach."

"How can Jonno hope to get back when Jonnan couldn't?" cried Ithleen.

"We made a serious error with Jonnan," said the wexter, "as we now realize. We sent him into non-existence immediately after a painful emotional experience; his mind was in a state of withdrawal. By the time he had completed his task, he was too dissociated from the existence he had left to be able to regain it. If Jonno is strongly enough motivated to search, to hold, and to return, and has no great emotional disturbances, he might be successful."

"Send me," said Jonno.

"You are very sure you wish to do this? Remember, you must not hesitate or you will be delayed; and time works against you."

"If you can get me to him," said Jonno quietly, "I'll bring him or send him back."

He and the wexter vanished.

Ithleen stood motionless, looking unseeingly at the spot where they had been.

The seconds, the minutes dragged by. No one in the room spoke again; even movement almost ceased. Ithleen remembered the plennors' comments that, 'We can control our actions, but not our wills.' And this depended entirely on willing. Could Jonno want this, however strong his affection for Jonnan. Could he hold his determination without a single moment of faltering?

And as the minutes passed and piled up, it began to seem he could not...

Then, finally, a shape began to appear: the silver shimmer of the wexter...and another figure...

Just one.

They solidified.

"Jonnan!" cried Ithleen.

For long heartbeats, he stood unmoving, a look of vacant horror slowly fading from his eyes. Then he focused on Ithleen and smiled, a bit shakily, taking the hands she was holding out. He glanced beside him, then looked sharply all around. "Spen! Where's Jonno?"

"For some reason, he gave up at the last minute. His will was strong as he searched, and as he held you until you had regathered yourself and sensed your direction out. But as this happened, he suddenly yielded up his own will and made no effort to return with you."

"Take me back! Fast!"

Ithleen caught her breath, her grip tightening on his hands.

"Spen!" said Mayne, before she could cry out her protest. "I'm re-anchored to reality now. Quick!"

They faded out again. Ithleen's hands closed spasmodically on nothing. She twisted them together and waited... again.

Once more the seconds dragged blankly, and mounted up. Silence, like rigid bonds, held the group. No one moved. Breaths were hushed. Eyes and ears strained to perceive a return; minds willed it; emotions screamed for it. Time passed, and time hung in stasis.

And then again, the wexter's silver shielding appeared... and this time it was accompanied by two figures. With a sob of released breath, Ithleen seized a hand of each plennor as they solidified before her.

Jonnan smiled at her. "I persuaded him to make the effort."

Jonno, looking worn, said, "I feel as if I've been beaten black and blue."

"You had no strength to fight back, because you were withdrawing from life. And it was wilful, not unrealizing, like mine. There wasn't time to argue the matter. I had to use force."

Spen told them, "I will report these successes." Ne vanished.

Mayne looked at Jonno and Ithleen and realizing they needed to speak privately, he excused himself and left the room.

Ithleen drew a deep breath to speak, but Jonno forestalled her. "I know, Ithleen. When I linked minds with Jonnan, our recent memories were blended. I felt his feelings, his love for you. And I also know that you also have the same feelings for him.

"Jonno..."

"It's all right. I've been half-expecting it. But when I was in that ...*place*, even a small shock was too much. I shrank from the knowledge and nearly finished myself; but Jonnan slammed me with shame for failing to face up to something, and forced me to come back." He took her gently in his arms. "I shall treasure even second-hand memories of you, Ithleen..."

"Jonno, what can I say?"

"Nothing, except goodbye."

"Oh, Jonno, no! You can't leave us!"

"For a while, Ithleen. I wish you both all happiness; but I can't face actually watching it, yet. I'll go back to my own world."

"You're not going to give up the multiverse, are you?"

"No; I'll go on working for the wexters, if they wish; and if you ever need me, Ithleen, I'll come; but for now, I'd rather be alone."

"I had better go now." He kissed her gently and then intensely as she responded to him. Finally he forced himself to release her, and took out his new rifkey.

"Jonno, you know that I do love you?" she cried brokenly.

"I know; though your love is both a comfort and a torment. Goodbye, Ithleen."

"Goodbye, for now."

He operated the rifkey and faded out.

***

Mayne had intended to get a hot drink and relax, but his mind was whirling with the attempt to try to think ahead; but there was no planning he could do at this time. There was the problem of keeping the multiverse secret from Polminander and Simao and the rest of Security. He also wondered if there would be more missions for the wexters. Or was this his last venture into the multiverse?

Looking at his watch calendar, he counted back. Less than five weeks since the wexter had first interrupted his comfortable life. If he had to give up the multiverse to protect it from his Earth, could he go back to that comfortable life? Without Ithleen and Jonno?

It would not be as empty a life, he reminded himself, as he had once before. He had come to appreciate the friendship his assistants freely gave him. Since his teens, he had been unable to trust people enough to permit companionship; but he knew he would miss any he lost now. That offered by Van and Davith might prove indispensable to him if he became confined to his own Earth again. And there was Robinaire, who was attentive and retentive. No substitute for a colleague to talk to, but she listened; and she had a charm about her...

But it was the thought of losing his analog and his partner in adventure that hurt the most. More even than giving up that adventuring. After all, that had its drawbacks in the agonies of fear for his newfound friends.

Served him right for getting attached to people. Even if he was able to keep the multiverse, he might lose Ithleen and Jonno, for could they go on facing the fear for each other that could spring up suddenly on any world?

***

When Mayne returned, he found Ithleen waiting alone in her study. She told him of Jonno's decision.

"He did promise to come back?"

"Yes."

They were both silent for long moments. Finally Ithleen stirred and said, "Spen came back again."

"Another mission, already?" cried Mayne.

"No, ne suggested we should take some time off. Ne said that after this latest event ne thought we needed some rest, and knew that *ne* did. Do you think ne's developing a sense of humour?"

"Spen?"

"Anything's possible in the multiverse."

He smiled down at her in quiet happiness. "Even us."

She returned his look. "It's as if everything we've done has happened just so that we could meet and..." she broke off.

He raised an eyebrow at her.

"My intuition just gave me a kick. It says perhaps I should think of that in reverse. Perhaps we've met just to cause something else to happen..."

The End

About The Author

Sansoucy Kathenor served in the Canadian Airforce as an aircraft armament systems mechanic and had a private pilot's licence. She also worked as an archaeologist, and had many hobbies, including lapidary, jewelry-making, and astronomy. Many of these elements are seen in her writing. She was a member of SFWA (Science Fiction Writers of America), and SF Canada. She received several awards for her fiction She also has published a collection of her poetry – *Temple Into Time*.

In 1980 she formed the writing group, Lyngarde, dedicated to critiquing on-going works, and completing writing exercises. Several members had successful publications including short stories, poetry and novels. The group continues to this day.

Though Sansoucy passed away in 2005, the legacy of her work lives on.

A Handful of Earths trilogy is her final contribution to the world of science fiction.

OTHER BOOKS BY THE AUTHOR

E-Books available from Barnes and Noble, Kobo and Apple Books.
Special bonus, Death and Taxes e-book is FREE!

For more information contact MultiversePress42@gmail.com

Lightning Source UK Ltd.
Milton Keynes UK
UKHW020641150921
390618UK00010B/373